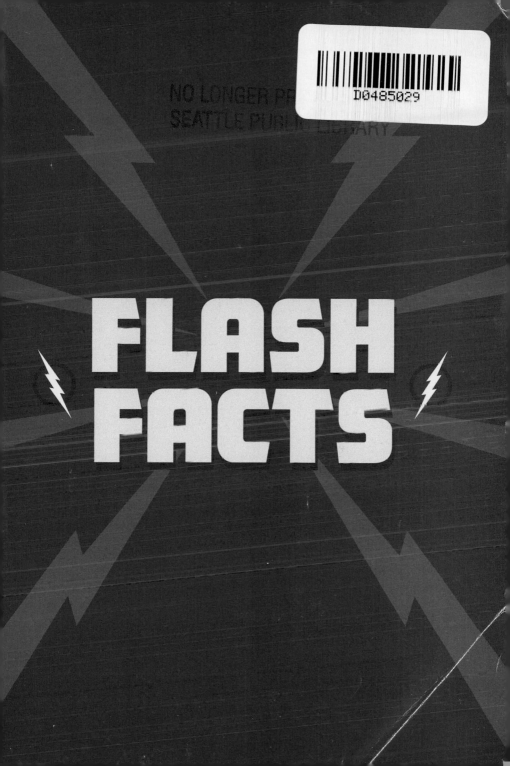

FLASH FACTS

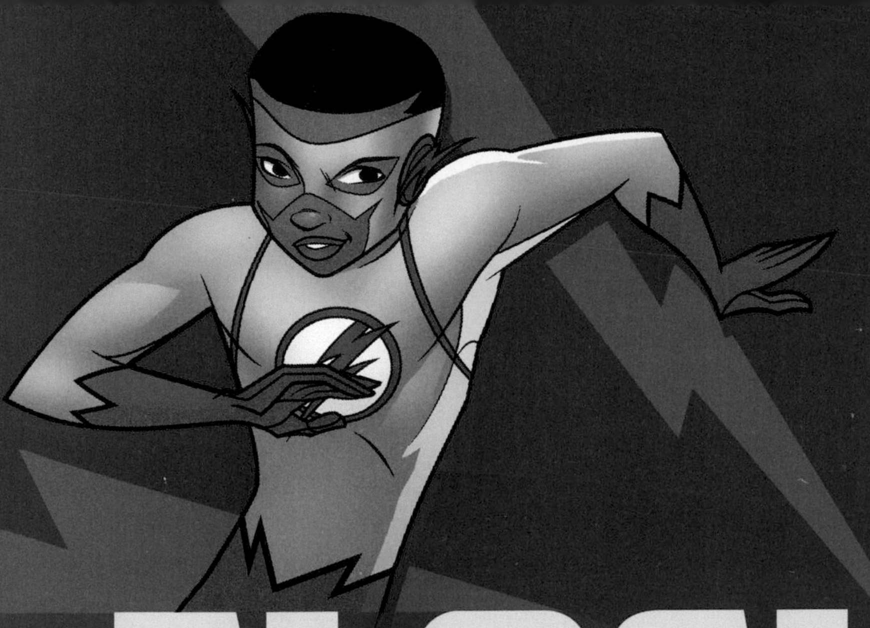

FLASH

EDITED BY

MAYIM BIALIK, PhD

WRITTEN BY

SHOLLY FISCH • VARIAN JOHNSON • DARIAN JOHNSON
AMY CHU • DUSTIN HANSEN • AMANDA DEIBERT
VITA AYALA • CECIL CASTELLUCCI • CORINNA BECHKO
MICHAEL NORTHROP • KIRK SCROGGS

ILLUSTRATED BY

ISAAC GOODHART • VIC REGIS • ILE GONZALEZ
DUSTIN HANSEN • ERICH OWEN • ANDIE TONG WITH
DEVYN HANSEN • GRETEL LUSKY • YESENIA MOISES
YANCEY LABAT WITH MONICA KUBINA • KIRK SCROGGS

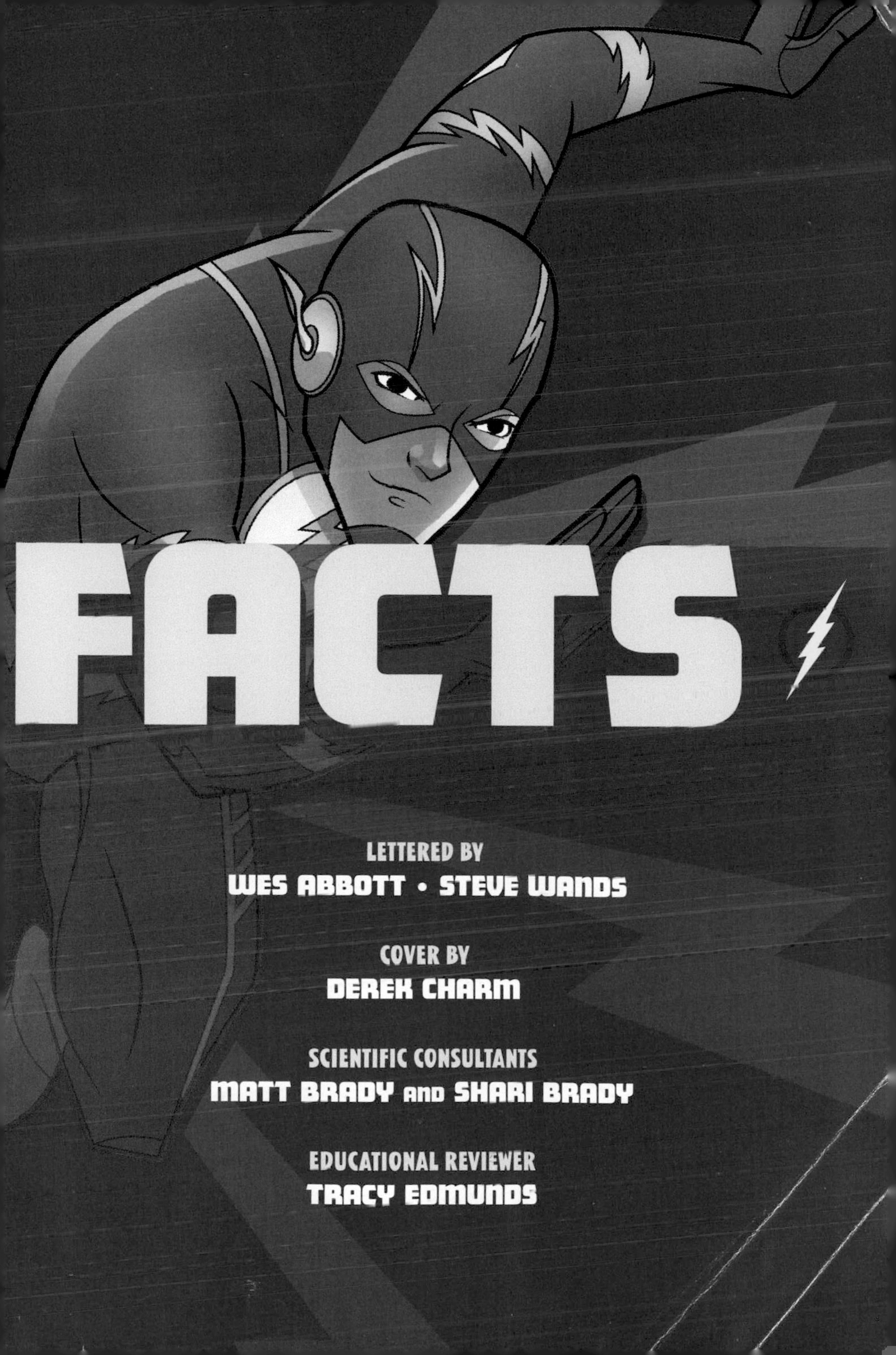

FACTS

LETTERED BY

WES ABBOTT • STEVE WANDS

COVER BY

DEREK CHARM

SCIENTIFIC CONSULTANTS

MATT BRADY AND SHARI BRADY

EDUCATIONAL REVIEWER

TRACY EDMUNDS

Michele R. Wells
VP & Executive Editor, Young Reader
Courtney Jordan
Assistant Editor
Steve Cook
Design Director – Books
Damian Ryland
Publication Design

Bob Harras
Senior VP – Editor-in-Chief, DC Comics

Jim Lee
Publisher & Chief Creative Officer
Bobbie Chase
VP – Global Publishing Initiatives & Digital Strategy
Don Falletti
VP – Manufacturing Operations & Workflow Management
Lawrence Ganem
VP – Talent Services
Alison Gill
Senior VP – Manufacturing & Operations
Hank Kanalz
Senior VP – Publishing Strategy & Support Services
Dan Miron
VP – Publishing Operations
Nick J. Napolitano
VP – Manufacturing Administration & Design
Nancy Spears
VP – Sales
Jonah Weiland
VP – Marketing & Creative Services

FLASH FACTS

DC Comics, 2900 West Alameda Ave., Burbank, CA 91505
Printed by LSC Communications, Crawfordsville, IN, USA. 12/25/20.
First Printing. ISBN: 978-1-77950-382-4.

Names: Fisch, Sholly, author. | Goodhart, Isaac, illustrator. | Bialik, Mayim, editor. Title: Flash facts / written by Sholly Fisch
[and ten others] ; illustrated by Isaac Goodhart [and eleven others] ; edited by Mayim Bialik, PhD ; lettered by Wes Abbott
and Steve Wands. Description: Burbank : DC Comics, 2021. | Audience: Ages 8-12 | Audience: Grades 4-6 | Summary:
"Have you ever wondered what's at the bottom of the sea? Why polar ice melts? Or which tools forensic scientists use to
solve a crime? Well look no further! Everyone's favorite Scarlet Speedster is here to answer all your burning questions!
Barry Allen, with the help of some of his close friends, will take readers on an exciting journey that examines everything
from the vast expanse of our galaxy to the smallest living organism known to man. Curated by award-winning actress and
author Mayim Bialik, PhD, and featuring stories created by an all-star cast of writers and illustrators, this anthology aligns
with Next Generation Science Standards and provides a helpful bridge between the lessons taught inside the classroom
and our everyday lives"-- Provided by publisher.
Identifiers: LCCN 2020040539 | ISBN 9781779503824 (trade paperback)
Subjects: LCSH: Science--Miscellanea--Juvenile literature. | Science--Study and teaching--Juvenile literature. | Science--
Comic books, strips, etc.
Classification: LCC Q163 .F45 2021 | DDC 500--dc23
LC record available at https://lccn.loc.gov/2020040539

FOREWORD

BY MAYIM BIALIK

When I was in elementary school, I knew two things: I liked comic books and I *didn't* like science. Flash forward a few decades and I have the unbelievable pleasure of writing a foreword to a comic book-inspired guide to science!

As a girl growing up in an overcrowded public school in Los Angeles in the 1980s, there was very little time for asking for things to be repeated if I didn't understand them. Classes were 30 kids and resources in my school were scarce. In addition, in math and science classes, we girls tended to shrink into our seats and if you didn't understand long division or fractions the first time through, many of us assumed that it just wasn't for us to understand. I excelled in storytelling and theater and I liked to dance and I sang in the choir and that all suited me fine—how much do I even need math and science?! At least that's what I thought then!

Despite crying over my times tables for what seemed like years, science always held an elusive allure for me. I was curious by nature, as most children are, and I loved animals and especially mammals of the sea. Was there a way I could ever have the ability to swim with them and learn from them? I checked out Jacques Cousteau books from the library and dreamed about descending into the depths of the ocean to discover amazing things. I was raised going to synagogue and believing in the forces of the universe and something inside of me wanted to believe that I could be one of the ones to really *get it*: to be able to describe the movement of the planets and the molecules that make up everything and to stand in awe of it all!

In high school, when I was 15, I got that opportunity. I was acting in a TV show called *Blossom* and a 19-year-old dental undergraduate student at UCLA answered an ad in the paper to tutor me. This amazing woman—who is now an oral surgeon—introduced me to the beauty and elegance of the scientific world and she gave me the skill set to succeed in the sciences. I owe her the path my life has taken and I am forever grateful to her! After I completed my work on *Blossom*, I went to UCLA in my hometown of Los Angeles and pursued an undergraduate degree and then a PhD in the study of the brain and the nervous system; I became a neuroscientist.

While my path has taken me from my PhD to raising two sons who are now a tween and a teen and back into the world of acting, I got to play a neurobiologist on *The Big Bang Theory* for almost 10 years! It was such a tremendous honor to get to show the world Amy Farrah Fowler: a quirky, passionate, and lovable scientist. And even though I make my living as an actor now, my heart belongs to the world of atoms, invisible forces, and unimaginable awesomeness. I have also taught neuroscience, biology, and chemistry and I devote my time to promoting the love and appreciation of STEM: Science, Technology, Engineering, and Mathematics. My passion is presenting the wonders of these worlds to as many young people as possible in ways that work for them. This book is a perfect way to do that!

Interestingly, the things I love about science are also the things comic books are made of, since comics are so linked to understanding the universe we live in. Whether it be in creating characters with abilities that test the laws of physics or using the accessibility of familiar personas we love to learn with and laugh with, the magic of the scientific world and the world of superheroes, robots, and mystery is ours to explore.

This book is your fun, fascinating, and fantastic guide to everything in the STEM world in a way you've never seen it before. It's not just Superman who can see inside of things—x-rays are real! It's not just Batman who knows how investigators track criminals—forensics is an entire field dedicated to tracking blood and understanding how everyone's genetics leaves a mark wherever they go. Invisible forces in the universe do exist and we can understand all about them with the use of specialized technology.

We are living in a scientific world and this book makes it easy and exciting to learn all about it in a way that will stick with you and inspire you and get you fired up about STEM. Buckle up and get ready to have your mind blown!

Mayim

TABLE OF CONTENTS

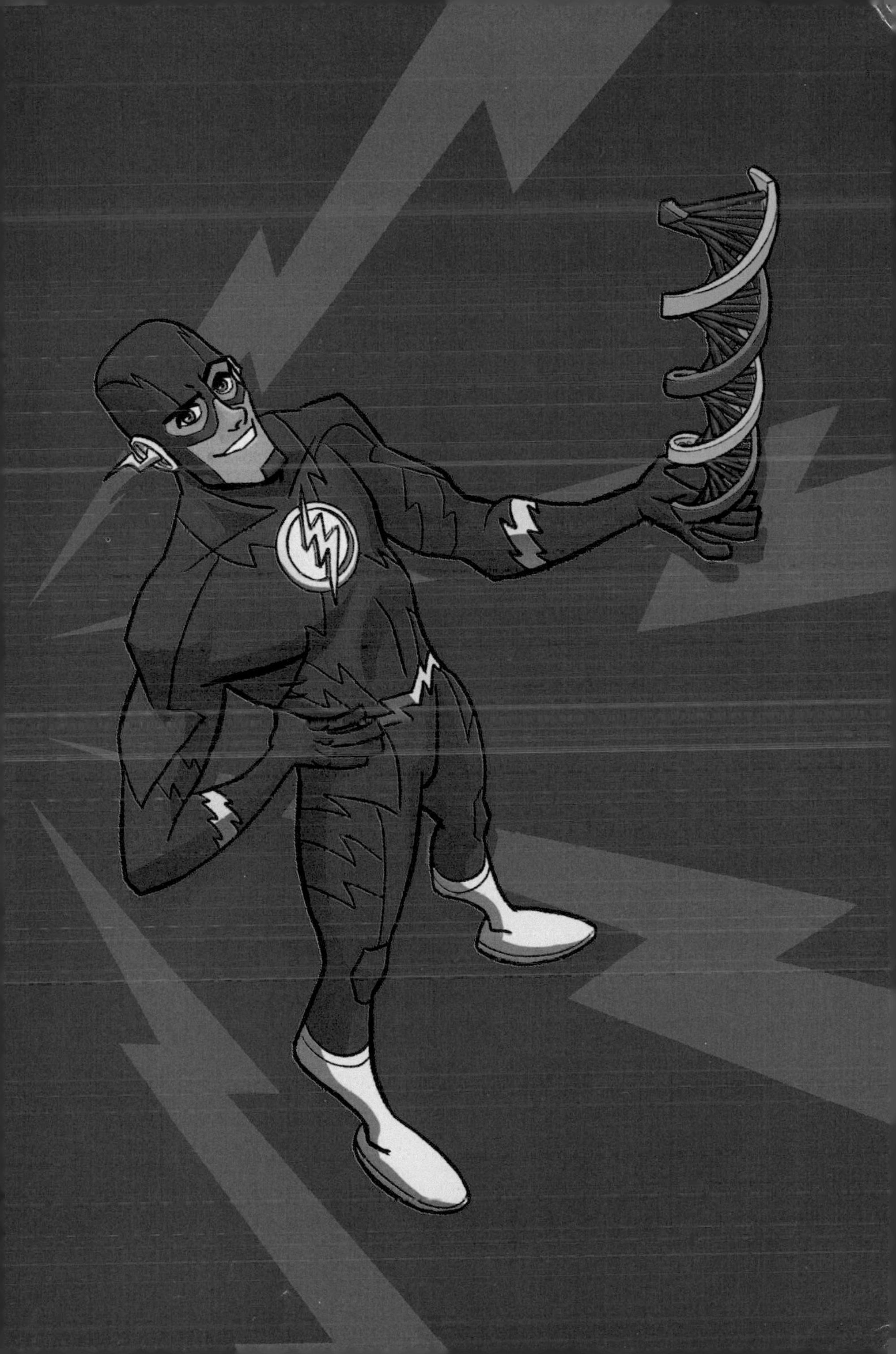

CHAPTER ONE
FAST TRACKS

WRITTEN BY **SHOLLY FISCH**

ILLUSTRATED BY **ISAAC GOODHART**

LETTERED BY **WES ABBOTT**

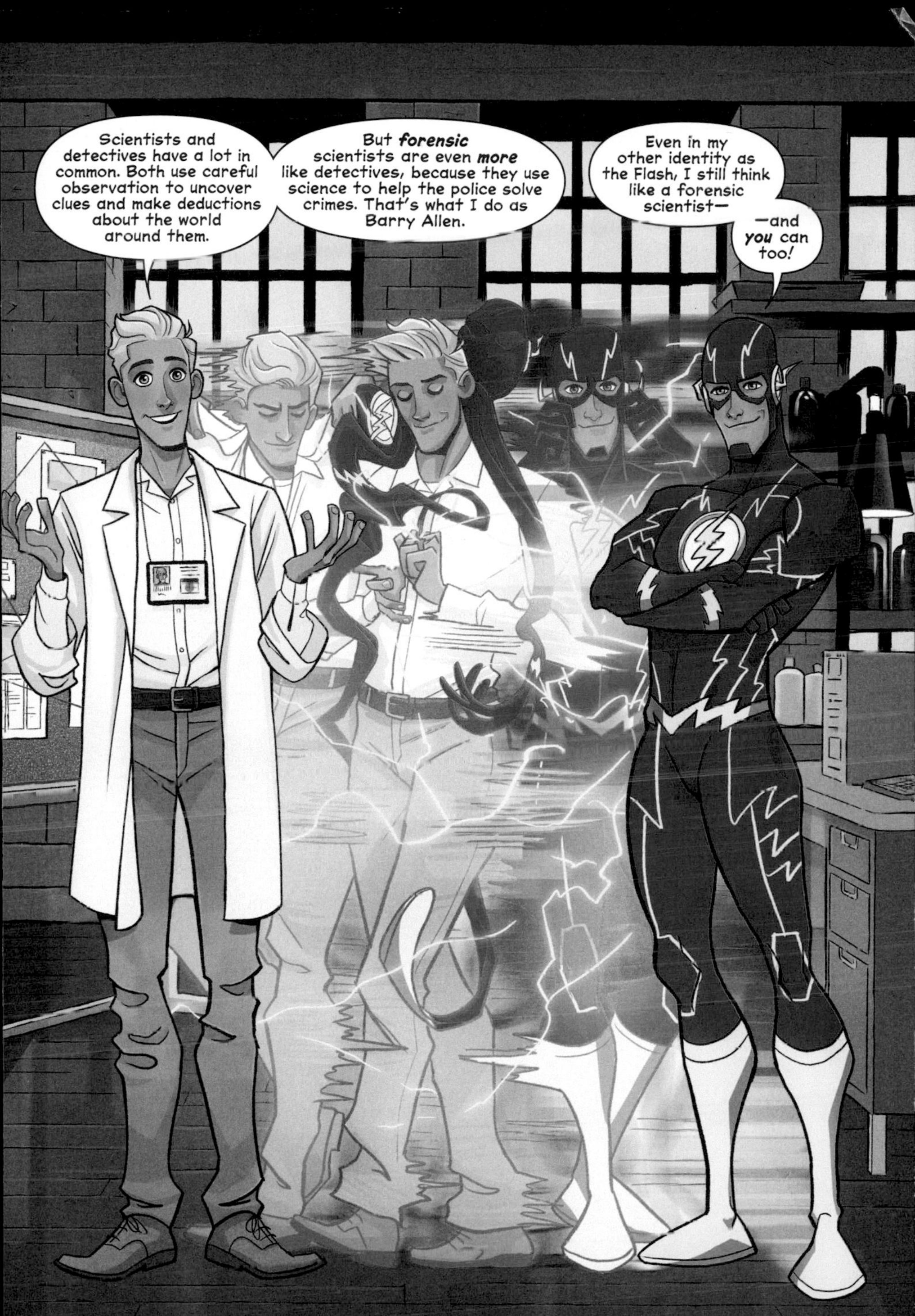
Scientists and detectives have a lot in common. Both use careful observation to uncover clues and make deductions about the world around them.
But *forensic* scientists are even *more* like detectives, because they use science to help the police solve crimes. That's what I do as Barry Allen.
Even in my other identity as the Flash, I still think like a forensic scientist—
—and *you* can too!

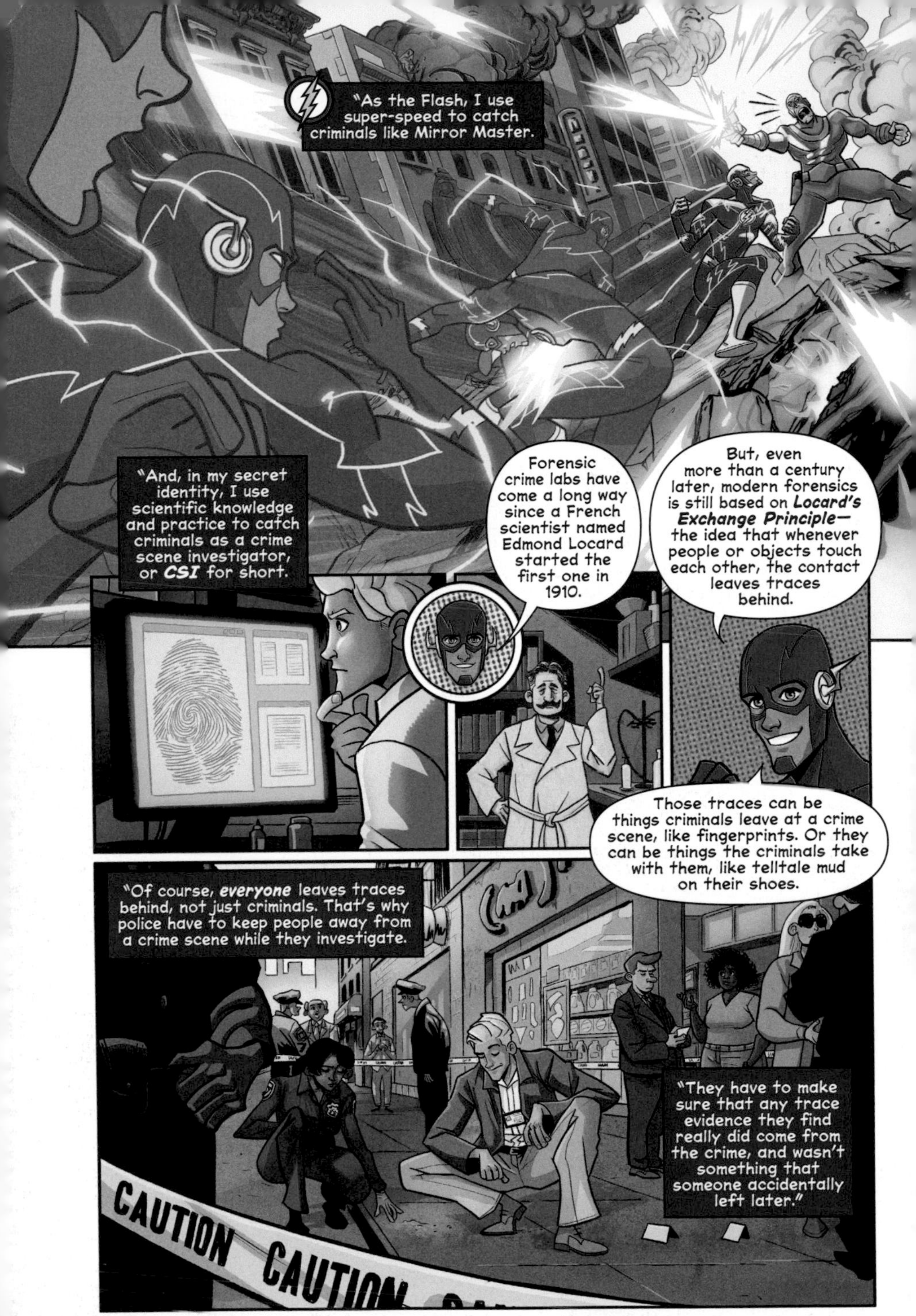
"As the Flash, I use super-speed to catch criminals like Mirror Master.
"And, in my secret identity, I use scientific knowledge and practice to catch criminals as a crime scene investigator, or CSI for short.
Forensic crime labs have come a long way since a French scientist named Edmond Locard started the first one in 1910.
But, even more than a century later, modern forensics is still based on Locard's Exchange Principle— the idea that whenever people or objects touch each other, the contact leaves traces behind.
Those traces can be things criminals leave at a crime scene, like fingerprints. Or they can be things the criminals take with them, like telltale mud on their shoes.
"Of course, everyone leaves traces behind, not just criminals. That's why police have to keep people away from a crime scene while they investigate.
"They have to make sure that any trace evidence they find really did come from the crime, and wasn't something that someone accidentally left later."
CAUTION
CAUTION

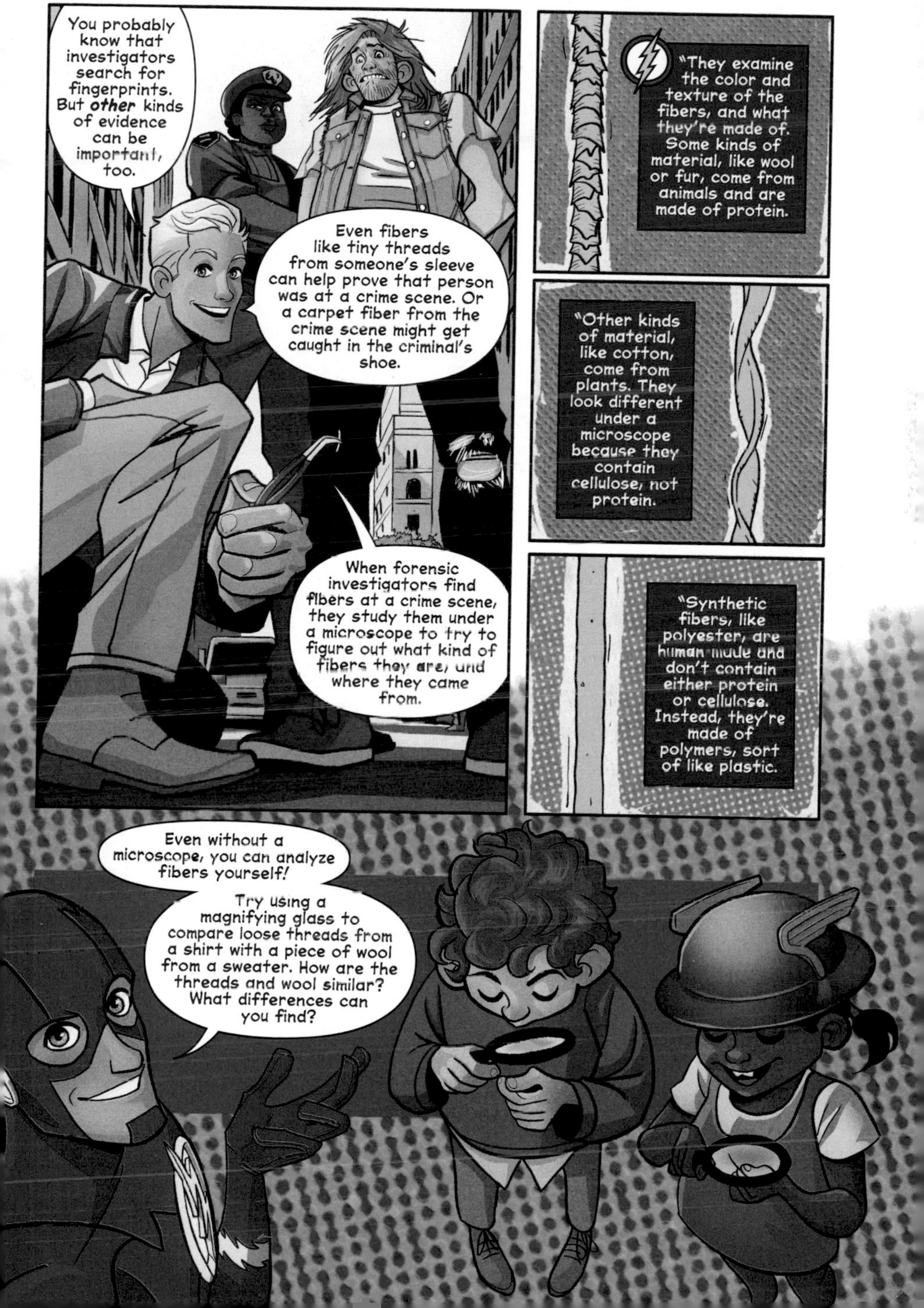
You probably know that investigators search for fingerprints. But *other* kinds of evidence can be important, too.
Even fibers like tiny threads from someone's sleeve can help prove that person was at a crime scene. Or a carpet fiber from the crime scene might get caught in the criminal's shoe.
When forensic investigators find fibers at a crime scene, they study them under a microscope to try to figure out what kind of fibers they are, and where they came from.
"They examine the color and texture of the fibers, and what they're made of. Some kinds of material, like wool or fur, come from animals and are made of protein.
"Other kinds of material, like cotton, come from plants. They look different under a microscope because they contain cellulose, not protein.
"Synthetic fibers, like polyester, are human made and don't contain either protein or cellulose. Instead, they're made of polymers, sort of like plastic.
Even without a microscope, you can analyze fibers yourself!
Try using a magnifying glass to compare loose threads from a shirt with a piece of wool from a sweater. How are the threads and wool similar? What differences can you find?

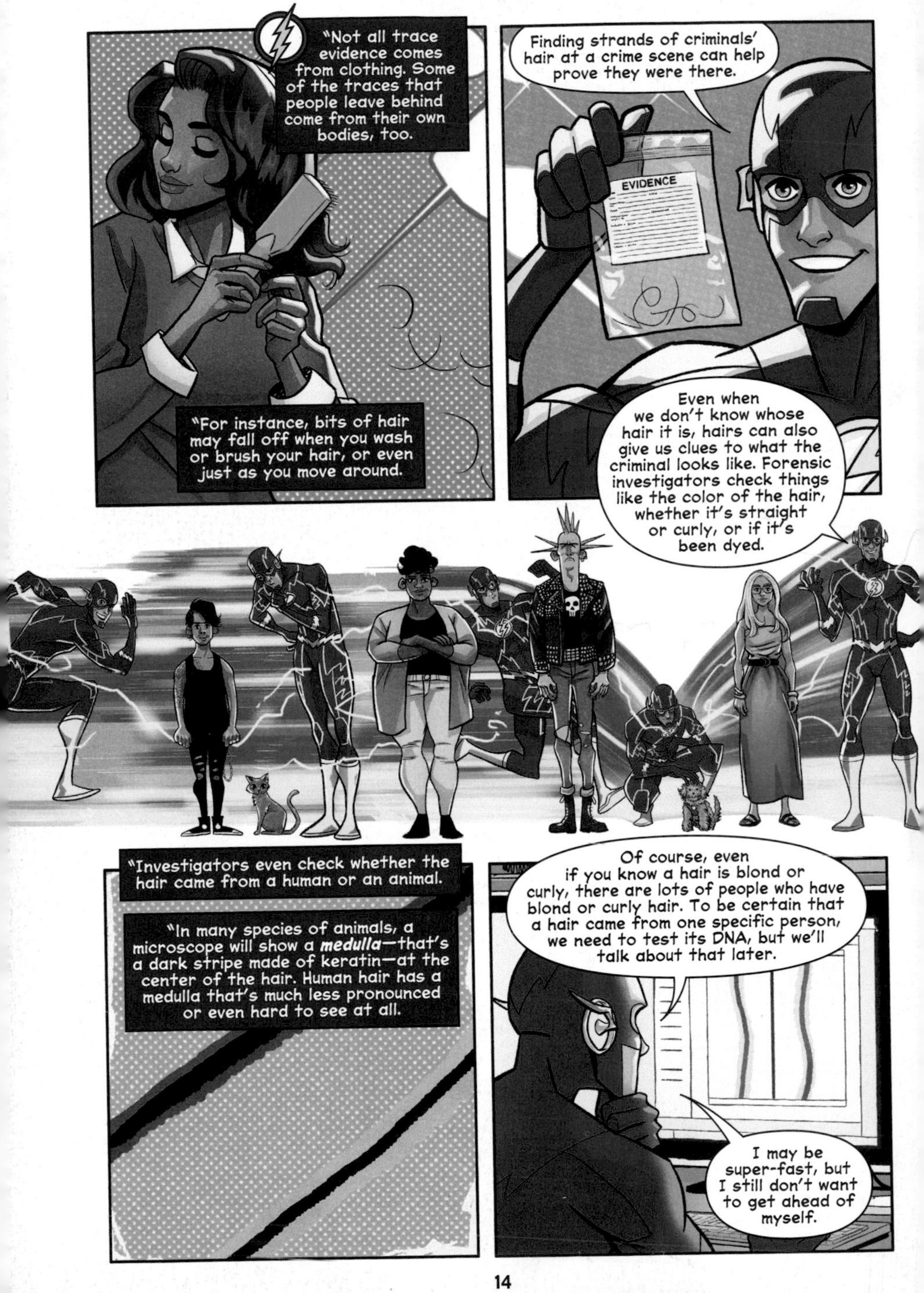
"Not all trace evidence comes from clothing. Some of the traces that people leave behind come from their own bodies, too.
"For instance, bits of hair may fall off when you wash or brush your hair, or even just as you move around.
Finding strands of criminals' hair at a crime scene can help prove they were there.
EVIDENCE
Even when we don't know whose hair it is, hairs can also give us clues to what the criminal looks like. Forensic investigators check things like the color of the hair, whether it's straight or curly, or if it's been dyed.
"Investigators even check whether the hair came from a human or an animal.
"In many species of animals, a microscope will show a *medulla*—that's a dark stripe made of keratin—at the center of the hair. Human hair has a medulla that's much less pronounced or even hard to see at all.
Of course, even if you know a hair is blond or curly, there are lots of people who have blond or curly hair. To be certain that a hair came from one specific person, we need to test its DNA, but we'll talk about that later.
I may be super-fast, but I still don't want to get ahead of myself.

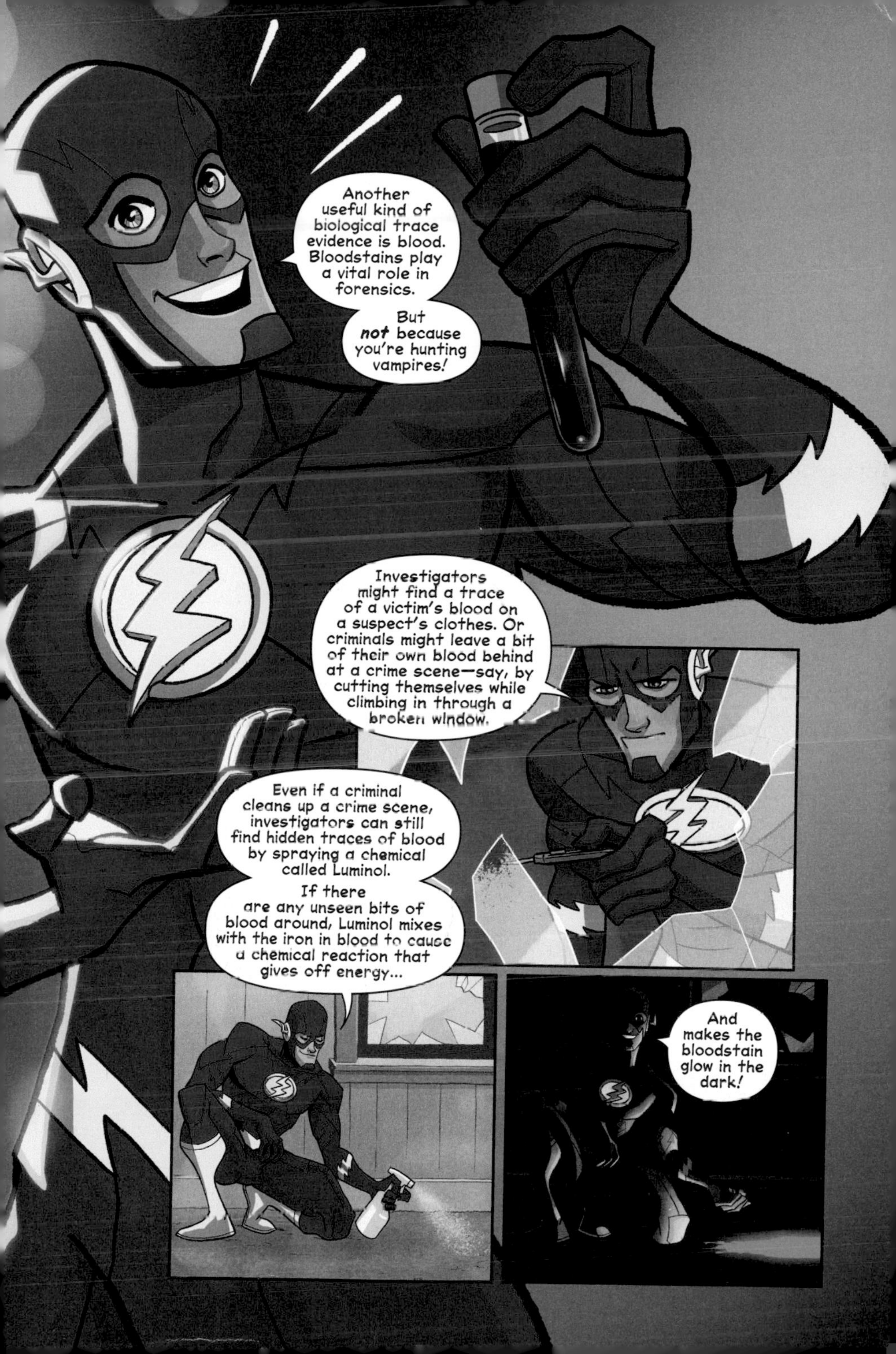

Another useful kind of biological trace evidence is blood. Bloodstains play a vital role in forensics.
But *not* because you're hunting vampires!
Investigators might find a trace of a victim's blood on a suspect's clothes. Or criminals might leave a bit of their own blood behind at a crime scene—say, by cutting themselves while climbing in through a broken window.
Even if a criminal cleans up a crime scene, investigators can still find hidden traces of blood by spraying a chemical called Luminol.
If there are any unseen bits of blood around, Luminol mixes with the iron in blood to cause a chemical reaction that gives off energy...
And makes the bloodstain glow in the dark!

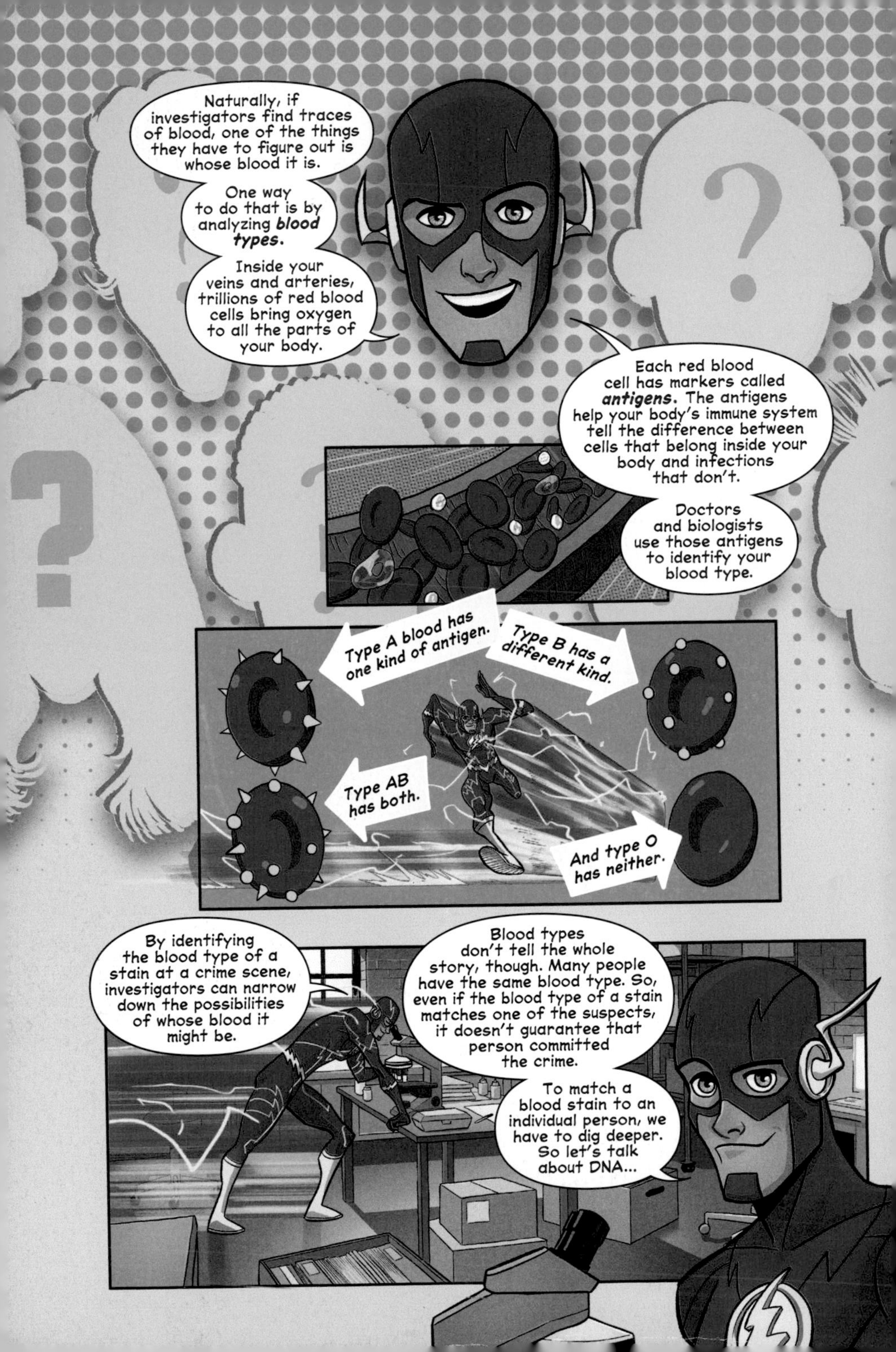
Naturally, if investigators find traces of blood, one of the things they have to figure out is whose blood it is.
One way to do that is by analyzing *blood types.*
Inside your veins and arteries, trillions of red blood cells bring oxygen to all the parts of your body.
Each red blood cell has markers called *antigens.* The antigens help your body's immune system tell the difference between cells that belong inside your body and infections that don't.
Doctors and biologists use those antigens to identify your blood type.
Type A blood has one kind of antigen.
Type B has a different kind.
Type AB has both.
And type O has neither.
By identifying the blood type of a stain at a crime scene, investigators can narrow down the possibilities of whose blood it might be.
Blood types don't tell the whole story, though. Many people have the same blood type. So, even if the blood type of a stain matches one of the suspects, it doesn't guarantee that person committed the crime.
To match a blood stain to an individual person, we have to dig deeper. So let's talk about DNA...

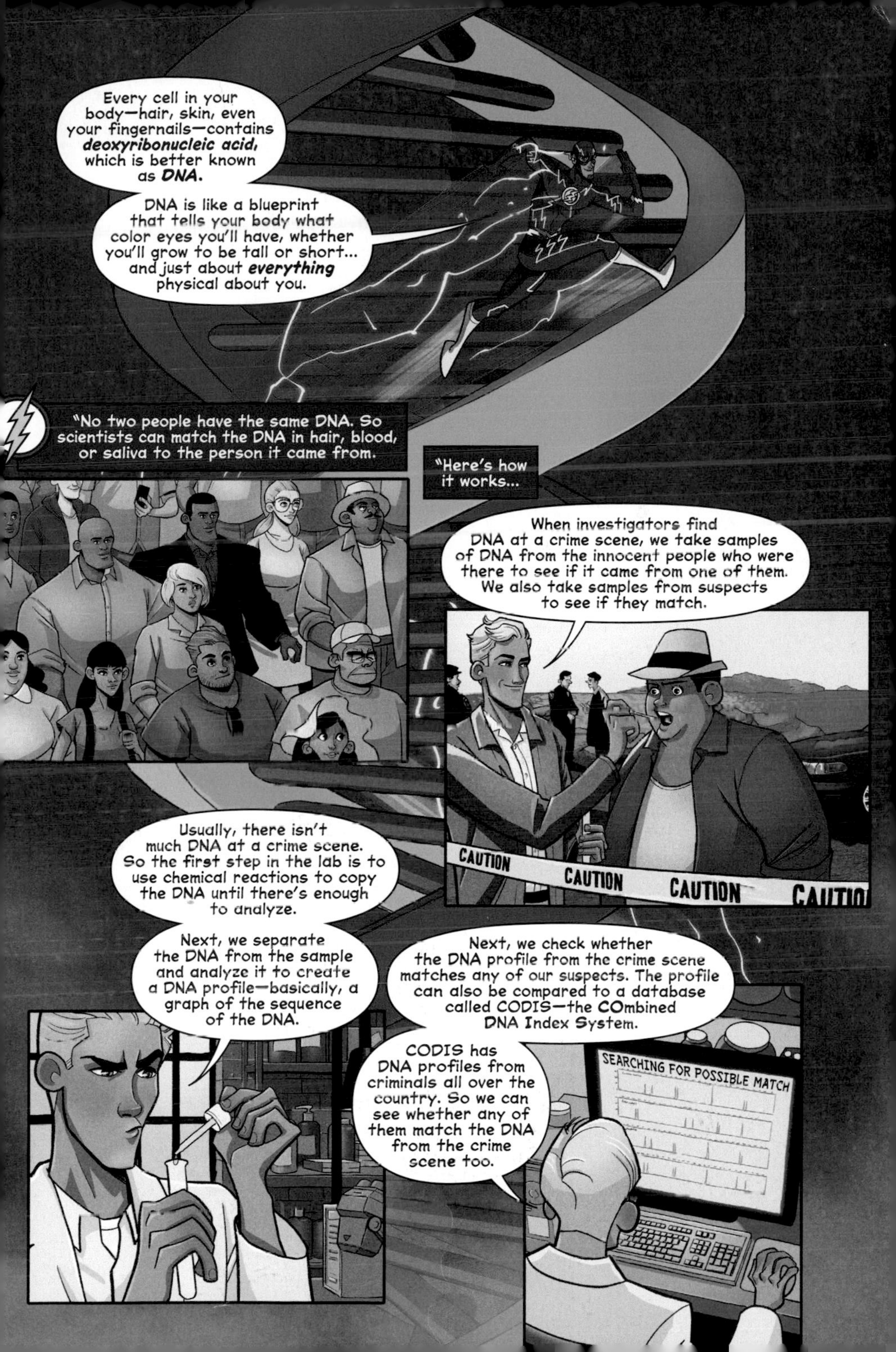
Every cell in your body—hair, skin, even your fingernails—contains ***deoxyribonucleic acid,*** which is better known as ***DNA.***
DNA is like a blueprint that tells your body what color eyes you'll have, whether you'll grow to be tall or short... and just about ***everything*** physical about you.
"No two people have the same DNA. So scientists can match the DNA in hair, blood, or saliva to the person it came from.
"Here's how it works...
When investigators find DNA at a crime scene, we take samples of DNA from the innocent people who were there to see if it came from one of them. We also take samples from suspects to see if they match.
CAUTION
CAUTION
CAUTION
CAUTIO
Usually, there isn't much DNA at a crime scene. So the first step in the lab is to use chemical reactions to copy the DNA until there's enough to analyze.
Next, we separate the DNA from the sample and analyze it to create a DNA profile—basically, a graph of the sequence of the DNA.
Next, we check whether the DNA profile from the crime scene matches any of our suspects. The profile can also be compared to a database called CODIS—the COmbined DNA Index System.
CODIS has DNA profiles from criminals all over the country. So we can see whether any of them match the DNA from the crime scene too.
SEARCHING FOR POSSIBLE MATCH

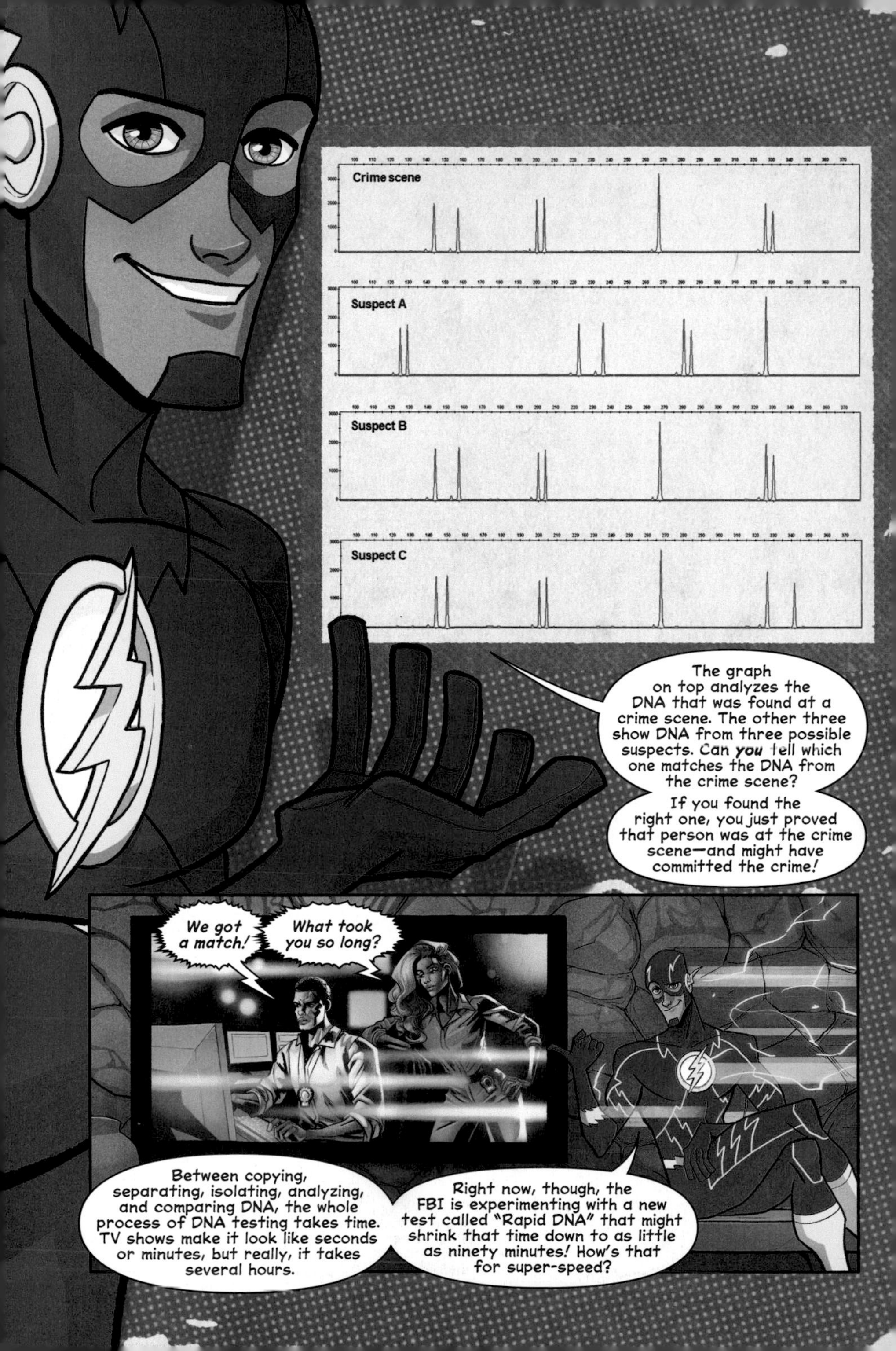
Crime scene
Suspect A
Suspect B
Suspect C
The graph on top analyzes the DNA that was found at a crime scene. The other three show DNA from three possible suspects. Can *you* tell which one matches the DNA from the crime scene?
If you found the right one, you just proved that person was at the crime scene—and might have committed the crime!
We got a match!
What took you so long?
Between copying, separating, isolating, analyzing, and comparing DNA, the whole process of DNA testing takes time. TV shows make it look like seconds or minutes, but really, it takes several hours.
Right now, though, the FBI is experimenting with a new test called "Rapid DNA" that might shrink that time down to as little as ninety minutes! How's that for super-speed?

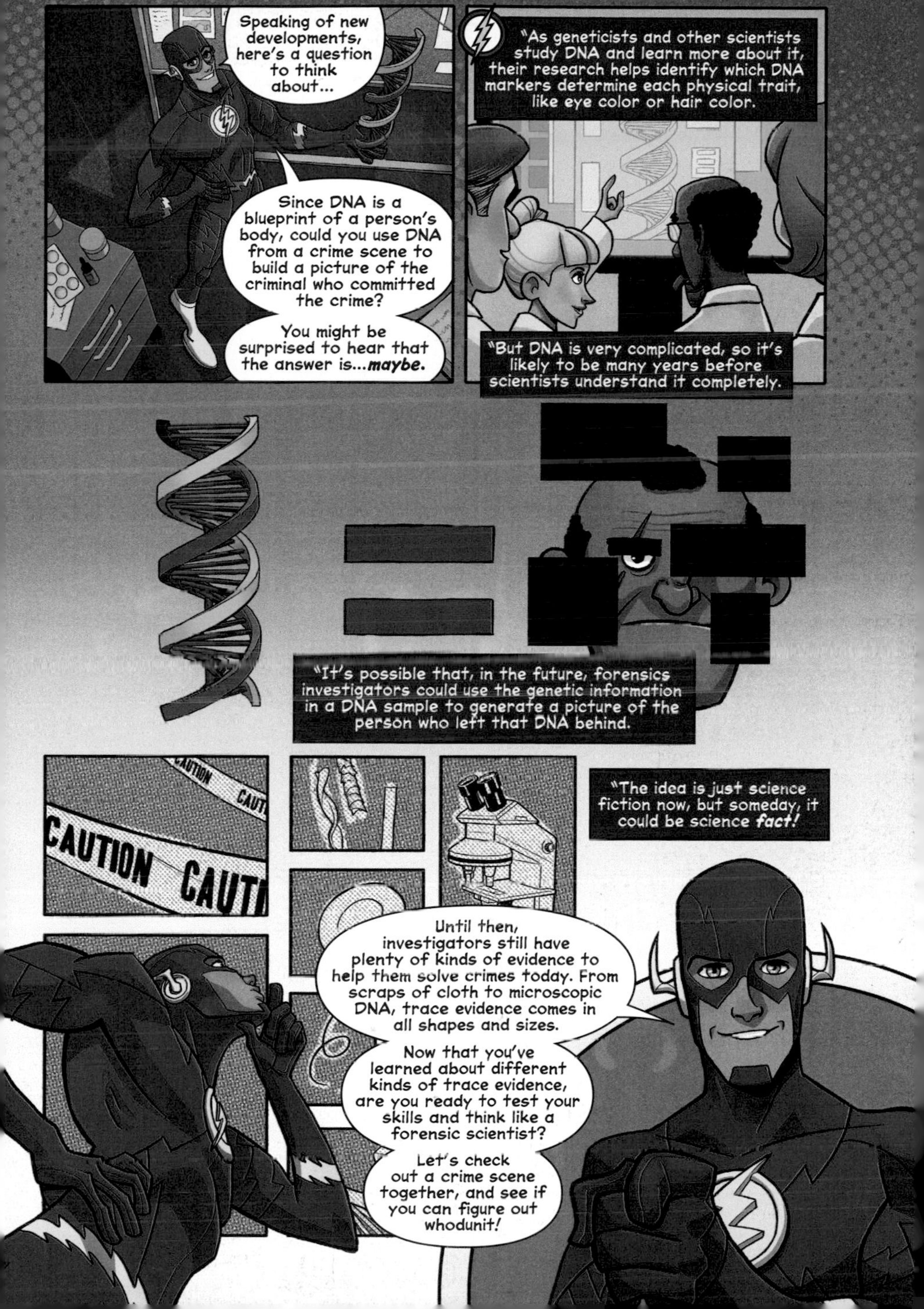
Speaking of new developments, here's a question to think about...
Since DNA is a blueprint of a person's body, could you use DNA from a crime scene to build a picture of the criminal who committed the crime?
You might be surprised to hear that the answer is...*maybe.*
"As geneticists and other scientists study DNA and learn more about it, their research helps identify which DNA markers determine each physical trait, like eye color or hair color.
"But DNA is very complicated, so it's likely to be many years before scientists understand it completely.
"It's possible that, in the future, forensics investigators could use the genetic information in a DNA sample to generate a picture of the person who left that DNA behind.
CAUTION CAUTI
"The idea is just science fiction now, but someday, it could be science *fact!*
Until then, investigators still have plenty of kinds of evidence to help them solve crimes today. From scraps of cloth to microscopic DNA, trace evidence comes in all shapes and sizes.
Now that you've learned about different kinds of trace evidence, are you ready to test your skills and think like a forensic scientist?
Let's check out a crime scene together, and see if you can figure out whodunit!

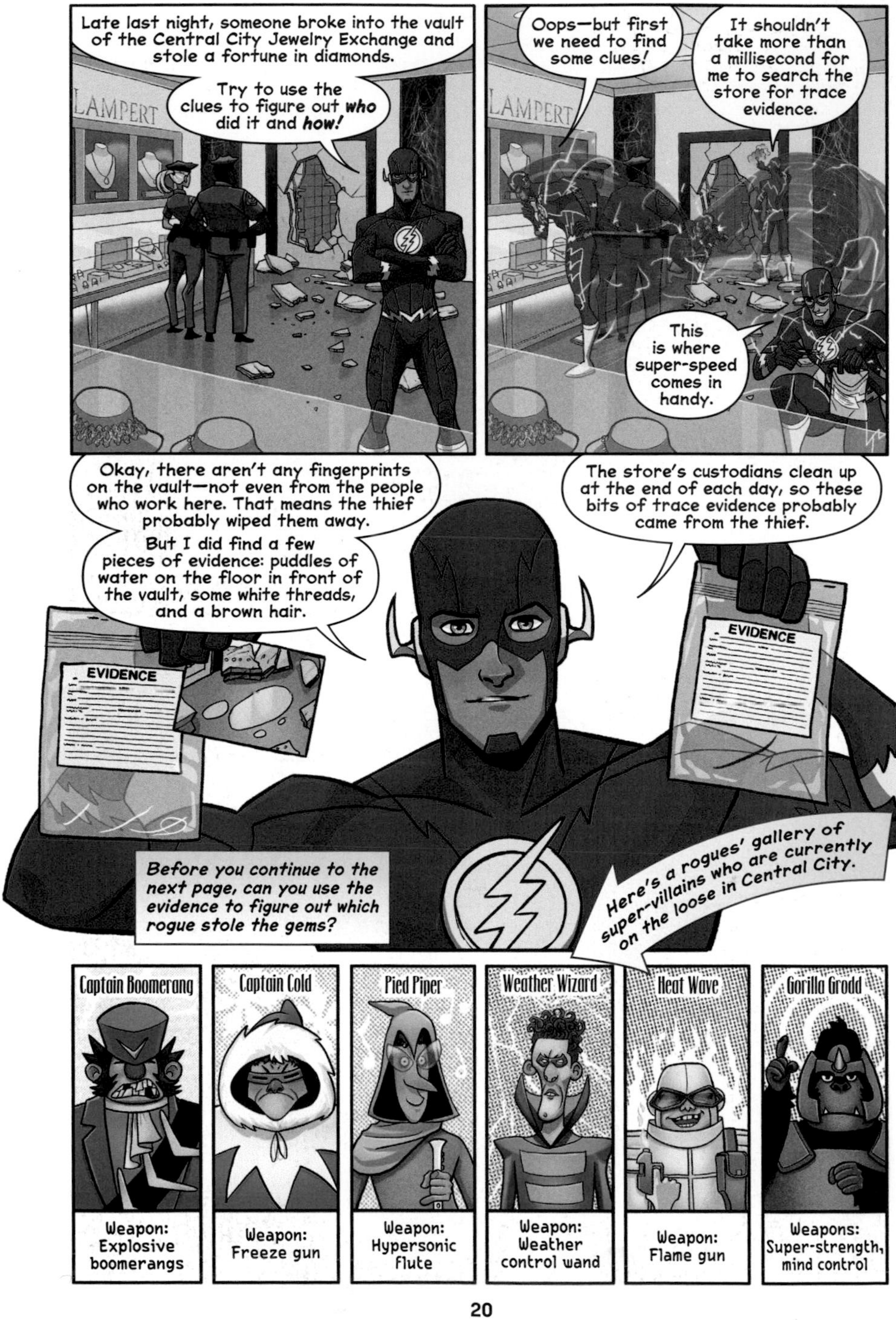
Late last night, someone broke into the vault of the Central City Jewelry Exchange and stole a fortune in diamonds.
Try to use the clues to figure out ***who*** did it and ***how!***
LAMPERT
Oops—but first we need to find some clues!
It shouldn't take more than a millisecond for me to search the store for trace evidence.
This is where super-speed comes in handy.
Okay, there aren't any fingerprints on the vault—not even from the people who work here. That means the thief probably wiped them away.
But I did find a few pieces of evidence: puddles of water on the floor in front of the vault, some white threads, and a brown hair.
The store's custodians clean up at the end of each day, so these bits of trace evidence probably came from the thief.
EVIDENCE
EVIDENCE
Before you continue to the next page, can you use the evidence to figure out which rogue stole the gems?
Here's a rogues' gallery of super-villains who are currently on the loose in Central City.
Captain Boomerang
Weapon: Explosive boomerangs
Captain Cold
Weapon: Freeze gun
Pied Piper
Weapon: Hypersonic flute
Weather Wizard
Weapon: Weather control wand
Heat Wave
Weapon: Flame gun
Gorilla Grodd
Weapons: Super-strength, mind control

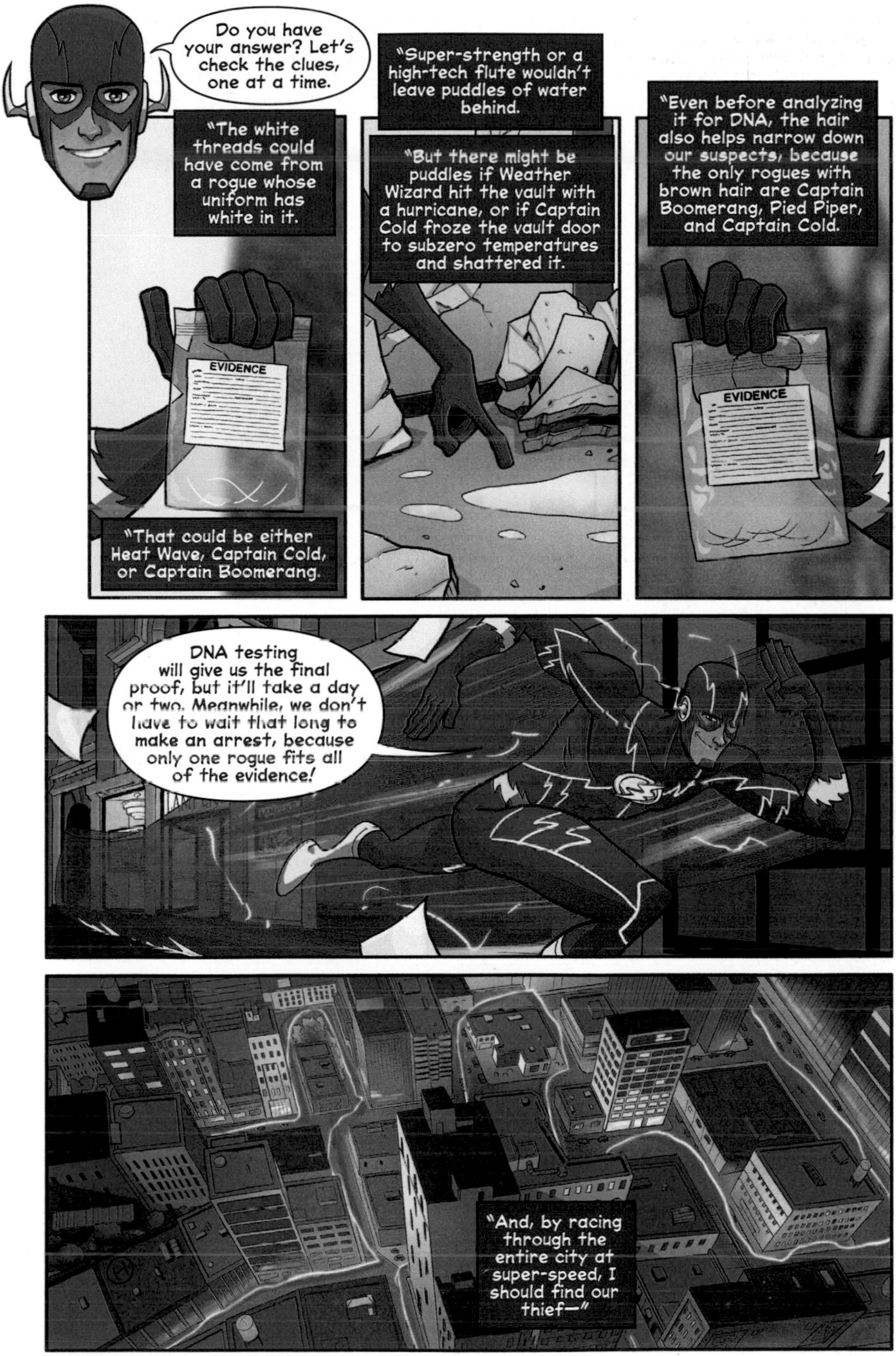
Do you have your answer? Let's check the clues, one at a time.
"The white threads could have come from a rogue whose uniform has white in it.
EVIDENCE
"That could be either Heat Wave, Captain Cold, or Captain Boomerang.
"Super-strength or a high-tech flute wouldn't leave puddles of water behind.
"But there might be puddles if Weather Wizard hit the vault with a hurricane, or if Captain Cold froze the vault door to subzero temperatures and shattered it.
"Even before analyzing it for DNA, the hair also helps narrow down our suspects, because the only rogues with brown hair are Captain Boomerang, Pied Piper, and Captain Cold.
EVIDENCE
DNA testing will give us the final proof, but it'll take a day or two. Meanwhile, we don't have to wait that long to make an arrest, because only one rogue fits all of the evidence!
"And, by racing through the entire city at super-speed, I should find our thief—"

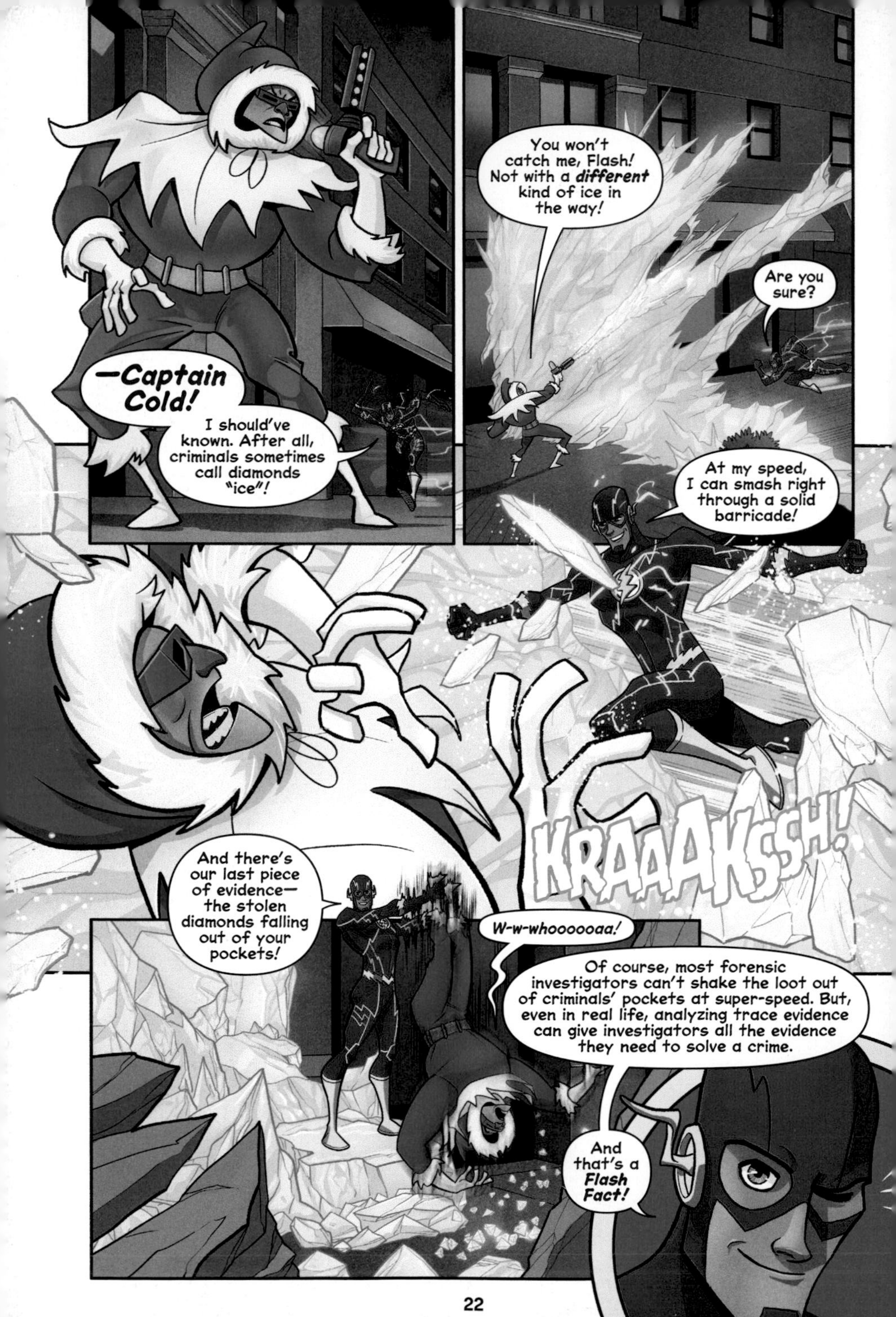
—Captain Cold!
I should've known. After all, criminals sometimes call diamonds "ice"!
You won't catch me, Flash! Not with a *different* kind of ice in the way!
Are you sure?
At my speed, I can smash right through a solid barricade!
KRAAAKSSH!
And there's our last piece of evidence— the stolen diamonds falling out of your pockets!
W-w-whoooooaa!
Of course, most forensic investigators can't shake the loot out of criminals' pockets at super-speed. But, even in real life, analyzing trace evidence can give investigators all the evidence they need to solve a crime.
And that's a *Flash Fact*!

CHAPTER TWO

IF YOU CAN'T TAKE
THE HEAT

WRITTEN BY **VARIAN JOHNSON** AND **DARIAN JOHNSON**

ILLUSTRATED BY **VIC REGIS**

LETTERED BY **WES ABBOTT**

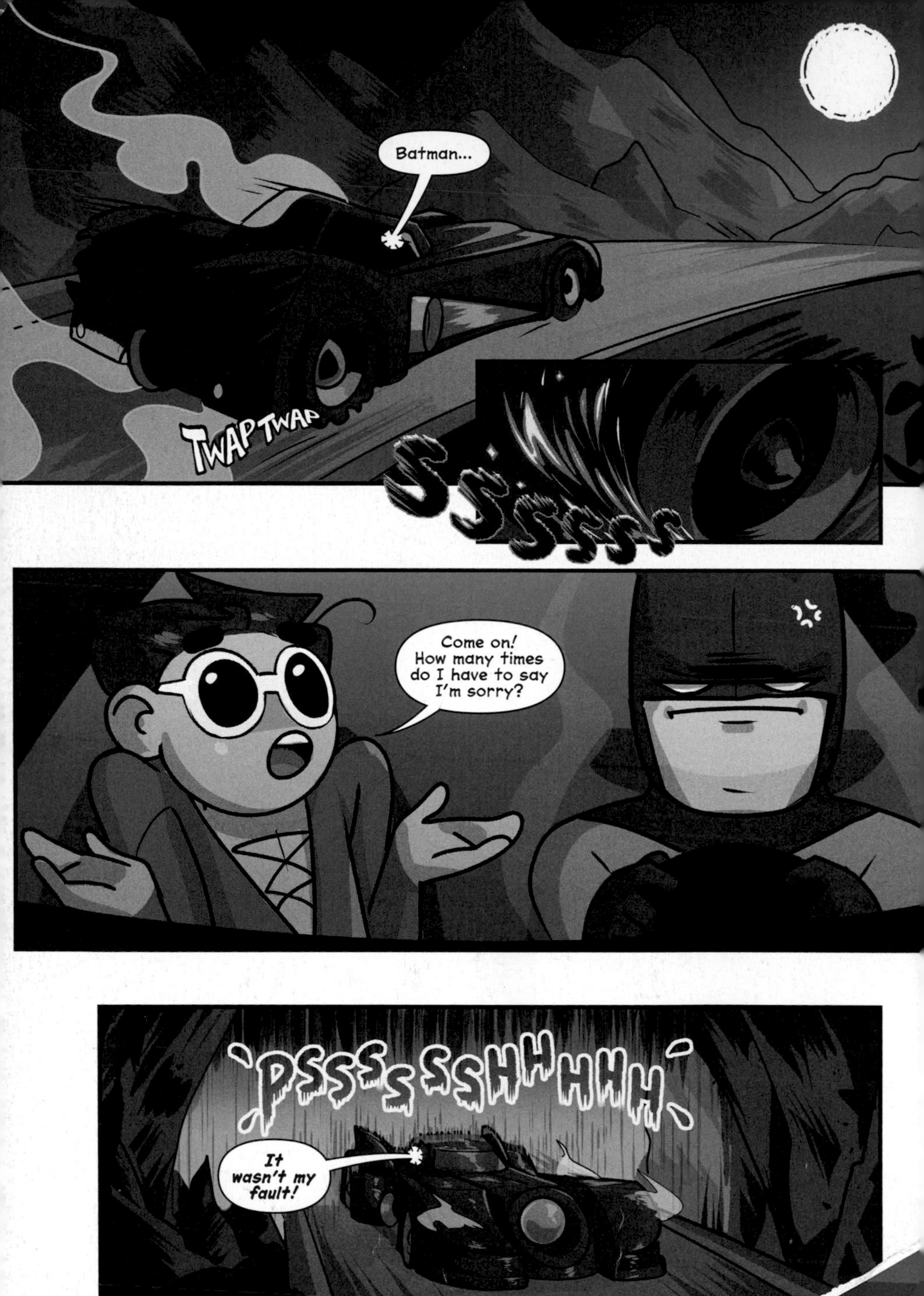
Batman...
TWAP TWAP
SSSSSSS
Come on! How many times do I have to say I'm sorry?
PSSSSSHHHHHH
It wasn't my fault!

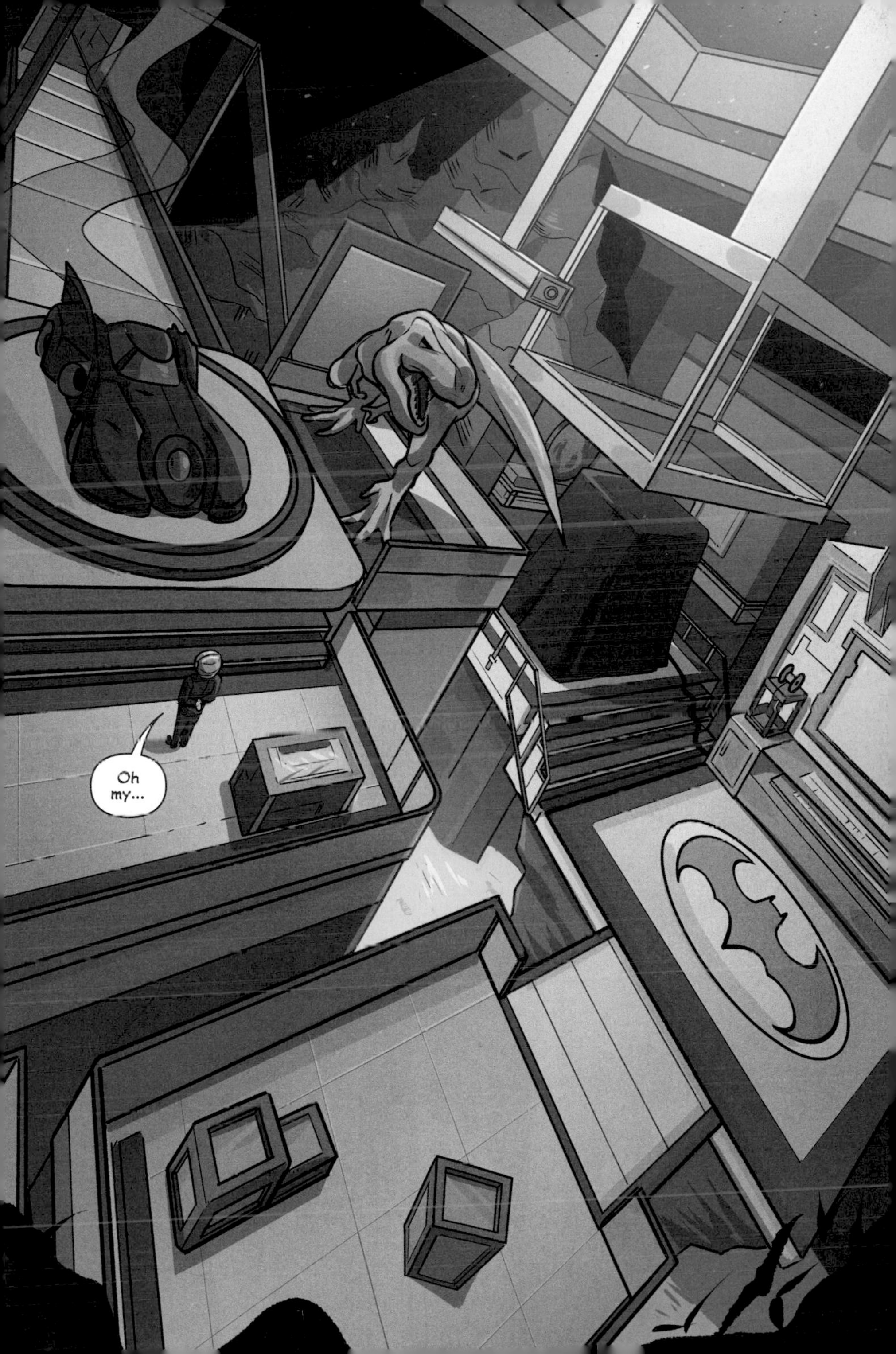
Oh my...

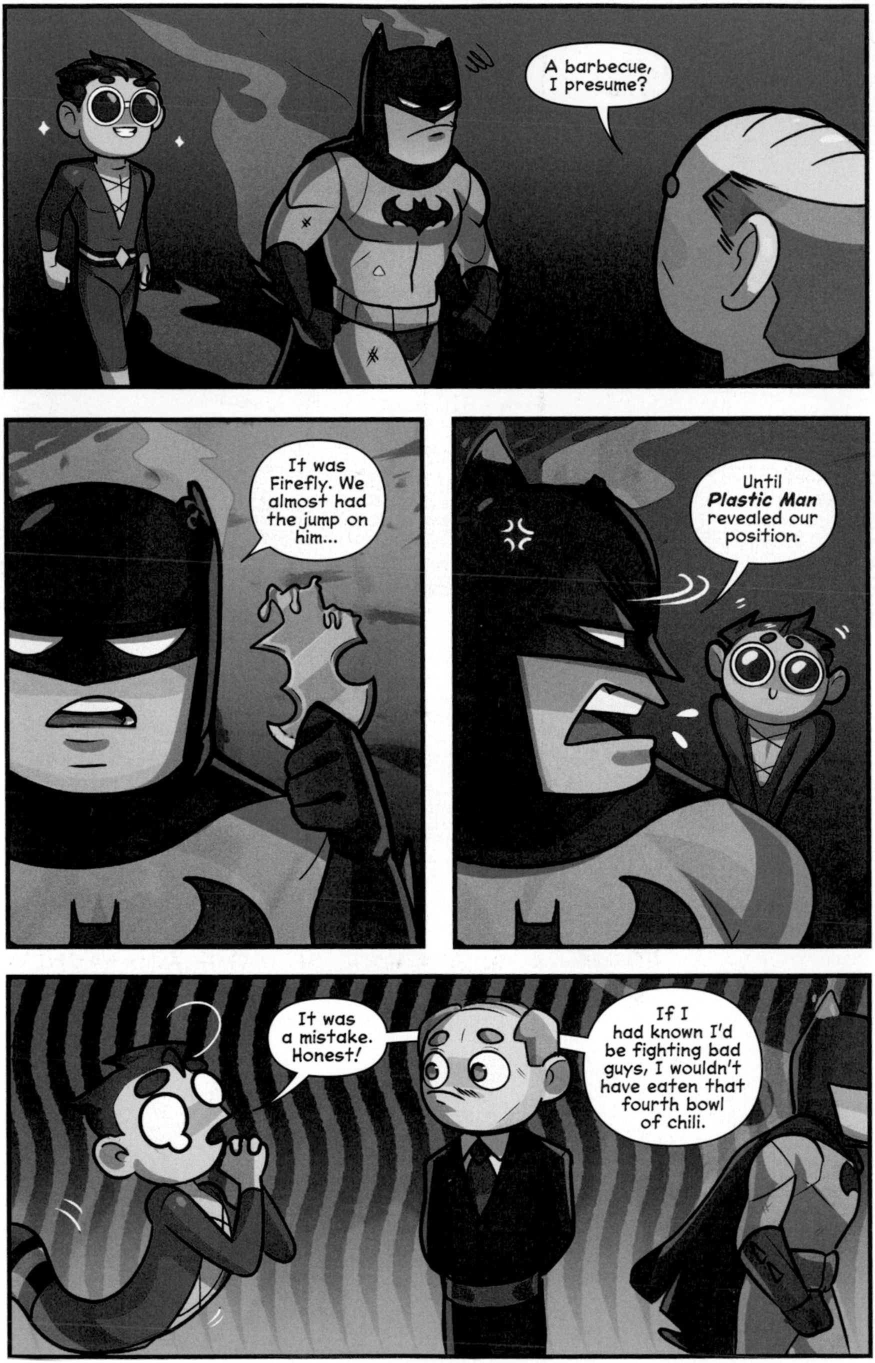
A barbecue, I presume?
It was Firefly. We almost had the jump on him...
Until *Plastic Man* revealed our position.
It was a mistake. Honest!
If I had known I'd be fighting bad guys, I wouldn't have eaten that fourth bowl of chili.

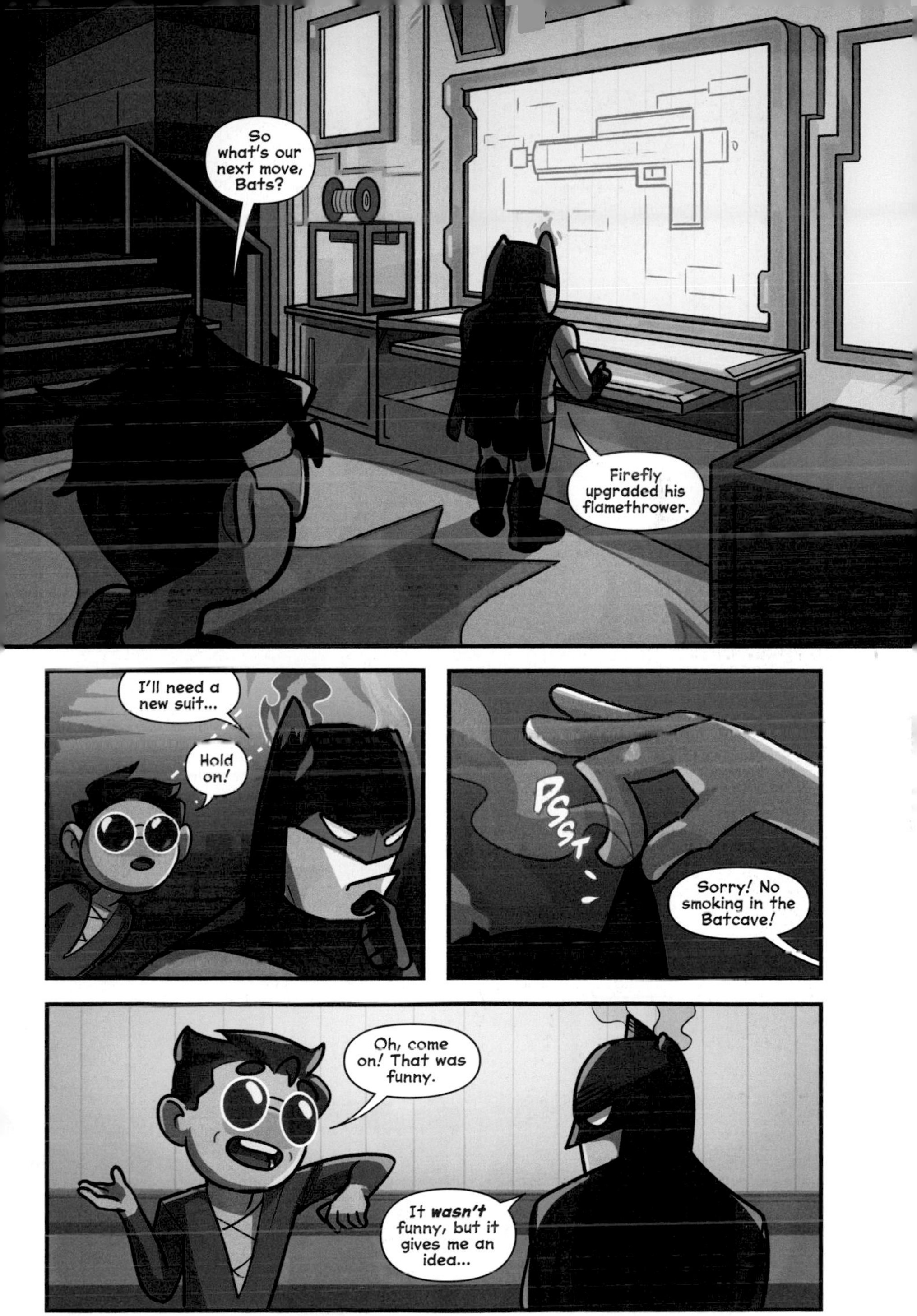
So what's our next move, Bats?
Firefly upgraded his flamethrower.
I'll need a new suit...
Hold on!
PSST
Sorry! No smoking in the Batcave!
Oh, come on! That was funny.
It *wasn't* funny, but it gives me an idea...

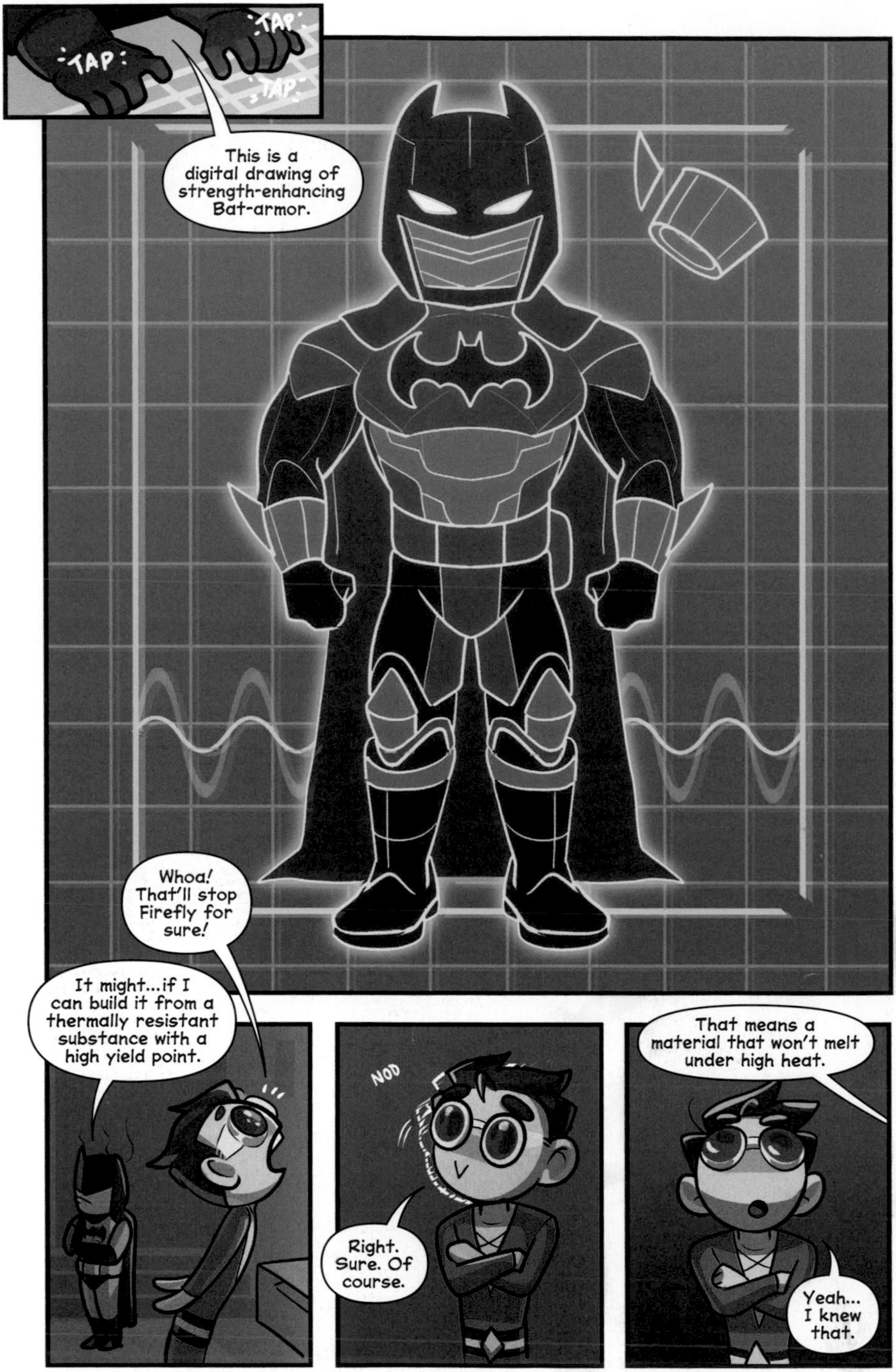
TAP
TAP
TAP
This is a digital drawing of strength-enhancing Bat-armor.
Whoa! That'll stop Firefly for sure!
It might...if I can build it from a thermally resistant substance with a high yield point.
NOD
Right. Sure. Of course.
That means a material that won't melt under high heat.
Yeah... I knew that.

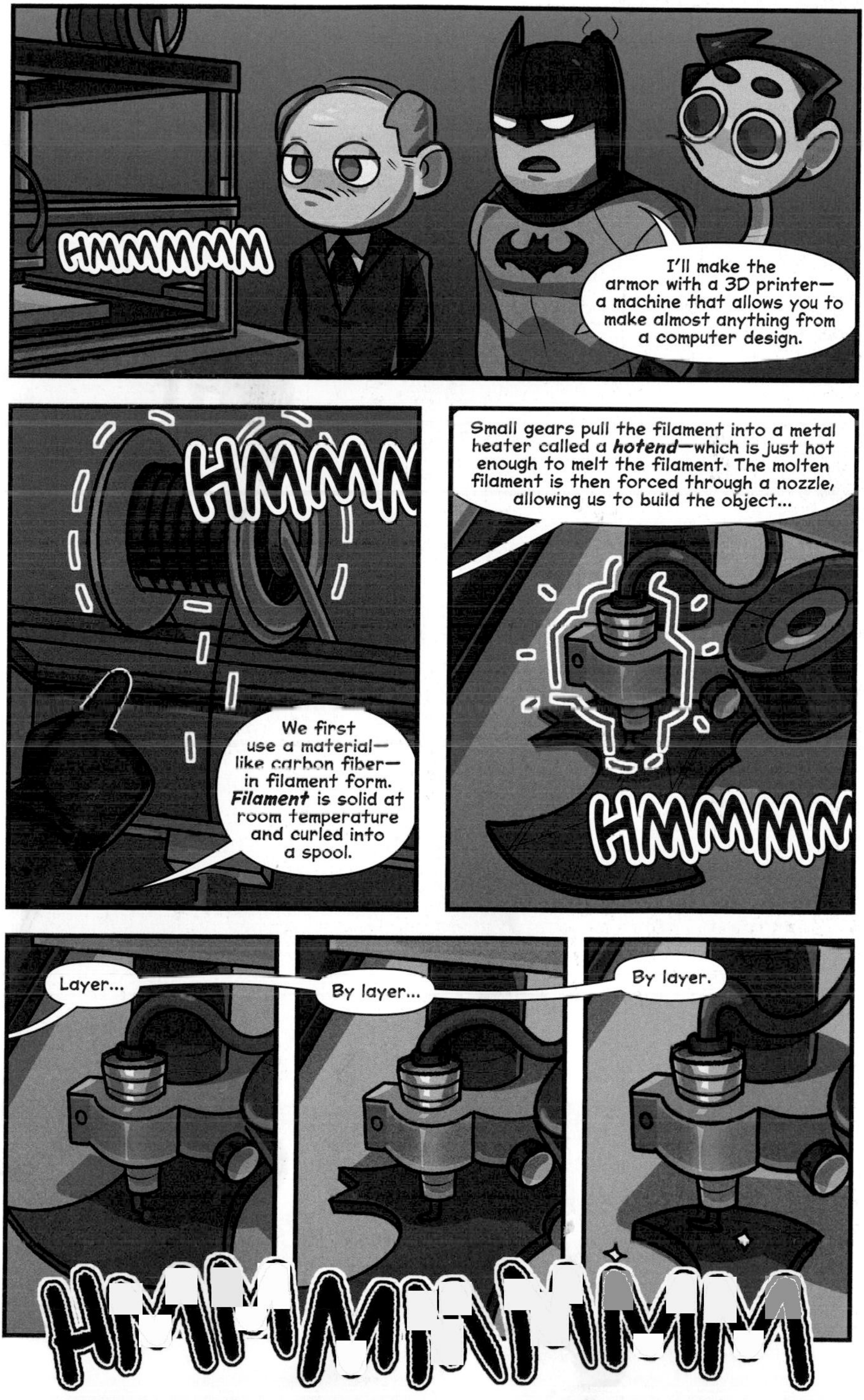
HMMMMMM
I'll make the armor with a 3D printer—a machine that allows you to make almost anything from a computer design.
HMMM
We first use a material—like carbon fiber—in filament form. *Filament* is solid at room temperature and curled into a spool.
Small gears pull the filament into a metal heater called a *hotend*—which is just hot enough to melt the filament. The molten filament is then forced through a nozzle, allowing us to build the object...
HMMMM
Layer...
By layer...
By layer.

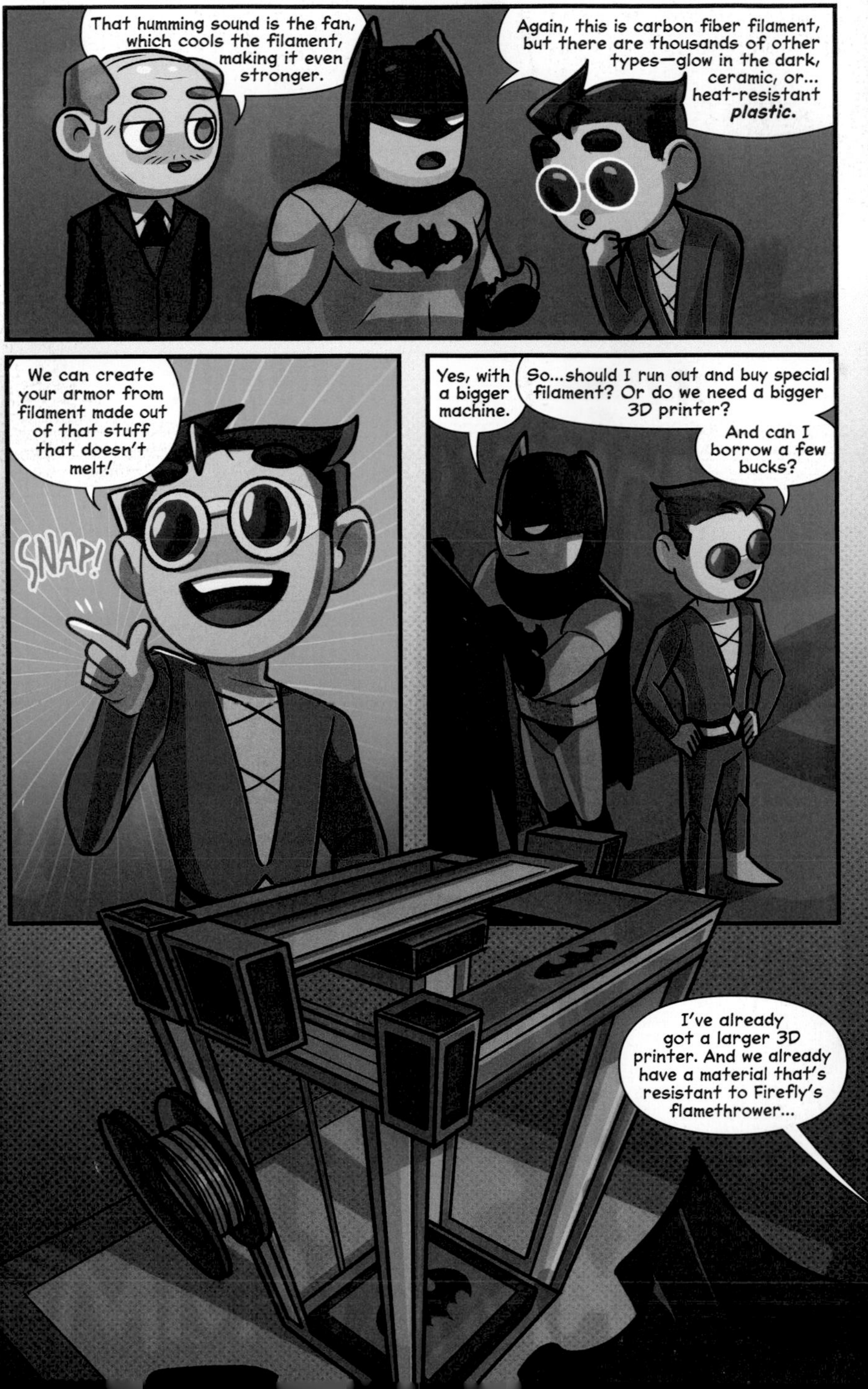
That humming sound is the fan, which cools the filament, making it even stronger.
Again, this is carbon fiber filament, but there are thousands of other types—glow in the dark, ceramic, or... heat-resistant ***plastic.***
We can create your armor from filament made out of that stuff that doesn't melt!
SNAP!
So...should I run out and buy special filament? Or do we need a bigger 3D printer?
Yes, with a bigger machine.
And can I borrow a few bucks?
I've already got a larger 3D printer. And we already have a material that's resistant to Firefly's flamethrower...

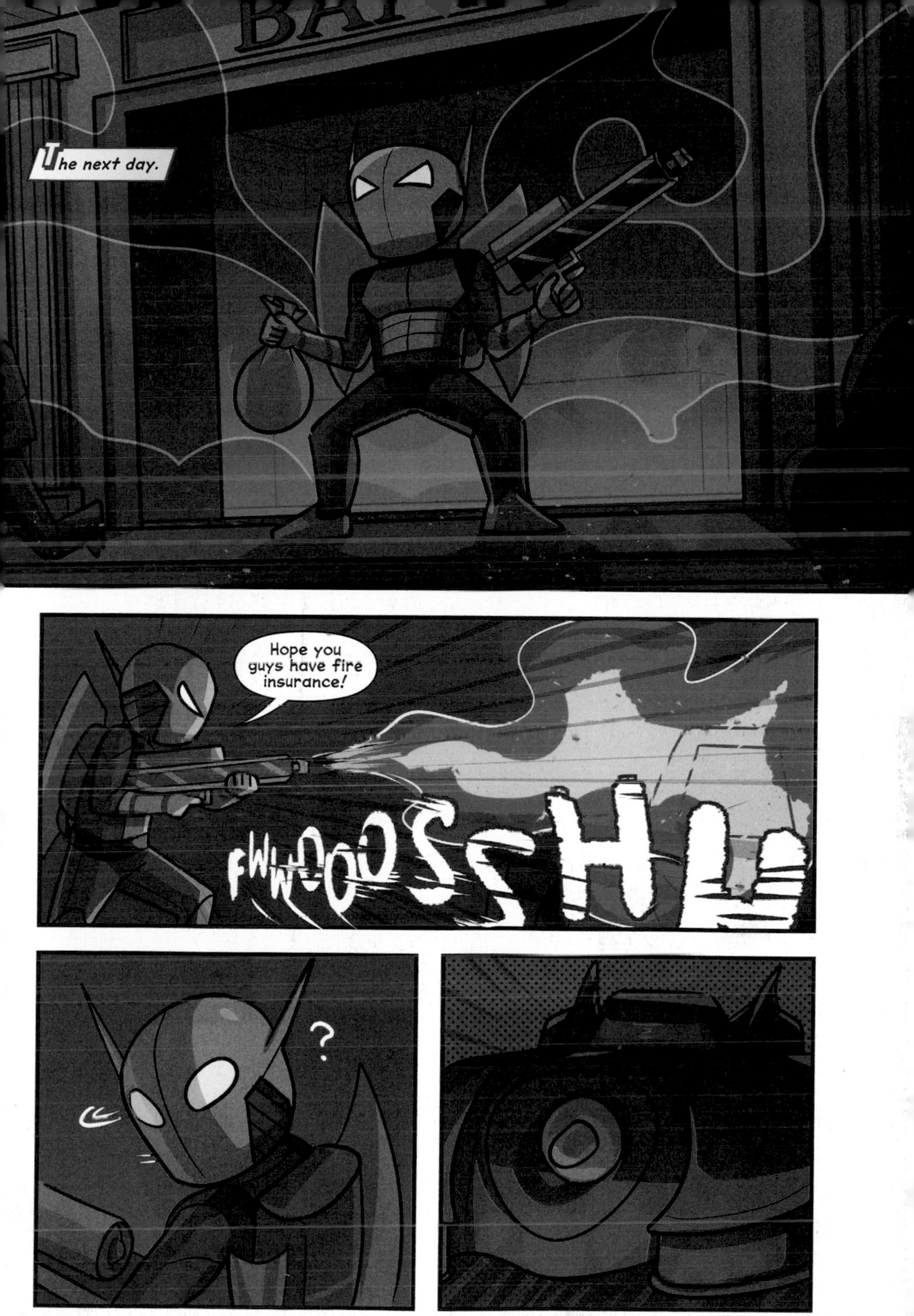
The next day.
Hope you guys have fire insurance!
FWWOOOSH
?

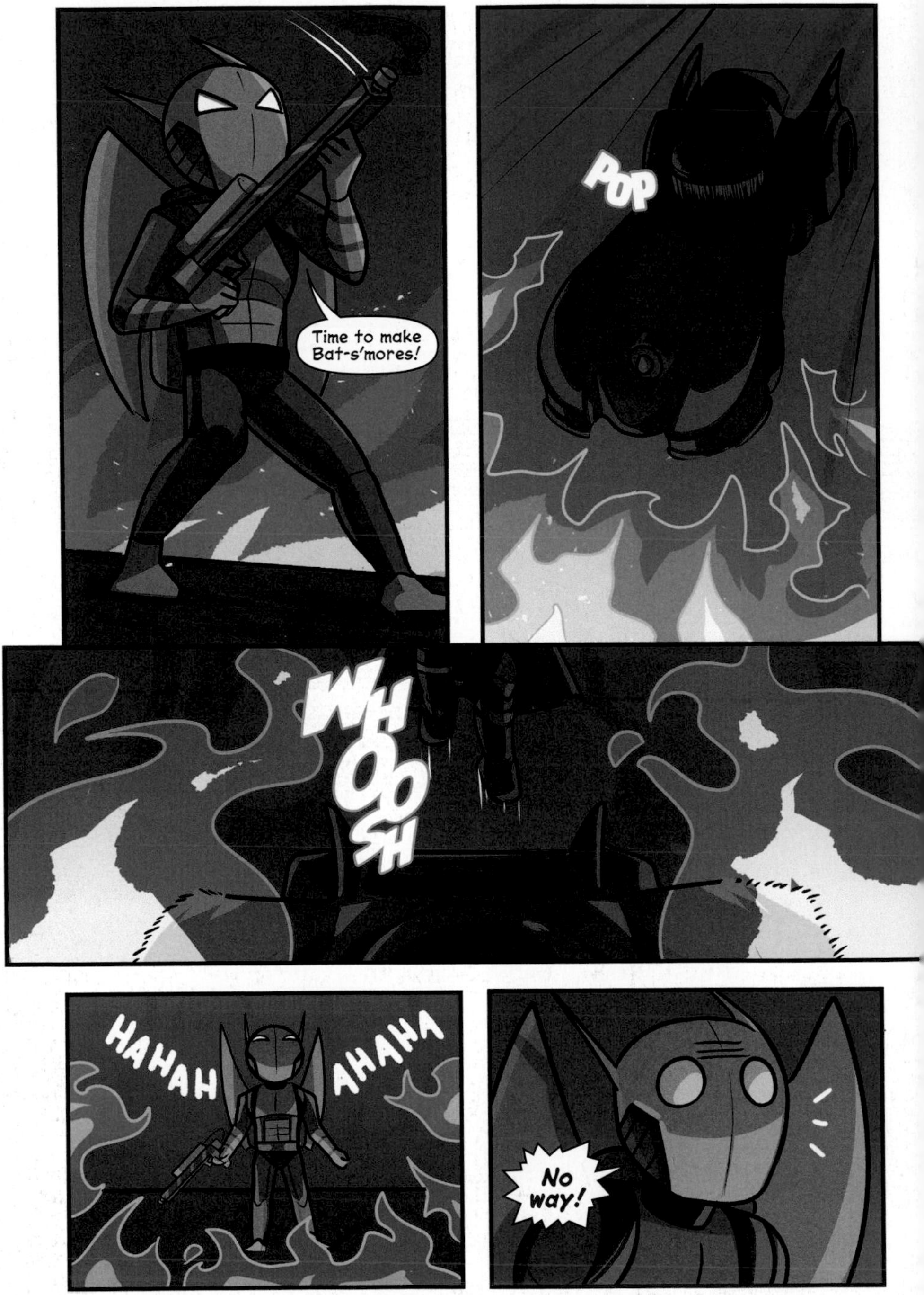
Time to make Bat-s'mores!
POP
WHOOOSH
HAHAH AHAHA
No way!

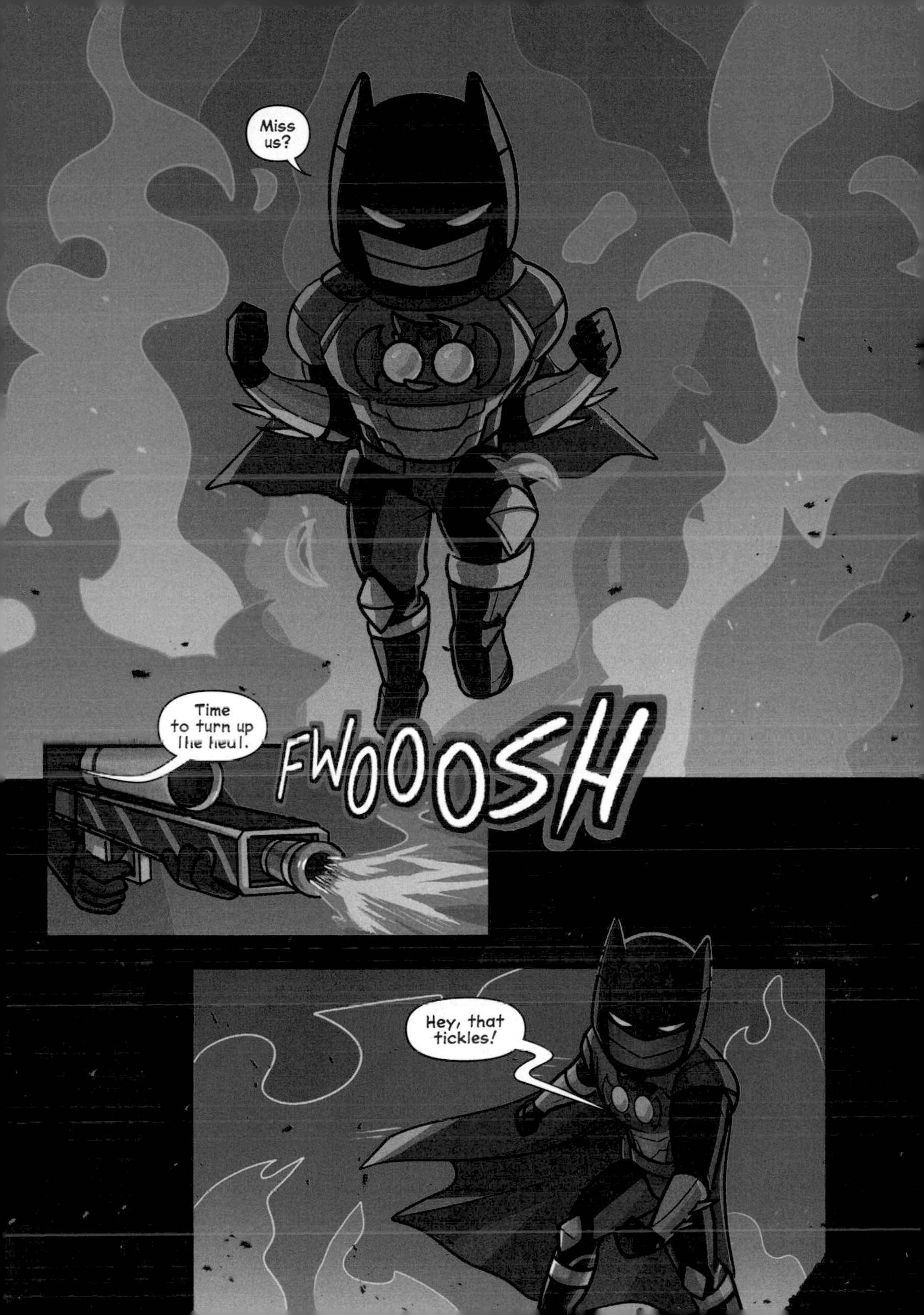
Miss us?
Time to turn up the heat.
FWOOOSH
Hey, that tickles!

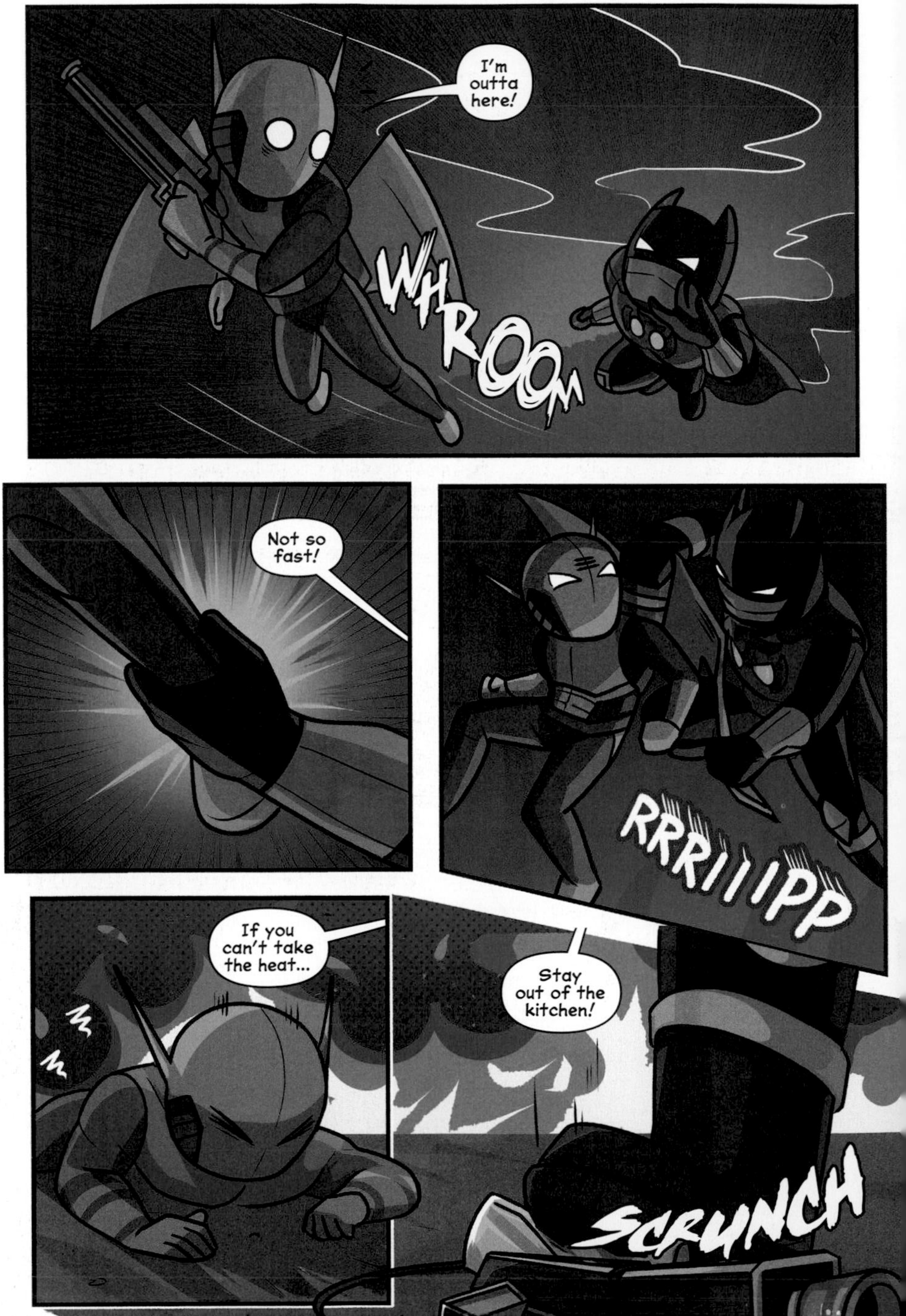
I'm outta here!
WHROOM
Not so fast!
RRRIIIPP
If you can't take the heat...
Stay out of the kitchen!
SCRUNCH

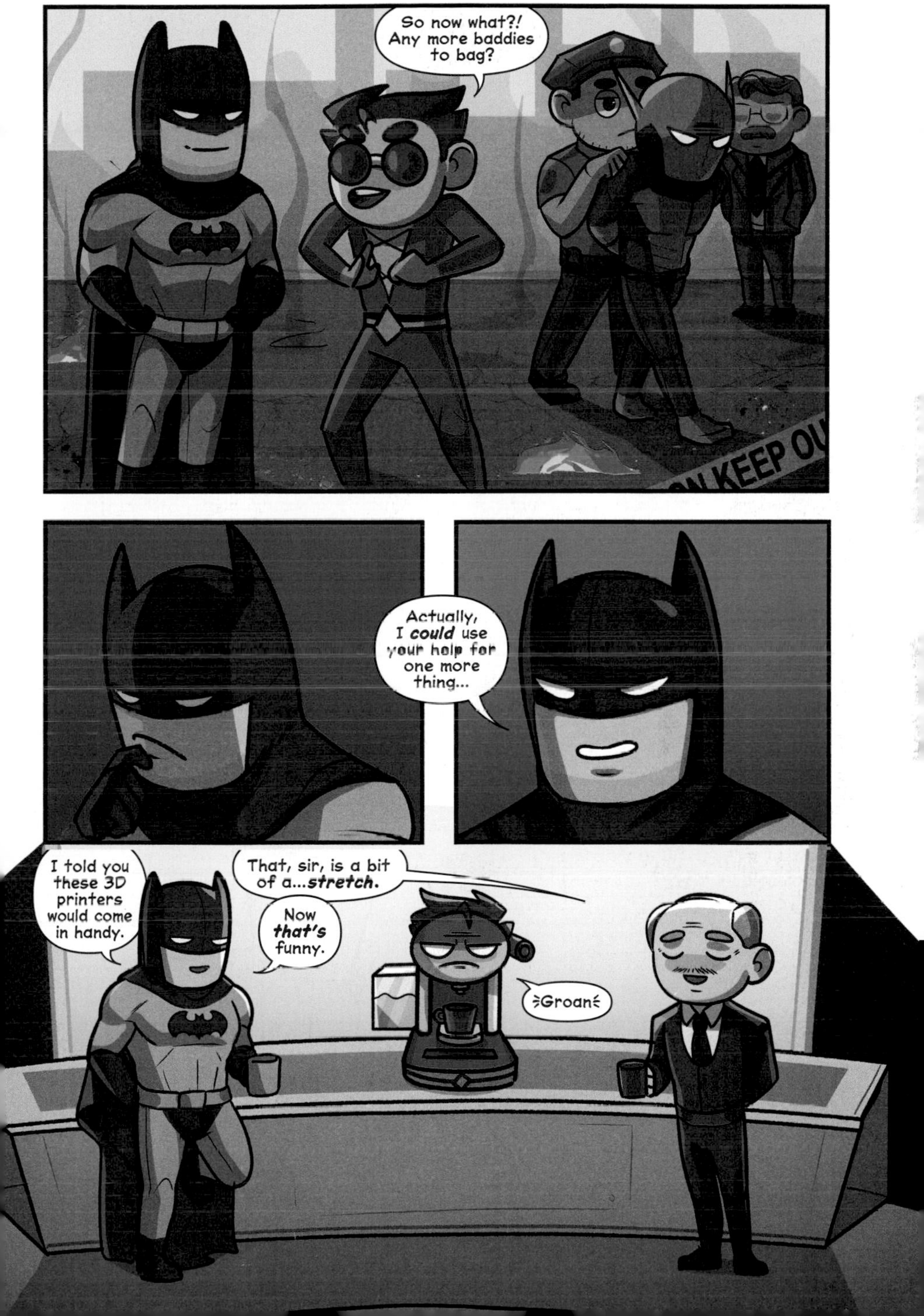

So now what?! Any more baddies to bag?
KEEP OU
Actually, I *could* use your help for one more thing...
I told you these 3D printers would come in handy.
That, sir, is a bit of a...*stretch.*
Now *that's* funny.
Groan

CHAPTER THREE

THE FACTS OF LIFE

WRITTEN BY **AMY CHU**

ILLUSTRATED BY **ILE GONZALEZ**

LETTERED BY **WES ABBOTT**

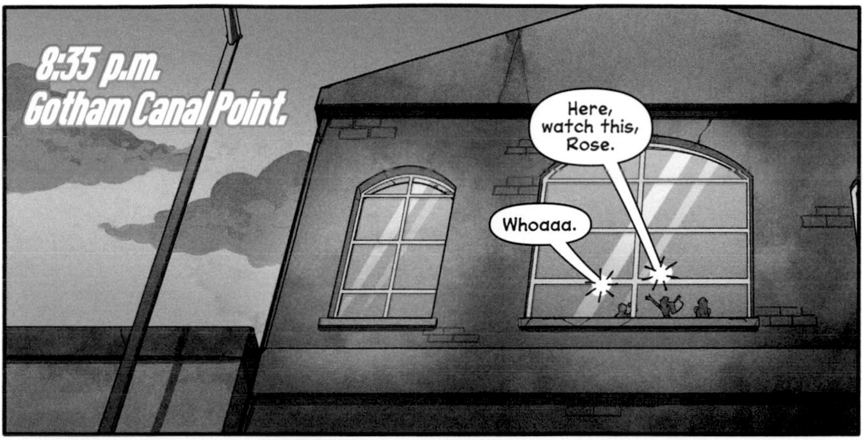
8:35 p.m.
Gotham Canal Point.
Here, watch this, Rose.
Whoaaa.

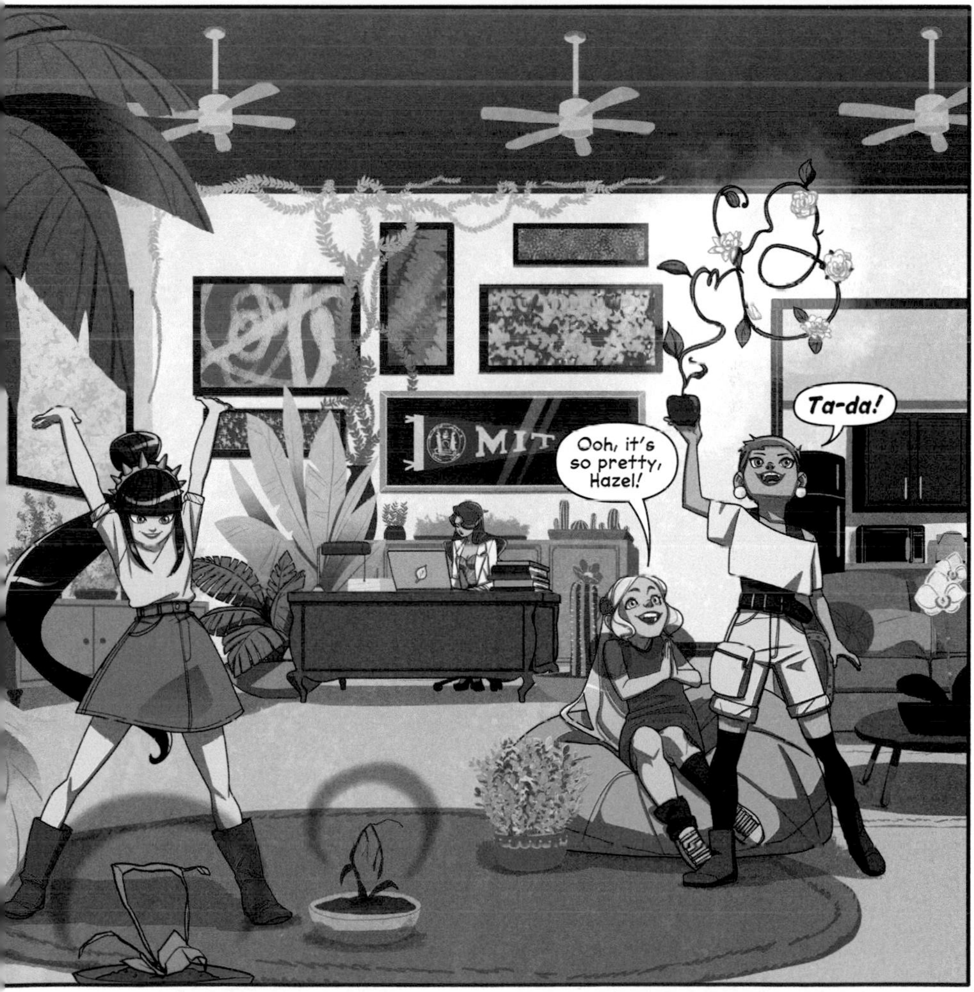
MIT
Ta-da!
Ooh, it's so pretty, Hazel!

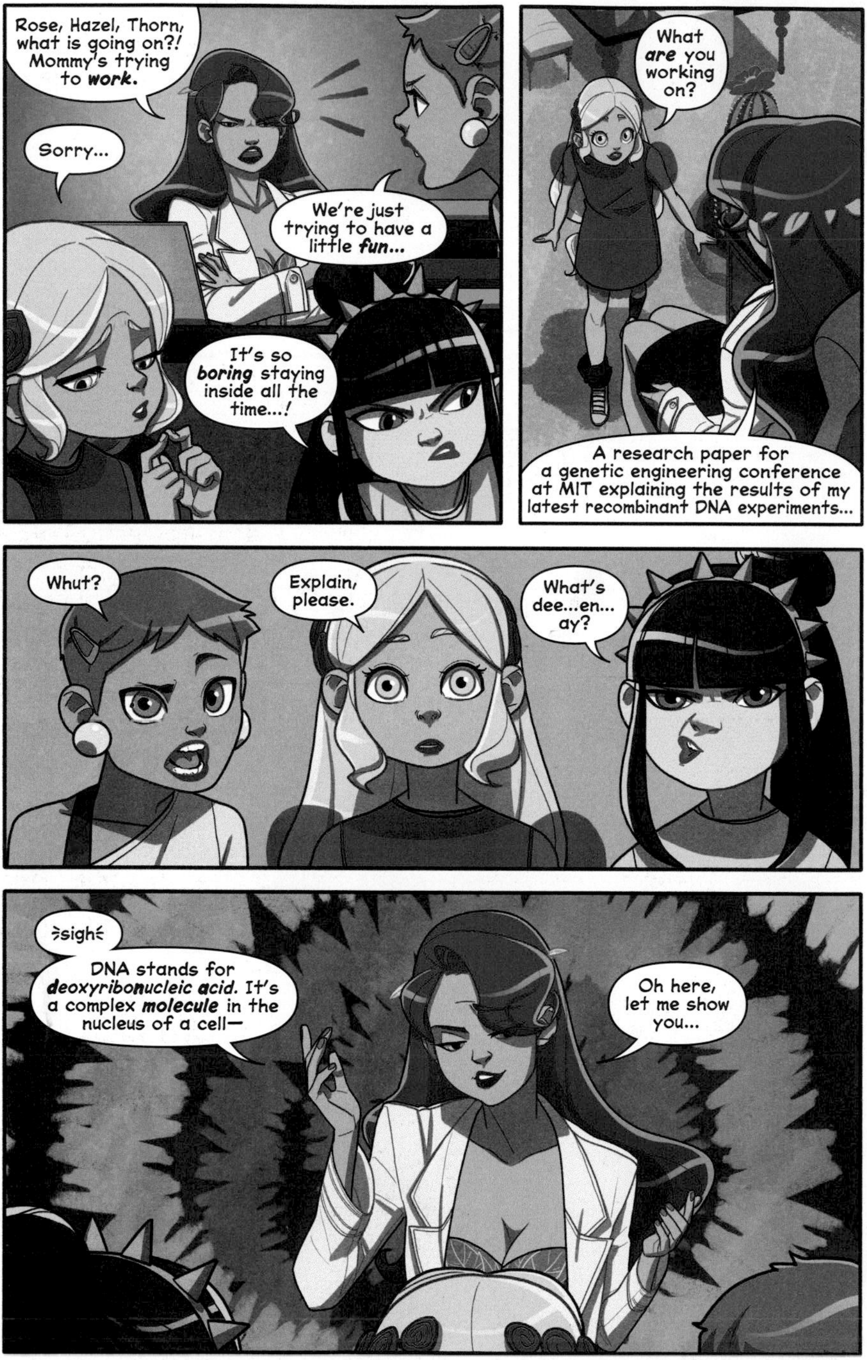
Rose, Hazel, Thorn, what is going on?! Mommy's trying to **work.**
Sorry...
We're just trying to have a little **fun...**
It's so **boring** staying inside all the time...!
What **are** you working on?
A research paper for a genetic engineering conference at MIT explaining the results of my latest recombinant DNA experiments...
Whut?
Explain, please.
What's dee...en... ay?
⋟sigh⋞
DNA stands for **deoxyribonucleic acid.** It's a complex **molecule** in the nucleus of a cell—
Oh here, let me show you...

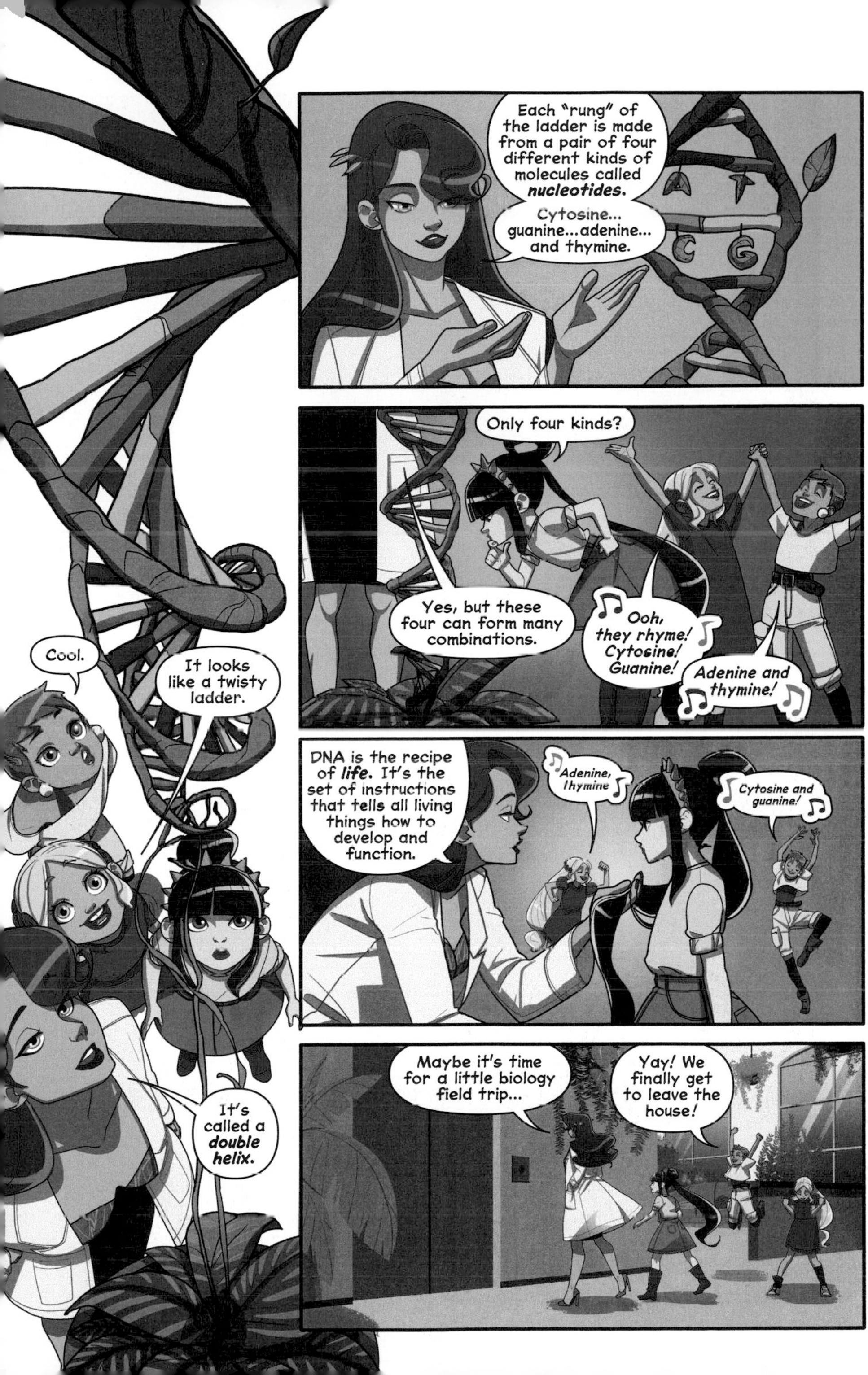

Each "rung" of the ladder is made from a pair of four different kinds of molecules called **nucleotides.**
Cytosine... guanine...adenine... and thymine.
Only four kinds?
Yes, but these four can form many combinations.
Ooh, they rhyme! Cytosine! Guanine!
Adenine and thymine!
Cool.
It looks like a twisty ladder.
DNA is the recipe of **life.** It's the set of instructions that tells all living things how to develop and function.
Adenine, thymine
Cytosine and guanine!
It's called a **double helix.**
Maybe it's time for a little biology field trip...
Yay! We finally get to leave the house!

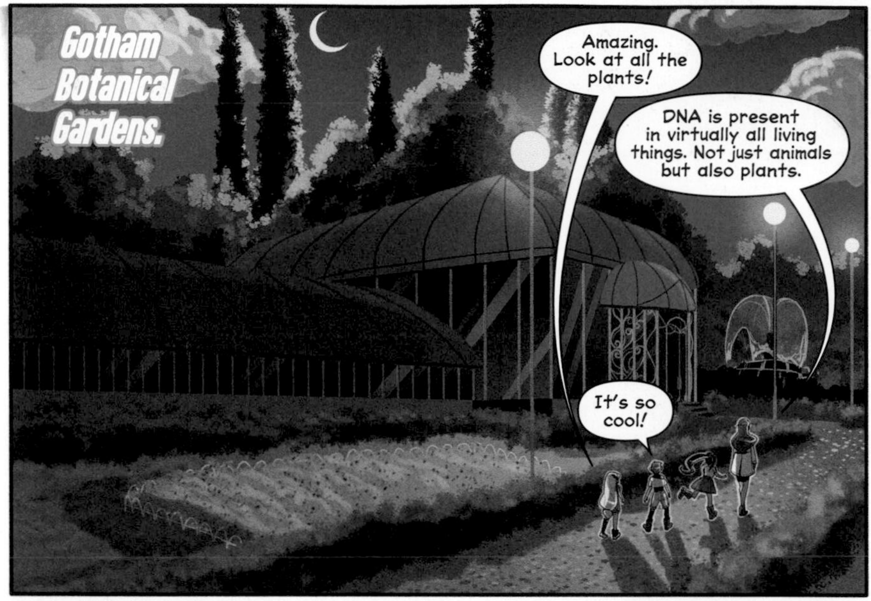
Gotham Botanical Gardens.
Amazing. Look at all the plants!
DNA is present in virtually all living things. Not just animals but also plants.
It's so cool!

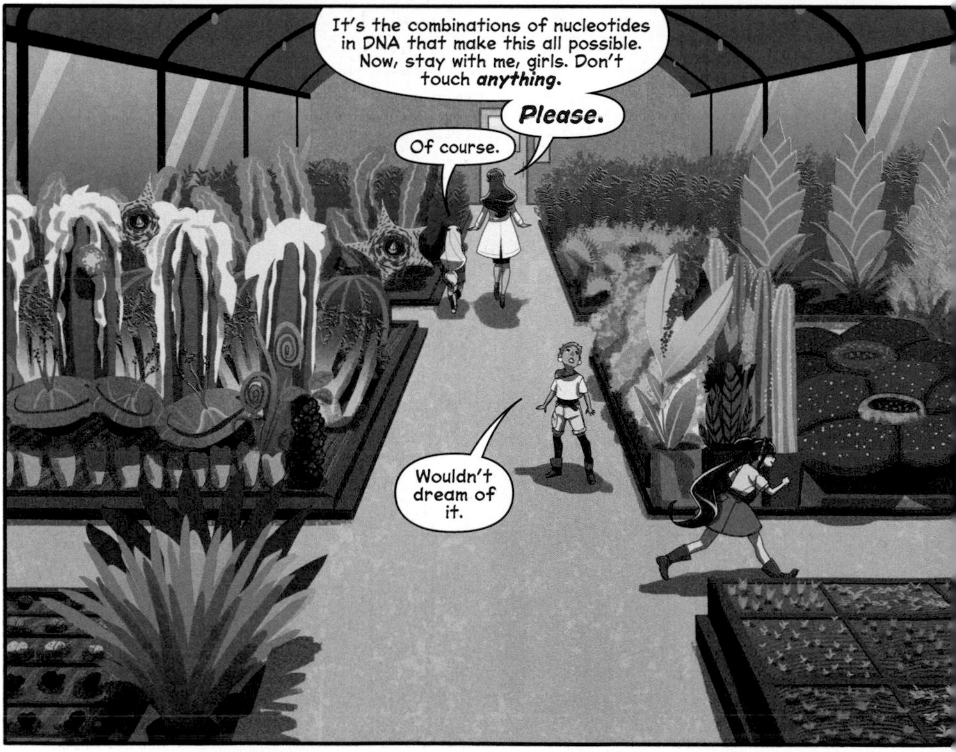
It's the combinations of nucleotides in DNA that make this all possible. Now, stay with me, girls. Don't touch *anything*.
Please.
Of course.
Wouldn't dream of it.

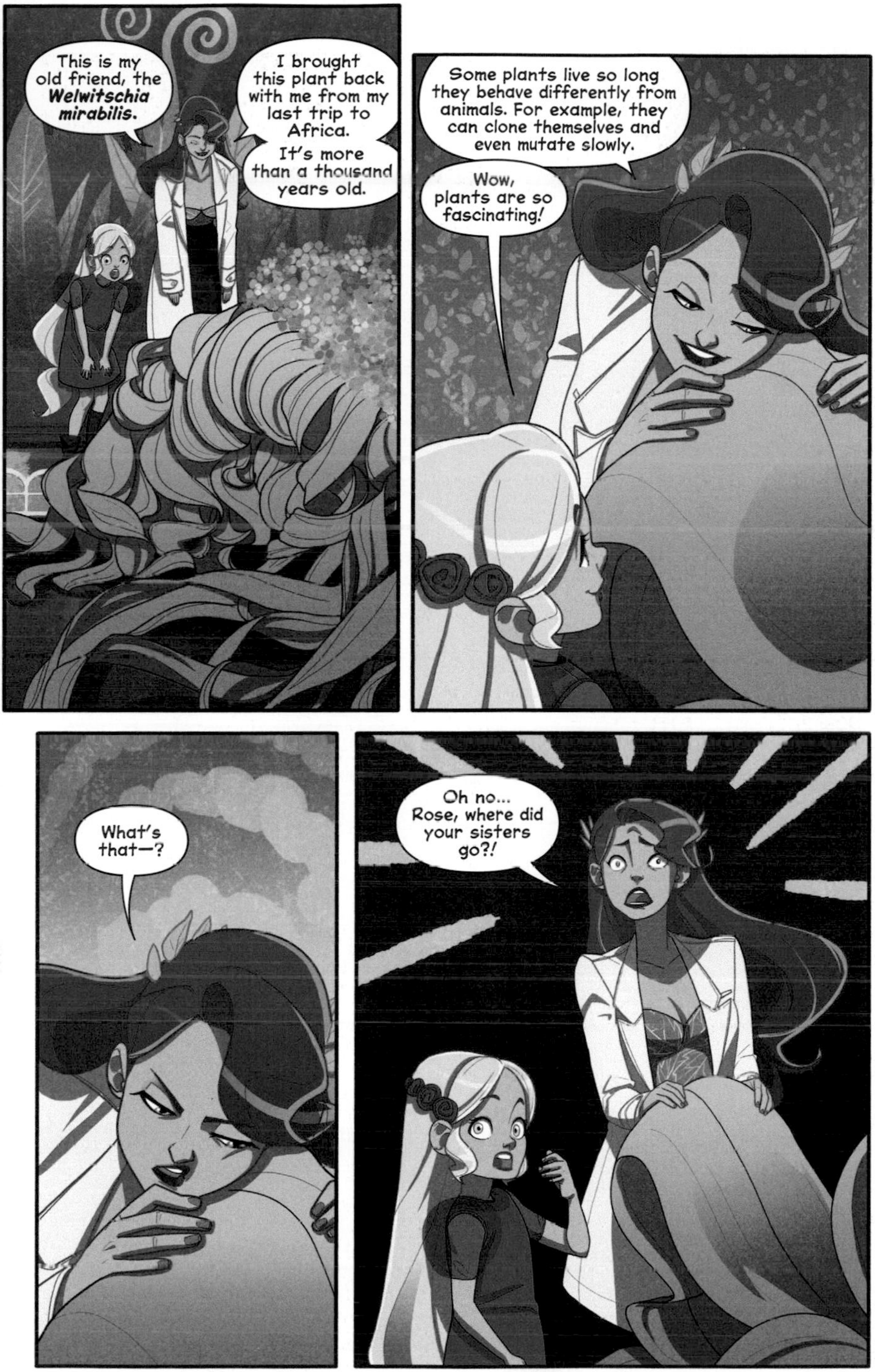
This is my old friend, the *Welwitschia mirabilis.*
I brought this plant back with me from my last trip to Africa.
It's more than a thousand years old.
Some plants live so long they behave differently from animals. For example, they can clone themselves and even mutate slowly.
Wow, plants are so fascinating!
What's that—?
Oh no... Rose, where did your sisters go?!

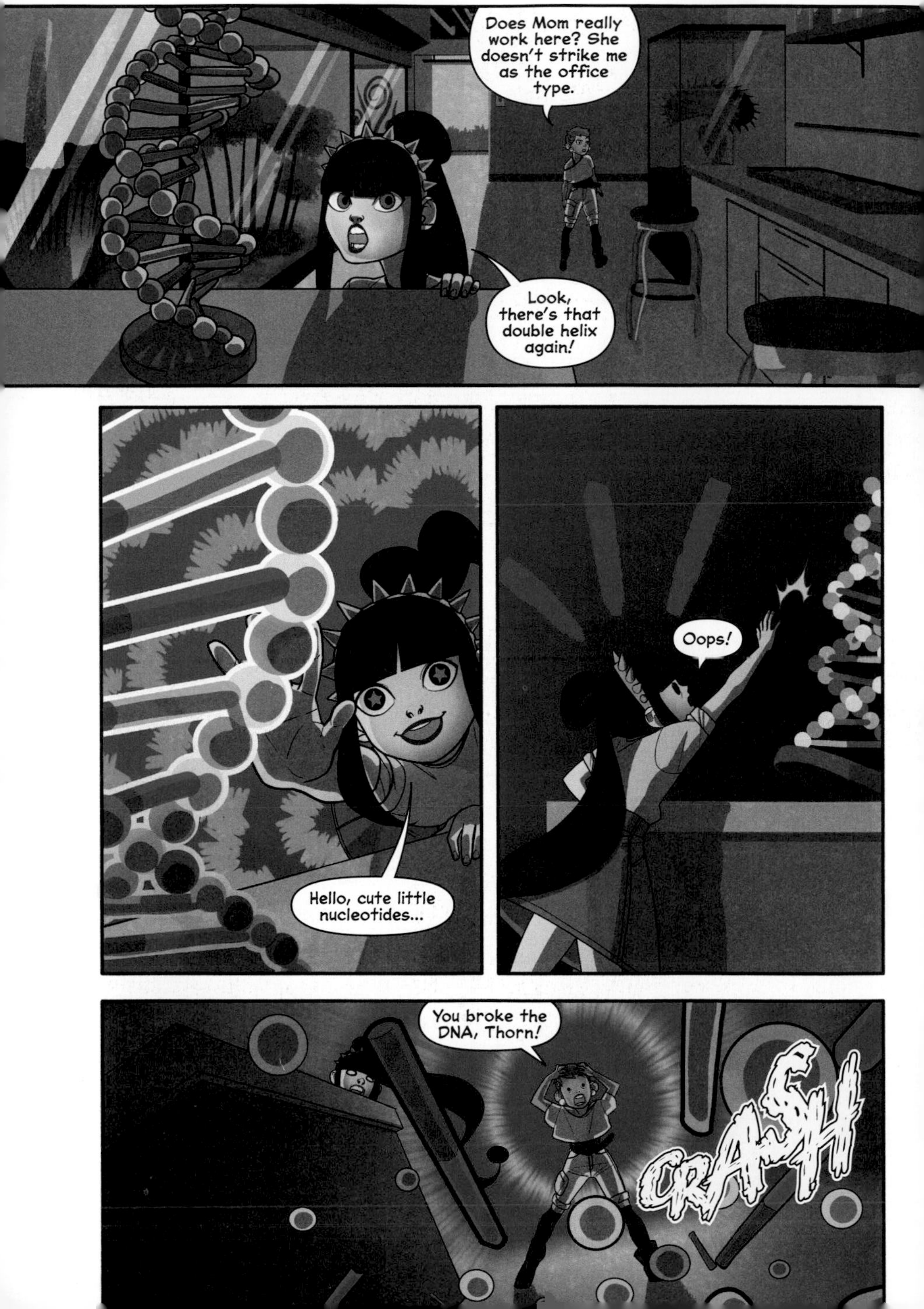
Does Mom really work here? She doesn't strike me as the office type.
Look, there's that double helix again!
Hello, cute little nucleotides...
Oops!
You broke the DNA, Thorn!
CRASH

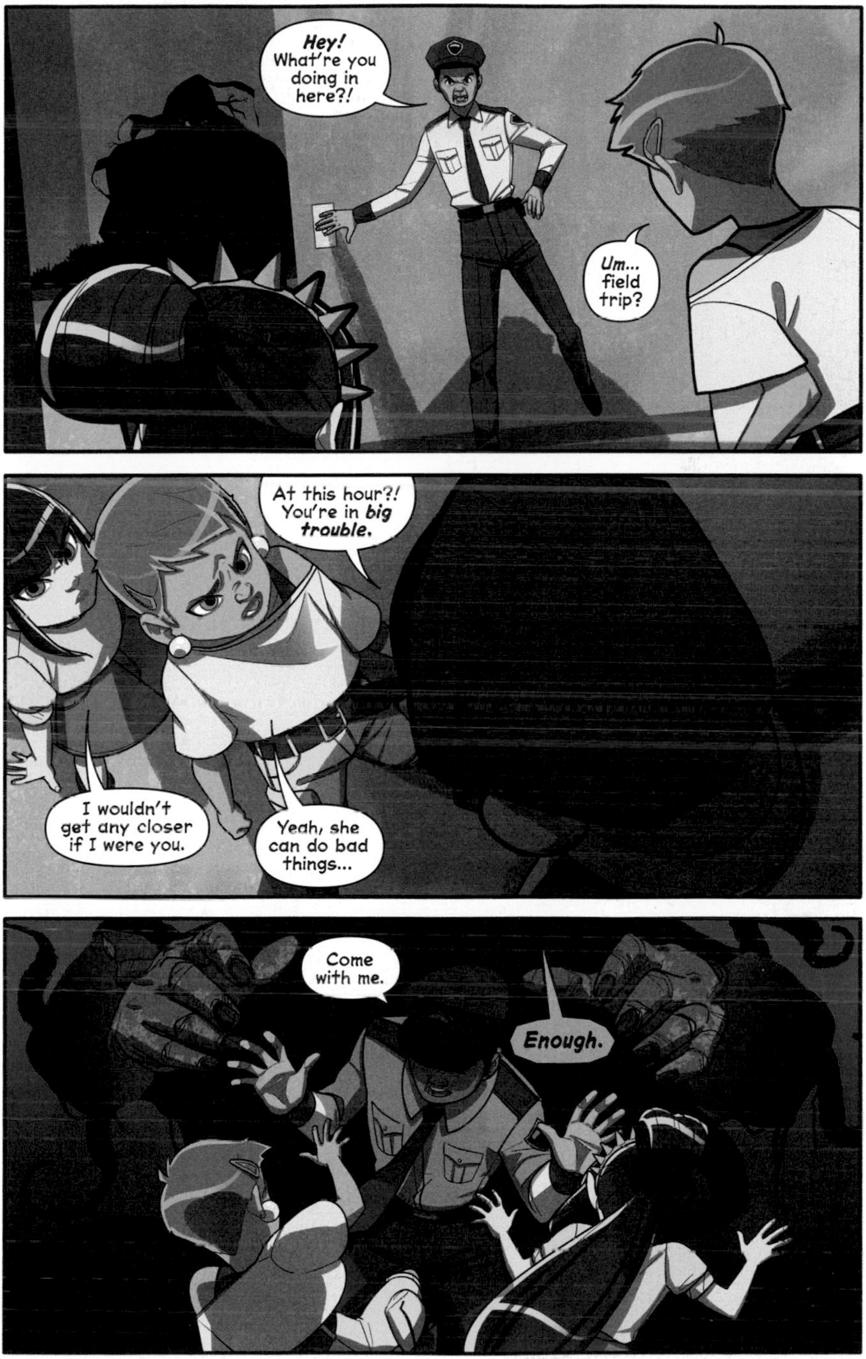
Hey! What're you doing in here?!
Um... field trip?
At this hour?! You're in big trouble.
I wouldn't get any closer if I were you.
Yeah, she can do bad things...
Come with me.
Enough.

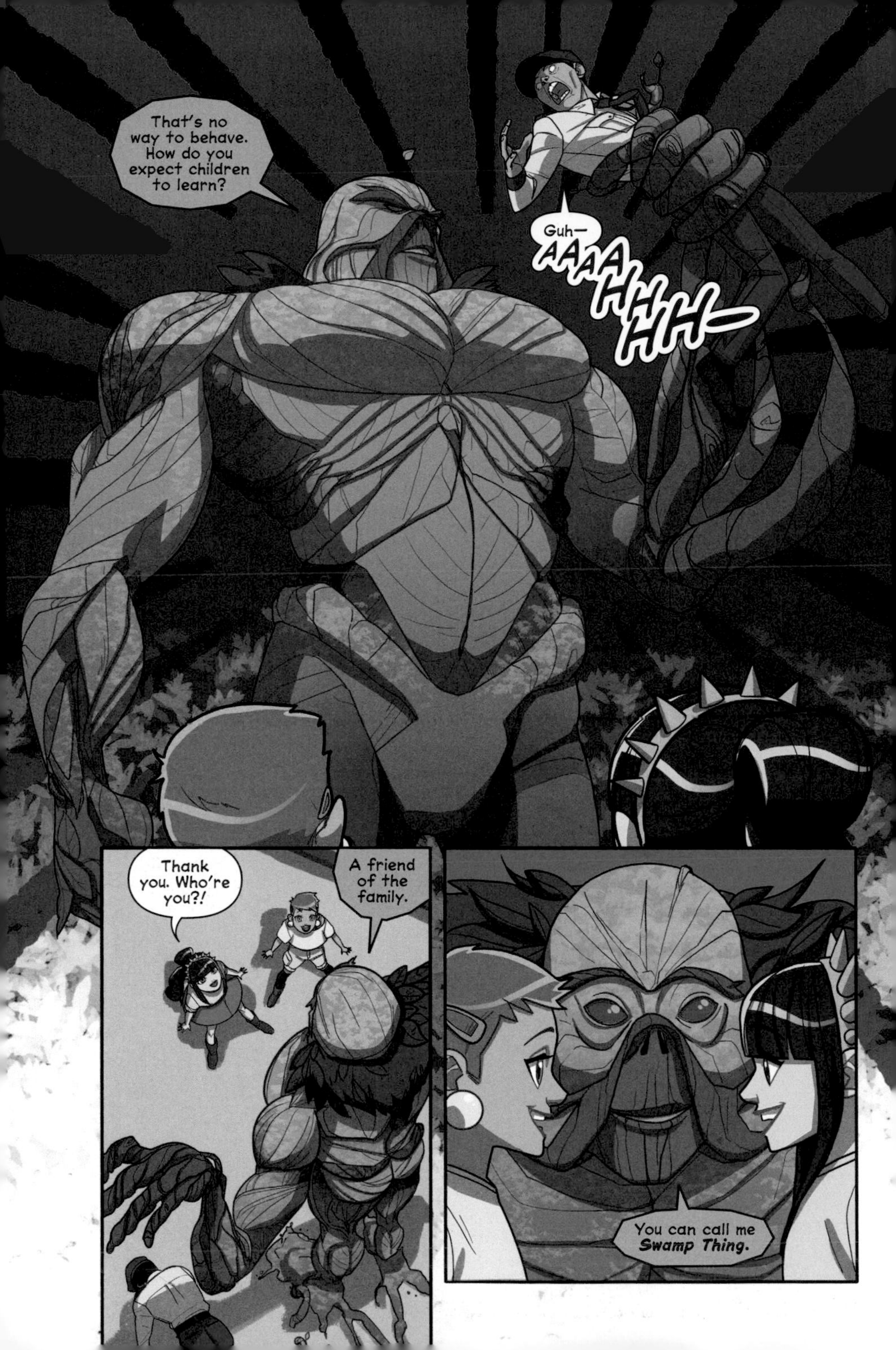
That's no way to behave. How do you expect children to learn?
Guh—
AAAAHHHHH—
Thank you. Who're you?!
A friend of the family.
You can call me Swamp Thing.

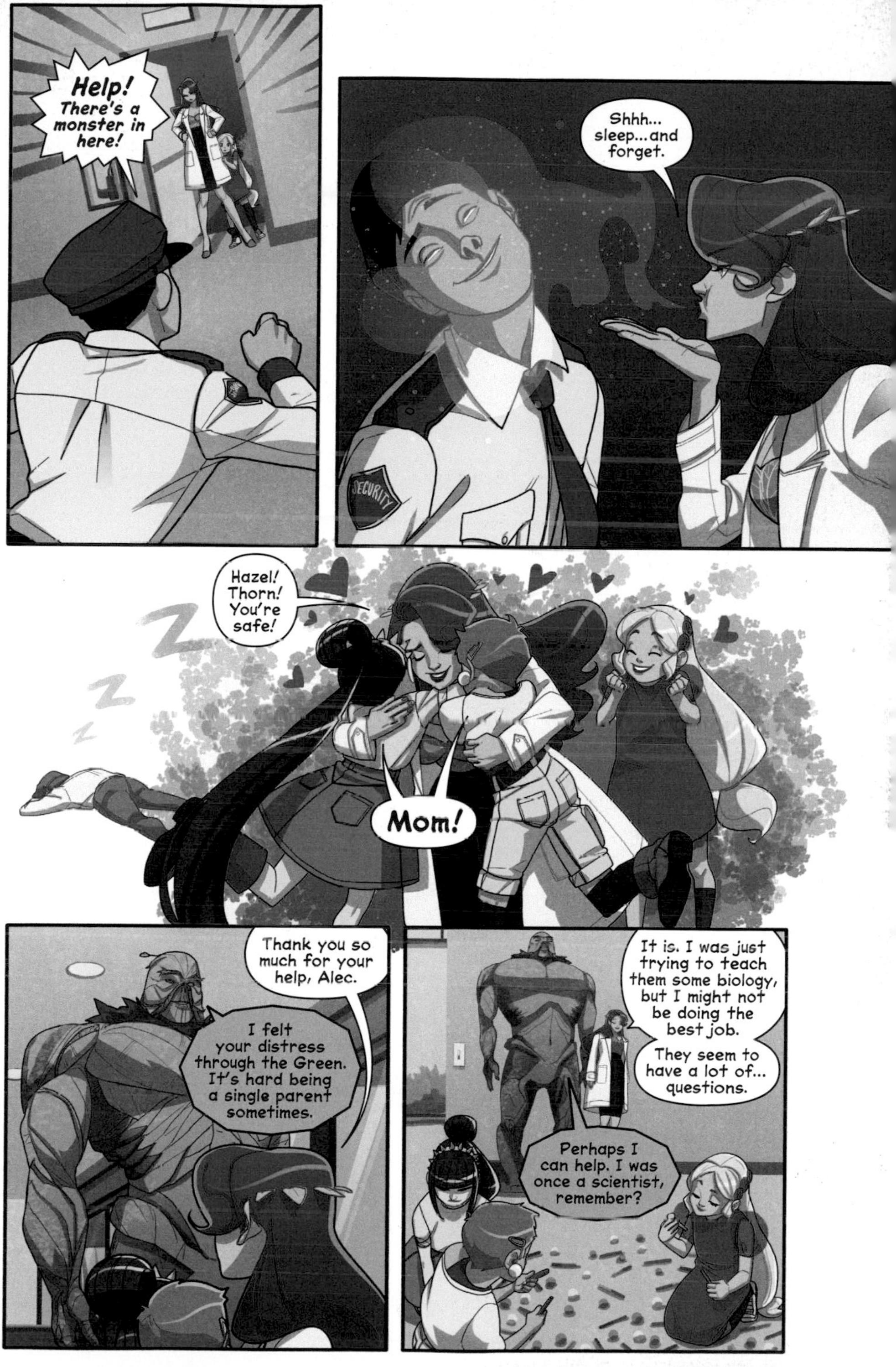
Help! There's a monster in here!
Shhh... sleep...and forget.
SECURITY
Hazel! Thorn! You're safe!
Z
Z
Z
Mom!
Thank you so much for your help, Alec.
I felt your distress through the Green. It's hard being a single parent sometimes.
It is. I was just trying to teach them some biology, but I might not be doing the best job.
They seem to have a lot of... questions.
Perhaps I can help. I was once a scientist, remember?

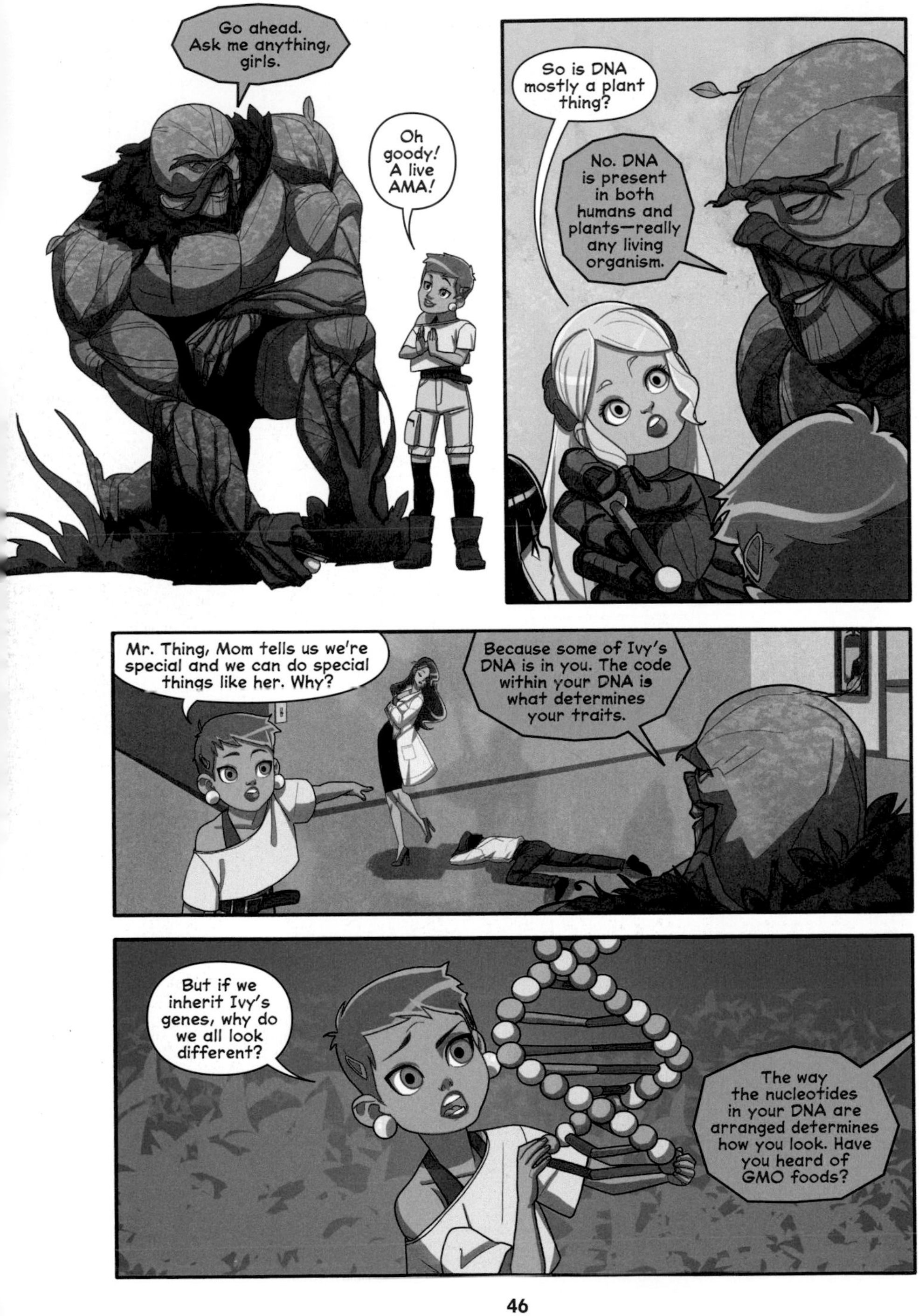
Go ahead. Ask me anything, girls.
Oh goody! A live AMA!
So is DNA mostly a plant thing?
No. DNA is present in both humans and plants—really any living organism.
Mr. Thing, Mom tells us we're special and we can do special things like her. Why?
Because some of Ivy's DNA is in you. The code within your DNA is what determines your traits.
But if we inherit Ivy's genes, why do we all look different?
The way the nucleotides in your DNA are arranged determines how you look. Have you heard of GMO foods?

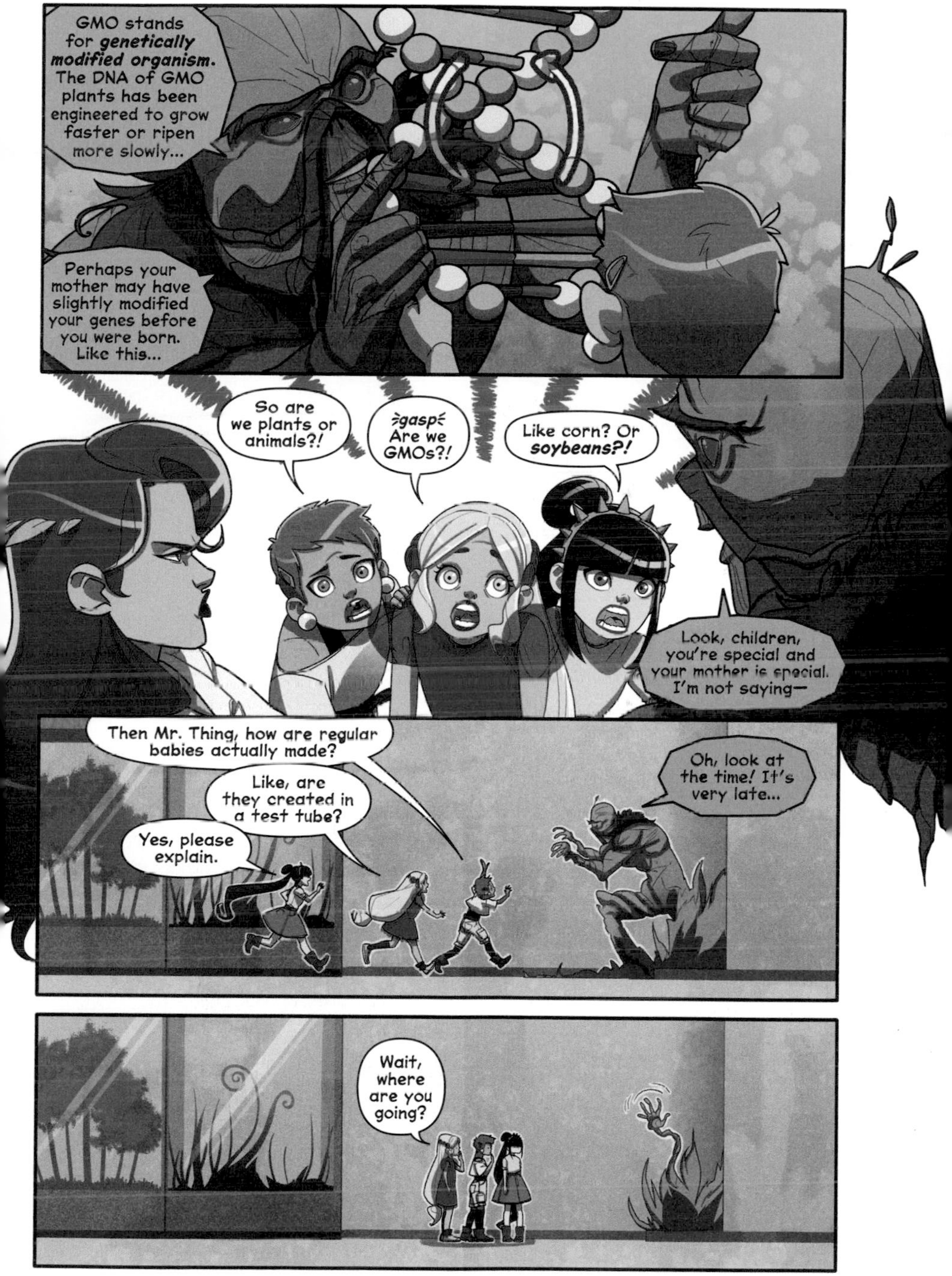

GMO stands for **genetically modified organism.** The DNA of GMO plants has been engineered to grow faster or ripen more slowly...
Perhaps your mother may have slightly modified your genes before you were born. Like this...
So are we plants or animals?!
gasp Are we GMOs?!
Like corn? Or **soybeans?!**
Look, children, you're special and your mother is special. I'm not saying—
Then Mr. Thing, how are regular babies actually made?
Like, are they created in a test tube?
Yes, please explain.
Oh, look at the time! It's very late...
Wait, where are you going?

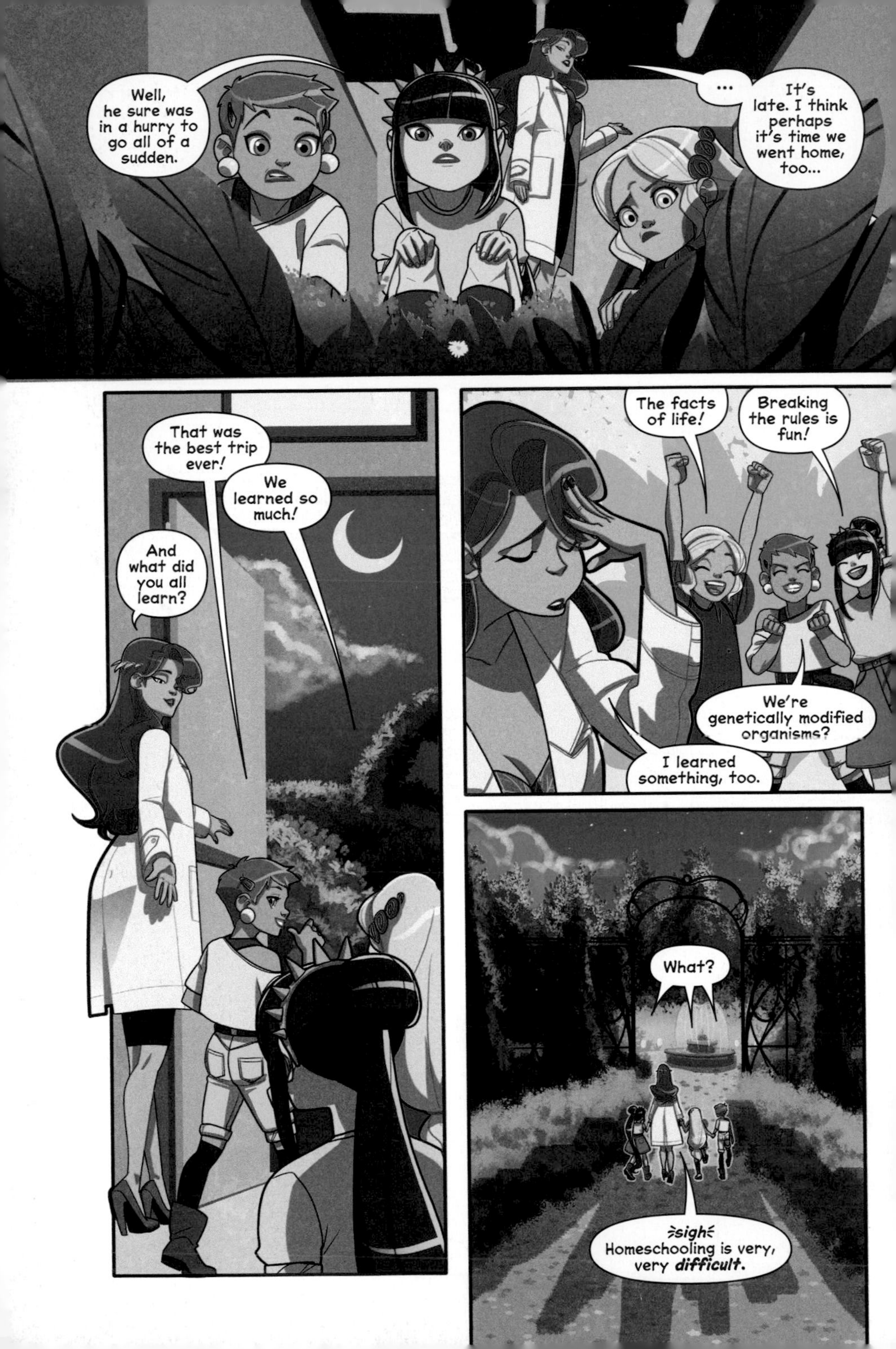
Well, he sure was in a hurry to go all of a sudden.
...
It's late. I think perhaps it's time we went home, too...
That was the best trip ever!
We learned so much!
And what did you all learn?
The facts of life!
Breaking the rules is fun!
We're genetically modified organisms?
I learned something, too.
What?
⸗sigh⸗ Homeschooling is very, very ***difficult***.

CHAPTER FOUR

MORE THAN MEETS THE EYE

WRITTEN AND ILLUSTRATED BY DUSTIN HANSEN
LETTERED BY WES ABBOTT

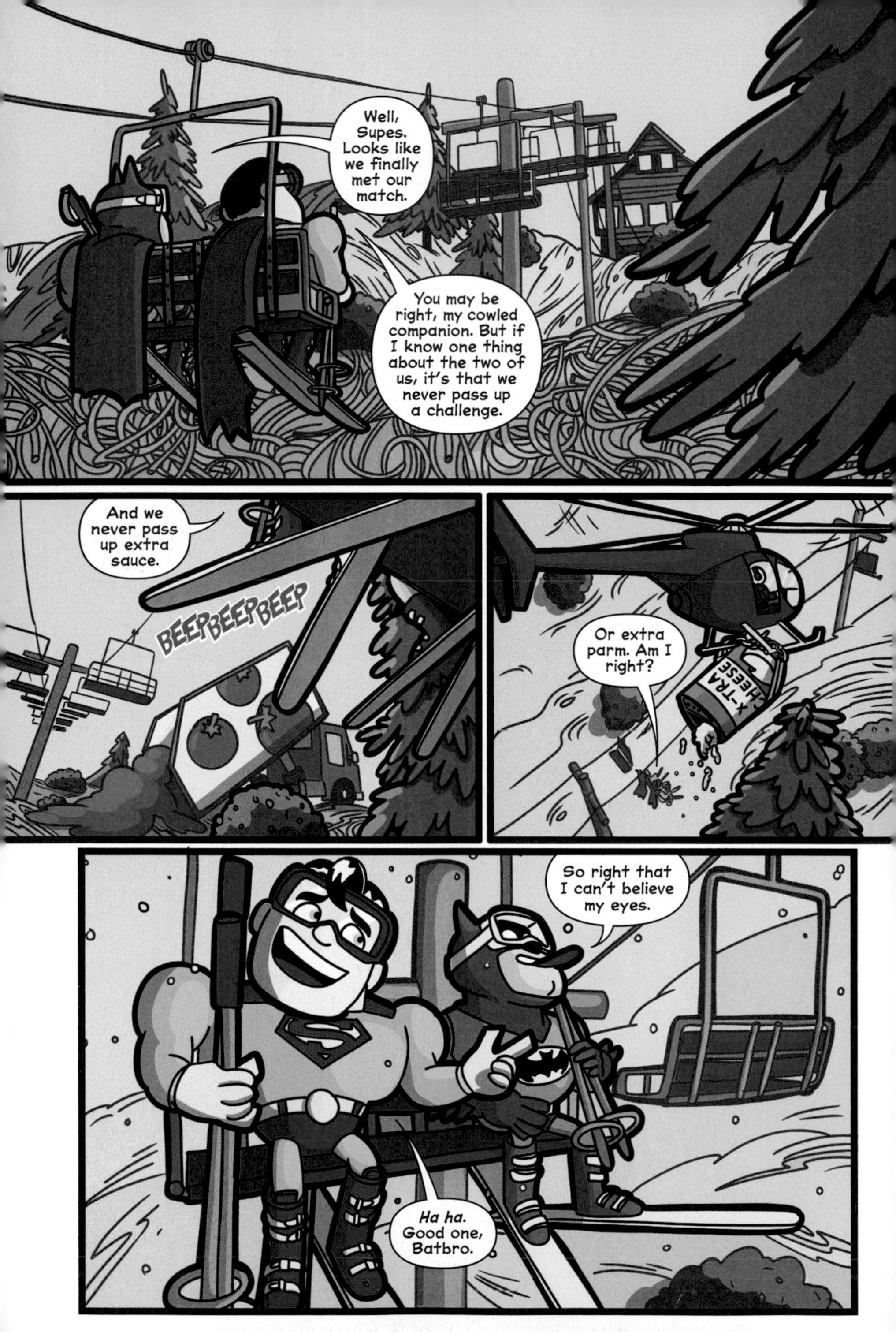
Well, Supes. Looks like we finally met our match.
You may be right, my cowled companion. But if I know one thing about the two of us, it's that we never pass up a challenge.
And we never pass up extra sauce.
BEEP BEEP BEEP
Or extra parm. Am I right?
X-TRA
So right that I can't believe my eyes.
Ha ha. Good one, Batbro.

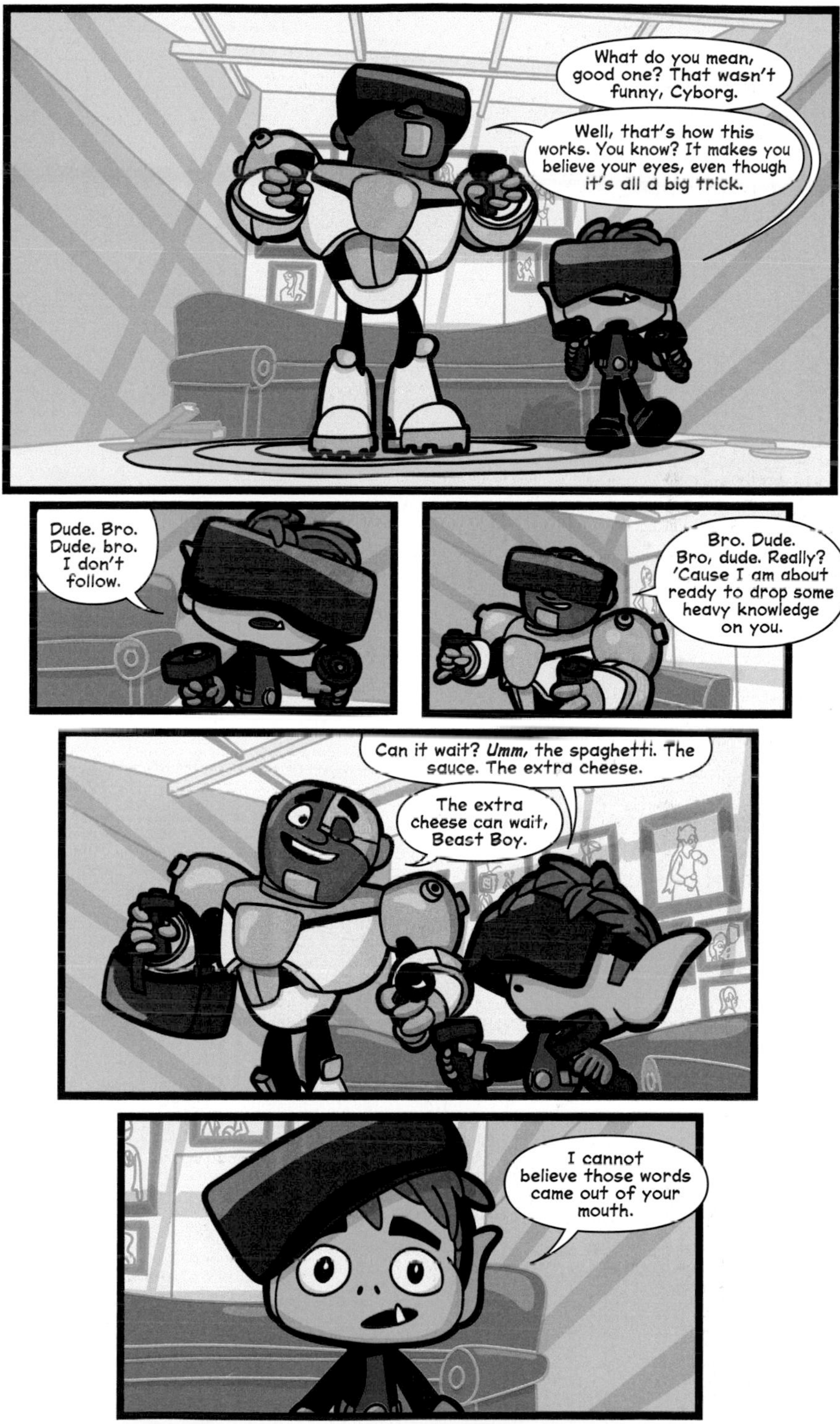
What do you mean, good one? That wasn't funny, Cyborg.
Well, that's how this works. You know? It makes you believe your eyes, even though it's all a big trick.
Dude. Bro. Dude, bro. I don't follow.
Bro. Dude. Bro, dude. Really? 'Cause I am about ready to drop some heavy knowledge on you.
Can it wait? *Umm,* the spaghetti. The sauce. The extra cheese.
The extra cheese can wait, Beast Boy.
I cannot believe those words came out of your mouth.

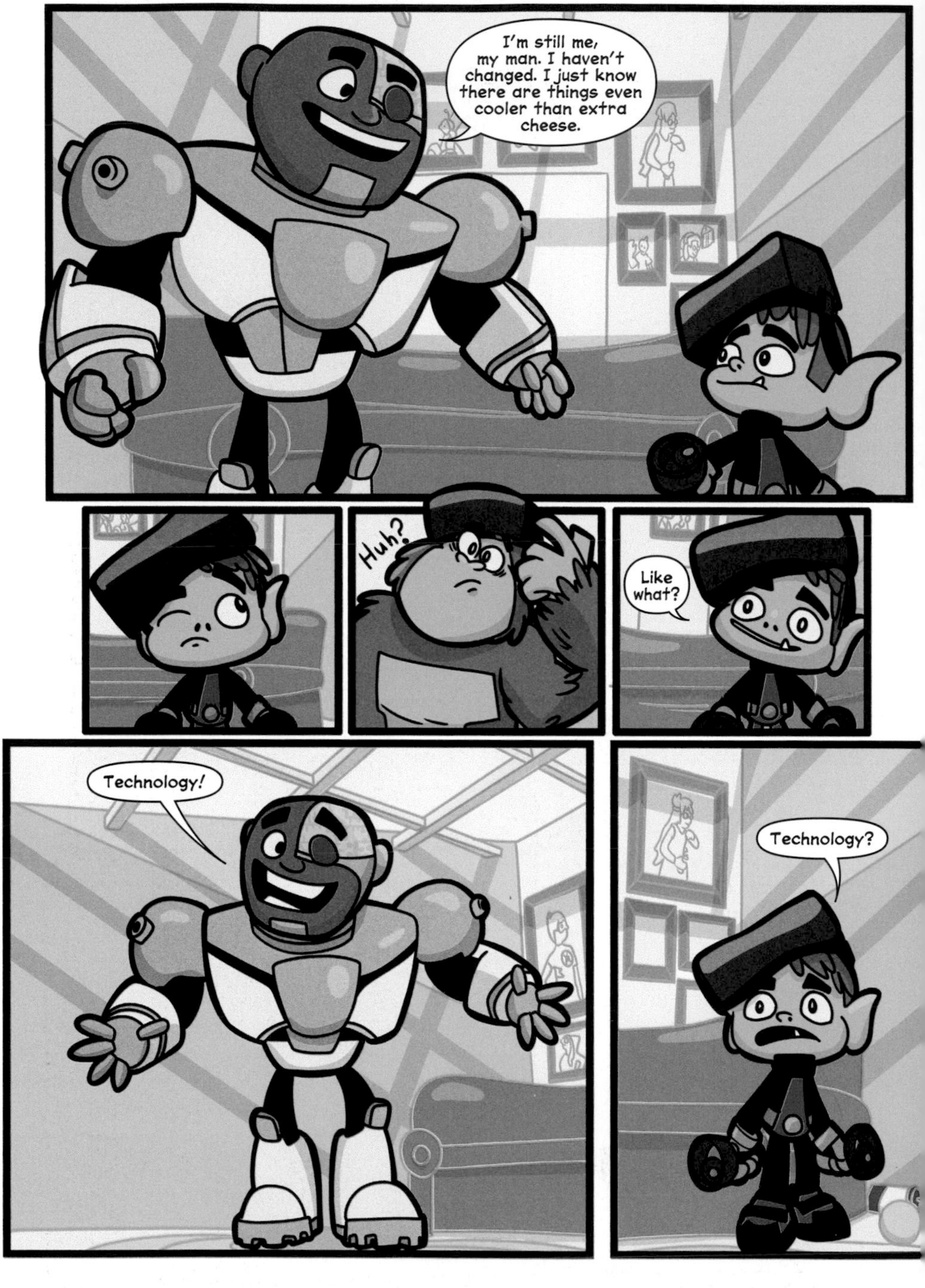
I'm still me, my man. I haven't changed. I just know there are things even cooler than extra cheese.
Huh?
Like what?
Technology!
Technology?

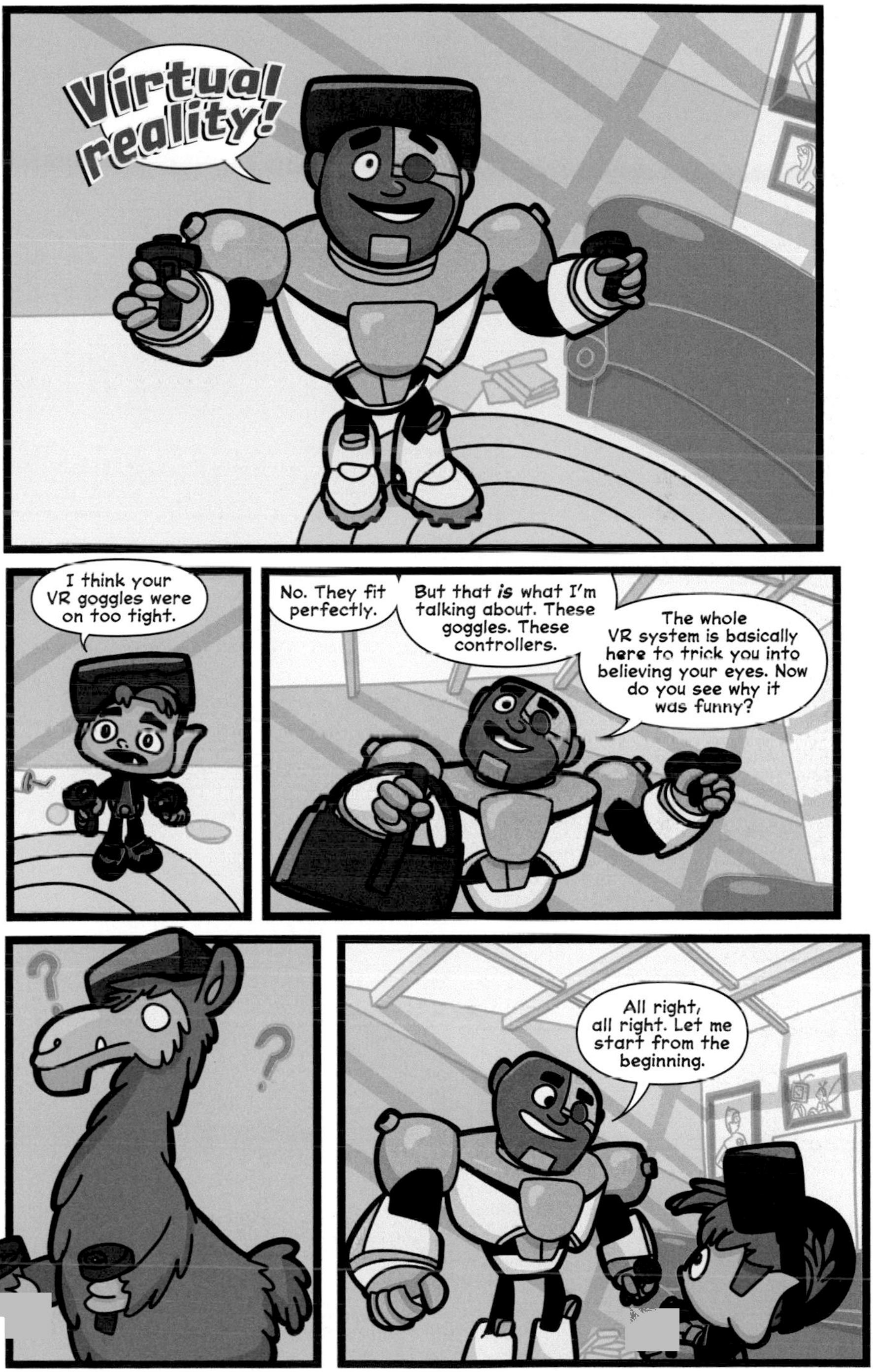
Virtual reality!
I think your VR goggles were on too tight.
No. They fit perfectly.
But that *is* what I'm talking about. These goggles. These controllers.
The whole VR system is basically here to trick you into believing your eyes. Now do you see why it was funny?
?
?
All right, all right. Let me start from the beginning.

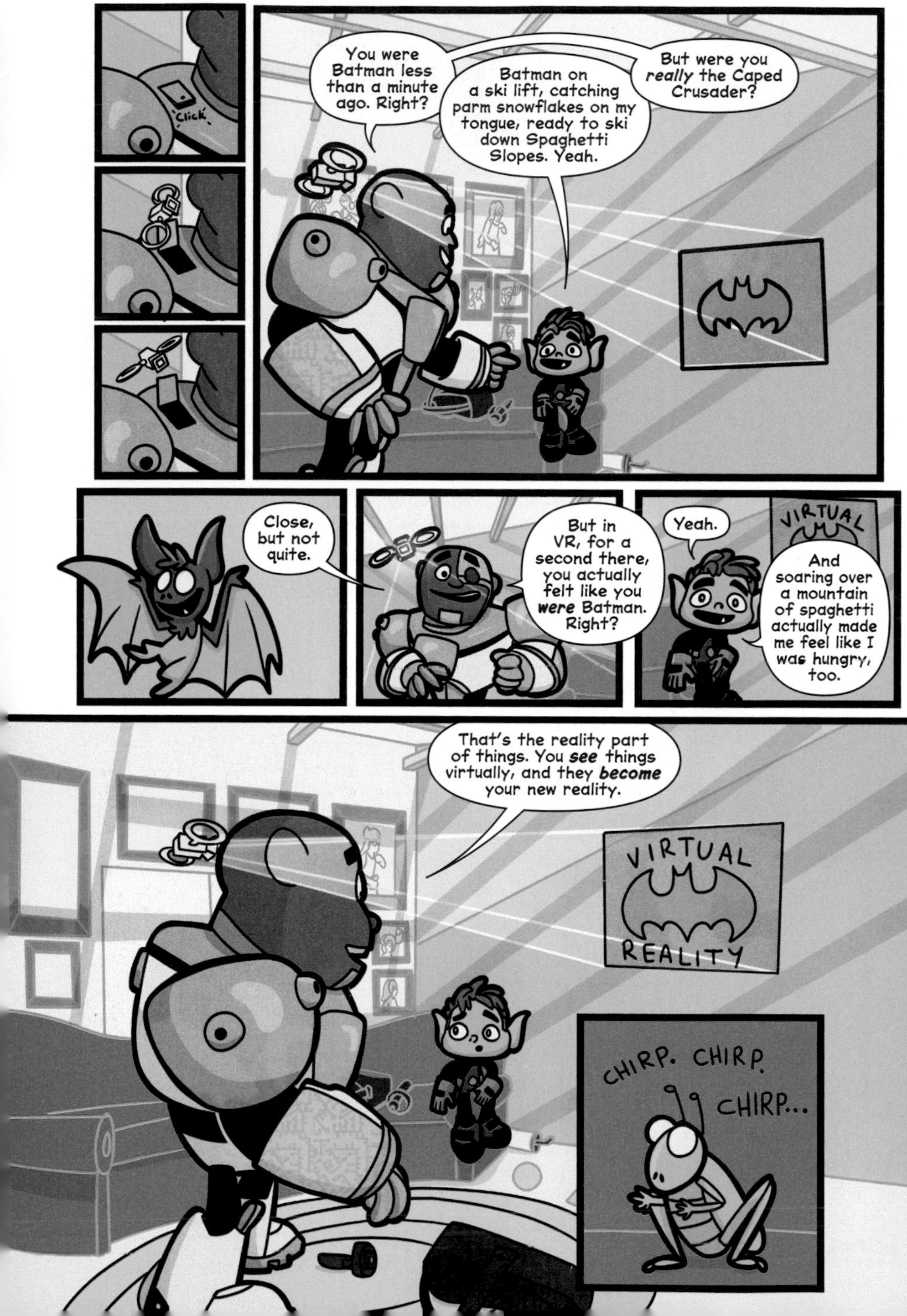
CLICK
You were Batman less than a minute ago. Right?
Batman on a ski lift, catching parm snowflakes on my tongue, ready to ski down Spaghetti Slopes. Yeah.
But were you *really* the Caped Crusader?
Close, but not quite.
But in VR, for a second there, you actually felt like you *were* Batman. Right?
Yeah.
And soaring over a mountain of spaghetti actually made me feel like I was hungry, too.
VIRTUAL
That's the reality part of things. You *see* things virtually, and they *become* your new reality.
VIRTUAL REALITY
CHIRP. CHIRP. CHIRP...

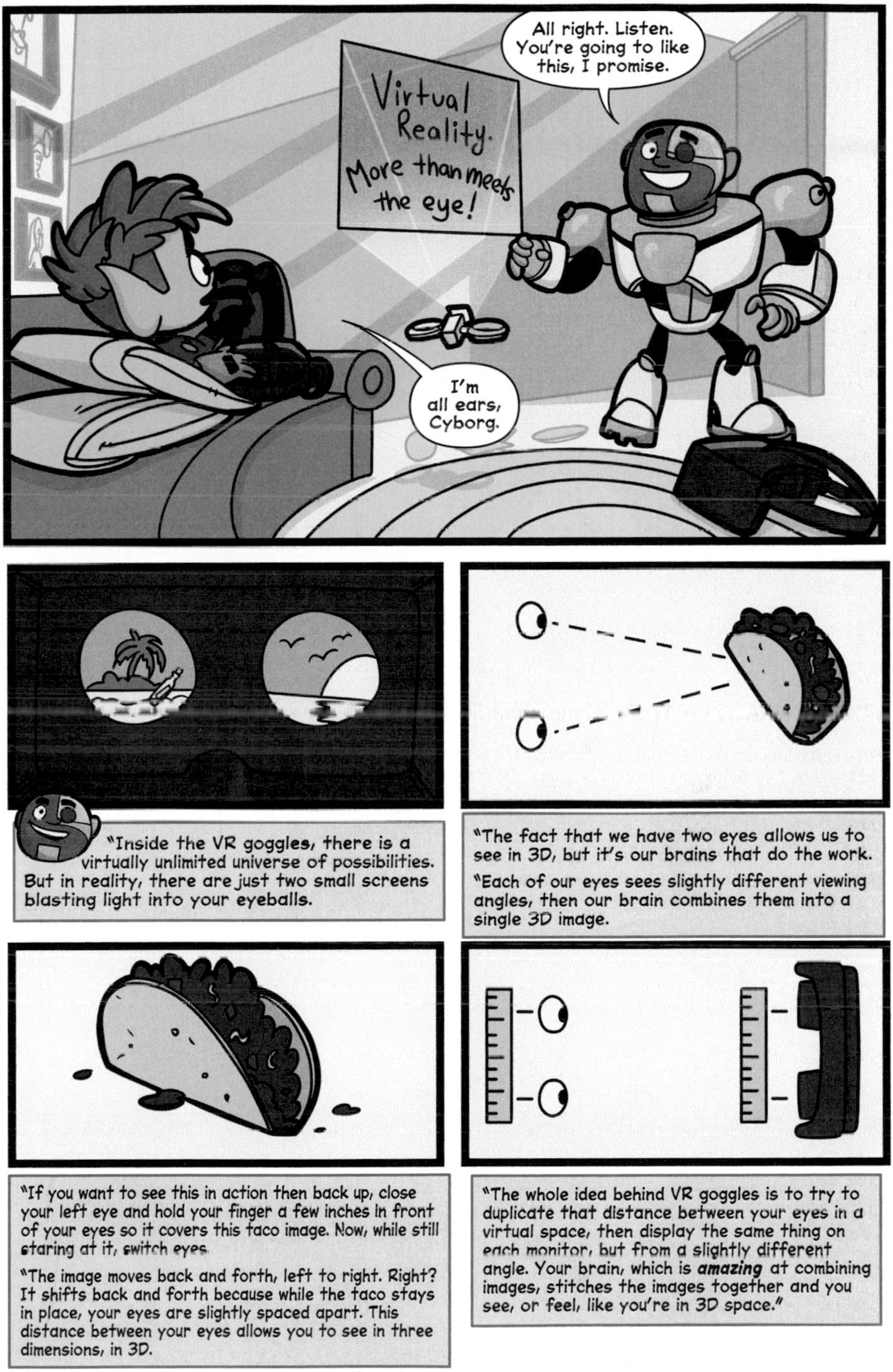
All right. Listen. You're going to like this, I promise.
Virtual Reality. More than meets the eye!
I'm all ears, Cyborg.
"Inside the VR goggles, there is a virtually unlimited universe of possibilities. But in reality, there are just two small screens blasting light into your eyeballs.
"The fact that we have two eyes allows us to see in 3D, but it's our brains that do the work.
"Each of our eyes sees slightly different viewing angles, then our brain combines them into a single 3D image.
"If you want to see this in action then back up, close your left eye and hold your finger a few inches in front of your eyes so it covers this taco image. Now, while still staring at it, switch eyes.
"The image moves back and forth, left to right. Right? It shifts back and forth because while the taco stays in place, your eyes are slightly spaced apart. This distance between your eyes allows you to see in three dimensions, in 3D.
"The whole idea behind VR goggles is to try to duplicate that distance between your eyes in a virtual space, then display the same thing on each monitor, but from a slightly different angle. Your brain, which is amazing at combining images, stitches the images together and you see, or feel, like you're in 3D space."

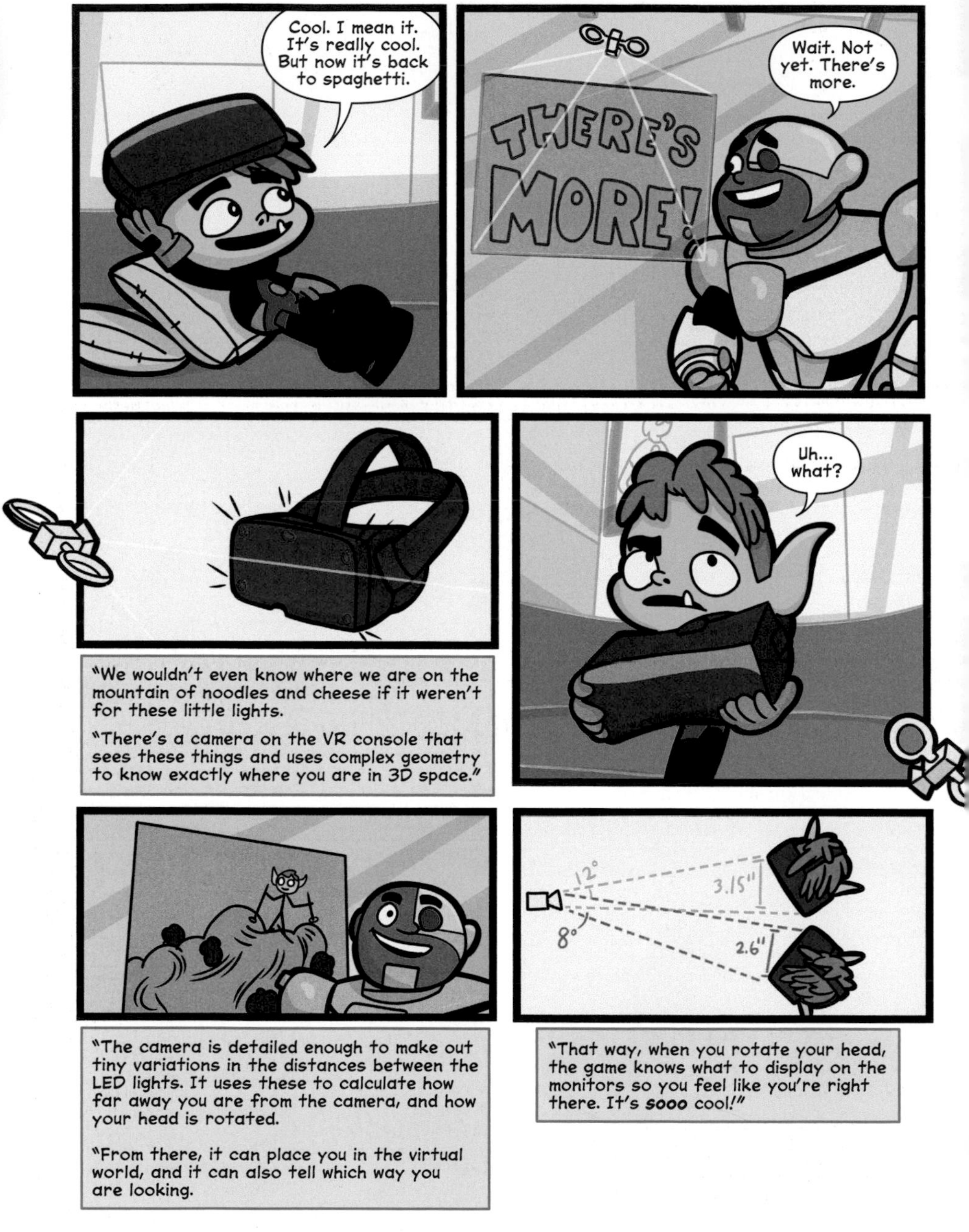
Cool. I mean it. It's really cool. But now it's back to spaghetti.
THERE'S MORE!
Wait. Not yet. There's more.
"We wouldn't even know where we are on the mountain of noodles and cheese if it weren't for these little lights.
"There's a camera on the VR console that sees these things and uses complex geometry to know exactly where you are in 3D space."
Uh... what?
"The camera is detailed enough to make out tiny variations in the distances between the LED lights. It uses these to calculate how far away you are from the camera, and how your head is rotated.
"From there, it can place you in the virtual world, and it can also tell which way you are looking.
12°
3.15"
8°
2.6"
"That way, when you rotate your head, the game knows what to display on the monitors so you feel like you're right there. It's ***sooo*** cool!"

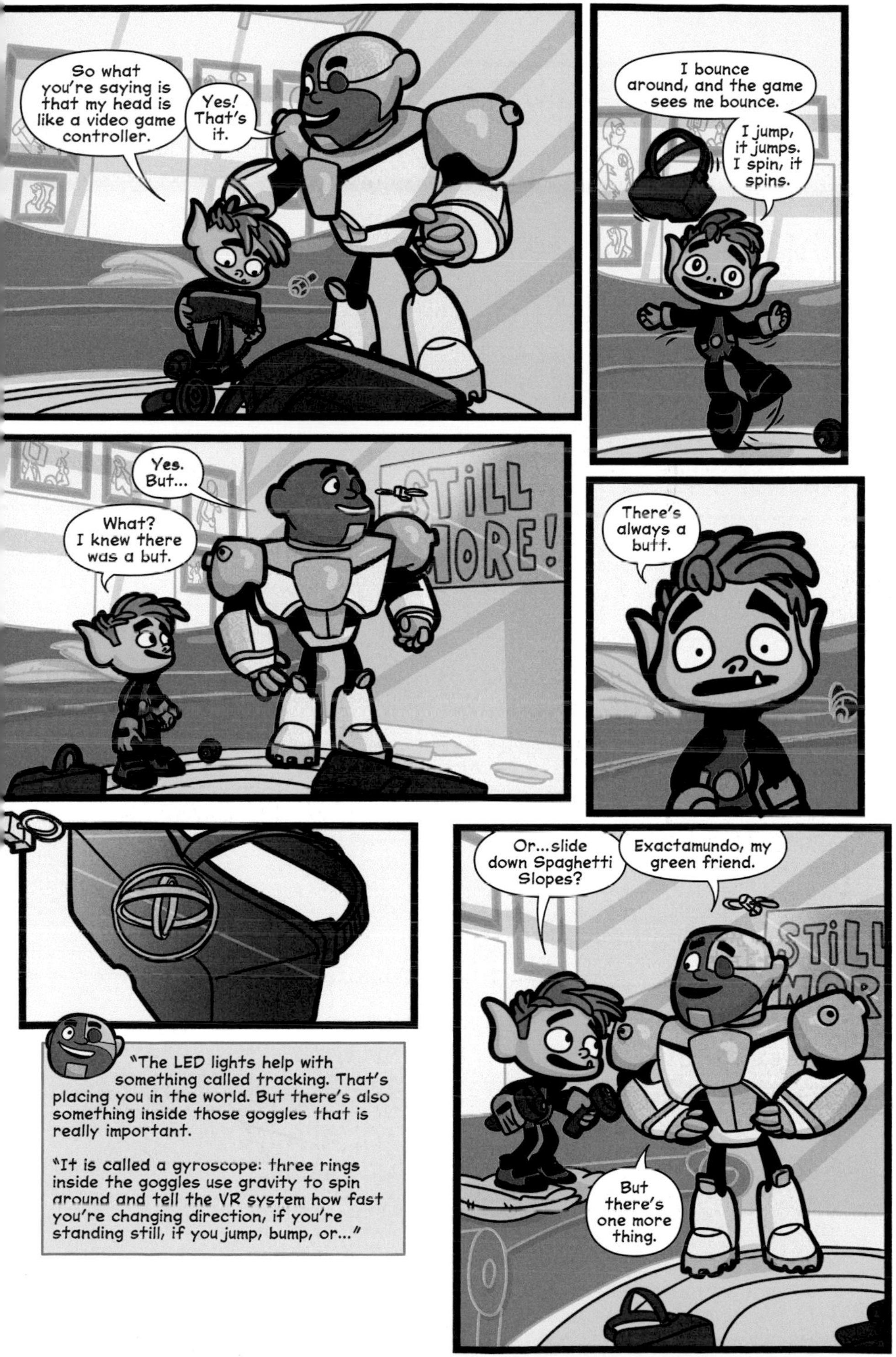
So what you're saying is that my head is like a video game controller.
Yes! That's it.
I bounce around, and the game sees me bounce.
I jump, it jumps. I spin, it spins.
Yes. But...
What? I knew there was a but.
There's always a butt.
"The LED lights help with something called tracking. That's placing you in the world. But there's also something inside those goggles that is really important.
"It is called a gyroscope: three rings inside the goggles use gravity to spin around and tell the VR system how fast you're changing direction, if you're standing still, if you jump, bump, or..."
Or...slide down Spaghetti Slopes?
Exactamundo, my green friend.
But there's one more thing.

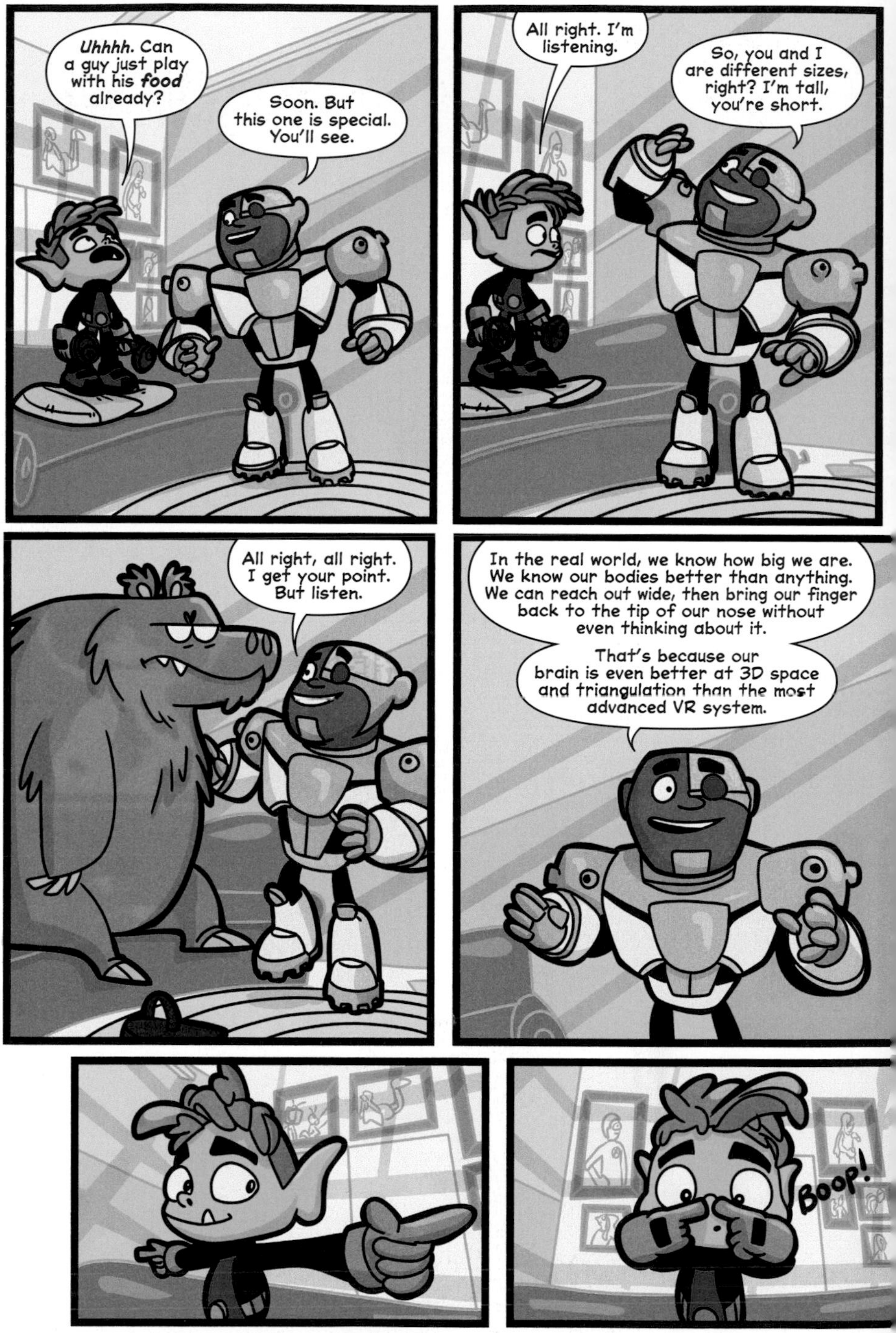

Uhhhh. Can a guy just play with his ***food*** already?
Soon. But this one is special. You'll see.
All right. I'm listening.
So, you and I are different sizes, right? I'm tall, you're short.
All right, all right. I get your point. But listen.
In the real world, we know how big we are. We know our bodies better than anything. We can reach out wide, then bring our finger back to the tip of our nose without even thinking about it.
That's because our brain is even better at 3D space and triangulation than the most advanced VR system.
BOOP!

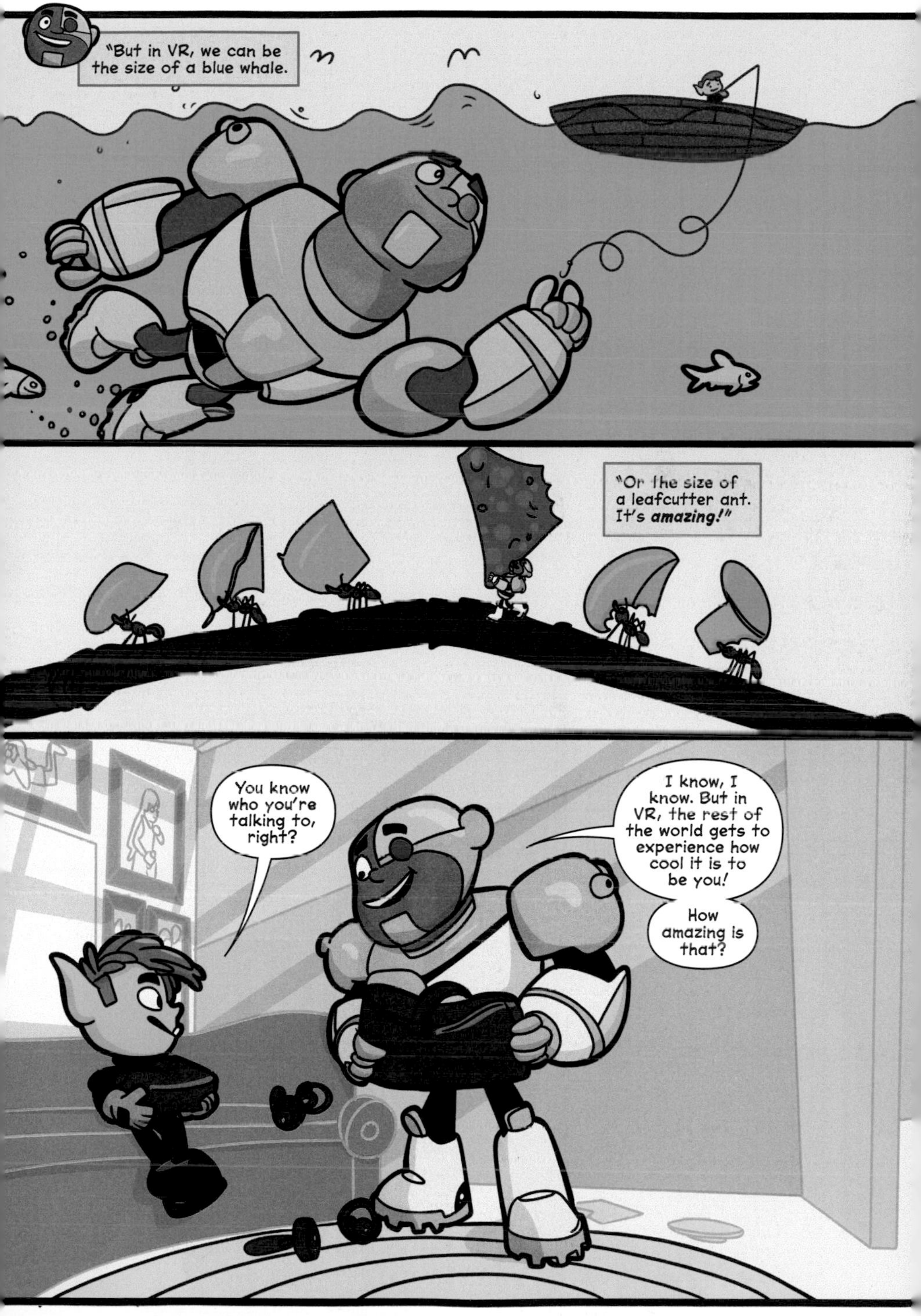
"But in VR, we can be the size of a blue whale.
"Or the size of a leafcutter ant. It's *amazing!*"
You know who you're talking to, right?
I know, I know. But in VR, the rest of the world gets to experience how cool it is to be you!
How amazing is that?

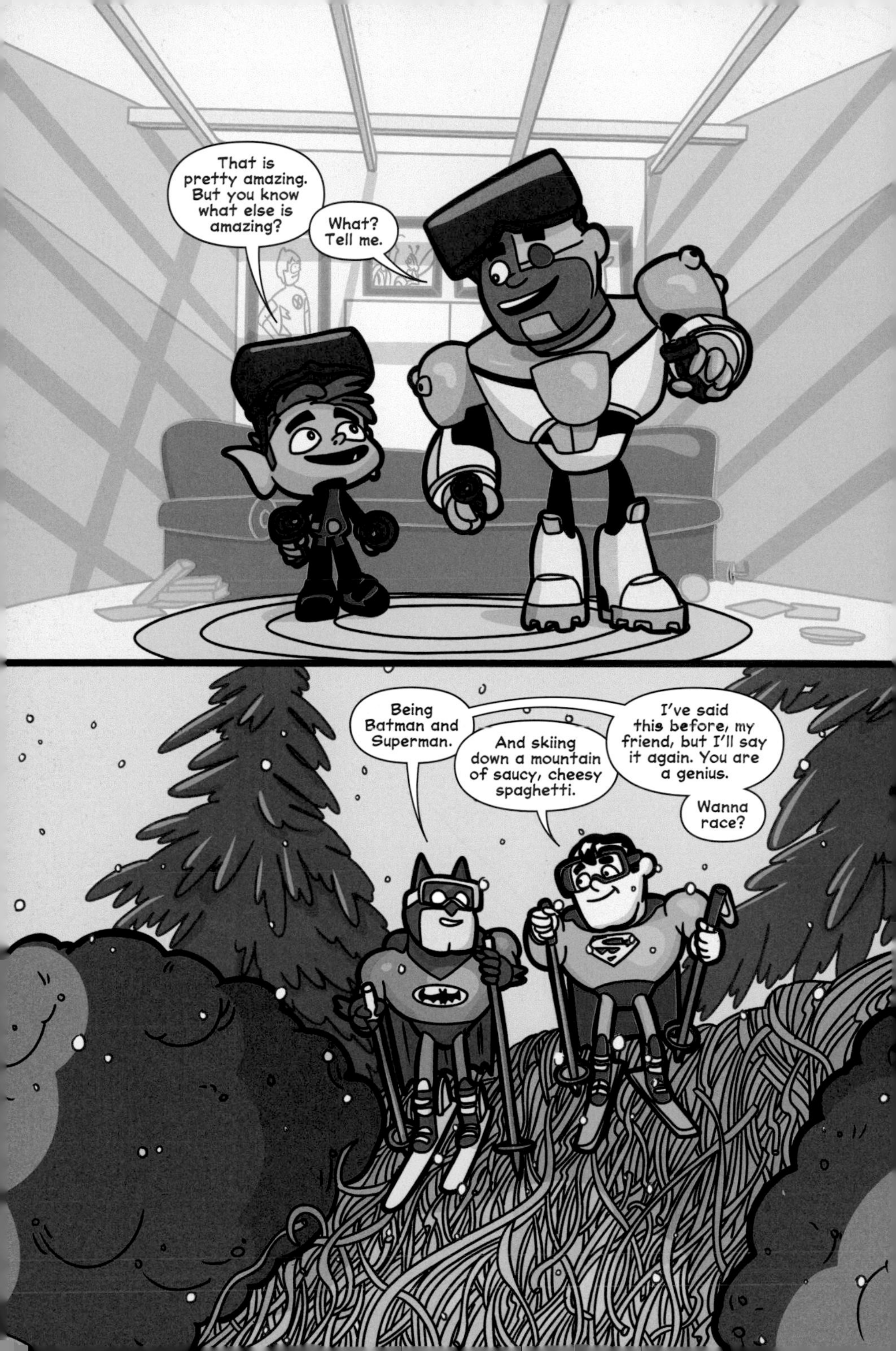
That is pretty amazing. But you know what else is amazing?
What? Tell me.
Being Batman and Superman.
And skiing down a mountain of saucy, cheesy spaghetti.
I've said this before, my friend, but I'll say it again. You are a genius.
Wanna race?

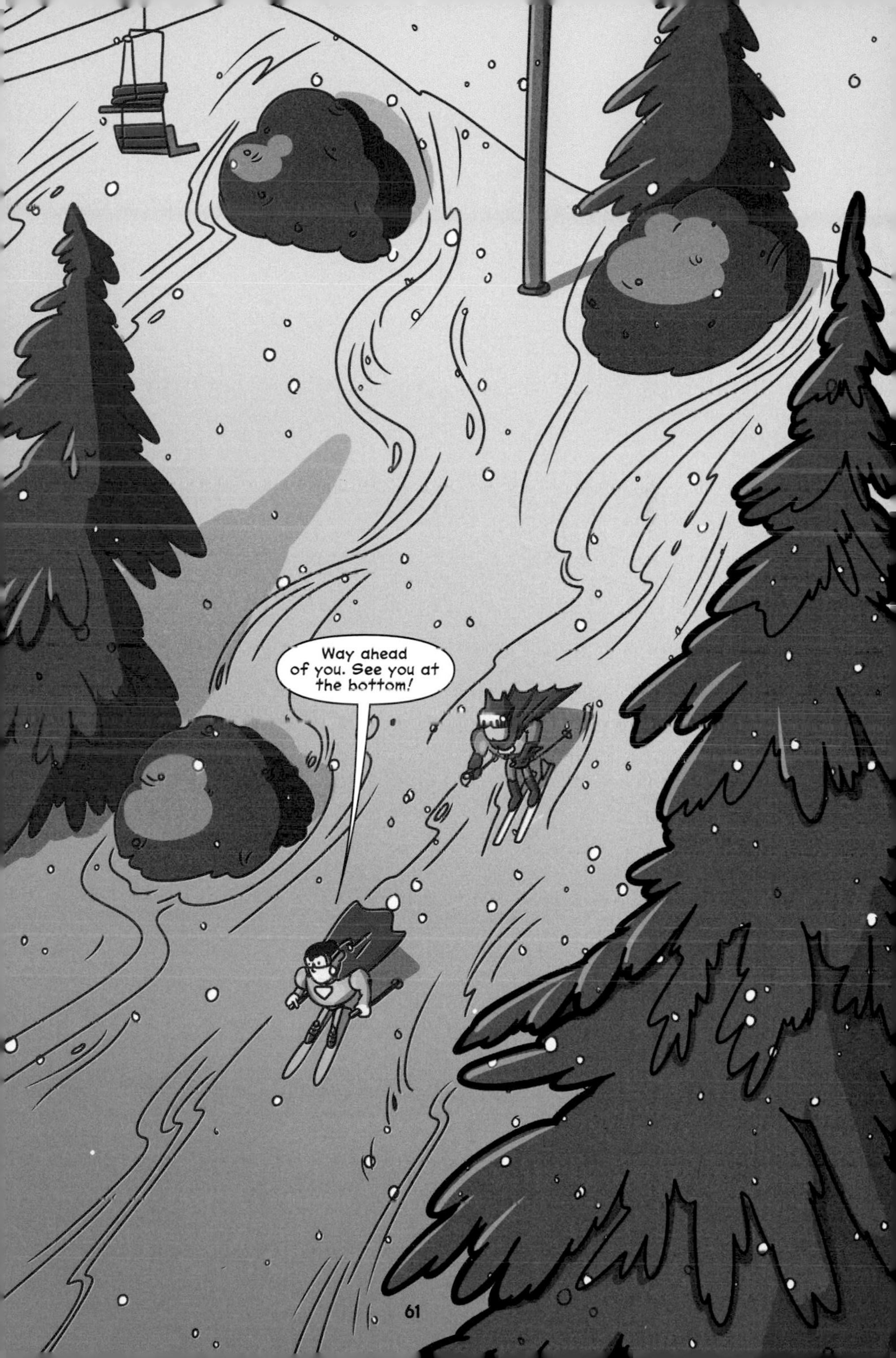
Way ahead of you. See you at the bottom!

CHAPTER FIVE

LIGHTS-OUT

WRITTEN BY **AMANDA DEIBERT**

ILLUSTRATED BY **ERICH OWEN**

LETTERED BY **WES ABBOTT**

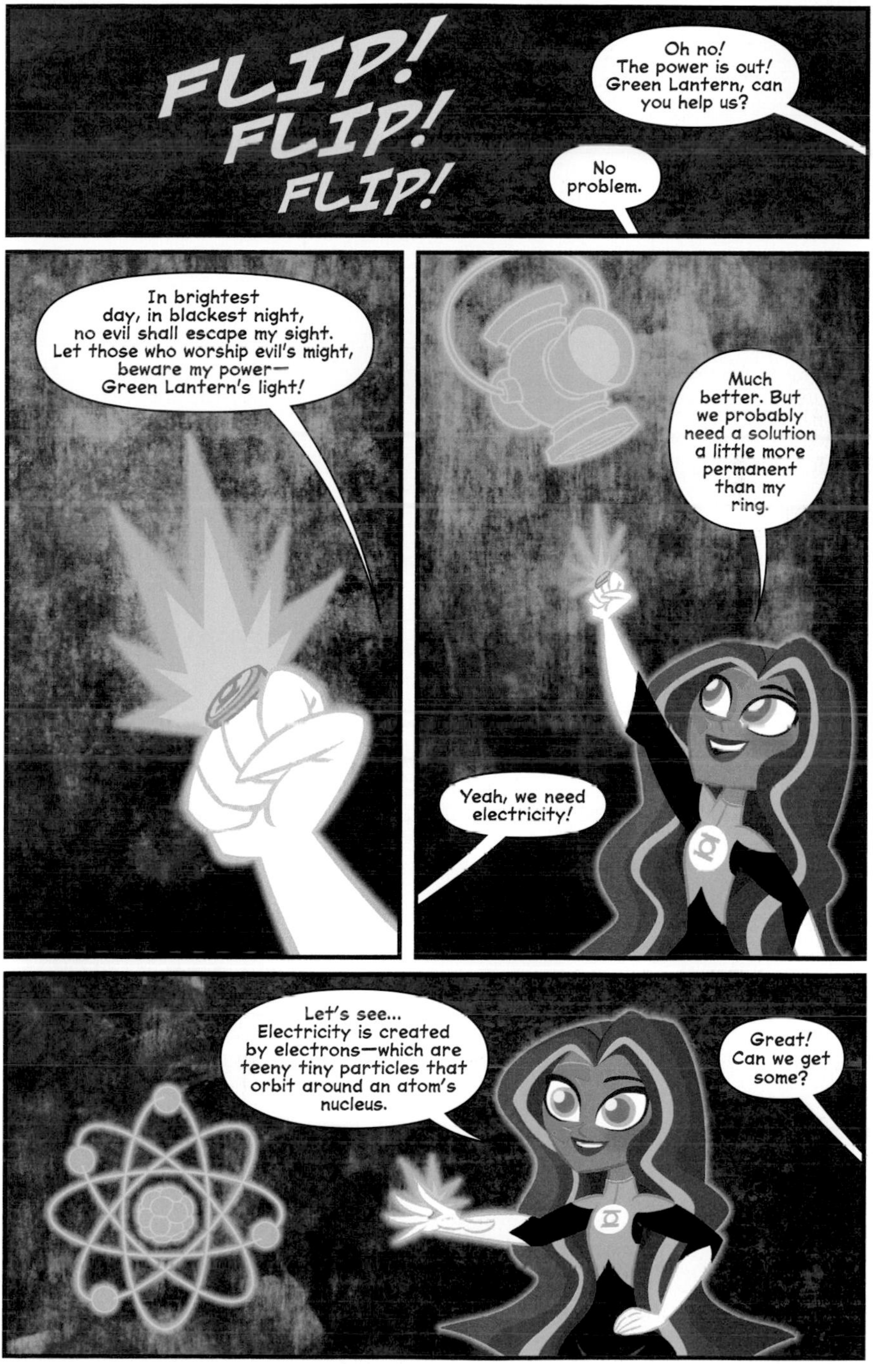
FLIP! FLIP! FLIP!
Oh no! The power is out! Green Lantern, can you help us?
No problem.
In brightest day, in blackest night, no evil shall escape my sight. Let those who worship evil's might, beware my power— Green Lantern's light!
Much better. But we probably need a solution a little more permanent than my ring.
Yeah, we need electricity!
Let's see... Electricity is created by electrons—which are teeny tiny particles that orbit around an atom's nucleus.
Great! Can we get some?

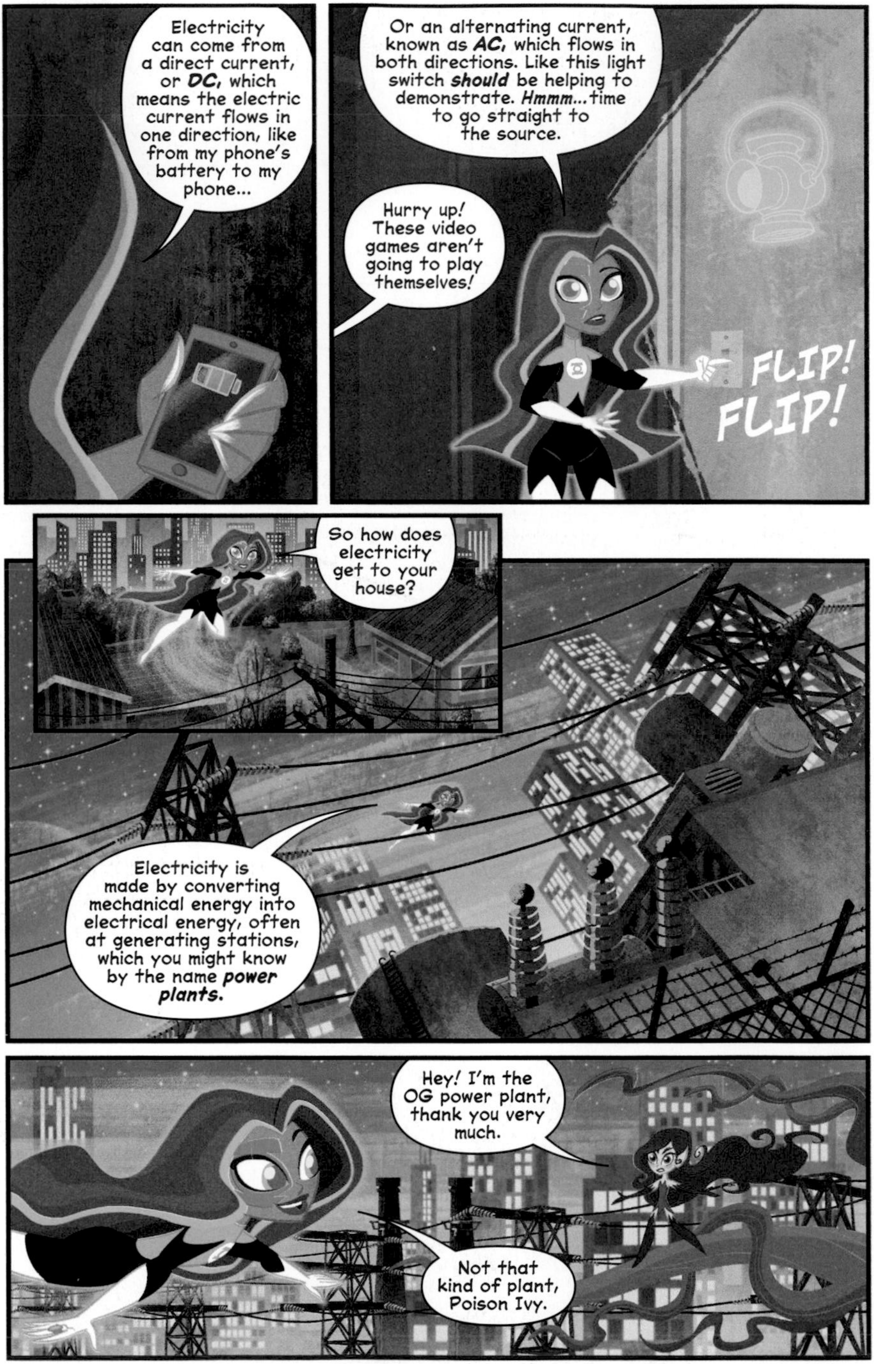
Electricity can come from a direct current, or *DC*, which means the electric current flows in one direction, like from my phone's battery to my phone...
Or an alternating current, known as *AC*, which flows in both directions. Like this light switch *should* be helping to demonstrate. *Hmmm...* time to go straight to the source.
Hurry up! These video games aren't going to play themselves!
FLIP! FLIP!
So how does electricity get to your house?
Electricity is made by converting mechanical energy into electrical energy, often at generating stations, which you might know by the name *power plants*.
Hey! I'm the OG power plant, thank you very much.
Not that kind of plant, Poison Ivy.

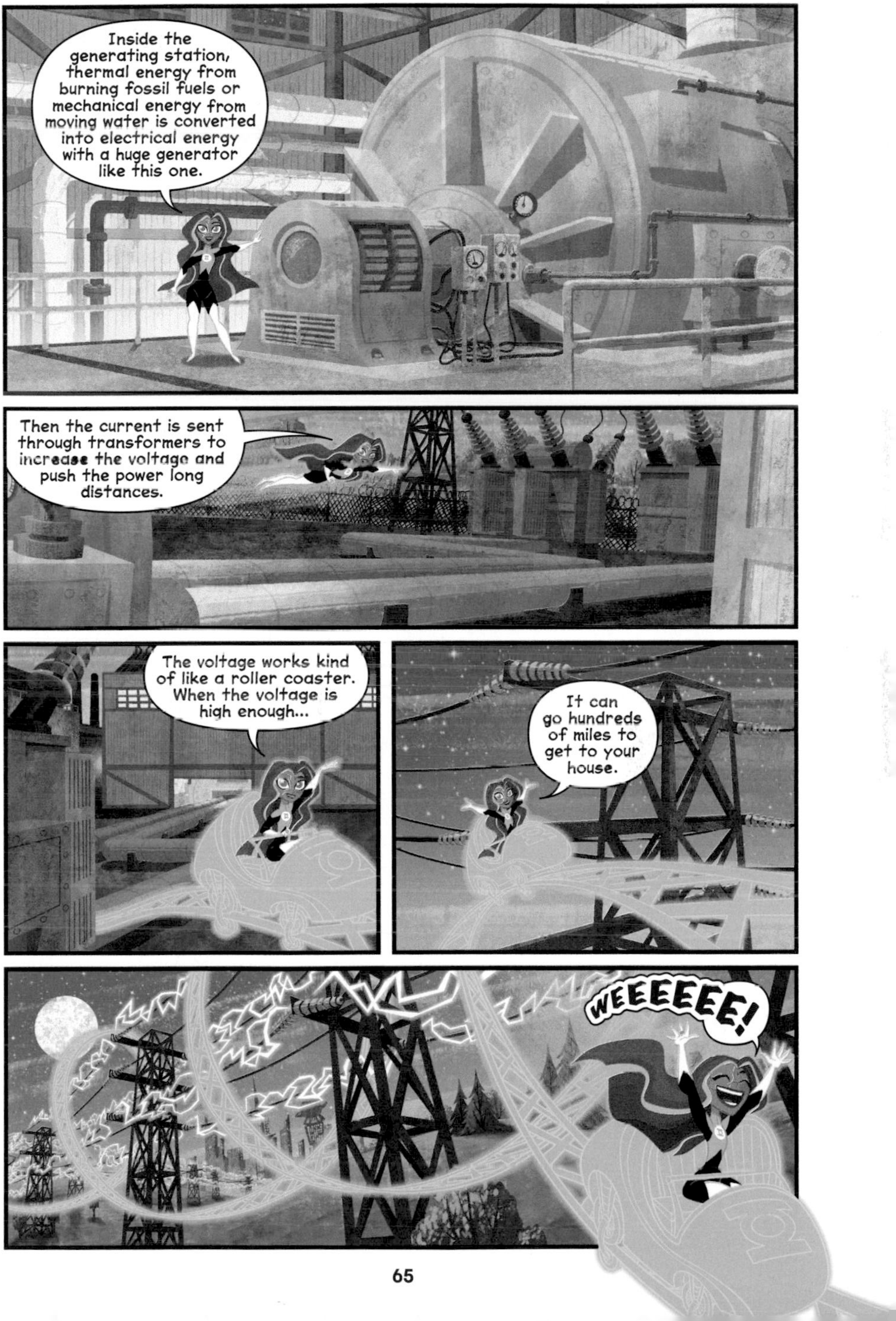
Inside the generating station, thermal energy from burning fossil fuels or mechanical energy from moving water is converted into electrical energy with a huge generator like this one.
Then the current is sent through transformers to increase the voltage and push the power long distances.
The voltage works kind of like a roller coaster. When the voltage is high enough...
It can go hundreds of miles to get to your house.
WEEEEEE!

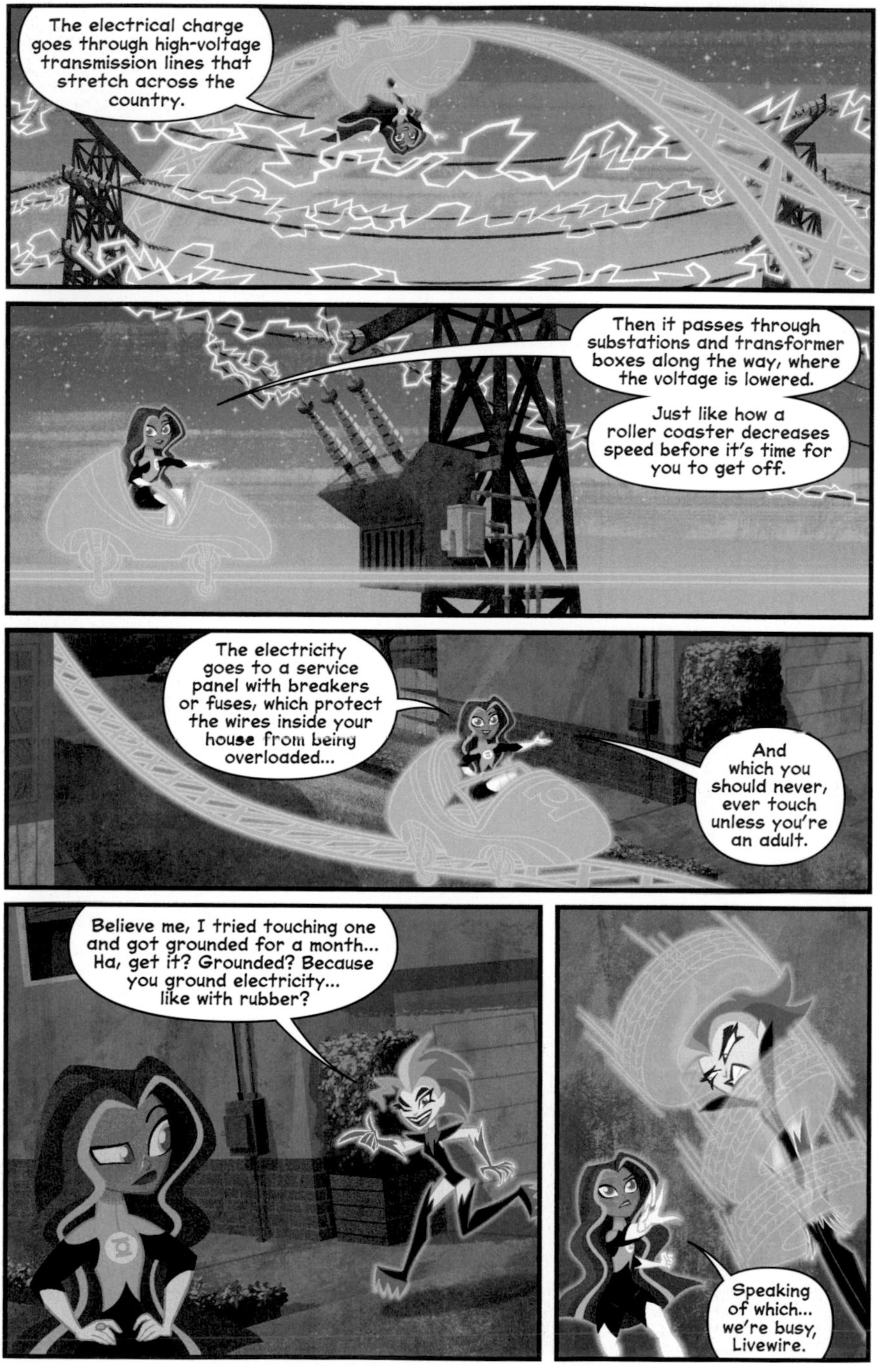
The electrical charge goes through high-voltage transmission lines that stretch across the country.
Then it passes through substations and transformer boxes along the way, where the voltage is lowered.
Just like how a roller coaster decreases speed before it's time for you to get off.
The electricity goes to a service panel with breakers or fuses, which protect the wires inside your house from being overloaded...
And which you should never, ever touch unless you're an adult.
Believe me, I tried touching one and got grounded for a month... Ha, get it? Grounded? Because you ground electricity... like with rubber?
Speaking of which... we're busy, Livewire.

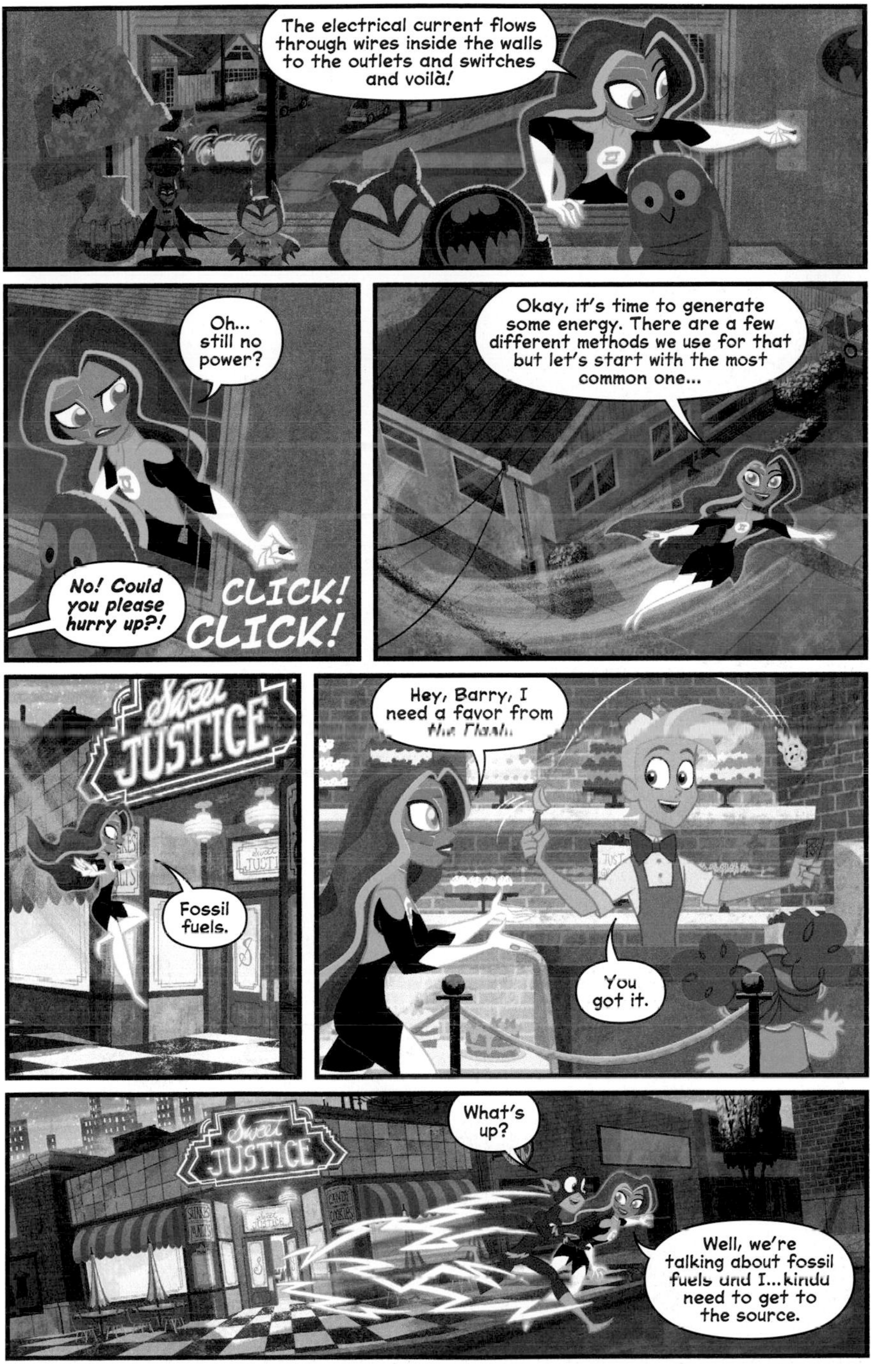

The electrical current flows through wires inside the walls to the outlets and switches and voilà!
Oh... still no power?
No! Could you please hurry up?!
CLICK! CLICK!
Okay, it's time to generate some energy. There are a few different methods we use for that but let's start with the most common one...
Sweet JUSTICE
Fossil fuels.
Hey, Barry, I need a favor from the Flash.
You got it.
Sweet JUSTICE
What's up?
Well, we're talking about fossil fuels and I...kinda need to get to the source.

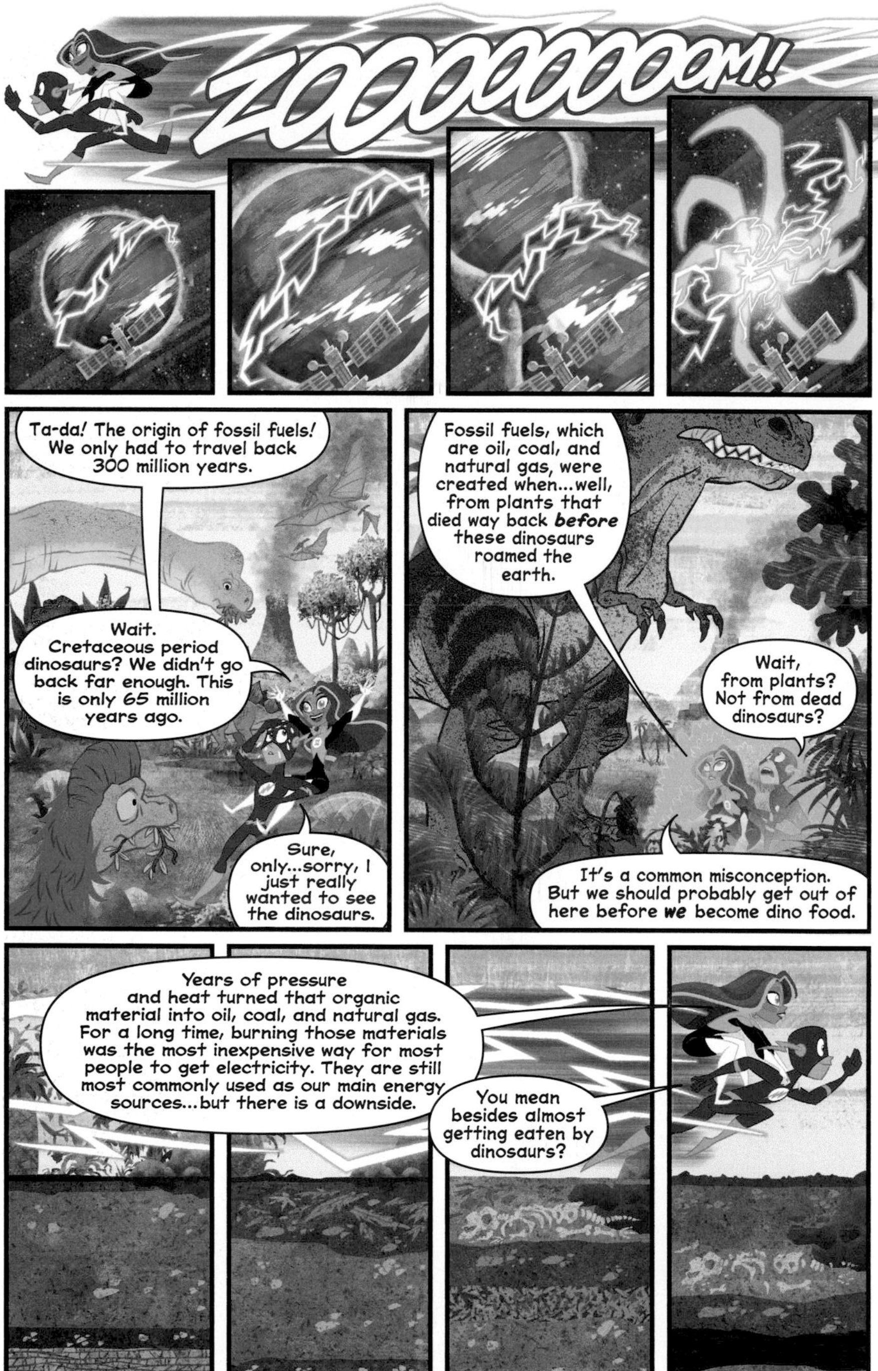
ZOOOOOOOOOM!
Ta-da! The origin of fossil fuels! We only had to travel back 300 million years.
Wait. Cretaceous period dinosaurs? We didn't go back far enough. This is only 65 million years ago.
Sure, only...sorry, I just really wanted to see the dinosaurs.
Fossil fuels, which are oil, coal, and natural gas, were created when...well, from plants that died way back before these dinosaurs roamed the earth.
Wait, from plants? Not from dead dinosaurs?
It's a common misconception. But we should probably get out of here before we become dino food.
Years of pressure and heat turned that organic material into oil, coal, and natural gas. For a long time, burning those materials was the most inexpensive way for most people to get electricity. They are still most commonly used as our main energy sources...but there is a downside.
You mean besides almost getting eaten by dinosaurs?

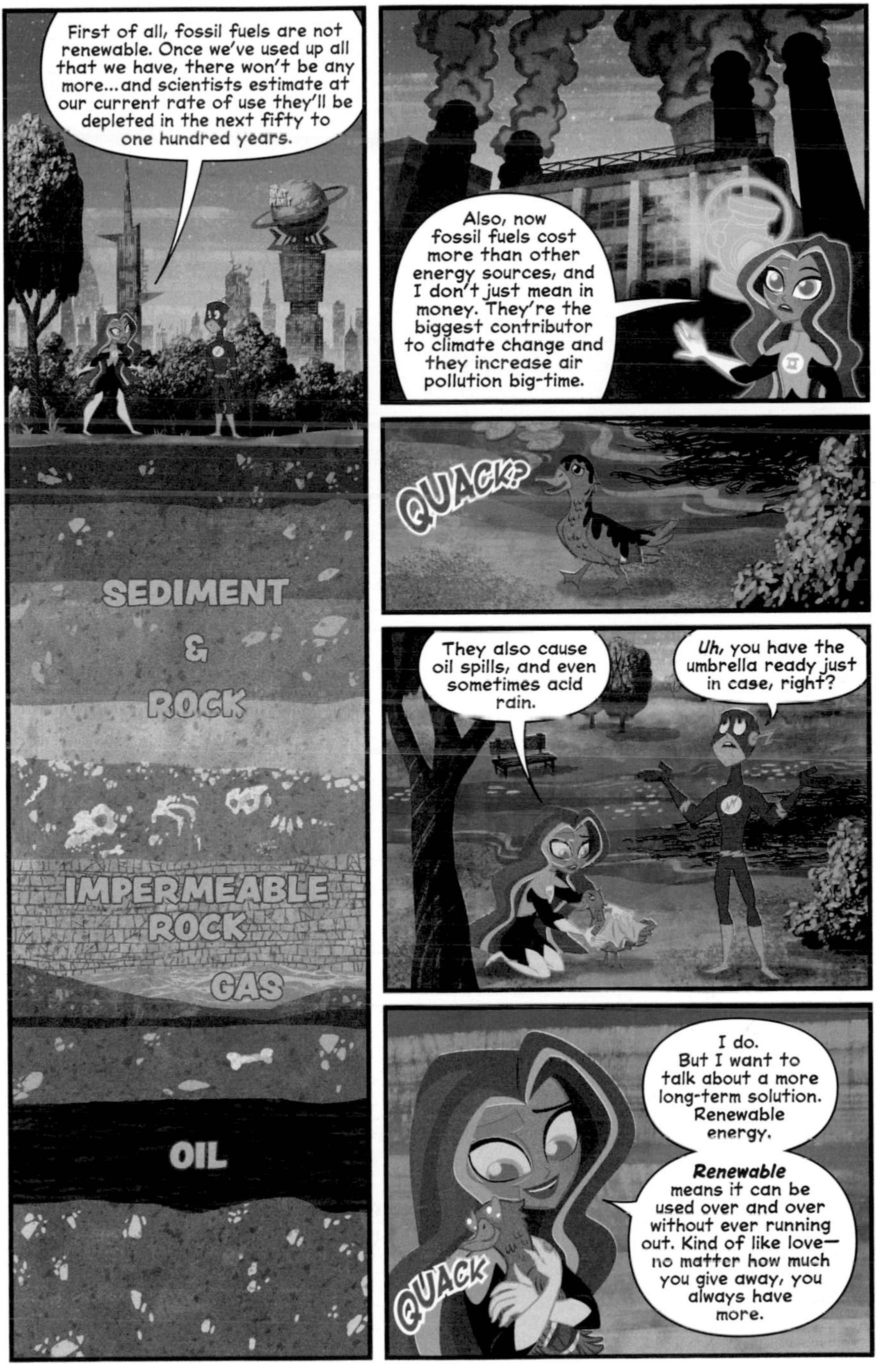

First of all, fossil fuels are not renewable. Once we've used up all that we have, there won't be any more...and scientists estimate at our current rate of use they'll be depleted in the next fifty to one hundred years.
SEDIMENT & ROCK
IMPERMEABLE ROCK
GAS
OIL
Also, now fossil fuels cost more than other energy sources, and I don't just mean in money. They're the biggest contributor to climate change and they increase air pollution big-time.
QUACK?
They also cause oil spills, and even sometimes acid rain.
Uh, you have the umbrella ready just in case, right?
I do. But I want to talk about a more long-term solution. Renewable energy.
Renewable means it can be used over and over without ever running out. Kind of like love—no matter how much you give away, you always have more.
QUACK

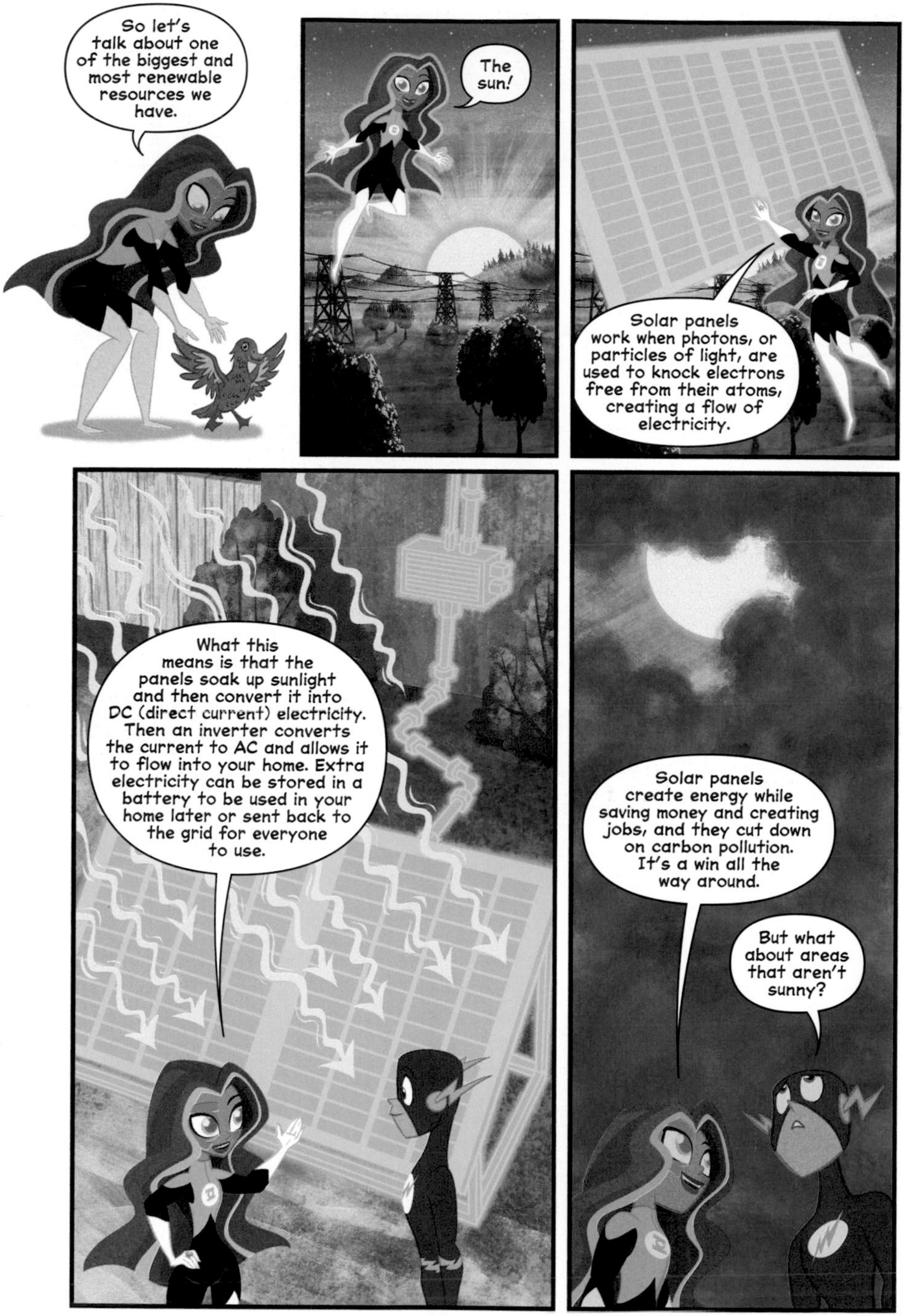
So let's talk about one of the biggest and most renewable resources we have.
The sun!
Solar panels work when photons, or particles of light, are used to knock electrons free from their atoms, creating a flow of electricity.
What this means is that the panels soak up sunlight and then convert it into DC (direct current) electricity. Then an inverter converts the current to AC and allows it to flow into your home. Extra electricity can be stored in a battery to be used in your home later or sent back to the grid for everyone to use.
Solar panels create energy while saving money and creating jobs, and they cut down on carbon pollution. It's a win all the way around.
But what about areas that aren't sunny?

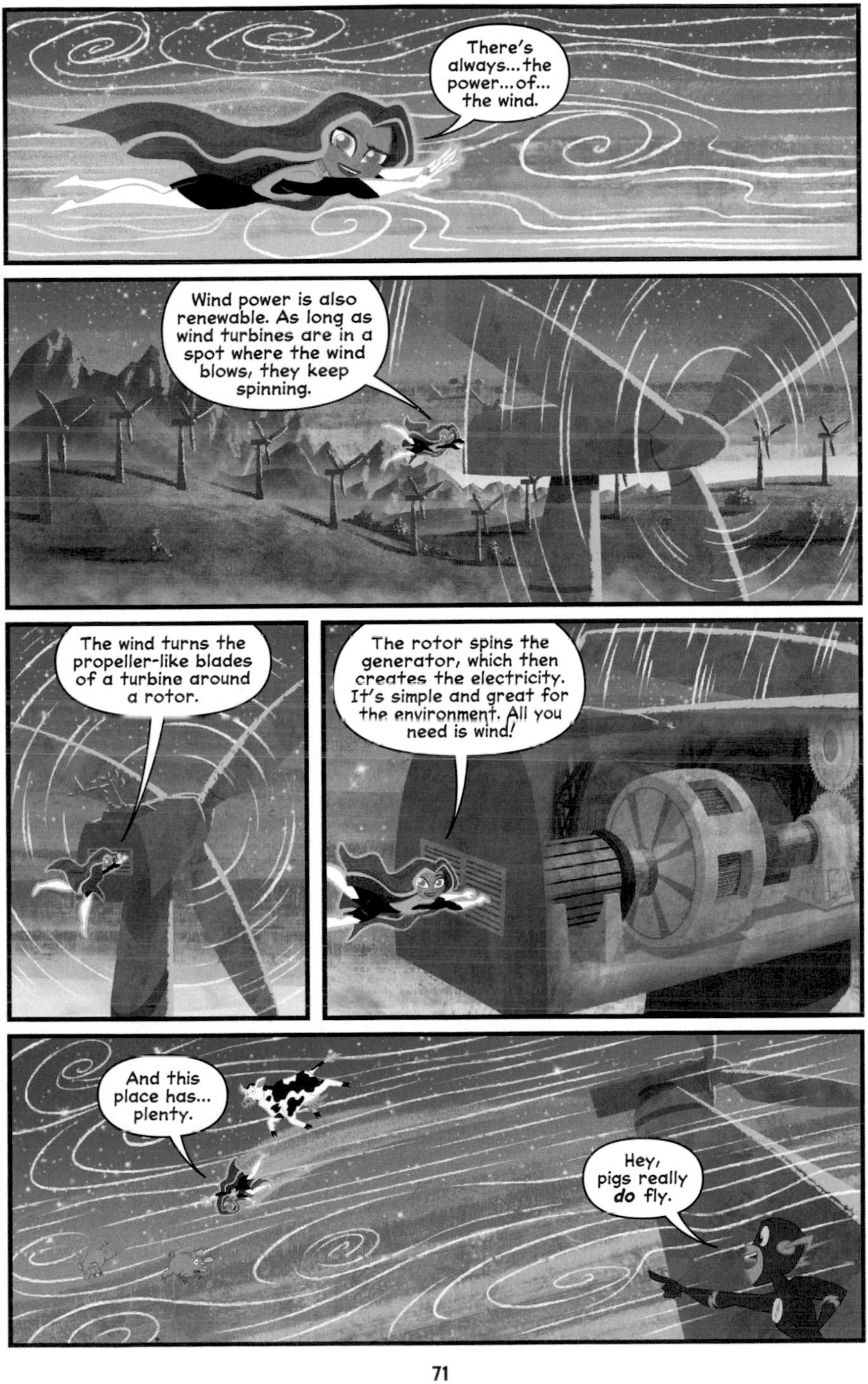
There's always...the power...of... the wind.
Wind power is also renewable. As long as wind turbines are in a spot where the wind blows, they keep spinning.
The wind turns the propeller-like blades of a turbine around a rotor.
The rotor spins the generator, which then creates the electricity. It's simple and great for the environment. All you need is wind!
And this place has... plenty.
Hey, pigs really *do* fly.

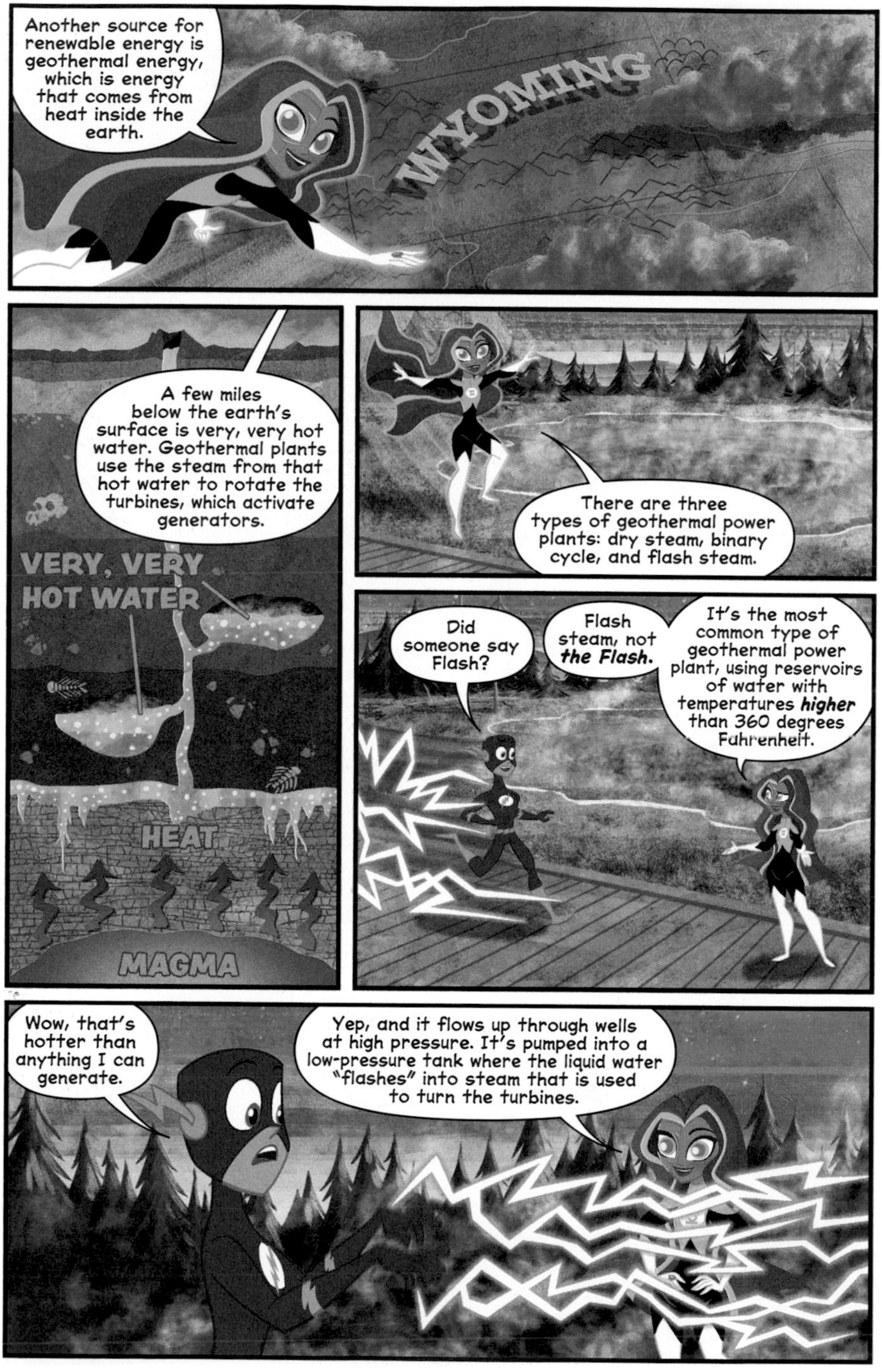
Another source for renewable energy is geothermal energy, which is energy that comes from heat inside the earth.
WYOMING
A few miles below the earth's surface is very, very hot water. Geothermal plants use the steam from that hot water to rotate the turbines, which activate generators.
VERY, VERY HOT WATER
HEAT
MAGMA
There are three types of geothermal power plants: dry steam, binary cycle, and flash steam.
Did someone say Flash?
Flash steam, not ***the Flash.***
It's the most common type of geothermal power plant, using reservoirs of water with temperatures ***higher*** than 360 degrees Fahrenheit.
Wow, that's hotter than anything I can generate.
Yep, and it flows up through wells at high pressure. It's pumped into a low-pressure tank where the liquid water "flashes" into steam that is used to turn the turbines.

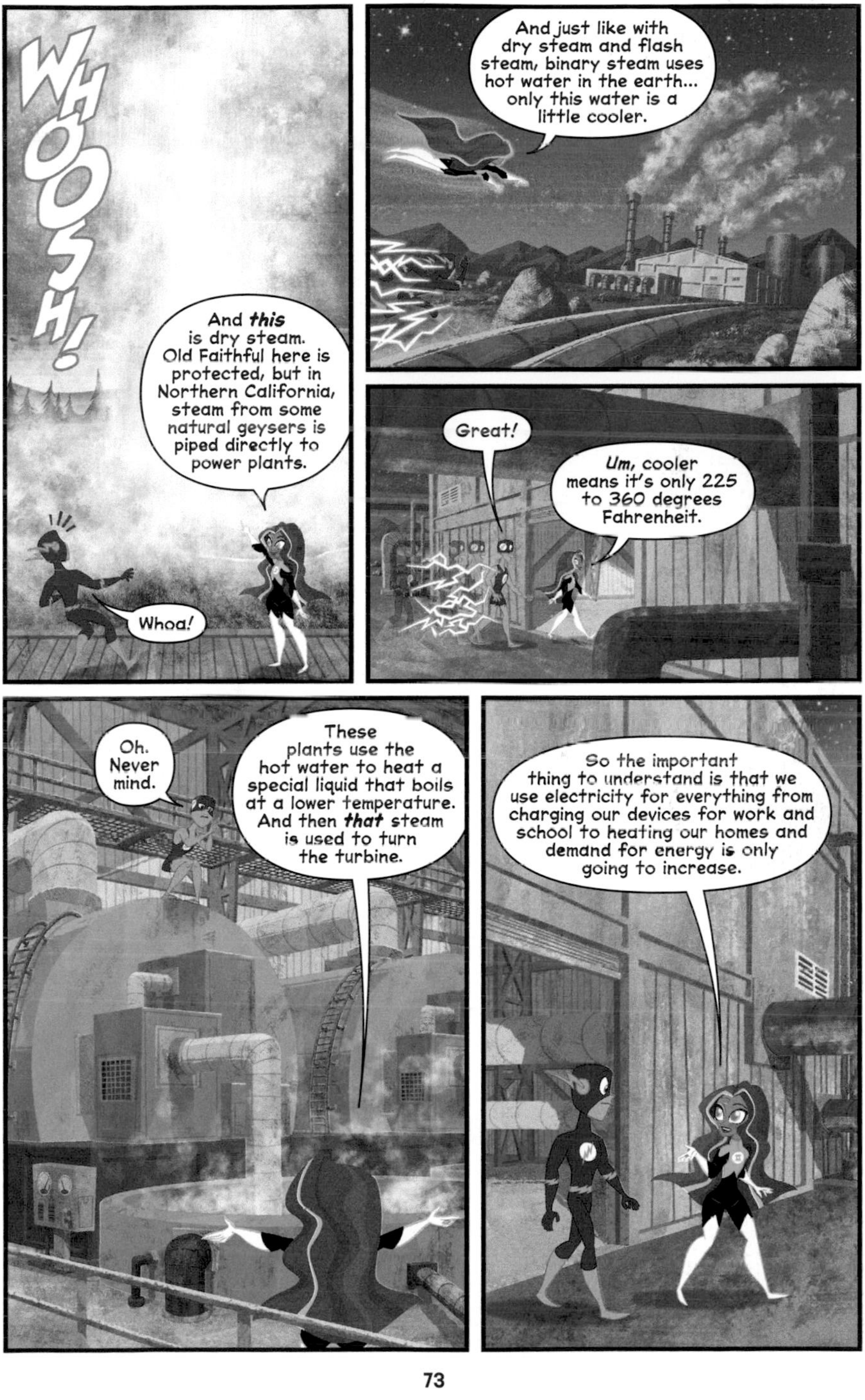

WHOOSH!
And *this* is dry steam. Old Faithful here is protected, but in Northern California, steam from some natural geysers is piped directly to power plants.
Whoa!
And just like with dry steam and flash steam, binary steam uses hot water in the earth... only this water is a little cooler.
Great!
Um, cooler means it's only 225 to 360 degrees Fahrenheit.
Oh. Never mind.
These plants use the hot water to heat a special liquid that boils at a lower temperature. And then *that* steam is used to turn the turbine.
So the important thing to understand is that we use electricity for everything from charging our devices for work and school to heating our homes and demand for energy is only going to increase.

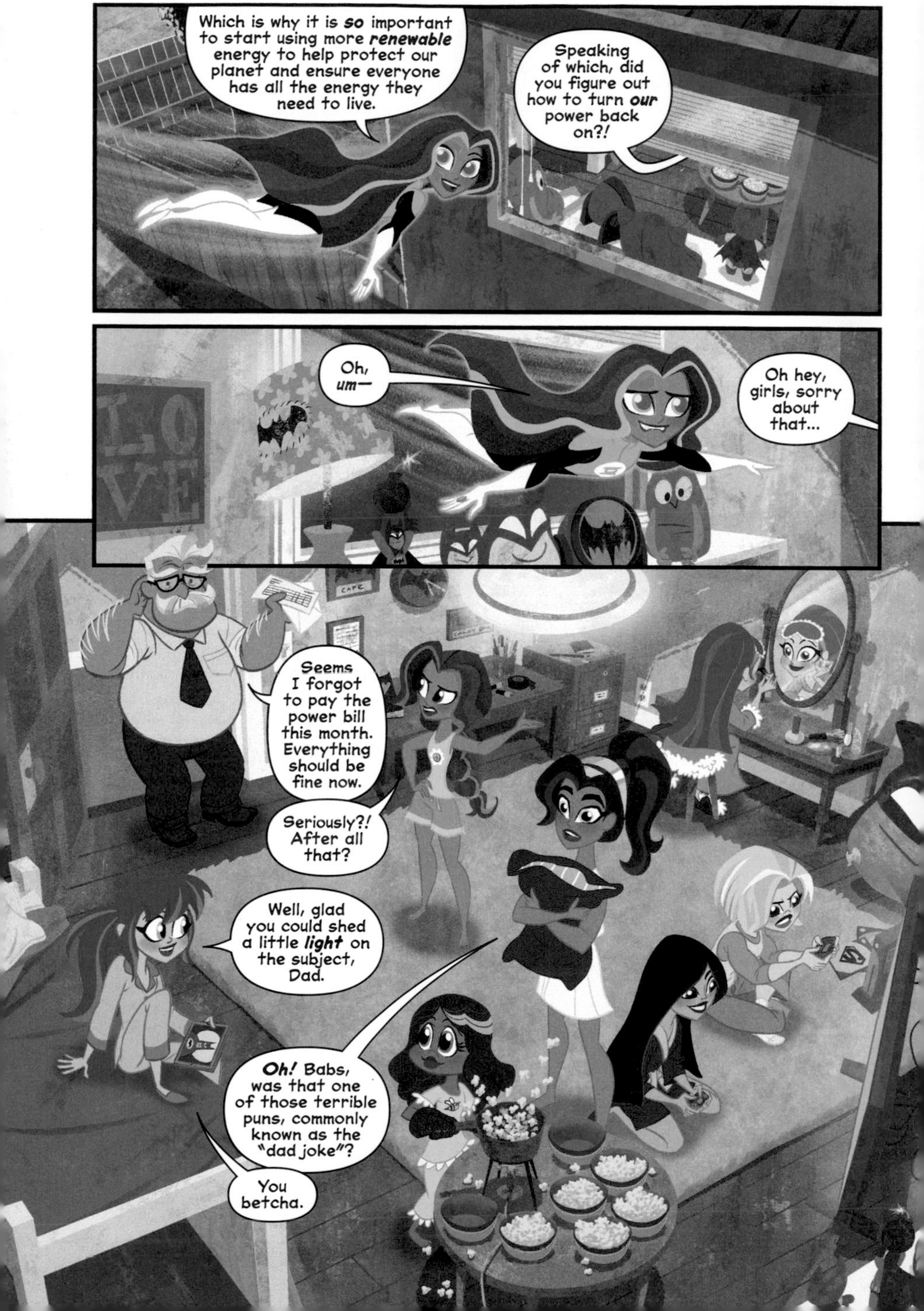

Which is why it is *so* important to start using more *renewable* energy to help protect our planet and ensure everyone has all the energy they need to live.
Speaking of which, did you figure out how to turn *our* power back on?!
Oh, *um*—
Oh hey, girls, sorry about that...
Seems I forgot to pay the power bill this month. Everything should be fine now.
Seriously?! After all that?
Well, glad you could shed a little *light* on the subject, Dad.
Oh! Babs, was that one of those terrible puns, commonly known as the "dad joke"?
You betcha.

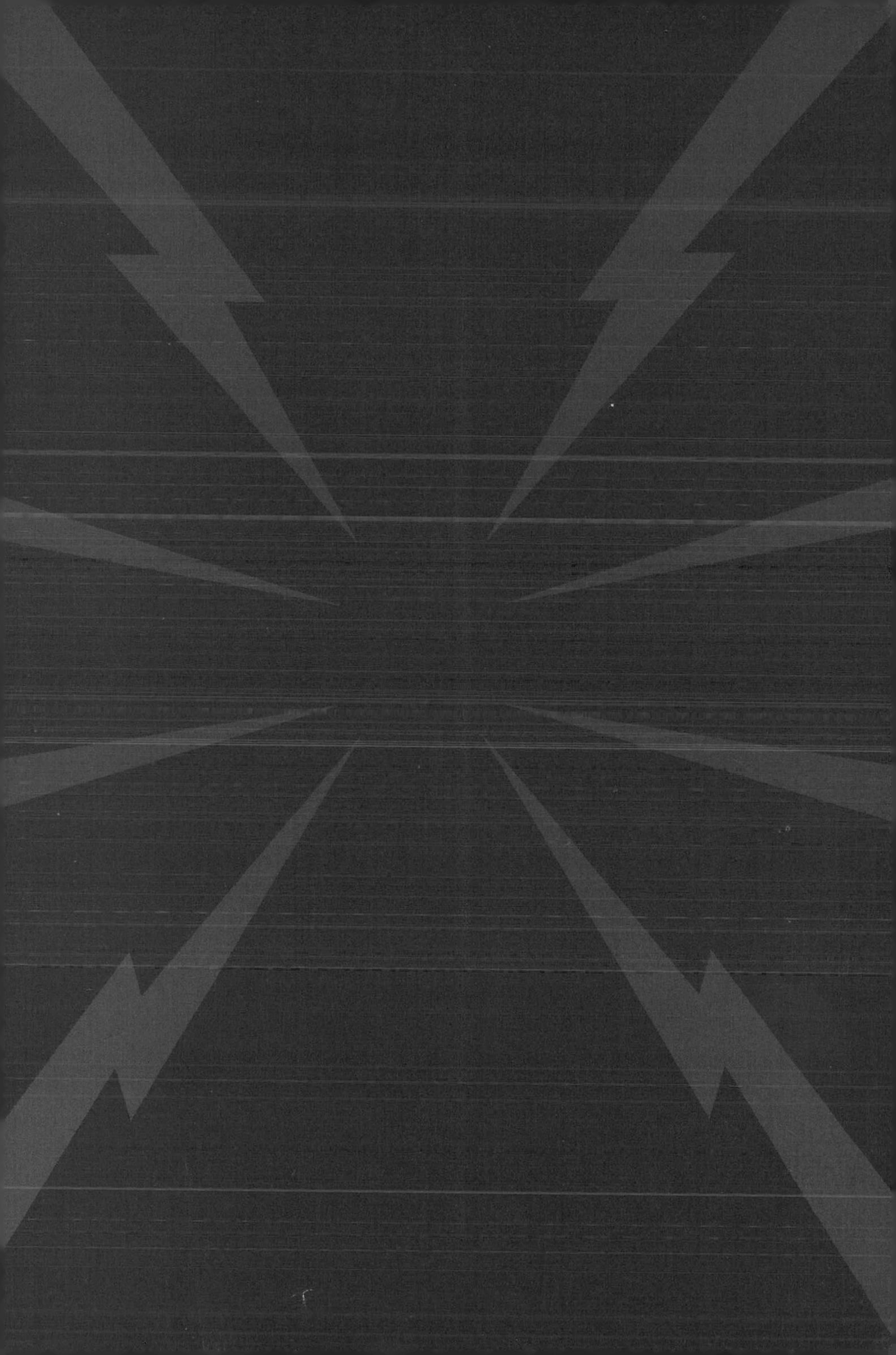

CHAPTER SIX

(SUB)ATOMIC

WRITTEN BY **VITA AYALA**
ILLUSTRATED BY **ANDIE TONG**
COLORED BY **DEVYN HANSEN**
LETTERED BY **WES ABBOTT**

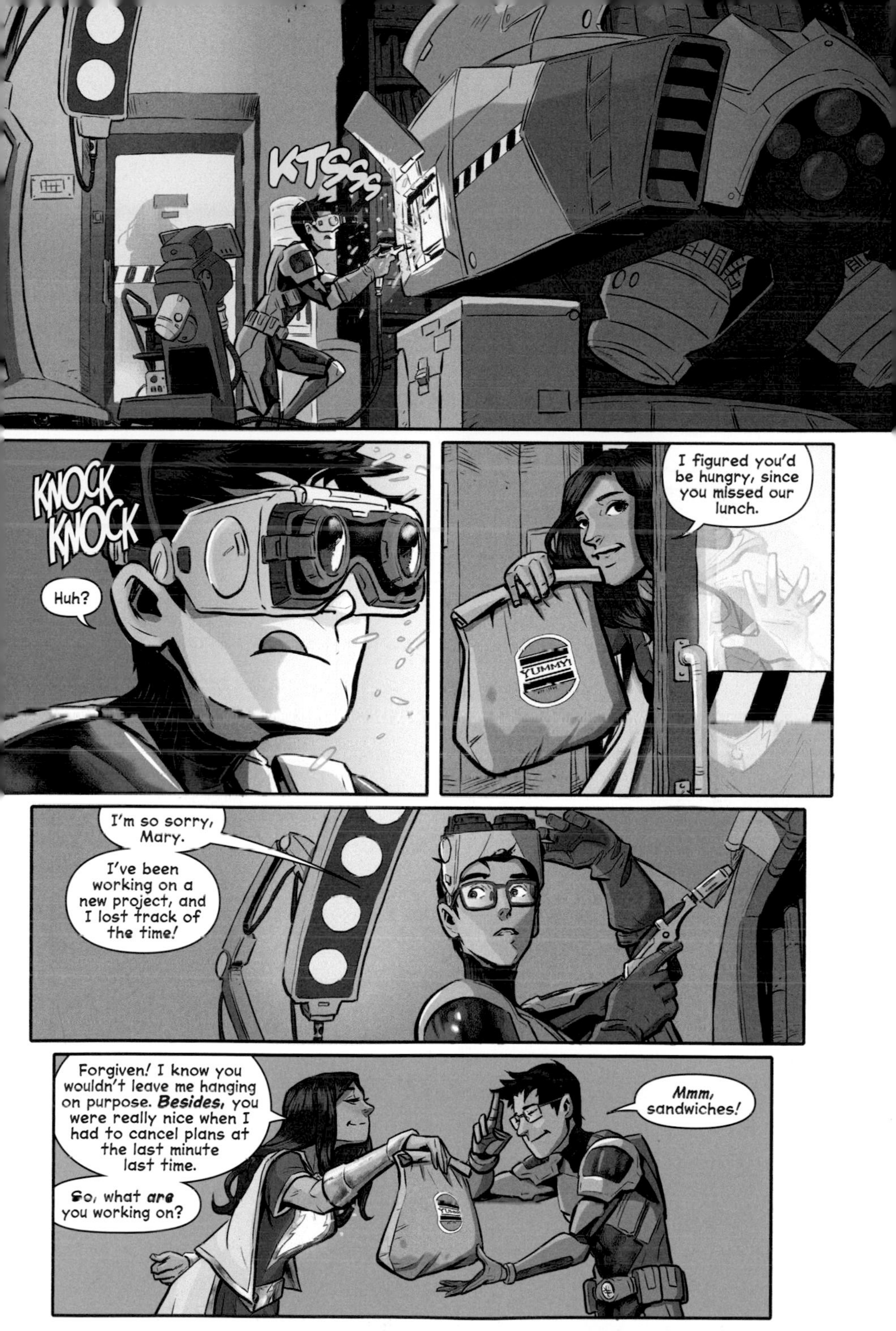
KTSSSS
KNOCK KNOCK
Huh?
I figured you'd be hungry, since you missed our lunch.
YUMMY!
I'm so sorry, Mary.
I've been working on a new project, and I lost track of the time!
Forgiven! I know you wouldn't leave me hanging on purpose. *Besides,* you were really nice when I had to cancel plans at the last minute last time.
So, what *are* you working on?
Mmm, sandwiches!

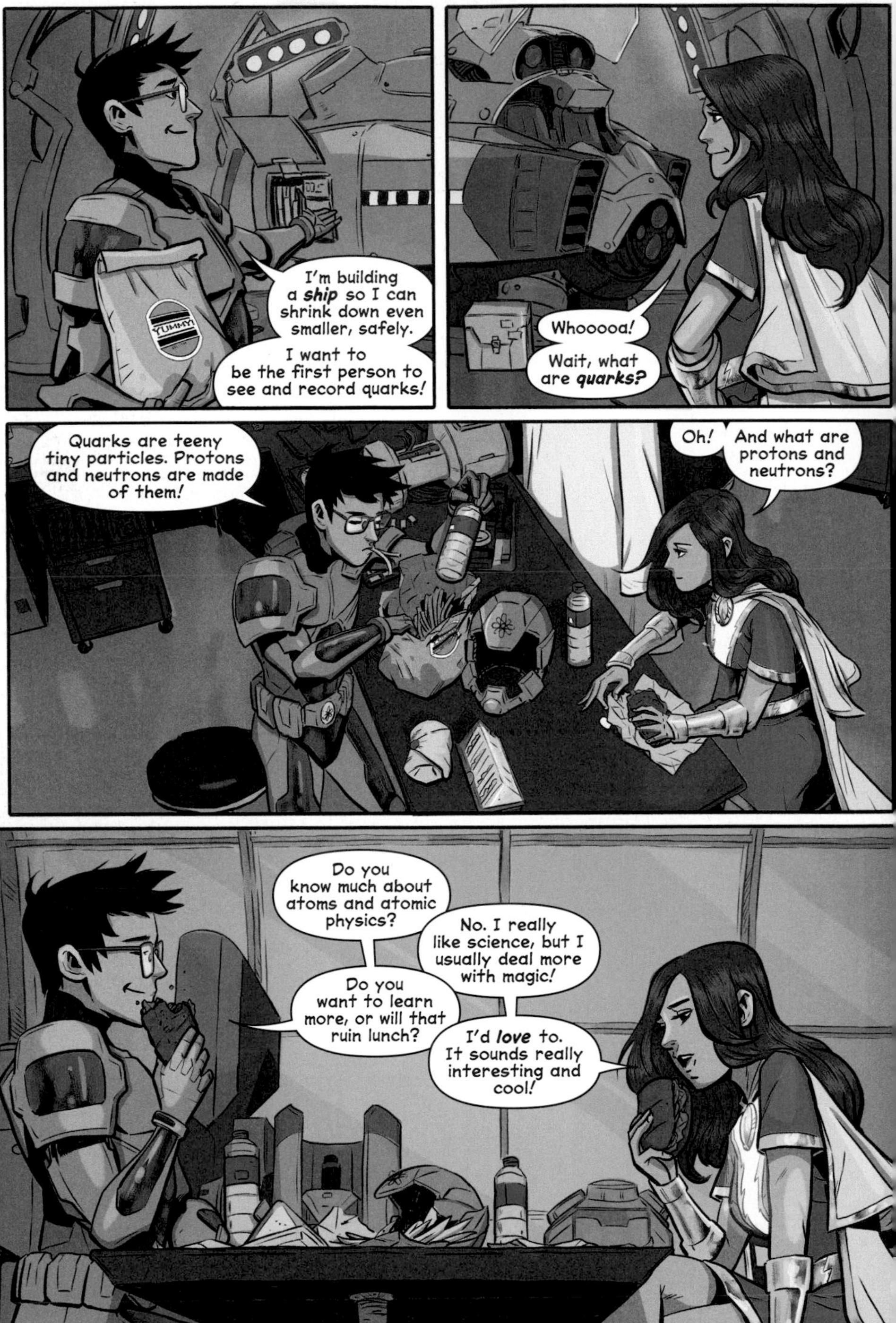
I'm building a ship so I can shrink down even smaller, safely.
I want to be the first person to see and record quarks!
YUMMY!
Whoooooa!
Wait, what are quarks?
Quarks are teeny tiny particles. Protons and neutrons are made of them!
Oh!
And what are protons and neutrons?
Do you know much about atoms and atomic physics?
No. I really like science, but I usually deal more with magic!
Do you want to learn more, or will that ruin lunch?
I'd love to. It sounds really interesting and cool!

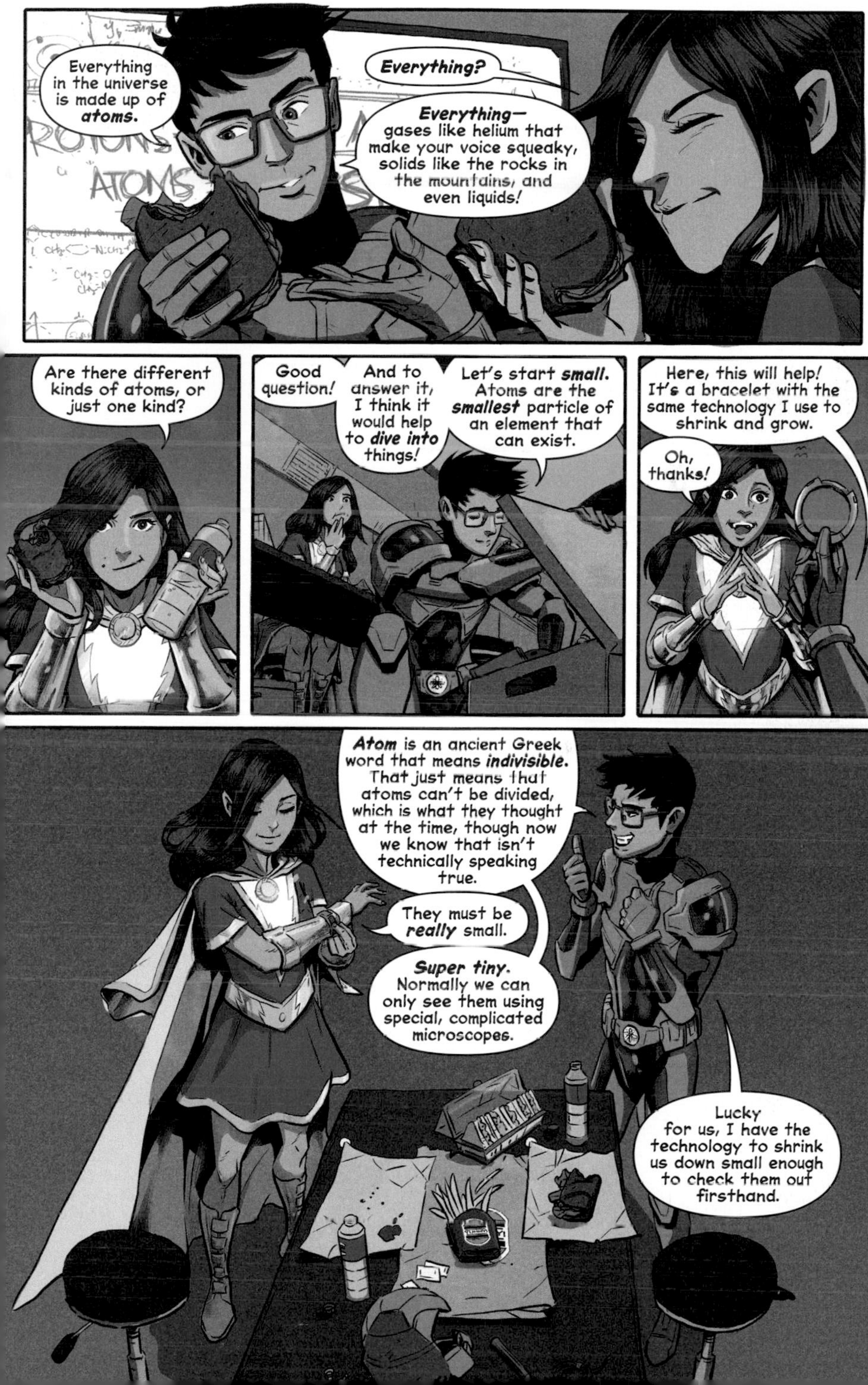
Everything in the universe is made up of atoms.
Everything?
Everything— gases like helium that make your voice squeaky, solids like the rocks in the mountains, and even liquids!
Are there different kinds of atoms, or just one kind?
Good question!
And to answer it, I think it would help to dive into things!
Let's start small. Atoms are the smallest particle of an element that can exist.
Here, this will help! It's a bracelet with the same technology I use to shrink and grow.
Oh, thanks!
Atom is an ancient Greek word that means indivisible. That just means that atoms can't be divided, which is what they thought at the time, though now we know that isn't technically speaking true.
They must be really small.
Super tiny. Normally we can only see them using special, complicated microscopes.
Lucky for us, I have the technology to shrink us down small enough to check them out firsthand.

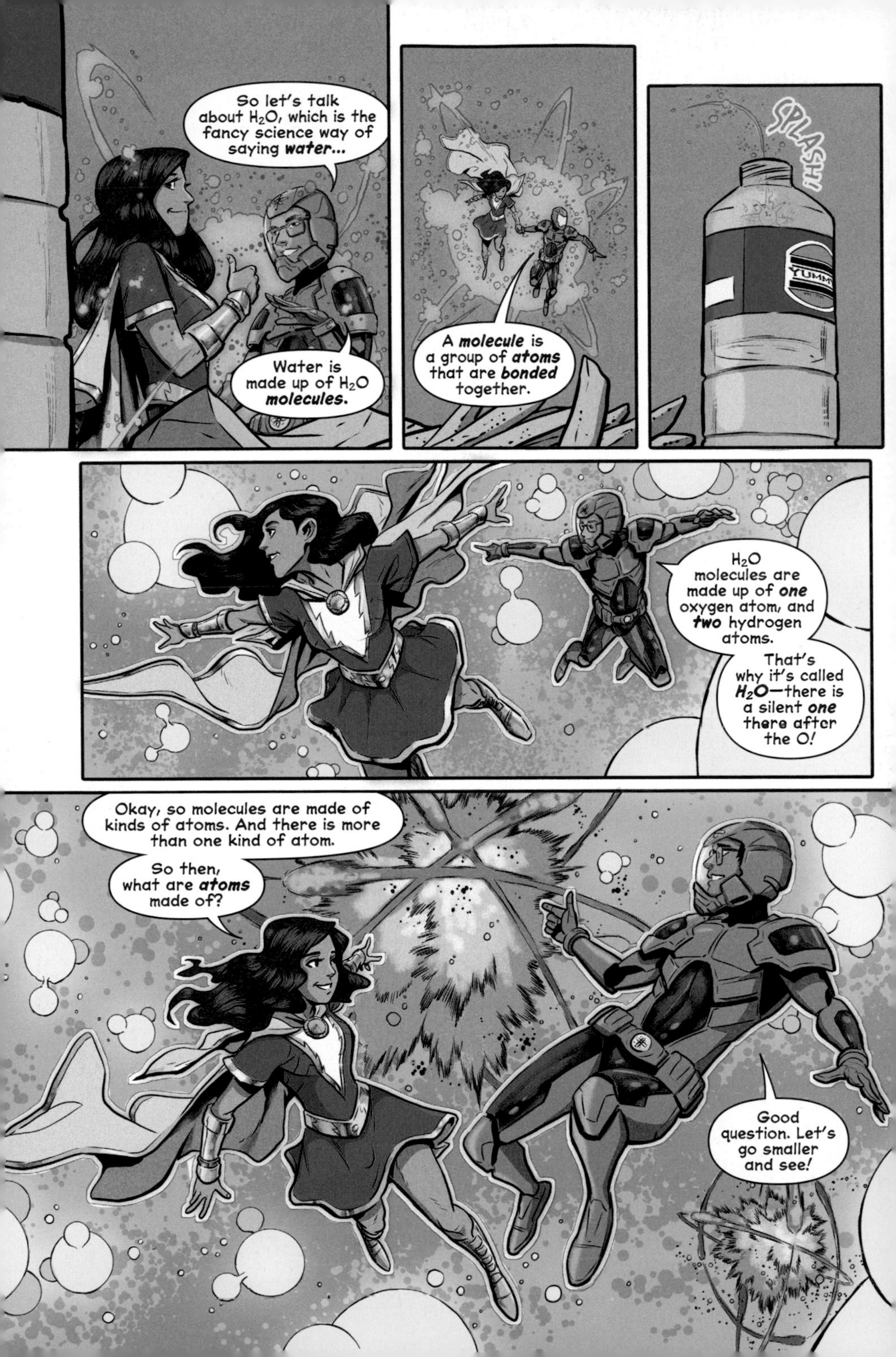

So let's talk about H_2O, which is the fancy science way of saying **water...**
Water is made up of H_2O **molecules.**
A **molecule** is a group of **atoms** that are **bonded** together.
SPLASH!
YUMM
H_2O molecules are made up of **one** oxygen atom, and **two** hydrogen atoms.
That's why it's called **H_2O**—there is a silent **one** there after the O!
Okay, so molecules are made of kinds of atoms. And there is more than one kind of atom.
So then, what are **atoms** made of?
Good question. Let's go smaller and see!

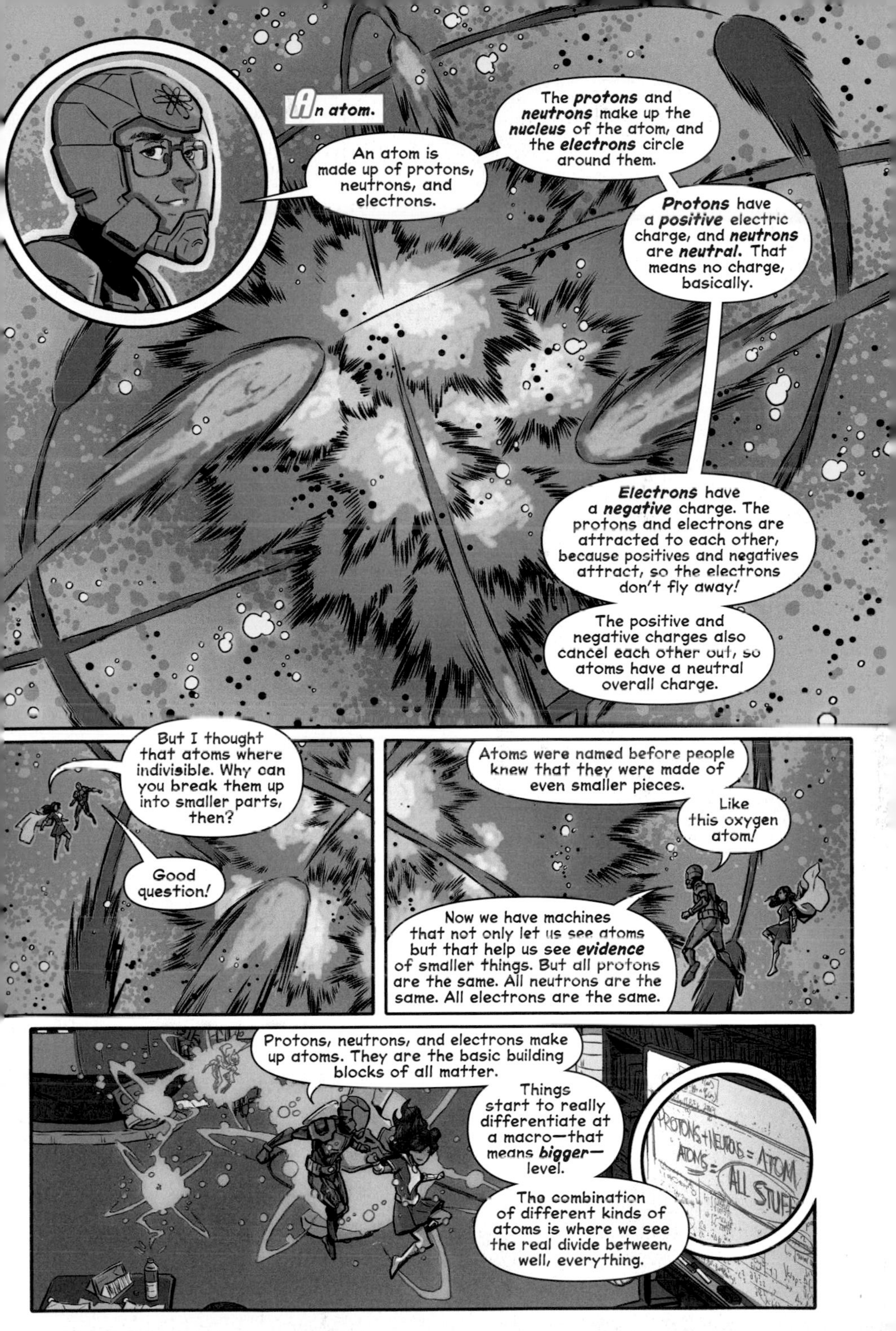
An atom.
An atom is made up of protons, neutrons, and electrons.
The ***protons*** and ***neutrons*** make up the ***nucleus*** of the atom, and the ***electrons*** circle around them.
Protons have a ***positive*** electric charge, and ***neutrons*** are ***neutral.*** That means no charge, basically.
Electrons have a ***negative*** charge. The protons and electrons are attracted to each other, because positives and negatives attract, so the electrons don't fly away!
The positive and negative charges also cancel each other out, so atoms have a neutral overall charge.
But I thought that atoms where indivisible. Why can you break them up into smaller parts, then?
Good question!
Atoms were named before people knew that they were made of even smaller pieces.
Like this oxygen atom!
Now we have machines that not only let us see atoms but that help us see ***evidence*** of smaller things. But all protons are the same. All neutrons are the same. All electrons are the same.
Protons, neutrons, and electrons make up atoms. They are the basic building blocks of all matter.
Things start to really differentiate at a macro—that means ***bigger***—level.
The combination of different kinds of atoms is where we see the real divide between, well, everything.
PROTONS+NEUTRONS = ATOM
ATOMS = ALL STUFF

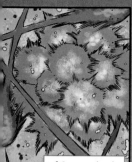

"So we start
with those
building blocks...

"...and we get to
the basic atoms...

"...which come together to
make all kinds of stuff...

"...things like the ocean we
swim in, the sand we stand
on, the air we breathe...

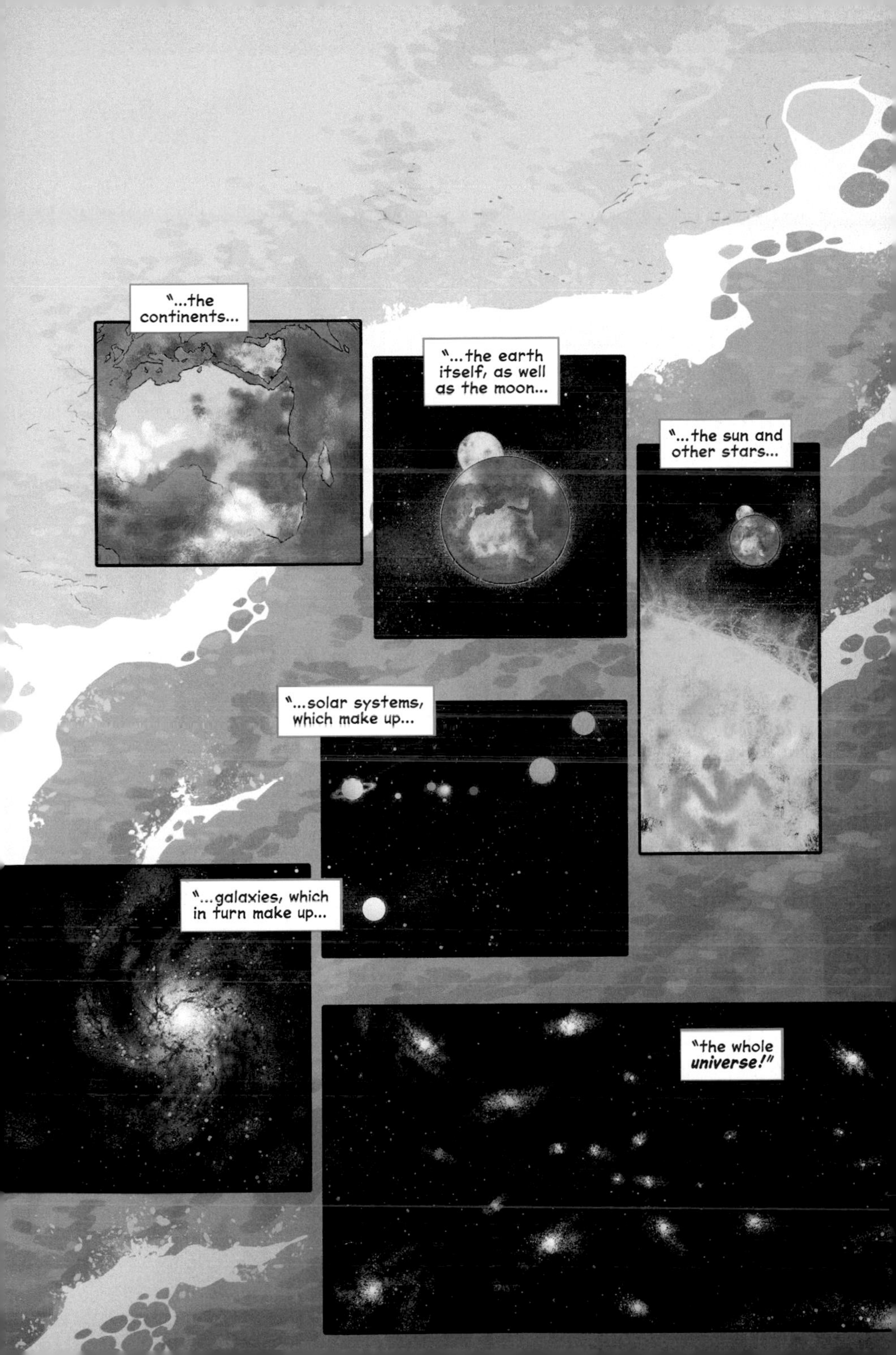
"...the continents...
"...the earth itself, as well as the moon...
"...the sun and other stars...
"...solar systems, which make up...
"...galaxies, which in turn make up...
"the whole *universe!*"

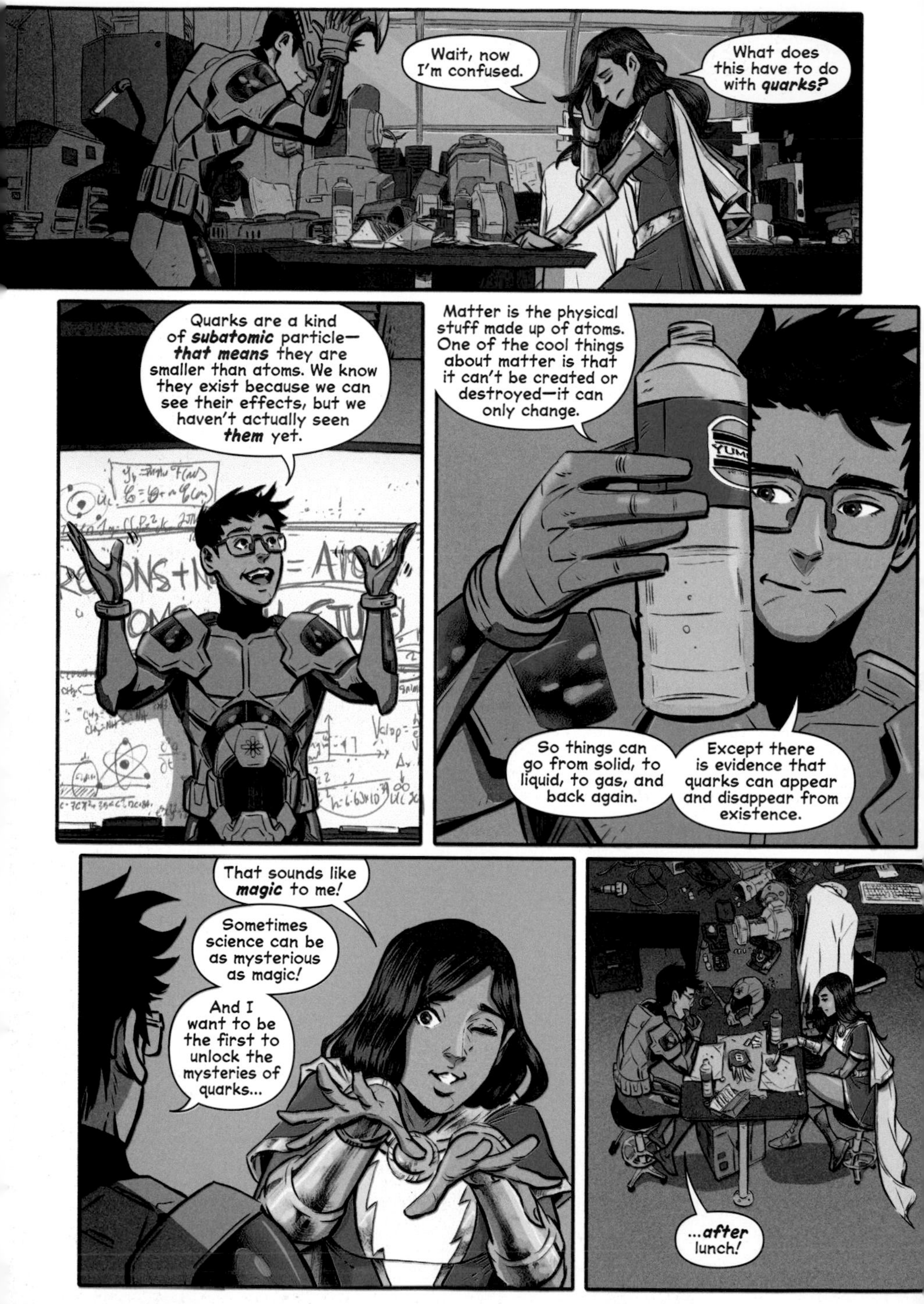
Wait, now I'm confused.
What does this have to do with ***quarks?***
Quarks are a kind of ***subatomic*** particle—***that means*** they are smaller than atoms. We know they exist because we can see their effects, but we haven't actually seen ***them*** yet.
Matter is the physical stuff made up of atoms. One of the cool things about matter is that it can't be created or destroyed—it can only change.
So things can go from solid, to liquid, to gas, and back again.
Except there is evidence that quarks can appear and disappear from existence.
That sounds like ***magic*** to me!
Sometimes science can be as mysterious as magic!
And I want to be the first to unlock the mysteries of quarks...
...***after*** lunch!

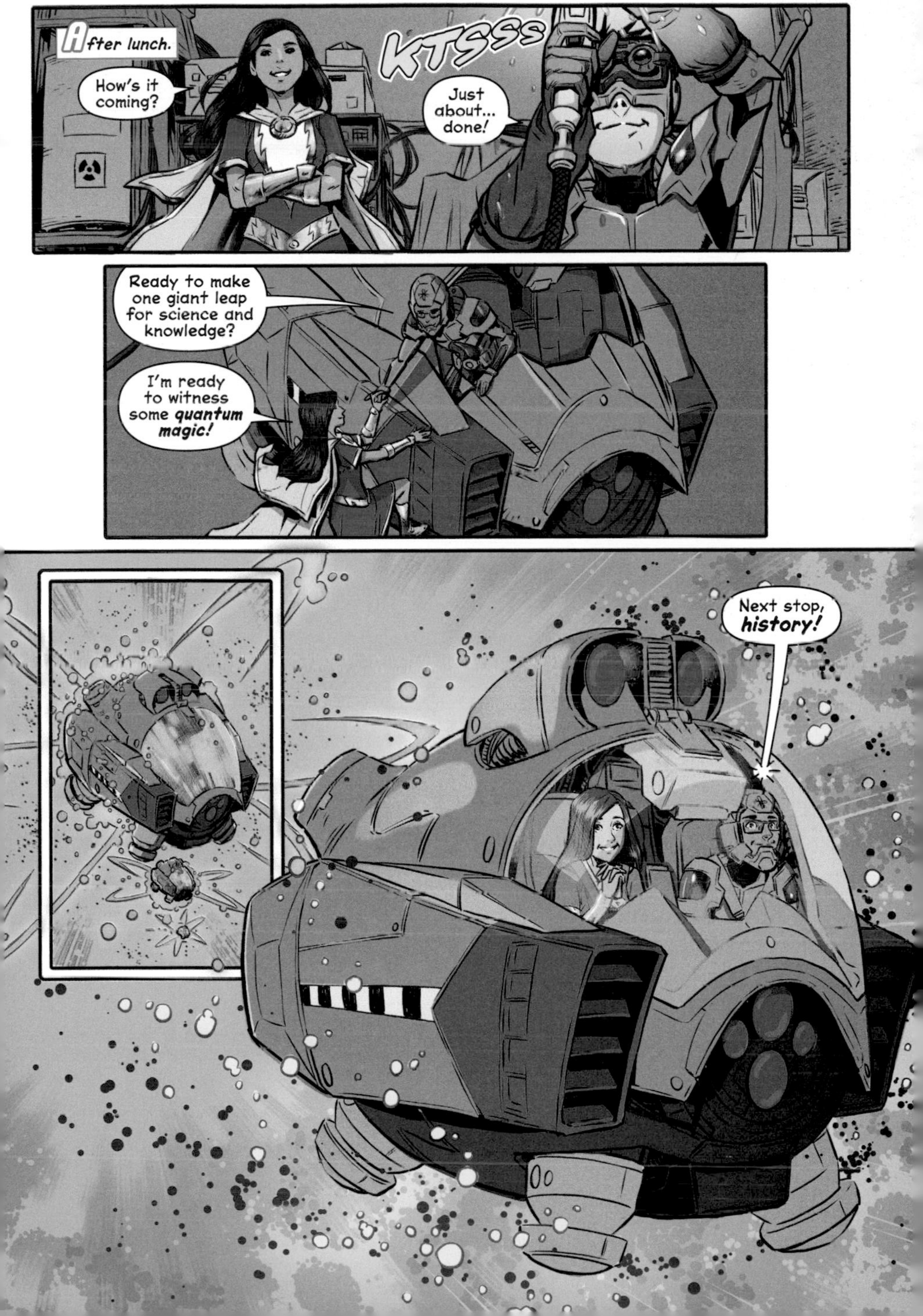
After lunch.
How's it coming?
KTSSS
Just about... done!
Ready to make one giant leap for science and knowledge?
I'm ready to witness some ***quantum magic!***
Next stop, ***history!***

CHAPTER SEVEN

HOME SWEET SPACE

WRITTEN BY **CECIL CASTELLUCCI**

ILLUSTRATED BY **GRETEL LUSKY**

LETTERED BY **WES ABBOTT**

SUPERGIRL BASED ON CHARACTERS CREATED BY JERRY SIEGEL AND JOE SHUSTER
BY SPECIAL ARRANGEMENT WITH THE JERRY SIEGEL FAMILY

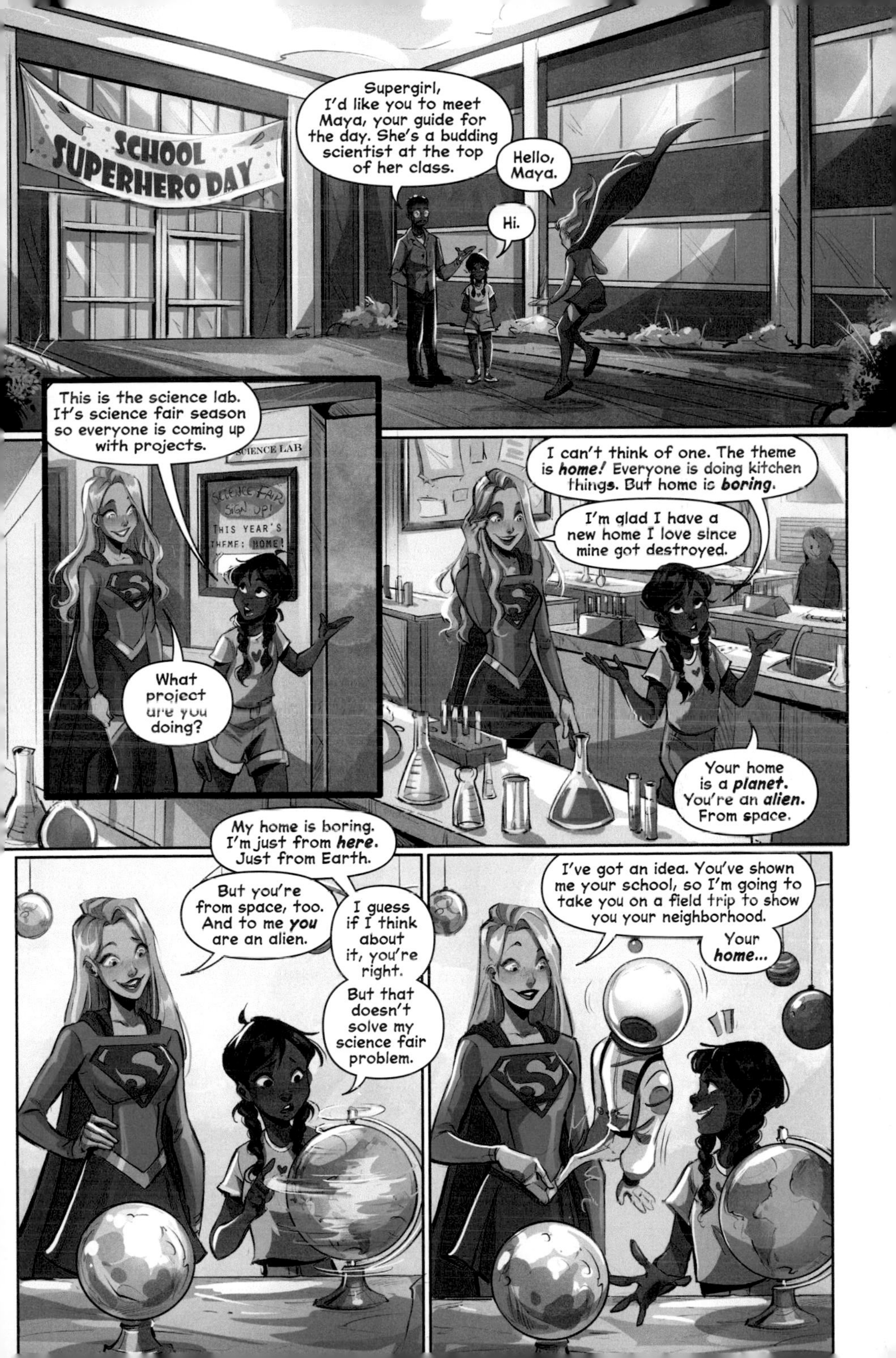
SCHOOL SUPERHERO DAY
Supergirl, I'd like you to meet Maya, your guide for the day. She's a budding scientist at the top of her class.
Hello, Maya.
Hi.
This is the science lab. It's science fair season so everyone is coming up with projects.
SCIENCE LAB
SCIENCE FAIR SIGN UP! THIS YEAR'S THEME: HOME!
What project are you doing?
I can't think of one. The theme is ***home!*** Everyone is doing kitchen things. But home is ***boring***.
I'm glad I have a new home I love since mine got destroyed.
Your home is a ***planet***. You're an ***alien***. From space.
My home is boring. I'm just from ***here***. Just from Earth.
But you're from space, too. And to me ***you*** are an alien.
I guess if I think about it, you're right.
But that doesn't solve my science fair problem.
I've got an idea. You've shown me your school, so I'm going to take you on a field trip to show you your neighborhood.
Your ***home***...

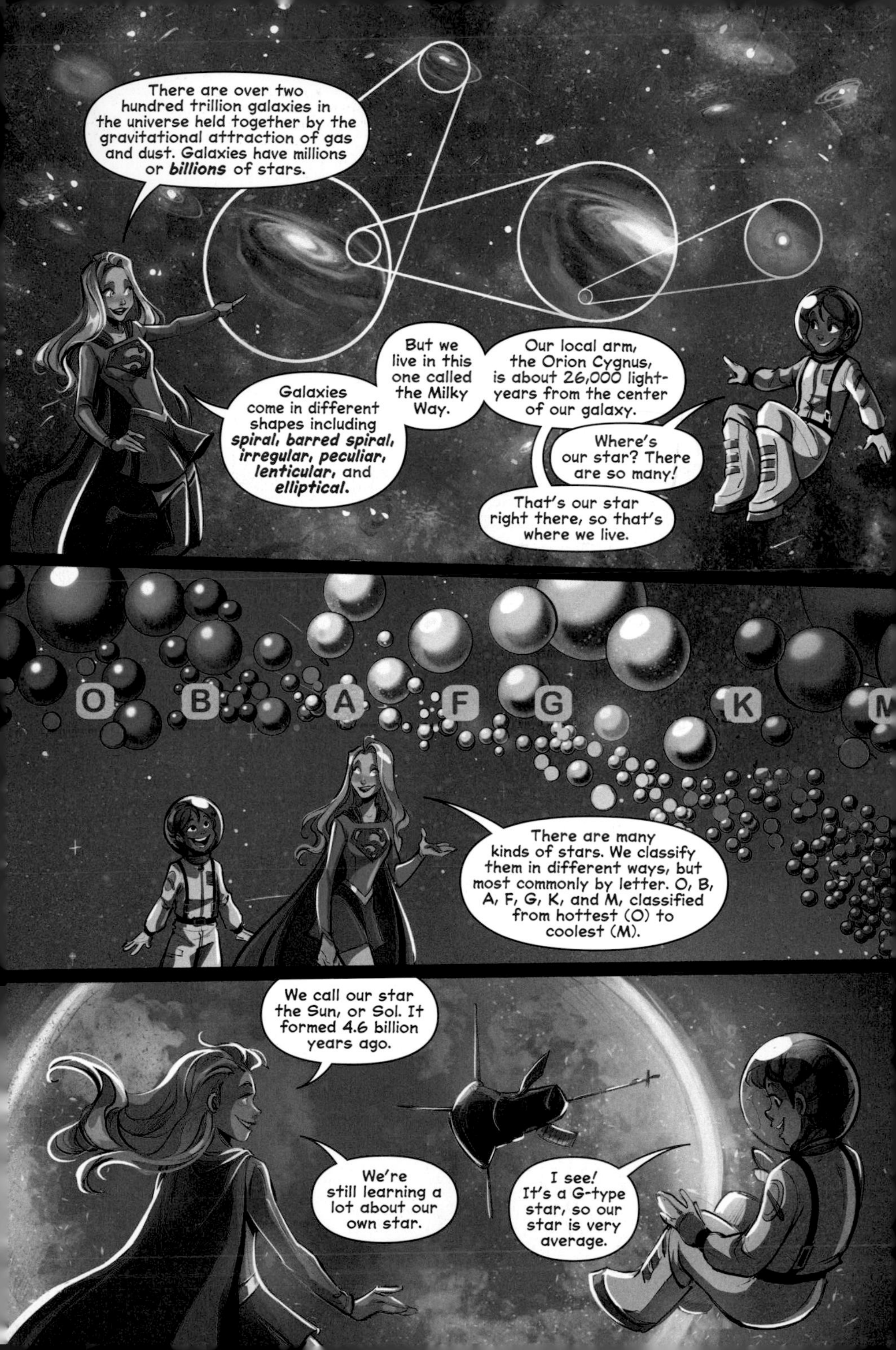

There are over two hundred trillion galaxies in the universe held together by the gravitational attraction of gas and dust. Galaxies have millions or ***billions*** of stars.
Galaxies come in different shapes including ***spiral, barred spiral, irregular, peculiar, lenticular,*** and ***elliptical.***
But we live in this one called the Milky Way.
Our local arm, the Orion Cygnus, is about 26,000 light-years from the center of our galaxy.
Where's our star? There are so many!
That's our star right there, so that's where we live.
O
B
A
F
G
K
M
There are many kinds of stars. We classify them in different ways, but most commonly by letter. O, B, A, F, G, K, and M, classified from hottest (O) to coolest (M).
We call our star the Sun, or Sol. It formed 4.6 billion years ago.
We're still learning a lot about our own star.
I see! It's a G-type star, so our star is very average.

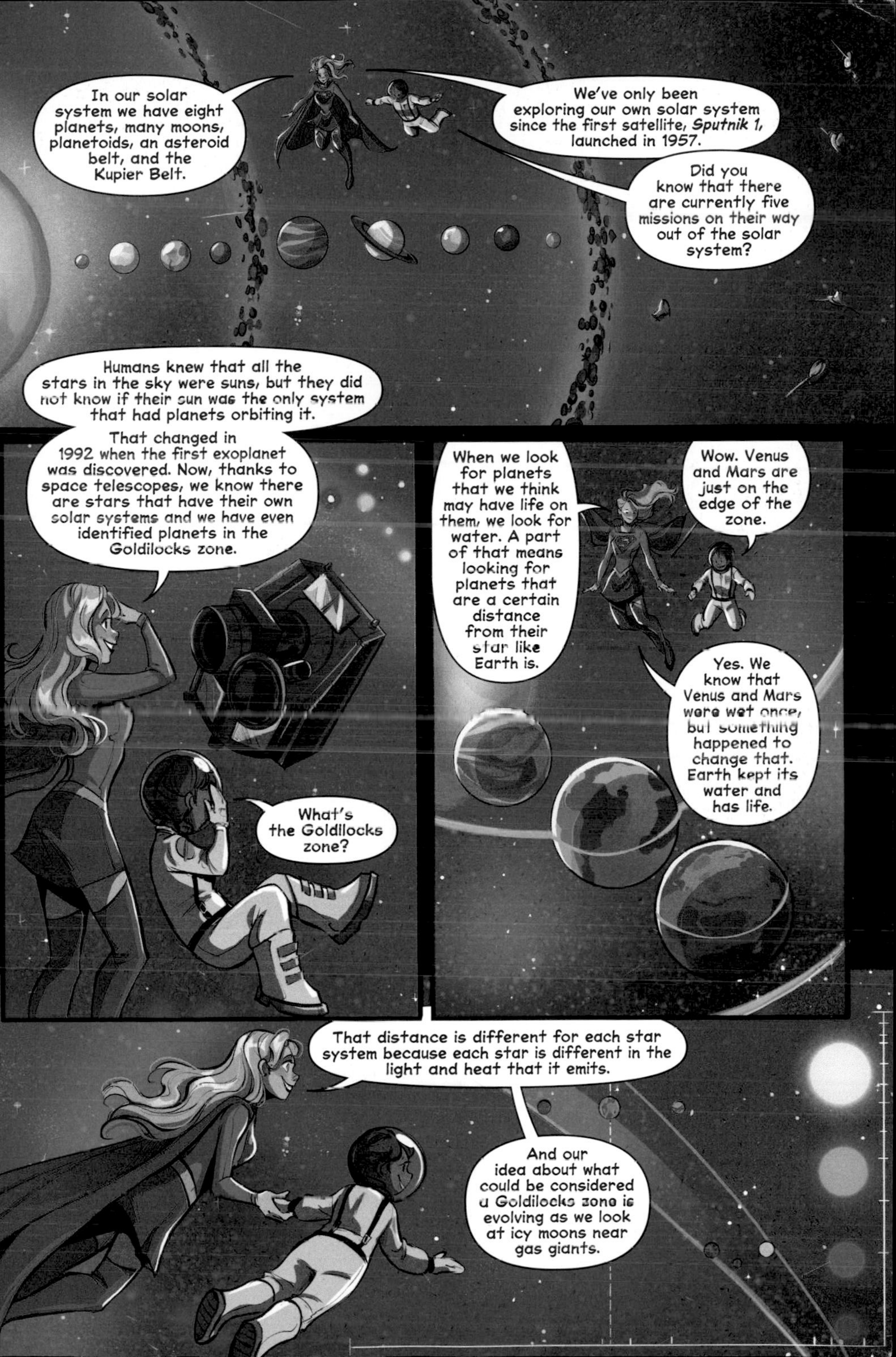
In our solar system we have eight planets, many moons, planetoids, an asteroid belt, and the Kupier Belt.
We've only been exploring our own solar system since the first satellite, *Sputnik 1*, launched in 1957.
Did you know that there are currently five missions on their way out of the solar system?
Humans knew that all the stars in the sky were suns, but they did not know if their sun was the only system that had planets orbiting it.
That changed in 1992 when the first exoplanet was discovered. Now, thanks to space telescopes, we know there are stars that have their own solar systems and we have even identified planets in the Goldilocks zone.
What's the Goldilocks zone?
When we look for planets that we think may have life on them, we look for water. A part of that means looking for planets that are a certain distance from their star like Earth is.
Wow. Venus and Mars are just on the edge of the zone.
Yes. We know that Venus and Mars were wet once, but something happened to change that. Earth kept its water and has life.
That distance is different for each star system because each star is different in the light and heat that it emits.
And our idea about what could be considered a Goldilocks zone is evolving as we look at icy moons near gas giants.

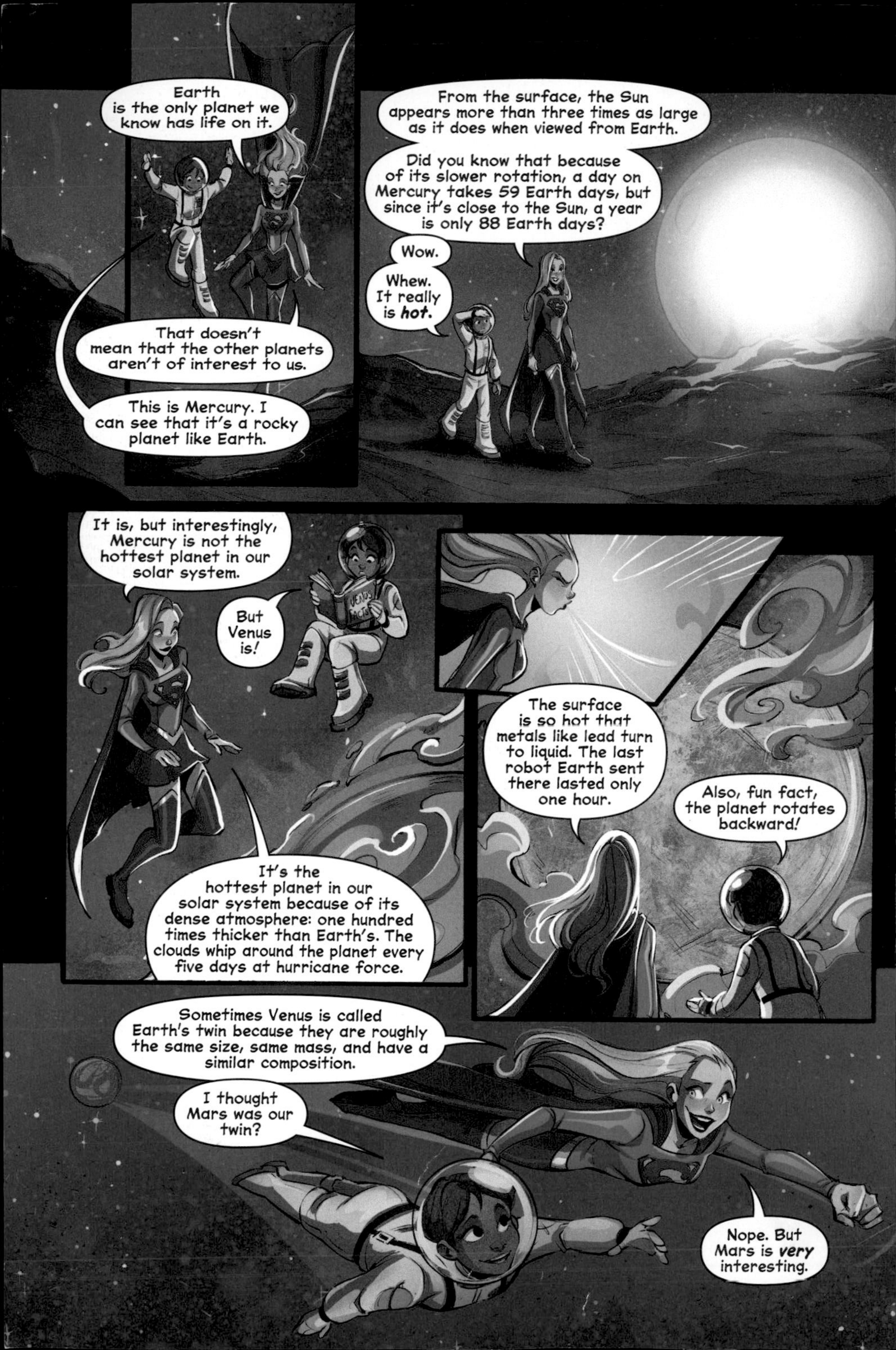

Earth is the only planet we know has life on it.
That doesn't mean that the other planets aren't of interest to us.
This is Mercury. I can see that it's a rocky planet like Earth.
From the surface, the Sun appears more than three times as large as it does when viewed from Earth.
Did you know that because of its slower rotation, a day on Mercury takes 59 Earth days, but since it's close to the Sun, a year is only 88 Earth days?
Wow.
Whew. It really is *hot*.
It is, but interestingly, Mercury is not the hottest planet in our solar system.
But Venus is!
VENUS FACTS
It's the hottest planet in our solar system because of its dense atmosphere: one hundred times thicker than Earth's. The clouds whip around the planet every five days at hurricane force.
The surface is so hot that metals like lead turn to liquid. The last robot Earth sent there lasted only one hour.
Also, fun fact, the planet rotates backward!
Sometimes Venus is called Earth's twin because they are roughly the same size, same mass, and have a similar composition.
I thought Mars was our twin?
Nope. But Mars is *very* interesting.

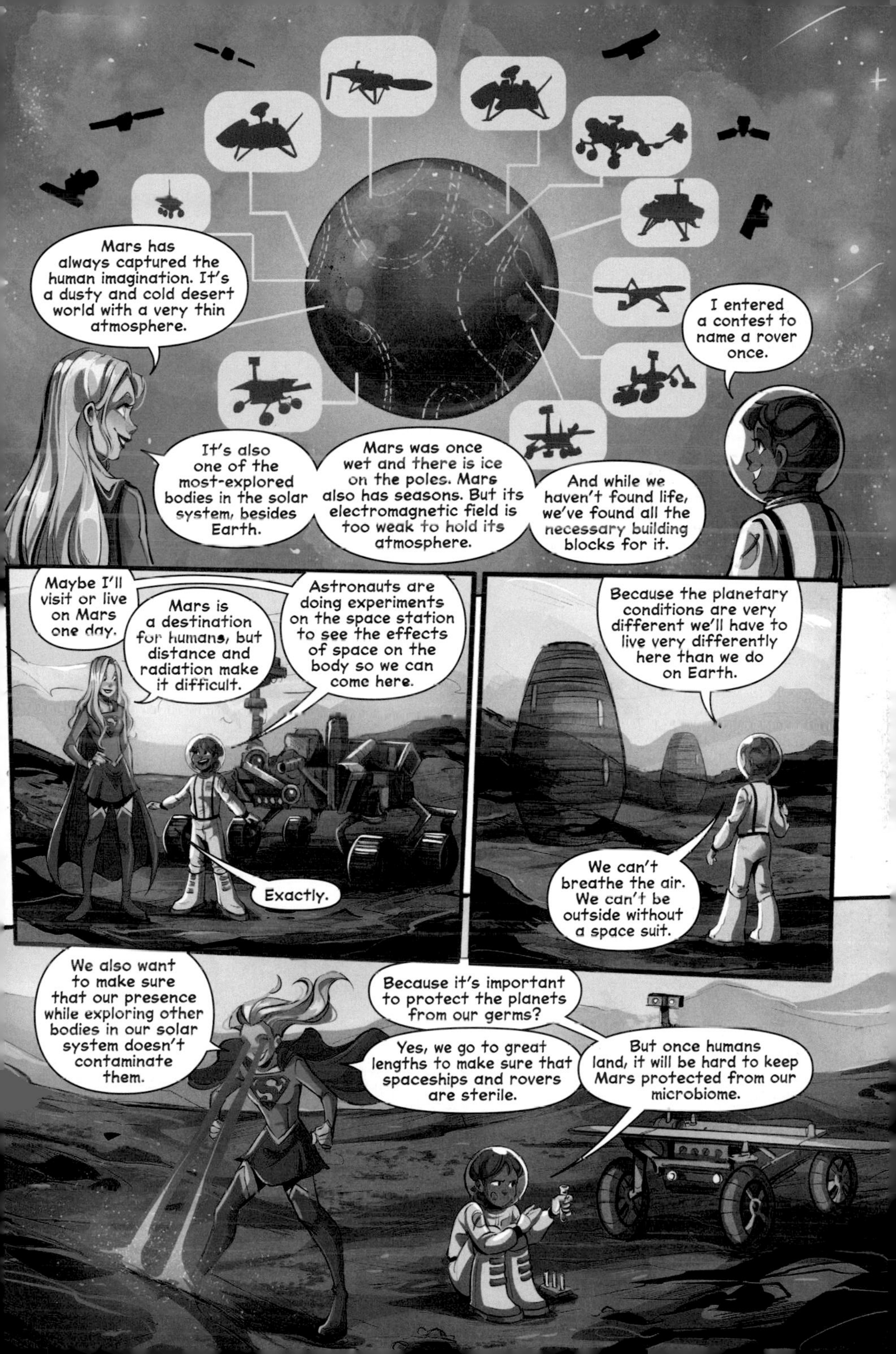

Mars has always captured the human imagination. It's a dusty and cold desert world with a very thin atmosphere.
I entered a contest to name a rover once.
It's also one of the most-explored bodies in the solar system, besides Earth.
Mars was once wet and there is ice on the poles. Mars also has seasons. But its electromagnetic field is too weak to hold its atmosphere.
And while we haven't found life, we've found all the necessary building blocks for it.
Maybe I'll visit or live on Mars one day.
Mars is a destination for humans, but distance and radiation make it difficult.
Astronauts are doing experiments on the space station to see the effects of space on the body so we can come here.
Exactly.
Because the planetary conditions are very different we'll have to live very differently here than we do on Earth.
We can't breathe the air. We can't be outside without a space suit.
We also want to make sure that our presence while exploring other bodies in our solar system doesn't contaminate them.
Because it's important to protect the planets from our germs?
Yes, we go to great lengths to make sure that spaceships and rovers are sterile.
But once humans land, it will be hard to keep Mars protected from our microbiome.

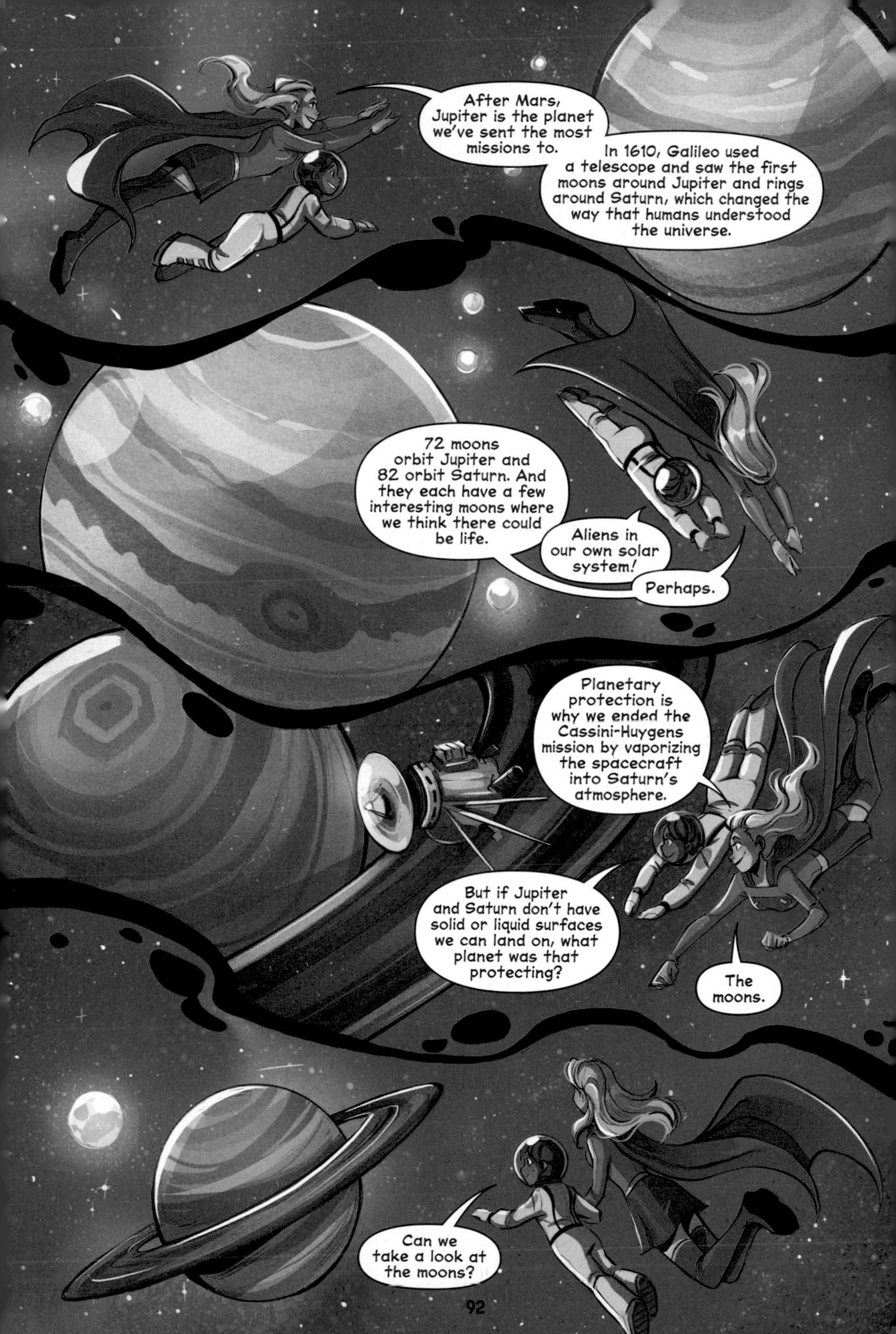
After Mars, Jupiter is the planet we've sent the most missions to.
In 1610, Galileo used a telescope and saw the first moons around Jupiter and rings around Saturn, which changed the way that humans understood the universe.
72 moons orbit Jupiter and 82 orbit Saturn. And they each have a few interesting moons where we think there could be life.
Aliens in our own solar system!
Perhaps.
Planetary protection is why we ended the Cassini-Huygens mission by vaporizing the spacecraft into Saturn's atmosphere.
But if Jupiter and Saturn don't have solid or liquid surfaces we can land on, what planet was that protecting?
The moons.
Can we take a look at the moons?

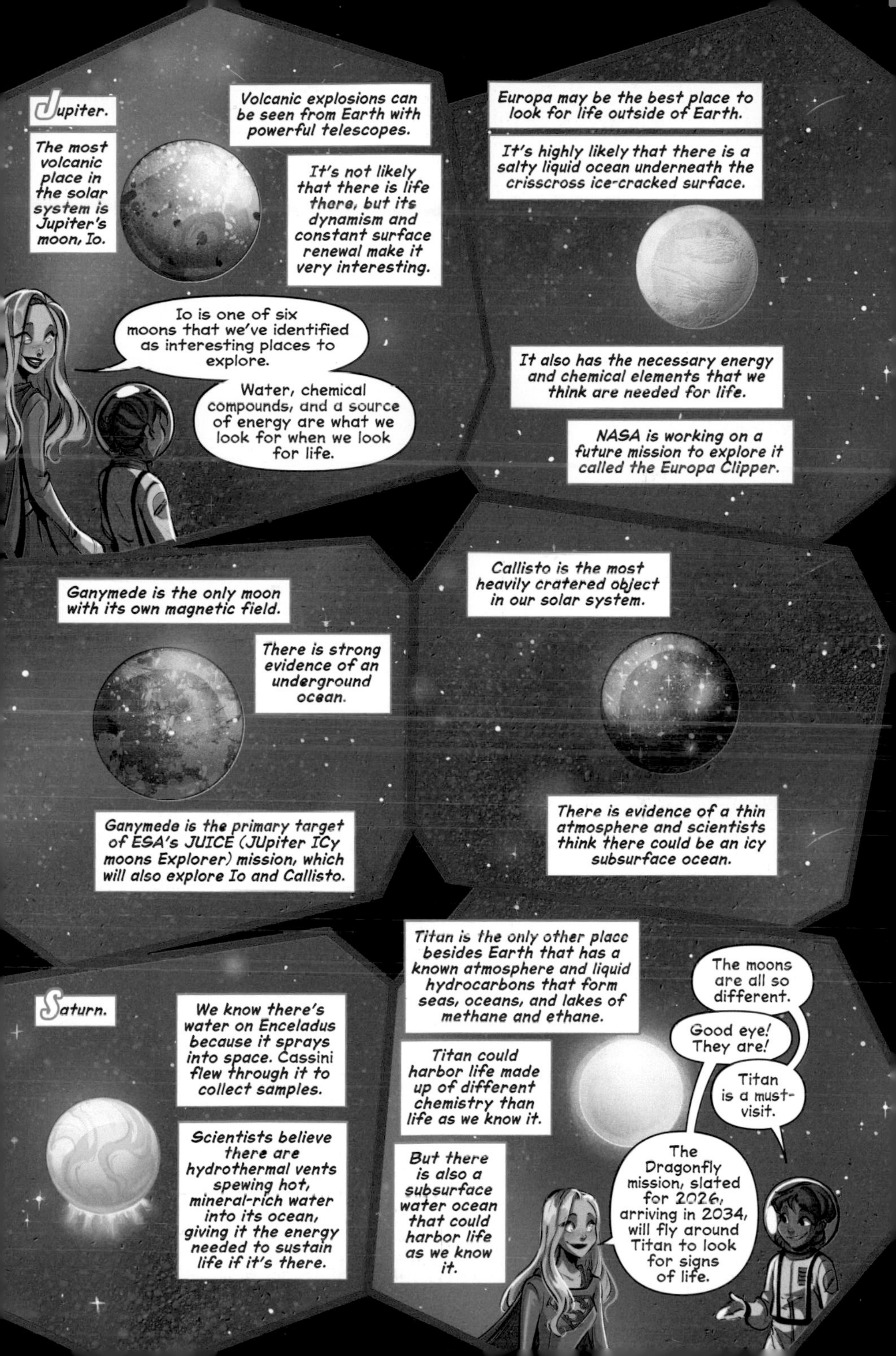

Jupiter.
The most volcanic place in the solar system is Jupiter's moon, Io.
Volcanic explosions can be seen from Earth with powerful telescopes.
It's not likely that there is life there, but its dynamism and constant surface renewal make it very interesting.
Io is one of six moons that we've identified as interesting places to explore.
Water, chemical compounds, and a source of energy are what we look for when we look for life.
Europa may be the best place to look for life outside of Earth.
It's highly likely that there is a salty liquid ocean underneath the crisscross ice-cracked surface.
It also has the necessary energy and chemical elements that we think are needed for life.
NASA is working on a future mission to explore it called the Europa Clipper.
Ganymede is the only moon with its own magnetic field.
There is strong evidence of an underground ocean.
Ganymede is the primary target of ESA's JUICE (JUpiter ICy moons Explorer) mission, which will also explore Io and Callisto.
Callisto is the most heavily cratered object in our solar system.
There is evidence of a thin atmosphere and scientists think there could be an icy subsurface ocean.
Saturn.
We know there's water on Enceladus because it sprays into space. Cassini flew through it to collect samples.
Scientists believe there are hydrothermal vents spewing hot, mineral-rich water into its ocean, giving it the energy needed to sustain life if it's there.
Titan is the only other place besides Earth that has a known atmosphere and liquid hydrocarbons that form seas, oceans, and lakes of methane and ethane.
Titan could harbor life made up of different chemistry than life as we know it.
But there is also a subsurface water ocean that could harbor life as we know it.
The moons are all so different.
Good eye! They are!
Titan is a must-visit.
The Dragonfly mission, slated for 2026, arriving in 2034, will fly around Titan to look for signs of life.

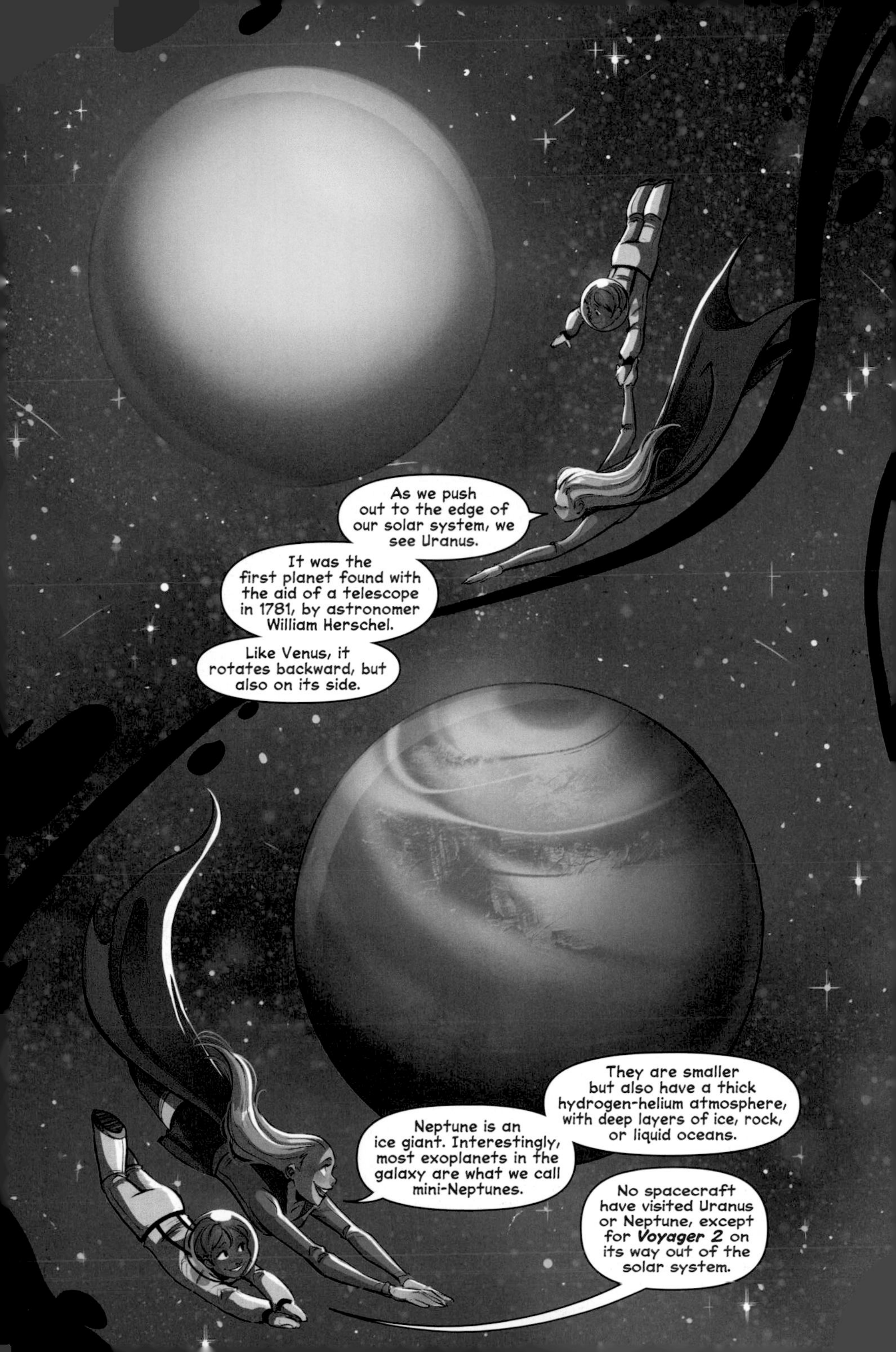

As we push out to the edge of our solar system, we see Uranus.
It was the first planet found with the aid of a telescope in 1781, by astronomer William Herschel.
Like Venus, it rotates backward, but also on its side.
Neptune is an ice giant. Interestingly, most exoplanets in the galaxy are what we call mini-Neptunes.
They are smaller but also have a thick hydrogen-helium atmosphere, with deep layers of ice, rock, or liquid oceans.
No spacecraft have visited Uranus or Neptune, except for ***Voyager 2*** on its way out of the solar system.

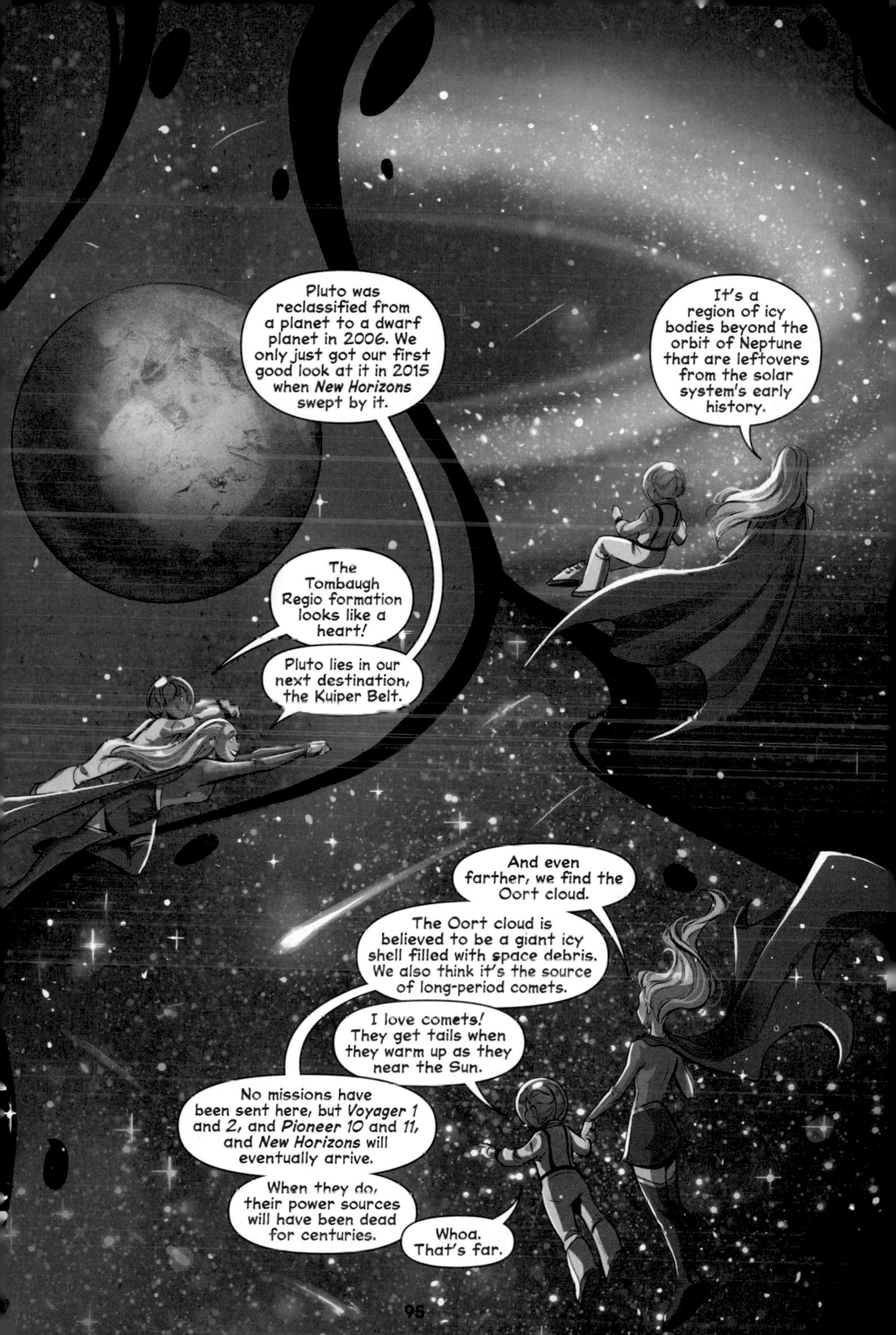

Pluto was reclassified from a planet to a dwarf planet in 2006. We only just got our first good look at it in 2015 when *New Horizons* swept by it.
The Tombaugh Regio formation looks like a heart!
Pluto lies in our next destination, the Kuiper Belt.
It's a region of icy bodies beyond the orbit of Neptune that are leftovers from the solar system's early history.
And even farther, we find the Oort cloud.
The Oort cloud is believed to be a giant icy shell filled with space debris. We also think it's the source of long-period comets.
I love comets! They get tails when they warm up as they near the Sun.
No missions have been sent here, but *Voyager 1* and *2*, and *Pioneer 10* and *11*, and *New Horizons* will eventually arrive.
When they do, their power sources will have been dead for centuries.
Whoa. That's far.

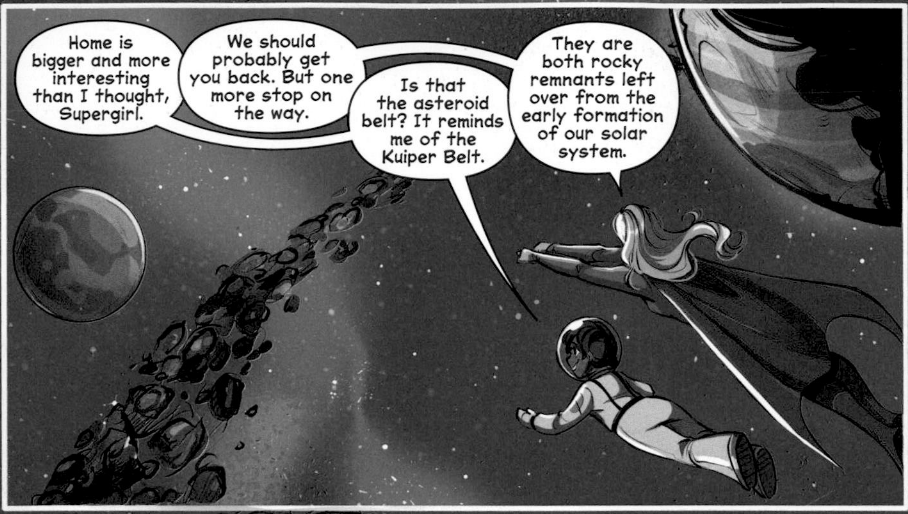
Home is bigger and more interesting than I thought, Supergirl.
We should probably get you back. But one more stop on the way.
Is that the asteroid belt? It reminds me of the Kuiper Belt.
They are both rocky remnants left over from the early formation of our solar system.

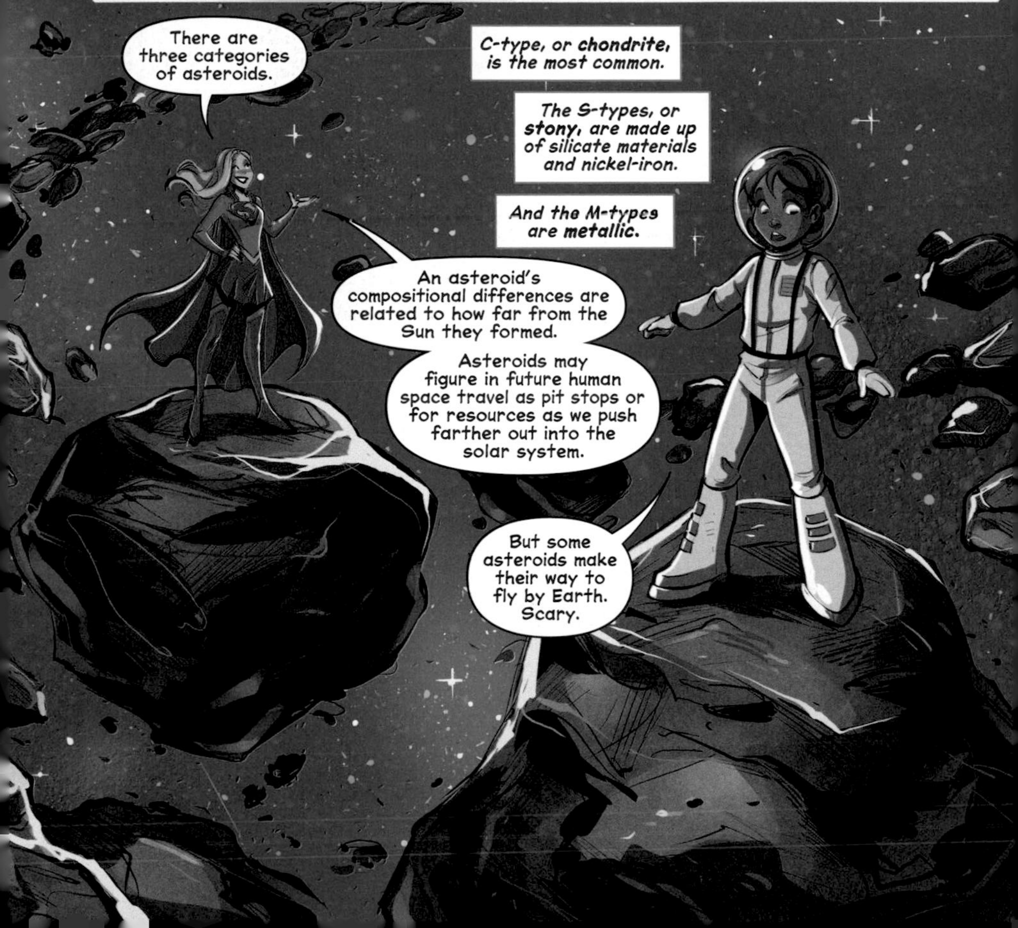
There are three categories of asteroids.
C-type, or chondrite, is the most common.
The S-types, or stony, are made up of silicate materials and nickel-iron.
And the M-types are metallic.
An asteroid's compositional differences are related to how far from the Sun they formed.
Asteroids may figure in future human space travel as pit stops or for resources as we push farther out into the solar system.
But some asteroids make their way to fly by Earth. Scary.

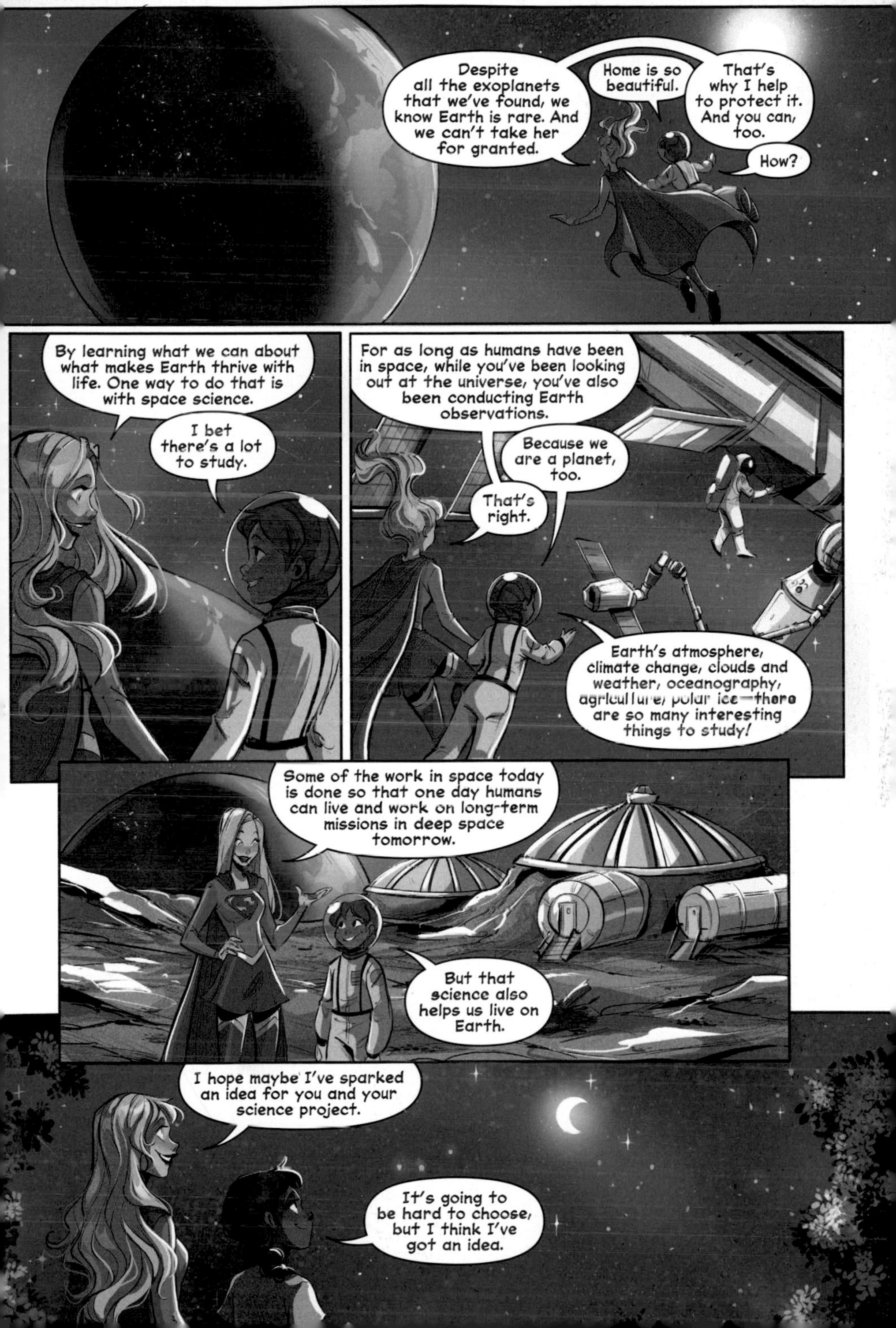
Despite all the exoplanets that we've found, we know Earth is rare. And we can't take her for granted.
Home is so beautiful.
That's why I help to protect it. And you can, too.
How?
By learning what we can about what makes Earth thrive with life. One way to do that is with space science.
I bet there's a lot to study.
For as long as humans have been in space, while you've been looking out at the universe, you've also been conducting Earth observations.
Because we are a planet, too.
That's right.
Earth's atmosphere, climate change, clouds and weather, oceanography, agriculture, polar ice—there are so many interesting things to study!
Some of the work in space today is done so that one day humans can live and work on long-term missions in deep space tomorrow.
But that science also helps us live on Earth.
I hope maybe I've sparked an idea for you and your science project.
It's going to be hard to choose, but I think I've got an idea.

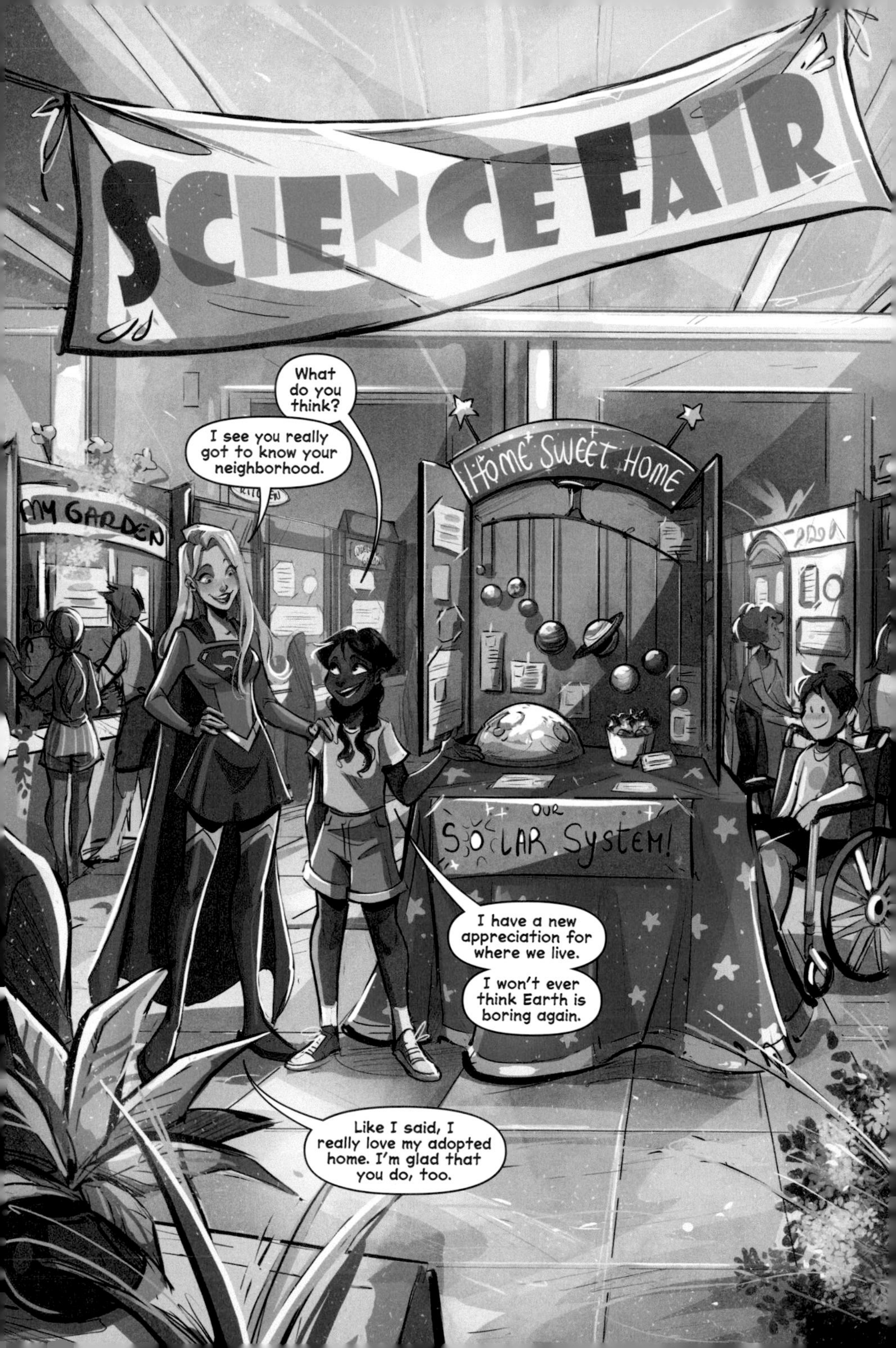
SCIENCE FAIR
MY GARDEN
HOME SWEET HOME
OUR SOLAR SYSTEM!
What do you think?
I see you really got to know your neighborhood.
I have a new appreciation for where we live.
I won't ever think Earth is boring again.
Like I said, I really love my adopted home. I'm glad that you do, too.

CHAPTER EIGHT

SEA
FOR YOURSELF

WRITTEN BY **CORINNA BECHKO**

ILLUSTRATED BY **YESENIA MOISES**

LETTERED BY **WES ABBOTT**

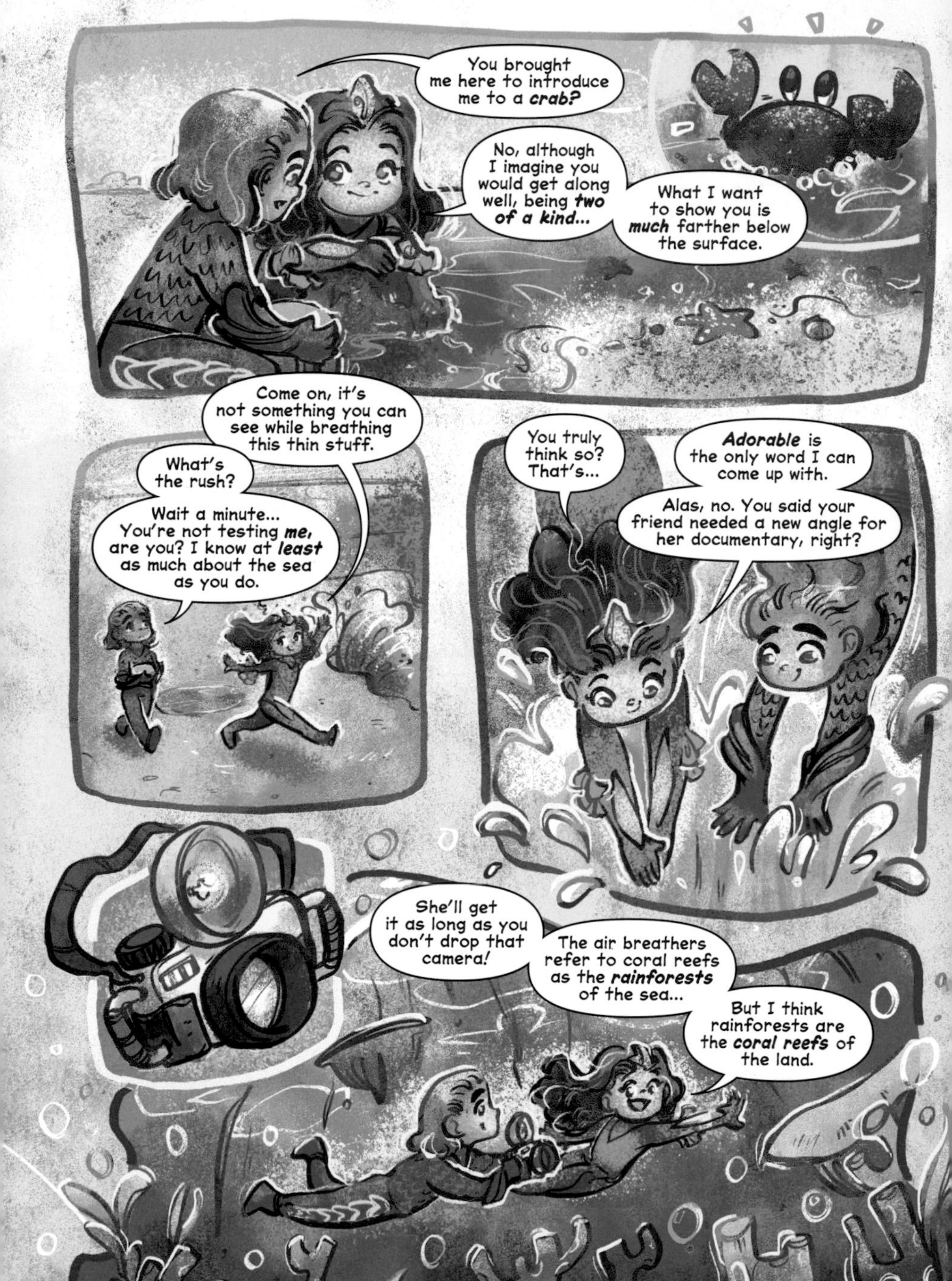
You brought me here to introduce me to a *crab?*
No, although I imagine you would get along well, being *two of a kind...*
What I want to show you is *much* farther below the surface.
What's the rush?
Come on, it's not something you can see while breathing this thin stuff.
Wait a minute... You're not testing *me,* are you? I know at *least* as much about the sea as you do.
You truly think so? That's...
Adorable is the only word I can come up with.
Alas, no. You said your friend needed a new angle for her documentary, right?
She'll get it as long as you don't drop that camera!
The air breathers refer to coral reefs as the *rainforests* of the sea...
But I think rainforests are the *coral reefs* of the land.

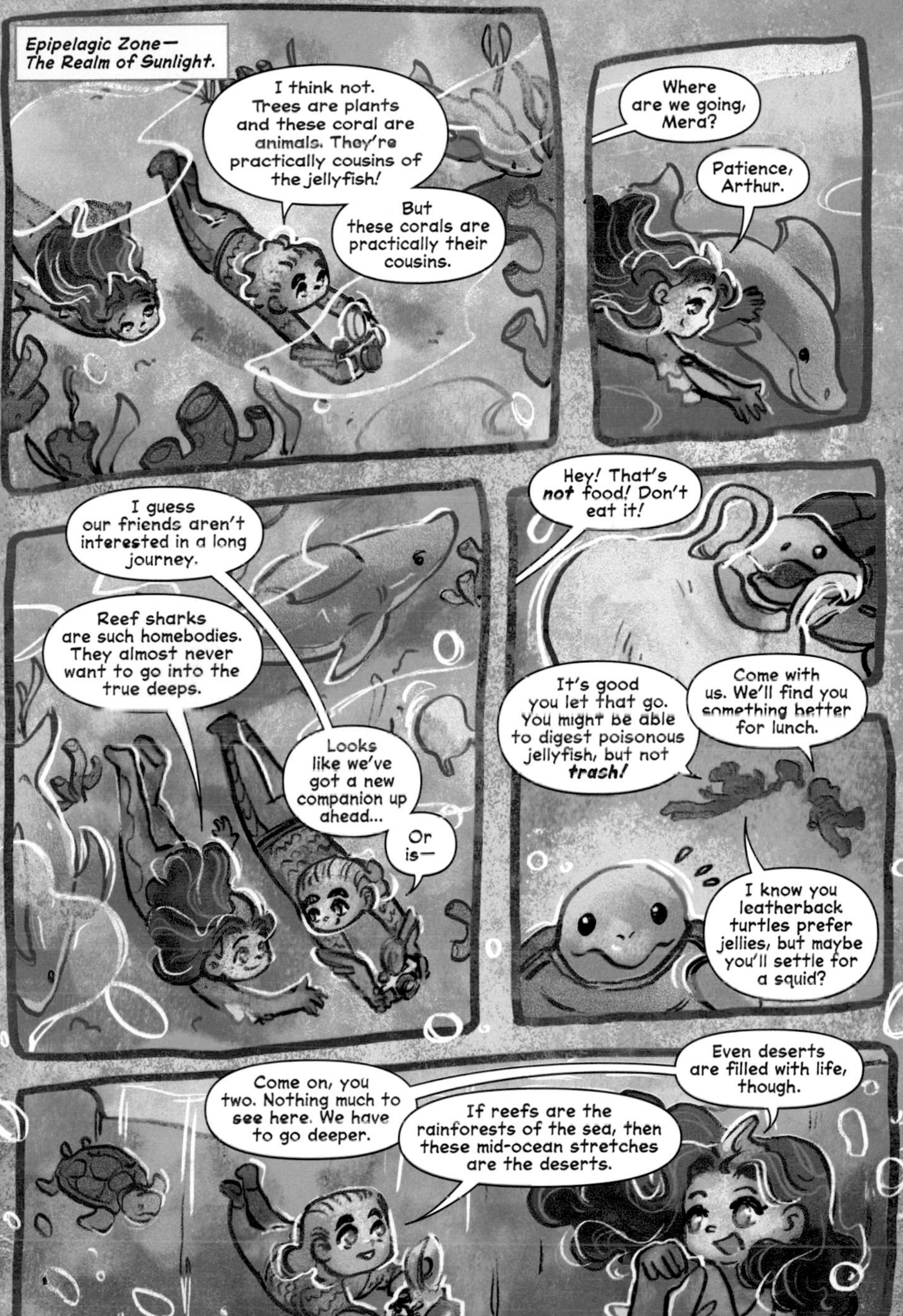
Epipelagic Zone— The Realm of Sunlight.
I think not. Trees are plants and these coral are animals. They're practically cousins of the jellyfish!
But these corals are practically their cousins.
Where are we going, Mera?
Patience, Arthur.
I guess our friends aren't interested in a long journey.
Reef sharks are such homebodies. They almost never want to go into the true deeps.
Looks like we've got a new companion up ahead...
Or is—
Hey! That's not food! Don't eat it!
It's good you let that go. You might be able to digest poisonous jellyfish, but not trash!
Come with us. We'll find you something better for lunch.
I know you leatherback turtles prefer jellies, but maybe you'll settle for a squid?
Come on, you two. Nothing much to see here. We have to go deeper.
If reefs are the rainforests of the sea, then these mid-ocean stretches are the deserts.
Even deserts are filled with life, though.

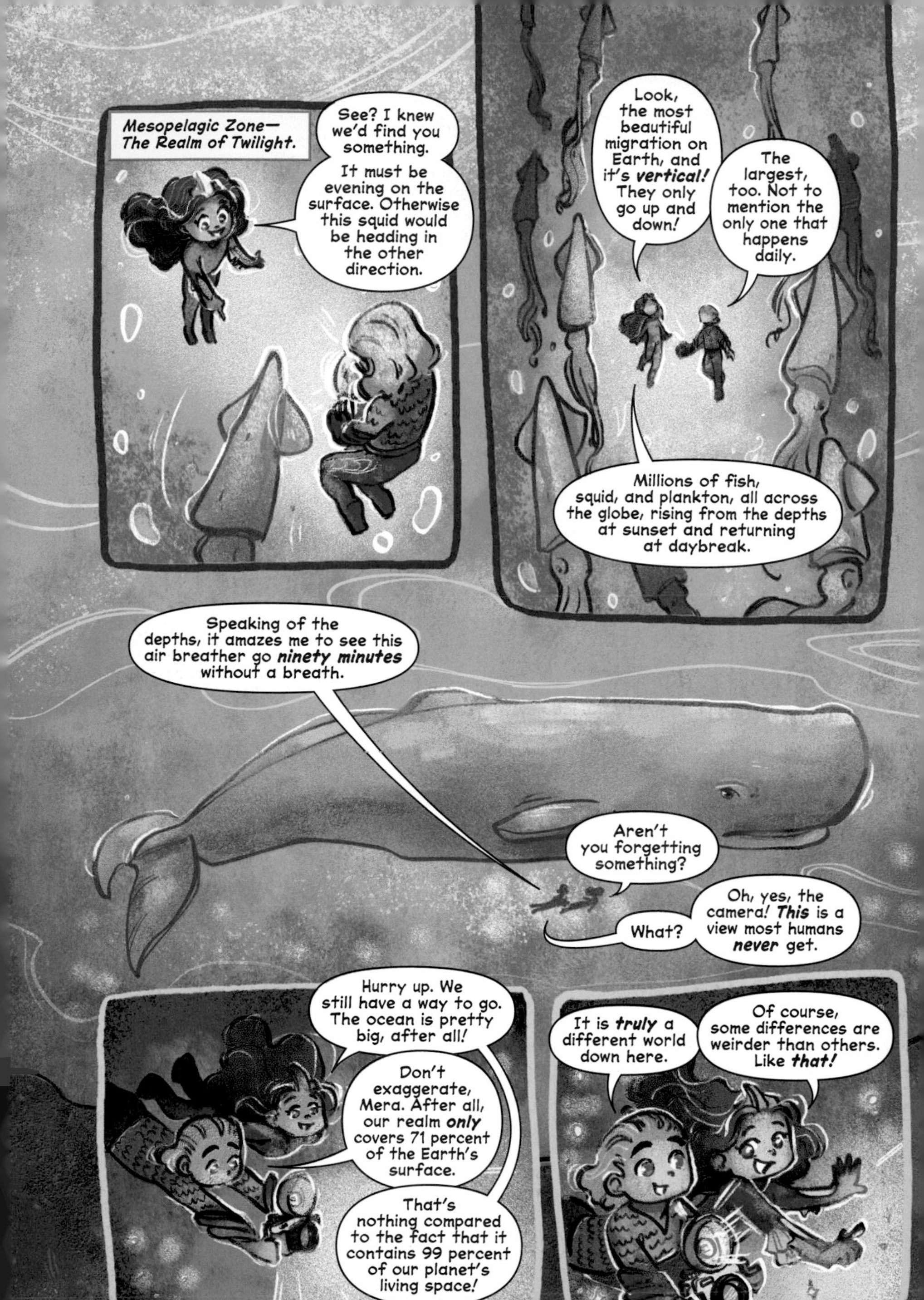

Mesopelagic Zone— The Realm of Twilight.
See? I knew we'd find you something.
It must be evening on the surface. Otherwise this squid would be heading in the other direction.
Look, the most beautiful migration on Earth, and it's vertical! They only go up and down!
The largest, too. Not to mention the only one that happens daily.
Millions of fish, squid, and plankton, all across the globe, rising from the depths at sunset and returning at daybreak.
Speaking of the depths, it amazes me to see this air breather go ninety minutes without a breath.
Aren't you forgetting something?
What?
Oh, yes, the camera! This is a view most humans never get.
Hurry up. We still have a way to go. The ocean is pretty big, after all!
Don't exaggerate, Mera. After all, our realm only covers 71 percent of the Earth's surface.
That's nothing compared to the fact that it contains 99 percent of our planet's living space!
It is truly a different world down here.
Of course, some differences are weirder than others. Like that!

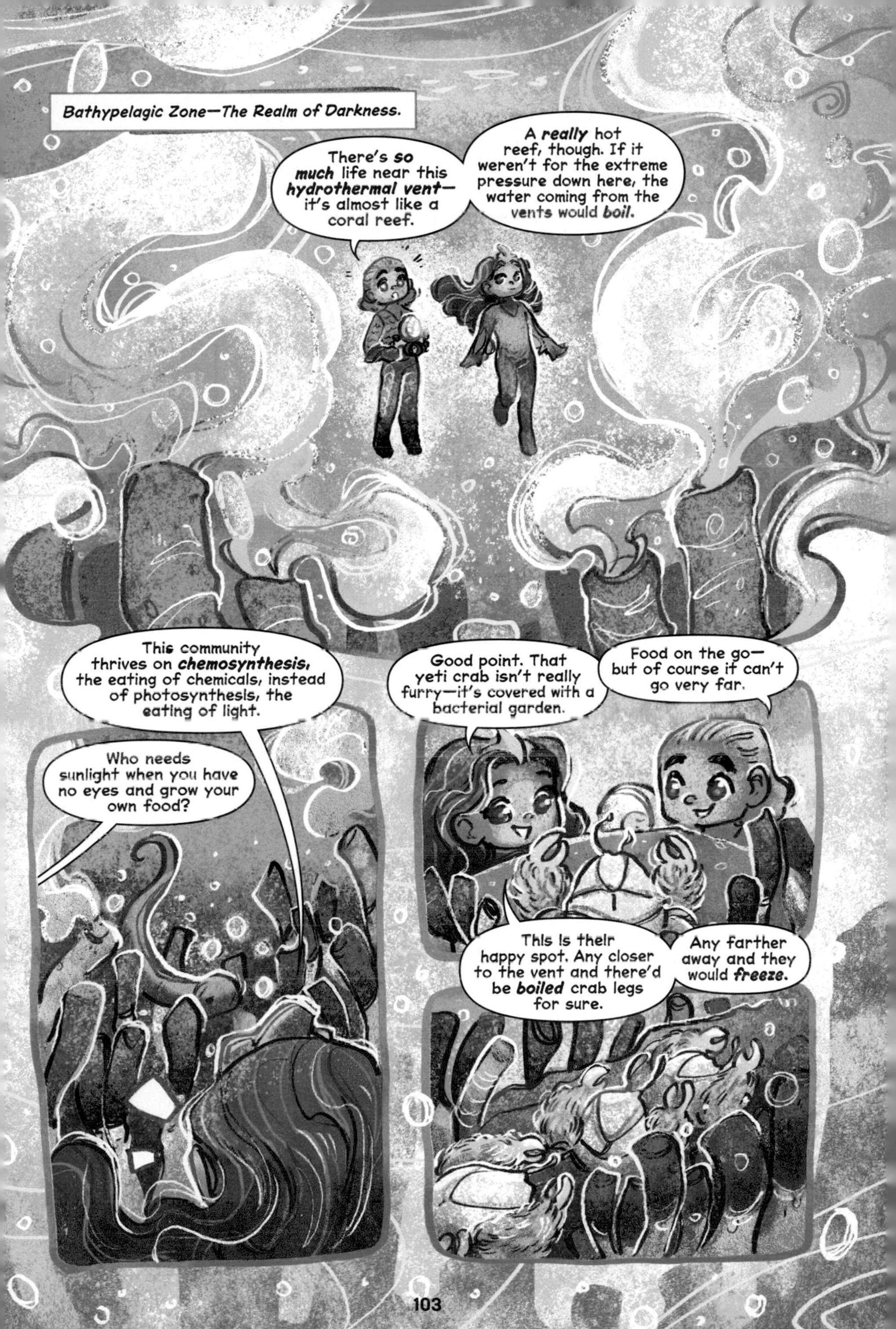
Bathypelagic Zone—The Realm of Darkness.
There's **so much** life near this ***hydrothermal vent***—it's almost like a coral reef.
A ***really*** hot reef, though. If it weren't for the extreme pressure down here, the water coming from the vents would ***boil.***
This community thrives on ***chemosynthesis,*** the eating of chemicals, instead of photosynthesis, the eating of light.
Who needs sunlight when you have no eyes and grow your own food?
Good point. That yeti crab isn't really furry—it's covered with a bacterial garden.
Food on the go—but of course it can't go very far.
This is their happy spot. Any closer to the vent and there'd be ***boiled*** crab legs for sure.
Any farther away and they would ***freeze.***

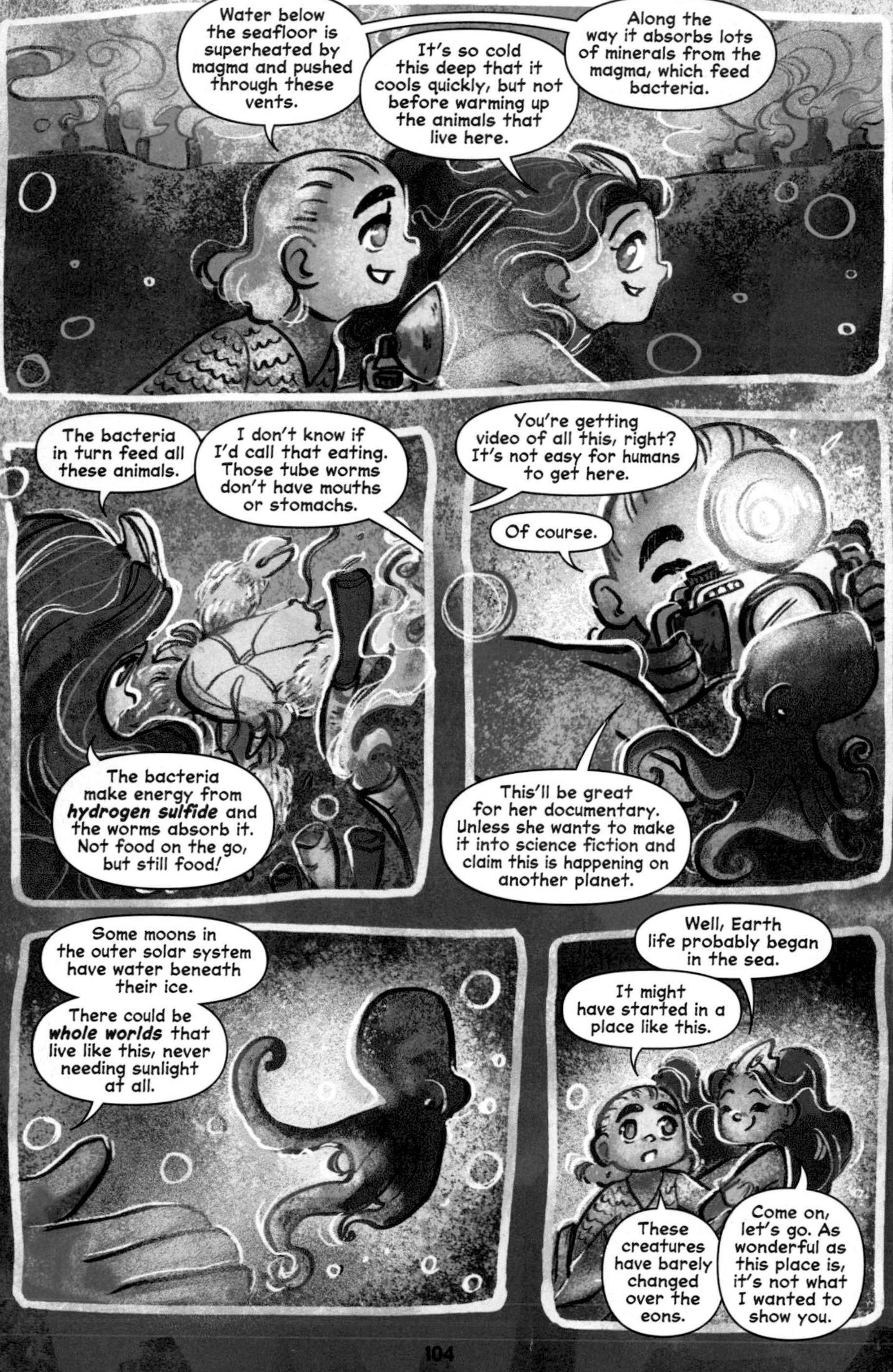
Water below the seafloor is superheated by magma and pushed through these vents.
It's so cold this deep that it cools quickly, but not before warming up the animals that live here.
Along the way it absorbs lots of minerals from the magma, which feed bacteria.
The bacteria in turn feed all these animals.
I don't know if I'd call that eating. Those tube worms don't have mouths or stomachs.
The bacteria make energy from ***hydrogen sulfide*** and the worms absorb it. Not food on the go, but still food!
You're getting video of all this, right? It's not easy for humans to get here.
Of course.
This'll be great for her documentary. Unless she wants to make it into science fiction and claim this is happening on another planet.
Some moons in the outer solar system have water beneath their ice.
There could be ***whole worlds*** that live like this, never needing sunlight at all.
Well, Earth life probably began in the sea.
It might have started in a place like this.
These creatures have barely changed over the eons.
Come on, let's go. As wonderful as this place is, it's not what I wanted to show you.

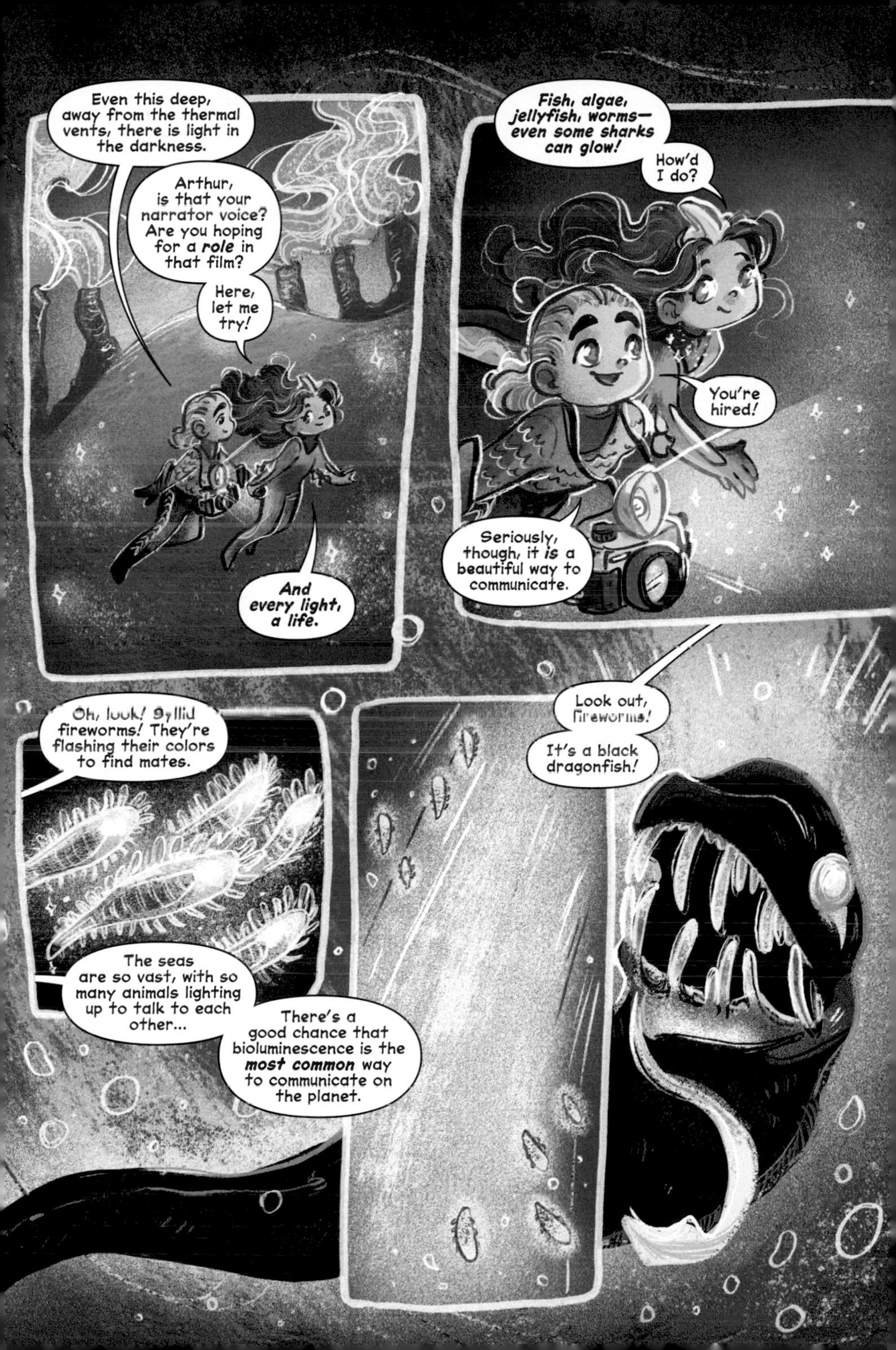

Even this deep, away from the thermal vents, there is light in the darkness.
Arthur, is that your narrator voice? Are you hoping for a *role* in that film?
Here, let me try!
And every light, a life.
Fish, algae, jellyfish, worms— even some sharks can glow!
How'd I do?
You're hired!
Seriously, though, it *is* a beautiful way to communicate.
Oh, look! Syllid fireworms! They're flashing their colors to find mates.
The seas are so vast, with so many animals lighting up to talk to each other...
There's a good chance that bioluminescence is the ***most common*** way to communicate on the planet.
Look out, fireworms!
It's a black dragonfish!

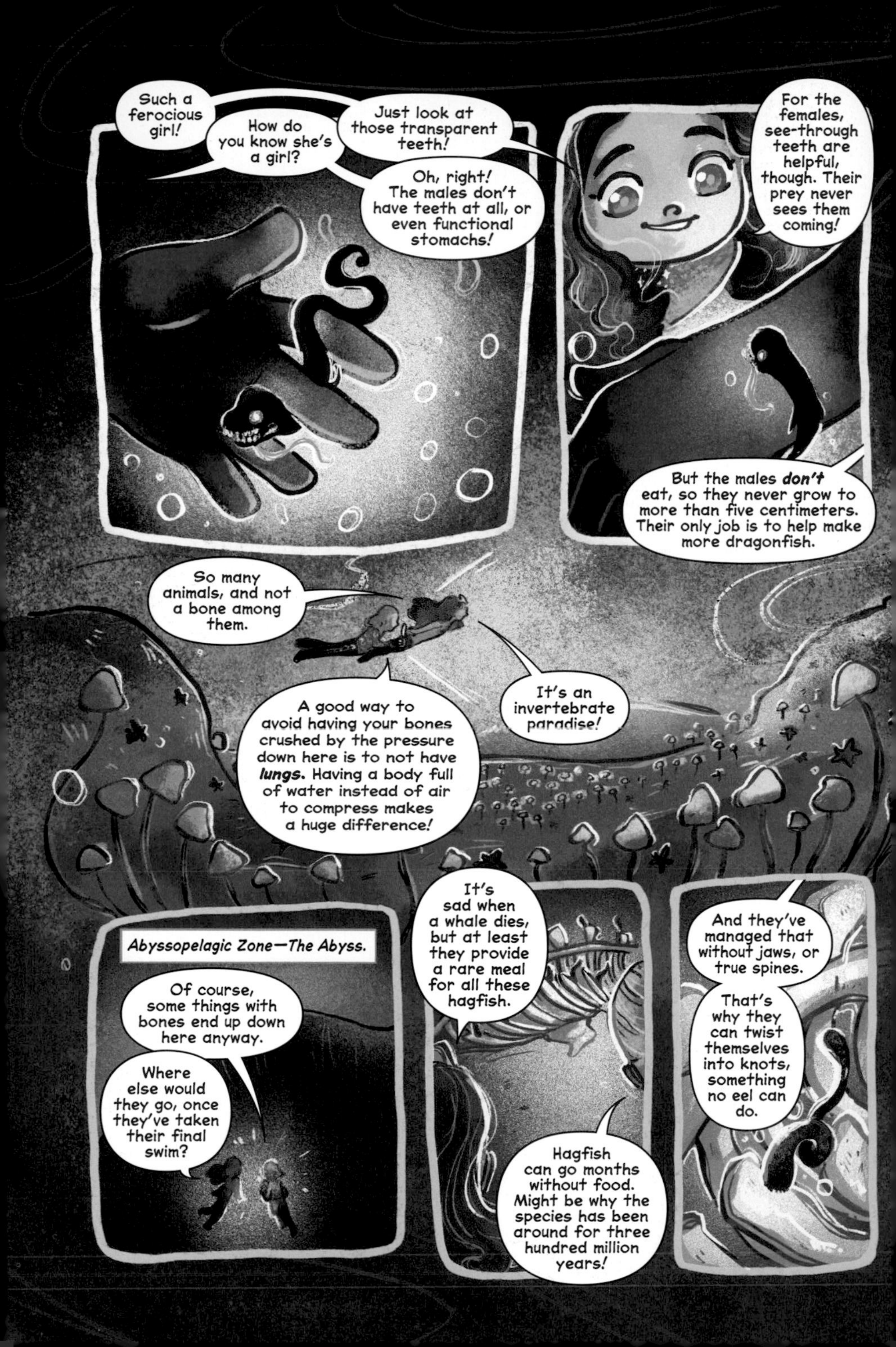
Such a ferocious girl!
How do you know she's a girl?
Just look at those transparent teeth!
Oh, right! The males don't have teeth at all, or even functional stomachs!
For the females, see-through teeth are helpful, though. Their prey never sees them coming!
But the males *don't* eat, so they never grow to more than five centimeters. Their only job is to help make more dragonfish.
So many animals, and not a bone among them.
It's an invertebrate paradise!
A good way to avoid having your bones crushed by the pressure down here is to not have *lungs.* Having a body full of water instead of air to compress makes a huge difference!
Abyssopelagic Zone—The Abyss.
Of course, some things with bones end up down here anyway.
Where else would they go, once they've taken their final swim?
It's sad when a whale dies, but at least they provide a rare meal for all these hagfish.
Hagfish can go months without food. Might be why the species has been around for three hundred million years!
And they've managed that without jaws, or true spines.
That's why they can twist themselves into knots, something no eel can do.

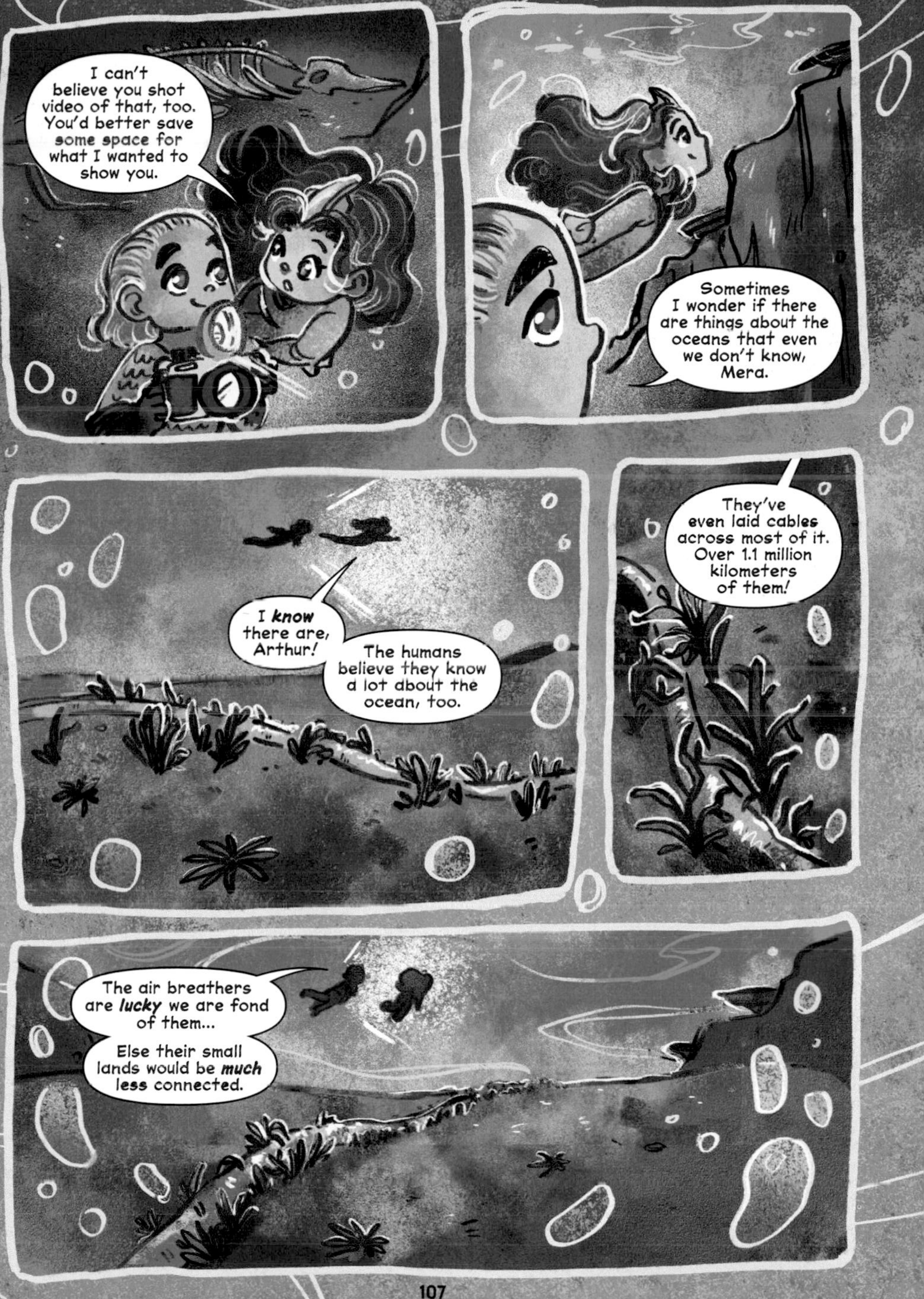
I can't believe you shot video of that, too. You'd better save some space for what I wanted to show you.
Sometimes I wonder if there are things about the oceans that even we don't know, Mera.
I *know* there are, Arthur!
The humans believe they know a lot about the ocean, too.
They've even laid cables across most of it. Over 1.1 million kilometers of them!
The air breathers are *lucky* we are fond of them...
Else their small lands would be *much* less connected.

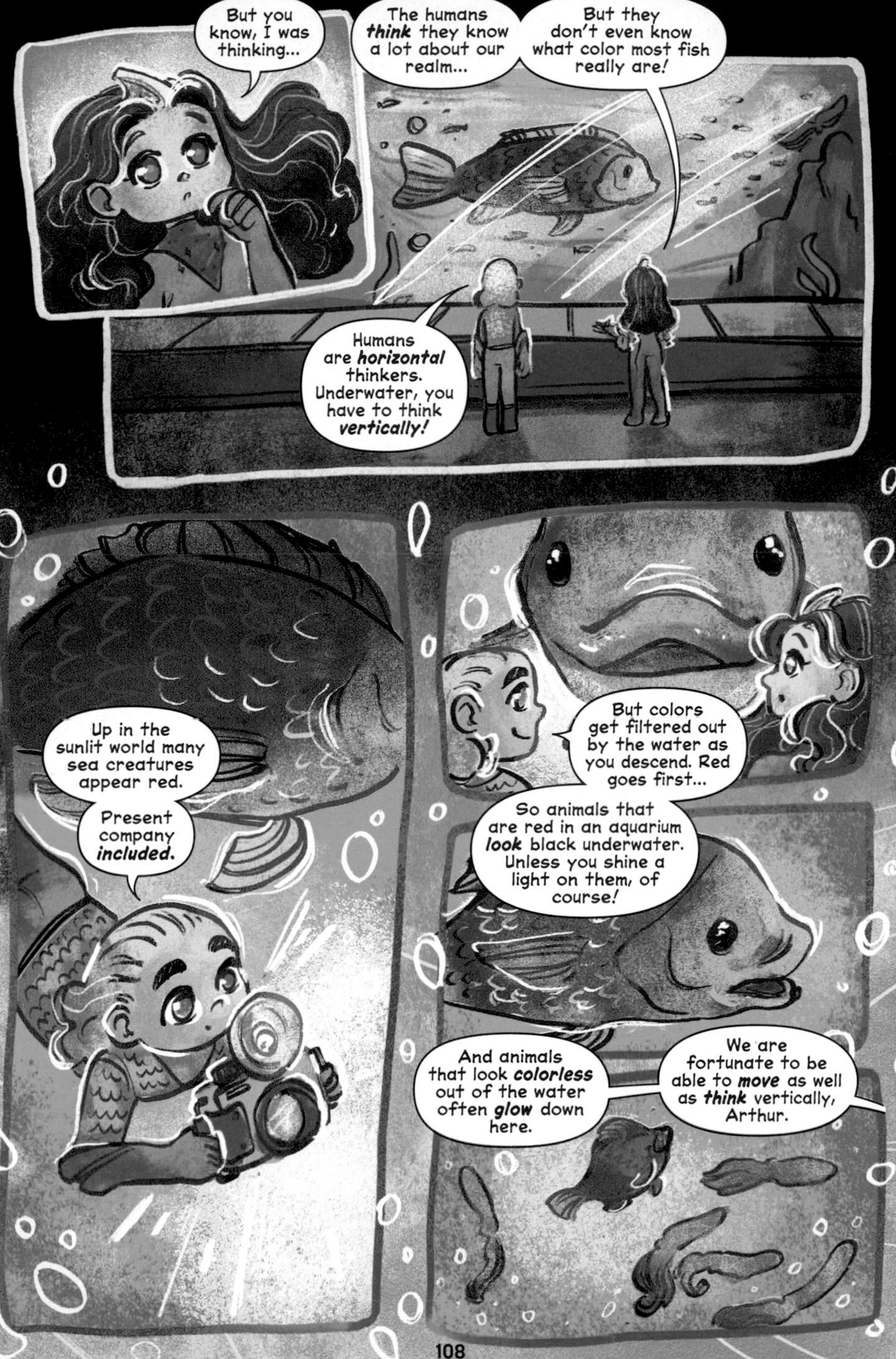
But you know, I was thinking...
The humans *think* they know a lot about our realm...
But they don't even know what color most fish really are!
Humans are *horizontal* thinkers. Underwater, you have to think *vertically!*
Up in the sunlit world many sea creatures appear red.
Present company *included.*
But colors get filtered out by the water as you descend. Red goes first...
So animals that are red in an aquarium *look* black underwater. Unless you shine a light on them, of course!
And animals that look *colorless* out of the water often *glow* down here.
We are fortunate to be able to *move* as well as *think* vertically, Arthur.

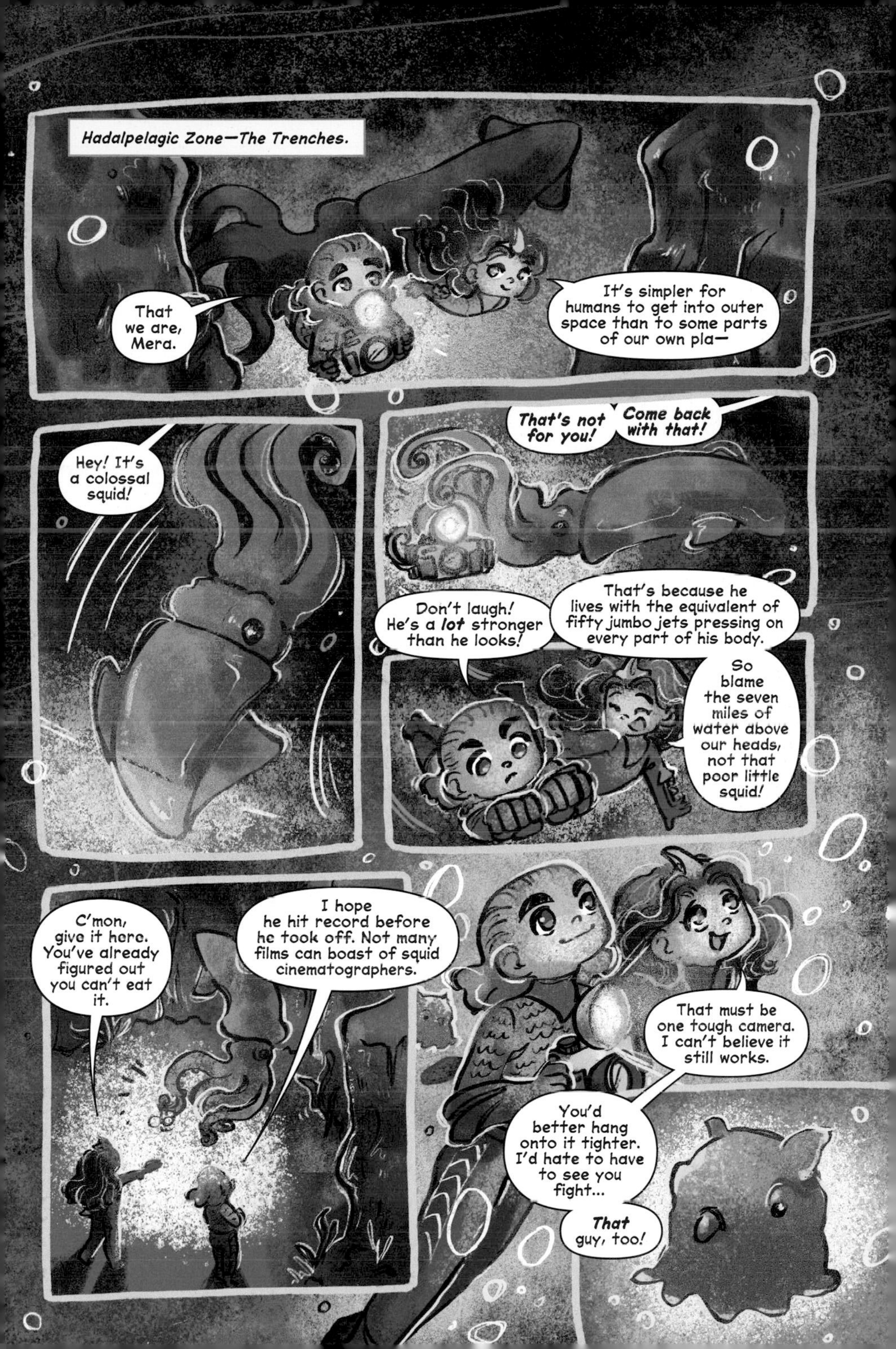
Hadalpelagic Zone—The Trenches.
It's simpler for humans to get into outer space than to some parts of our own pla—
That we are, Mera.
Hey! It's a colossal squid!
Come back with that!
That's not for you!
That's because he lives with the equivalent of fifty jumbo jets pressing on every part of his body.
Don't laugh! He's a *lot* stronger than he looks!
So blame the seven miles of water above our heads, not that poor little squid!
C'mon, give it here. You've already figured out you can't eat it.
I hope he hit record before he took off. Not many films can boast of squid cinematographers.
That must be one tough camera. I can't believe it still works.
You'd better hang onto it tighter. I'd hate to have to see you fight...
That guy, too!

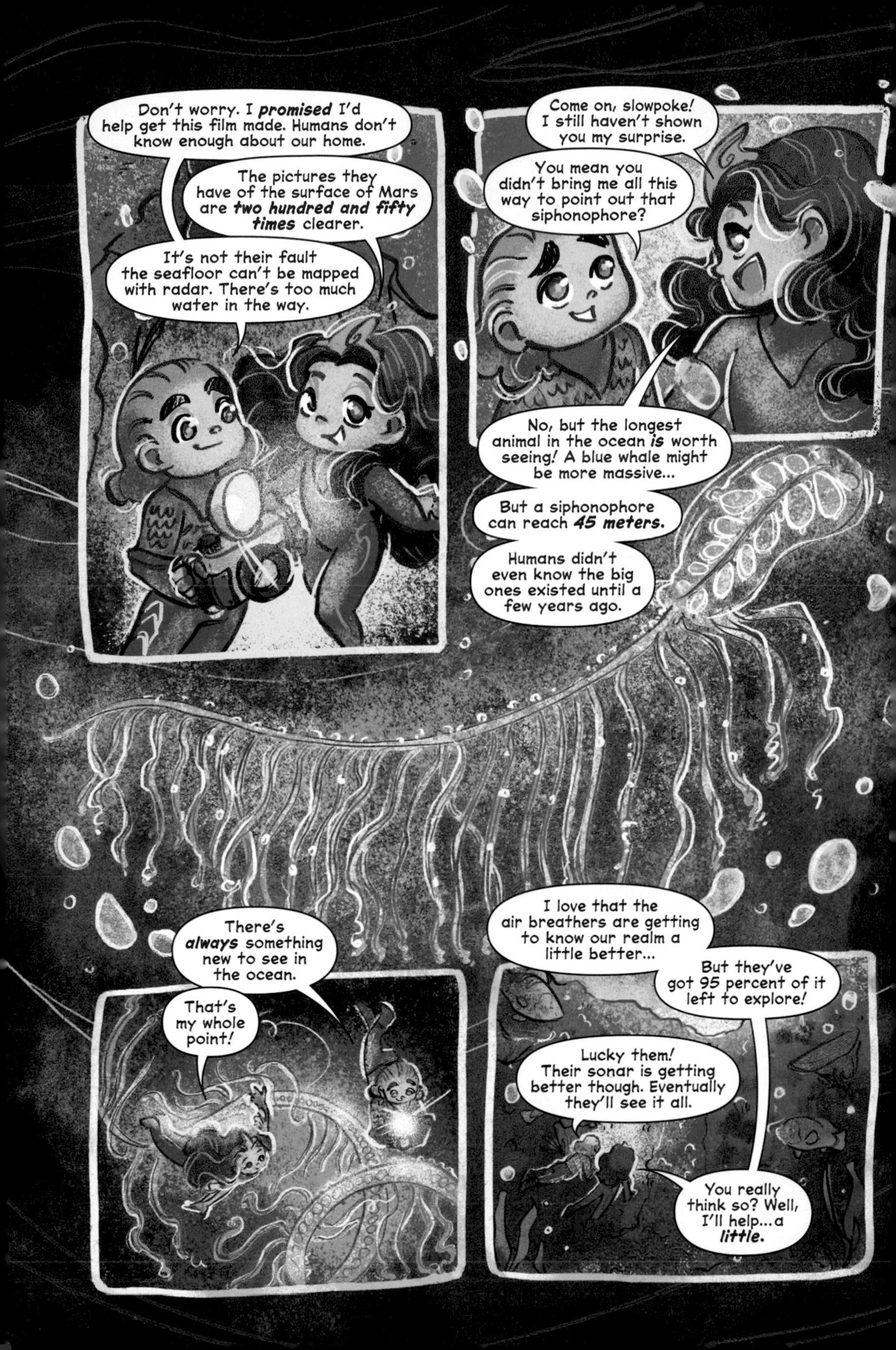
Don't worry. I **promised** I'd help get this film made. Humans don't know enough about our home.
The pictures they have of the surface of Mars are ***two hundred and fifty times*** clearer.
It's not their fault the seafloor can't be mapped with radar. There's too much water in the way.
Come on, slowpoke! I still haven't shown you my surprise.
You mean you didn't bring me all this way to point out that siphonophore?
No, but the longest animal in the ocean ***is*** worth seeing! A blue whale might be more massive...
But a siphonophore can reach ***45 meters.***
Humans didn't even know the big ones existed until a few years ago.
There's ***always*** something new to see in the ocean.
That's my whole point!
I love that the air breathers are getting to know our realm a little better...
But they've got 95 percent of it left to explore!
Lucky them! Their sonar is getting better though. Eventually they'll see it all.
You really think so? Well, I'll help...a ***little.***

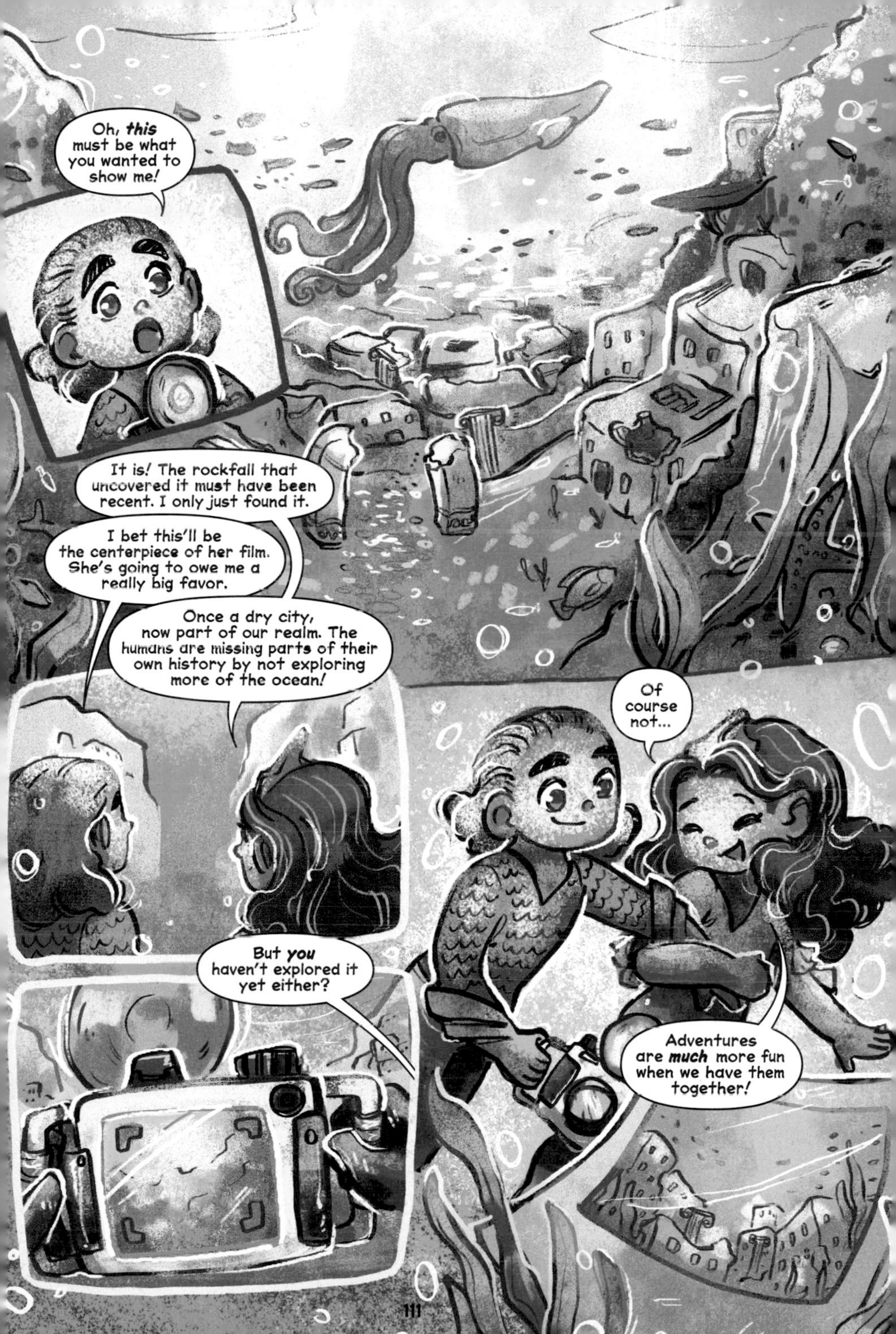
Oh, *this* must be what you wanted to show me!
It is! The rockfall that uncovered it must have been recent. I only just found it.
I bet this'll be the centerpiece of her film. She's going to owe me a really big favor.
Once a dry city, now part of our realm. The humans are missing parts of their own history by not exploring more of the ocean!
But *you* haven't explored it yet either?
Of course not...
Adventures are *much* more fun when we have them together!

CHAPTER NINE

WEATHER OR NOT...

WRITTEN BY **MICHAEL NORTHROP**

ILLUSTRATED BY **YANCEY LABAT**

COLORED BY **MONICA KUBINA**

LETTERED BY **WES ABBOTT**

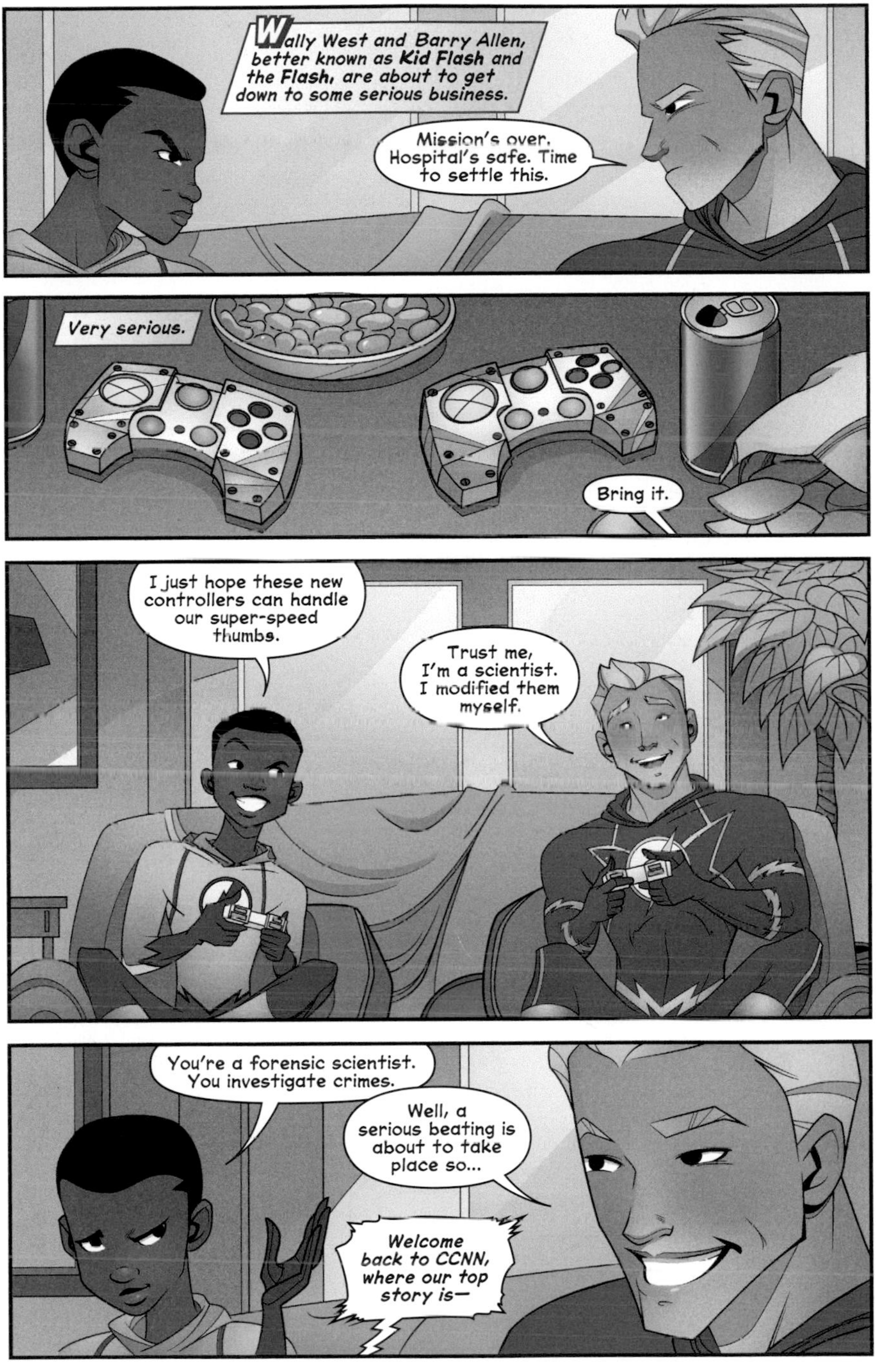
Wally West and Barry Allen, better known as **Kid Flash** and the **Flash**, are about to get down to some serious business.
Mission's over. Hospital's safe. Time to settle this.
Very serious.
Bring it.
I just hope these new controllers can handle our super-speed thumbs.
Trust me, I'm a scientist. I modified them myself.
You're a forensic scientist. You investigate crimes.
Well, a serious beating is about to take place so...
Welcome back to CCNN, where our top story is—

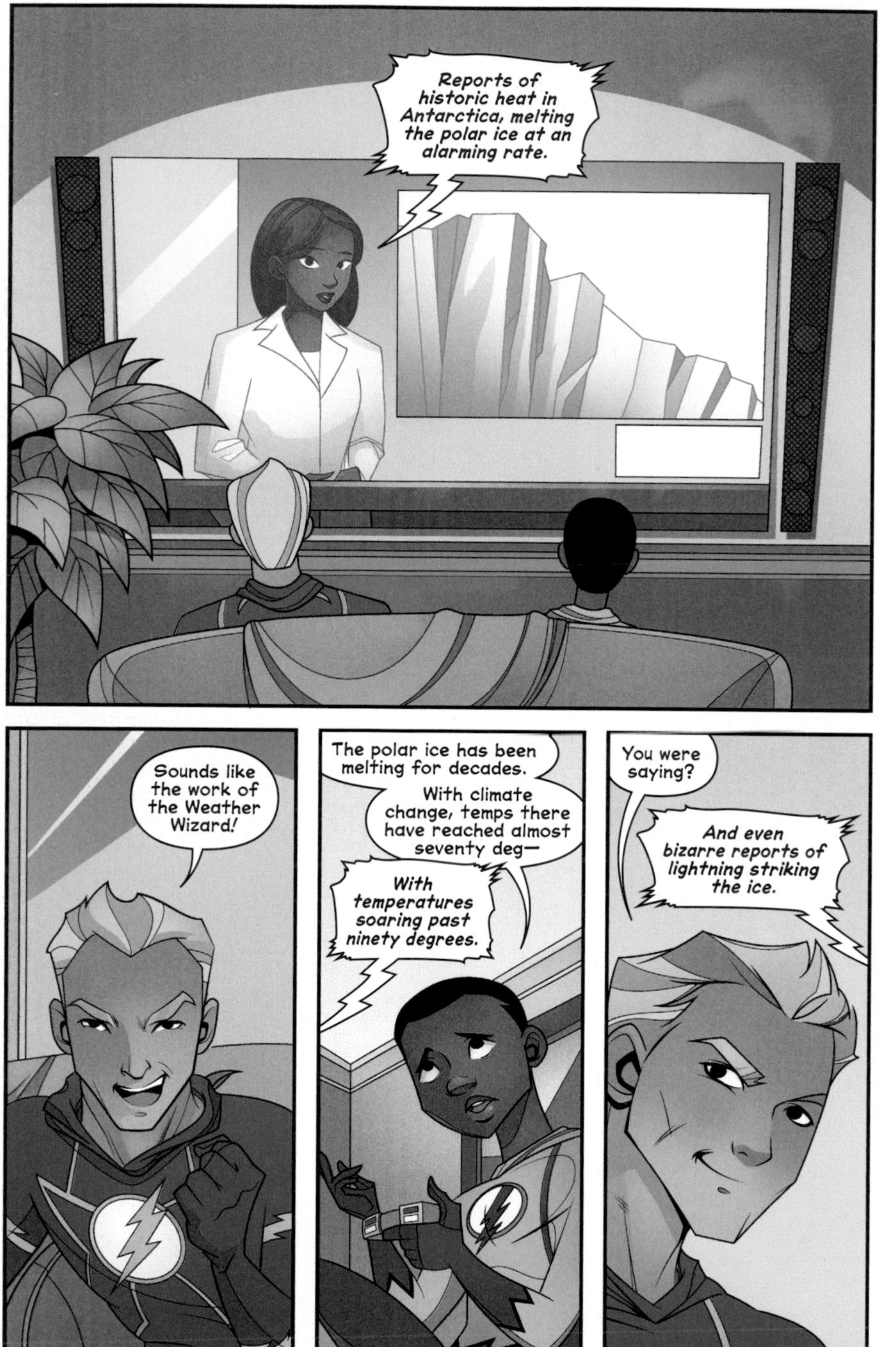
Reports of historic heat in Antarctica, melting the polar ice at an alarming rate.
Sounds like the work of the Weather Wizard!
The polar ice has been melting for decades.
With climate change, temps there have reached almost seventy deg—
With temperatures soaring past ninety degrees.
You were saying?
And even bizarre reports of lightning striking the ice.

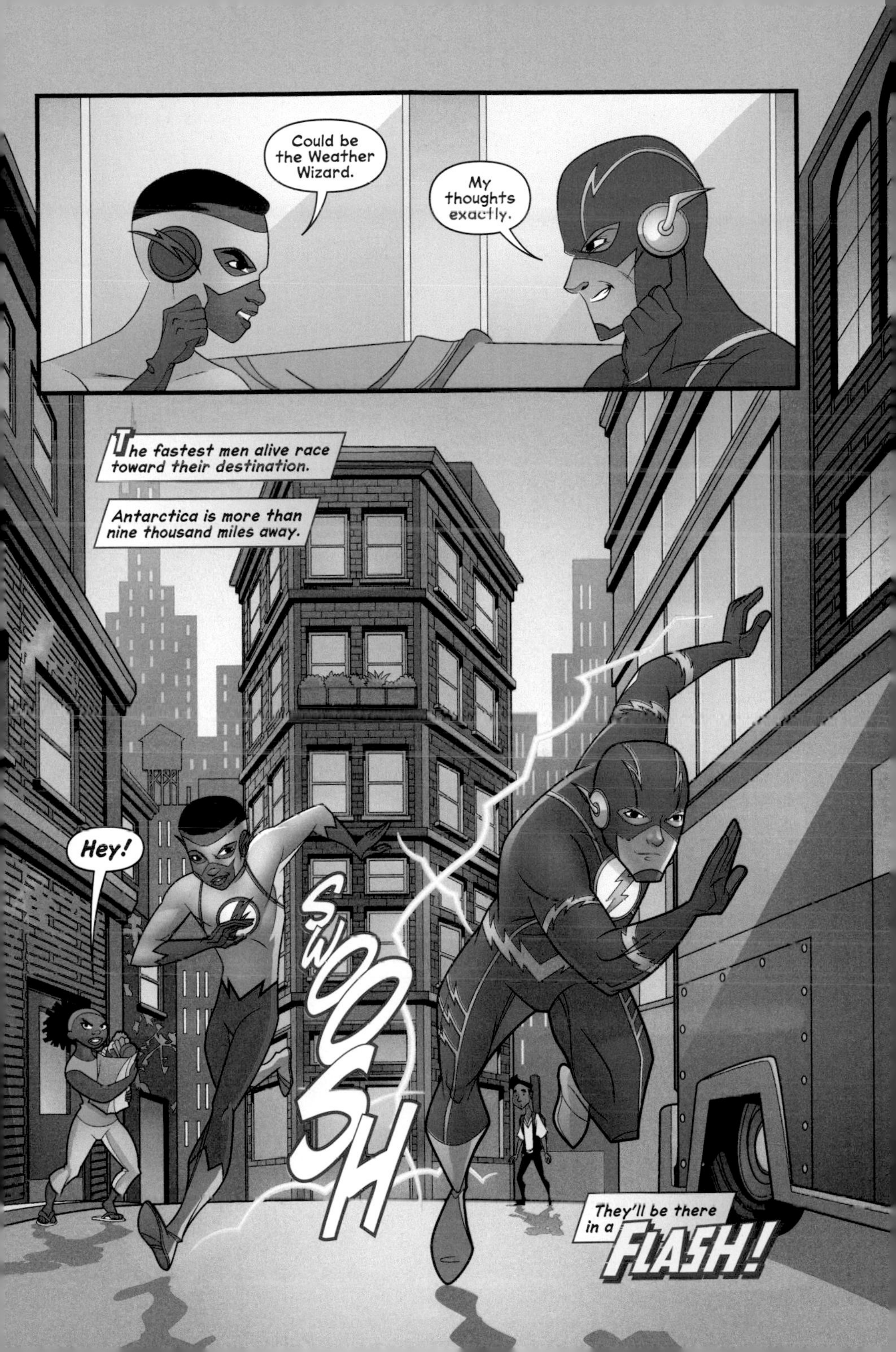
Could be the Weather Wizard.
My thoughts exactly.
The fastest men alive race toward their destination.
Antarctica is more than nine thousand miles away.
Hey!
SWOOOSH
They'll be there in a FLASH!

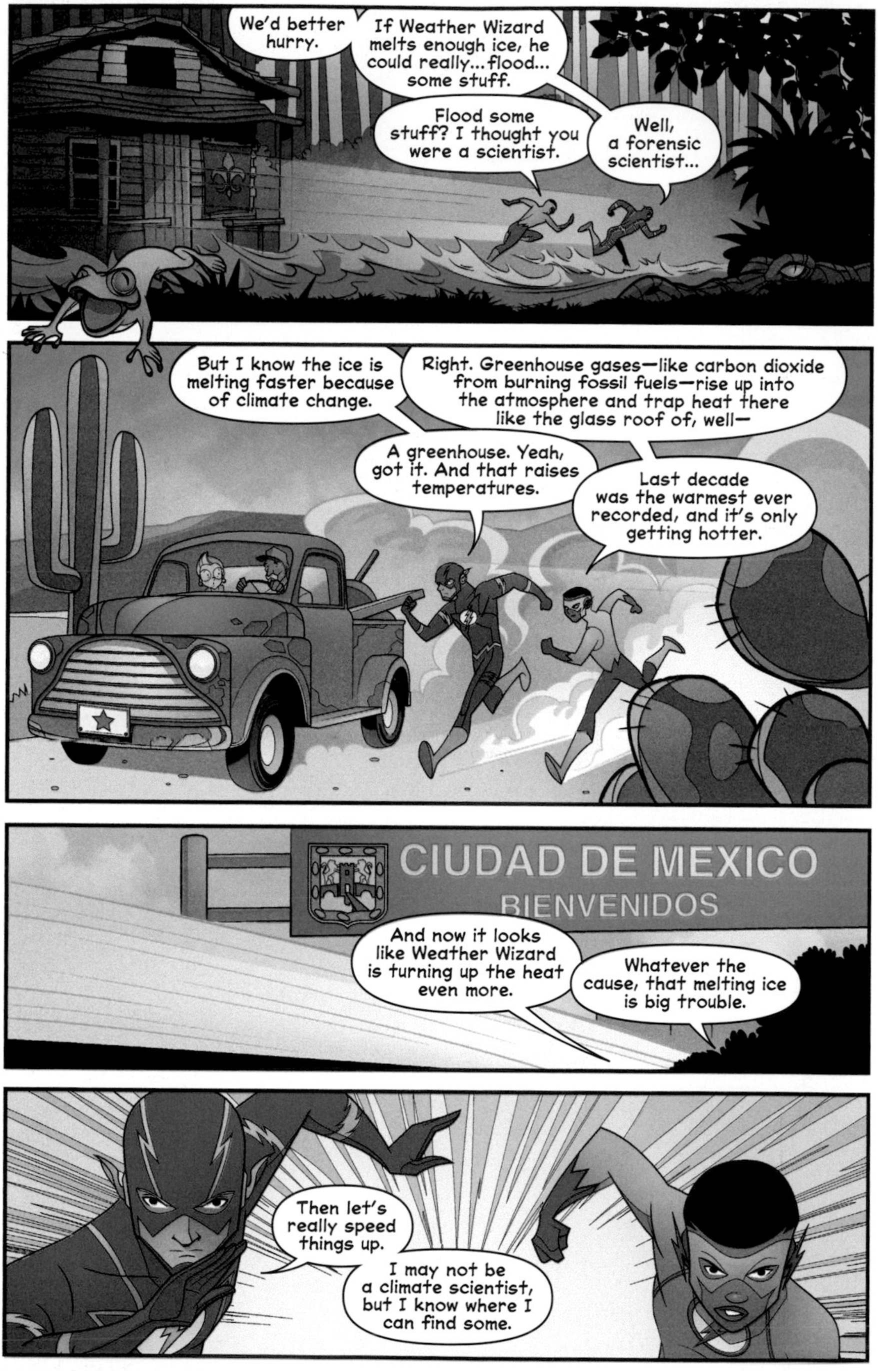
We'd better hurry.
If Weather Wizard melts enough ice, he could really...flood... some stuff.
Flood some stuff? I thought you were a scientist.
Well, a forensic scientist...
But I know the ice is melting faster because of climate change.
Right. Greenhouse gases—like carbon dioxide from burning fossil fuels—rise up into the atmosphere and trap heat there like the glass roof of, well—
A greenhouse. Yeah, got it. And that raises temperatures.
Last decade was the warmest ever recorded, and it's only getting hotter.
CIUDAD DE MEXICO
BIENVENIDOS
And now it looks like Weather Wizard is turning up the heat even more.
Whatever the cause, that melting ice is big trouble.
Then let's really speed things up.
I may not be a climate scientist, but I know where I can find some.

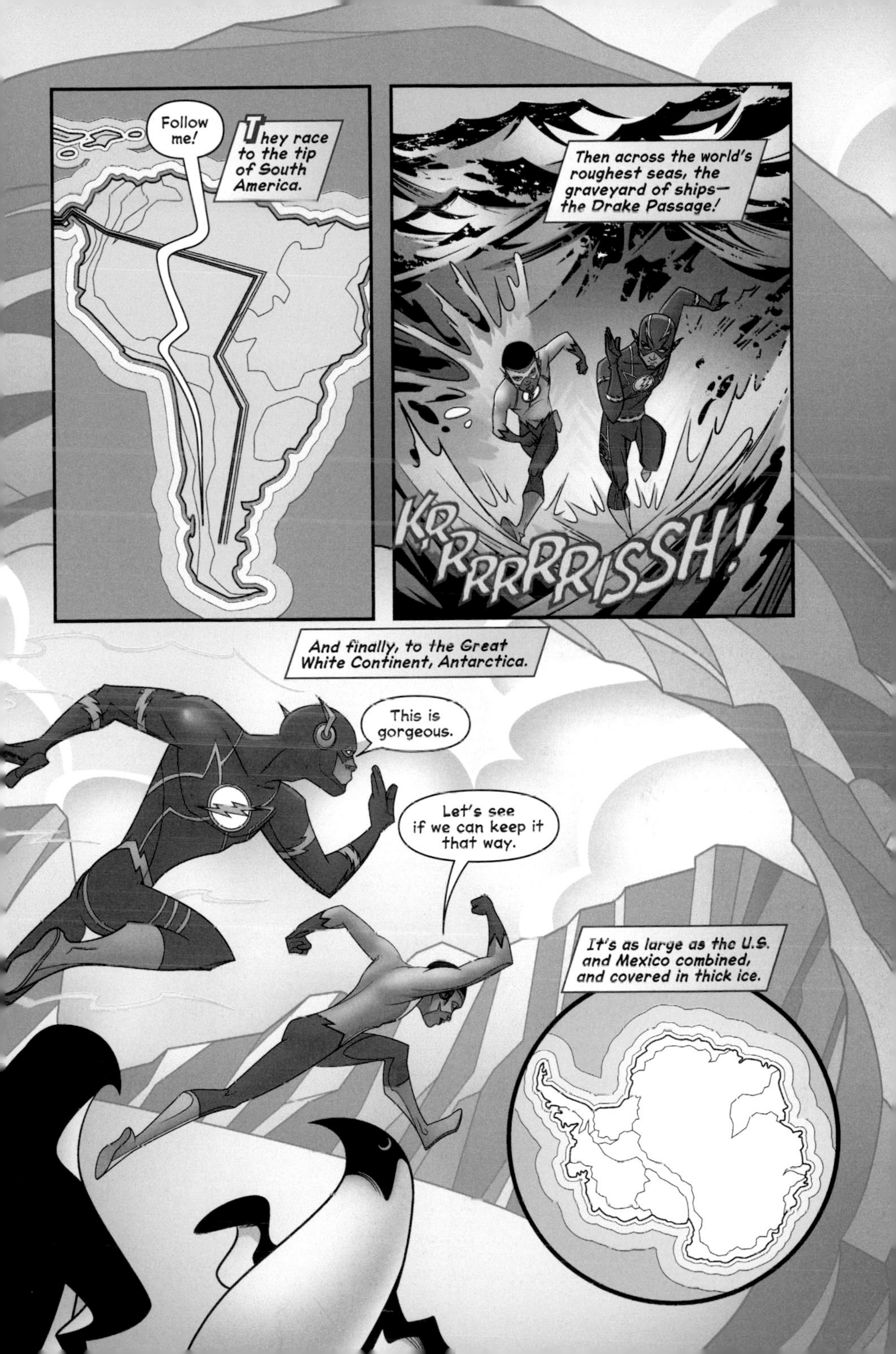
Follow me!
They race to the tip of South America.
Then across the world's roughest seas, the graveyard of ships—the Drake Passage!
KRRRRRRRISSH!
And finally, to the Great White Continent, Antarctica.
This is gorgeous.
Let's see if we can keep it that way.
It's as large as the U.S. and Mexico combined, and covered in thick ice.

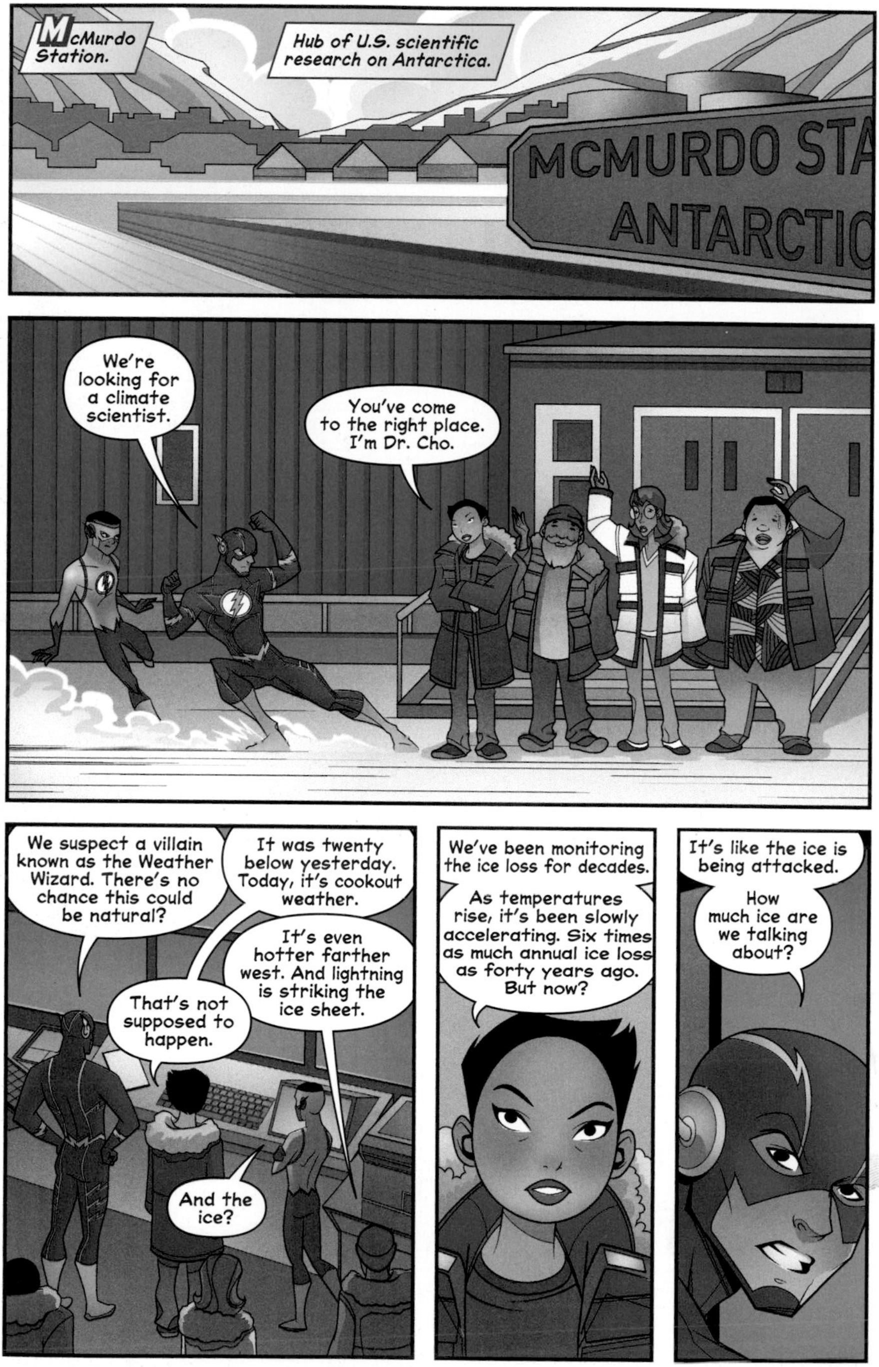
McMurdo Station.
Hub of U.S. scientific research on Antarctica.
MCMURDO STA
ANTARCTIC
We're looking for a climate scientist.
You've come to the right place. I'm Dr. Cho.
We suspect a villain known as the Weather Wizard. There's no chance this could be natural?
It was twenty below yesterday. Today, it's cookout weather.
It's even hotter farther west. And lightning is striking the ice sheet.
That's not supposed to happen.
And the ice?
We've been monitoring the ice loss for decades.
As temperatures rise, it's been slowly accelerating. Six times as much annual ice loss as forty years ago. But now?
It's like the ice is being attacked.
How much ice are we talking about?

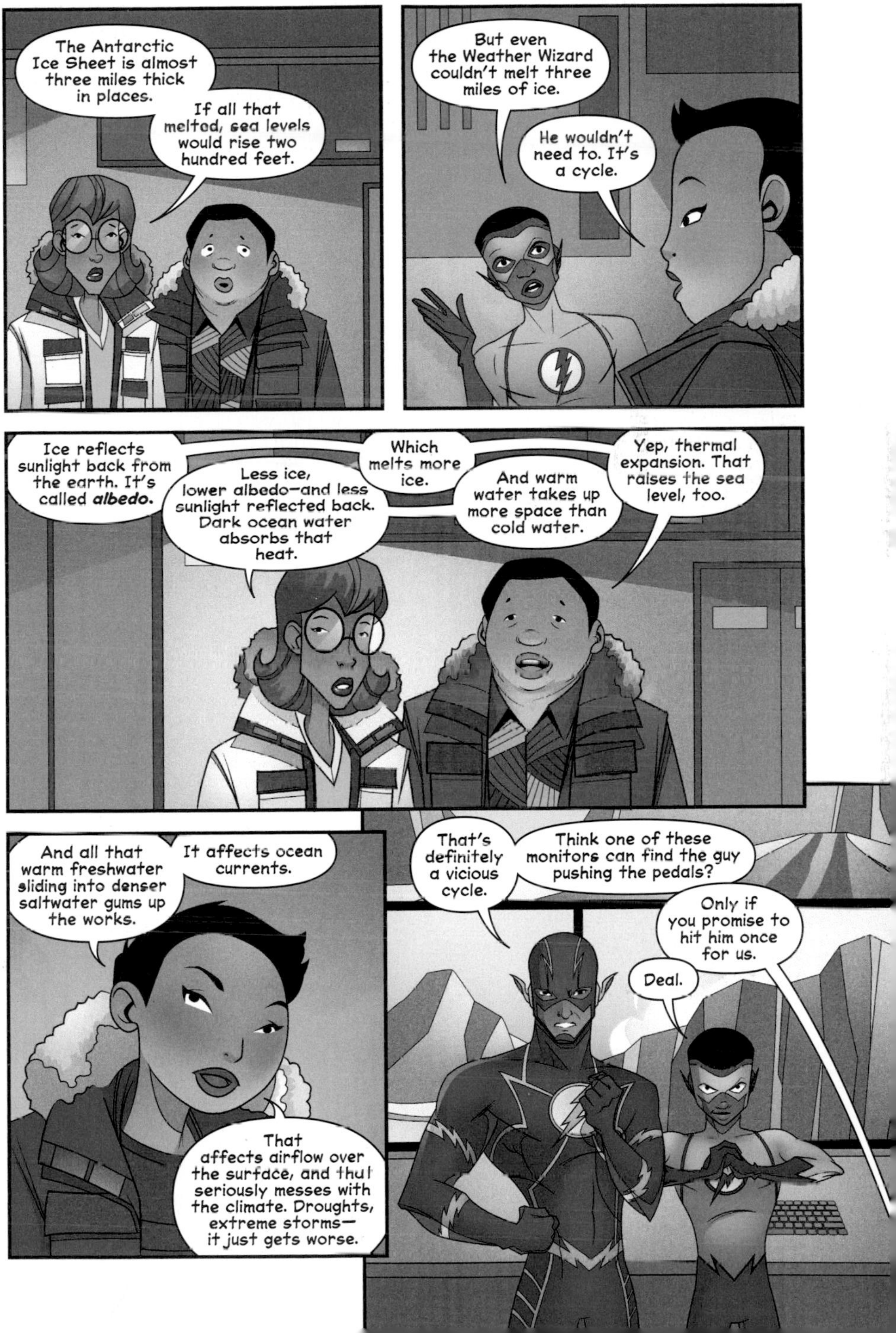
The Antarctic Ice Sheet is almost three miles thick in places.
If all that melted, sea levels would rise two hundred feet.
But even the Weather Wizard couldn't melt three miles of ice.
He wouldn't need to. It's a cycle.
Ice reflects sunlight back from the earth. It's called *albedo.*
Less ice, lower albedo—and less sunlight reflected back. Dark ocean water absorbs that heat.
Which melts more ice.
And warm water takes up more space than cold water.
Yep, thermal expansion. That raises the sea level, too.
And all that warm freshwater sliding into denser saltwater gums up the works.
It affects ocean currents.
That affects airflow over the surface, and that seriously messes with the climate. Droughts, extreme storms—it just gets worse.
That's definitely a vicious cycle.
Think one of these monitors can find the guy pushing the pedals?
Only if you promise to hit him once for us.
Deal.

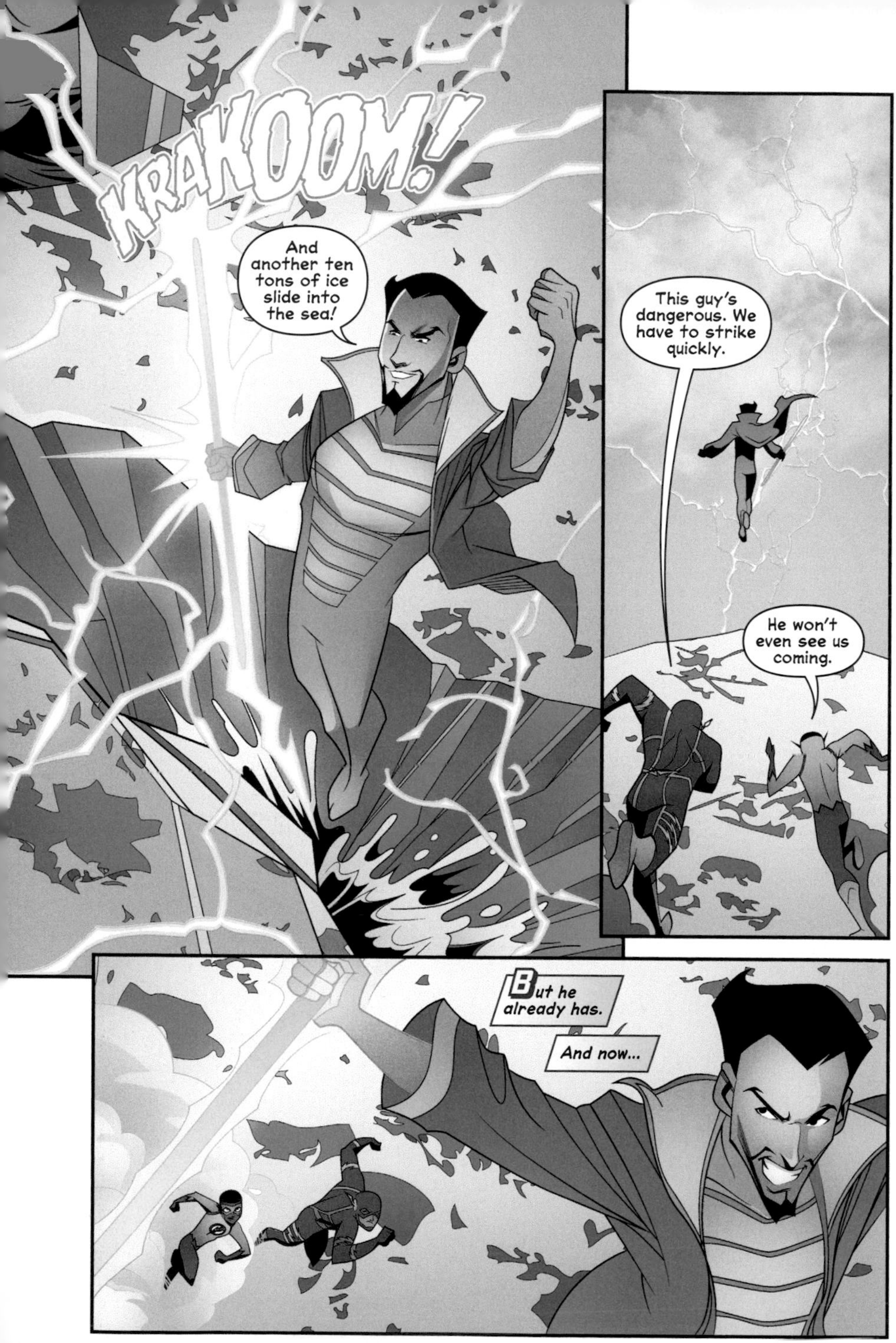
KRAKOOM!
And another ten tons of ice slide into the sea!
This guy's dangerous. We have to strike quickly.
He won't even see us coming.
But he already has.
And now...

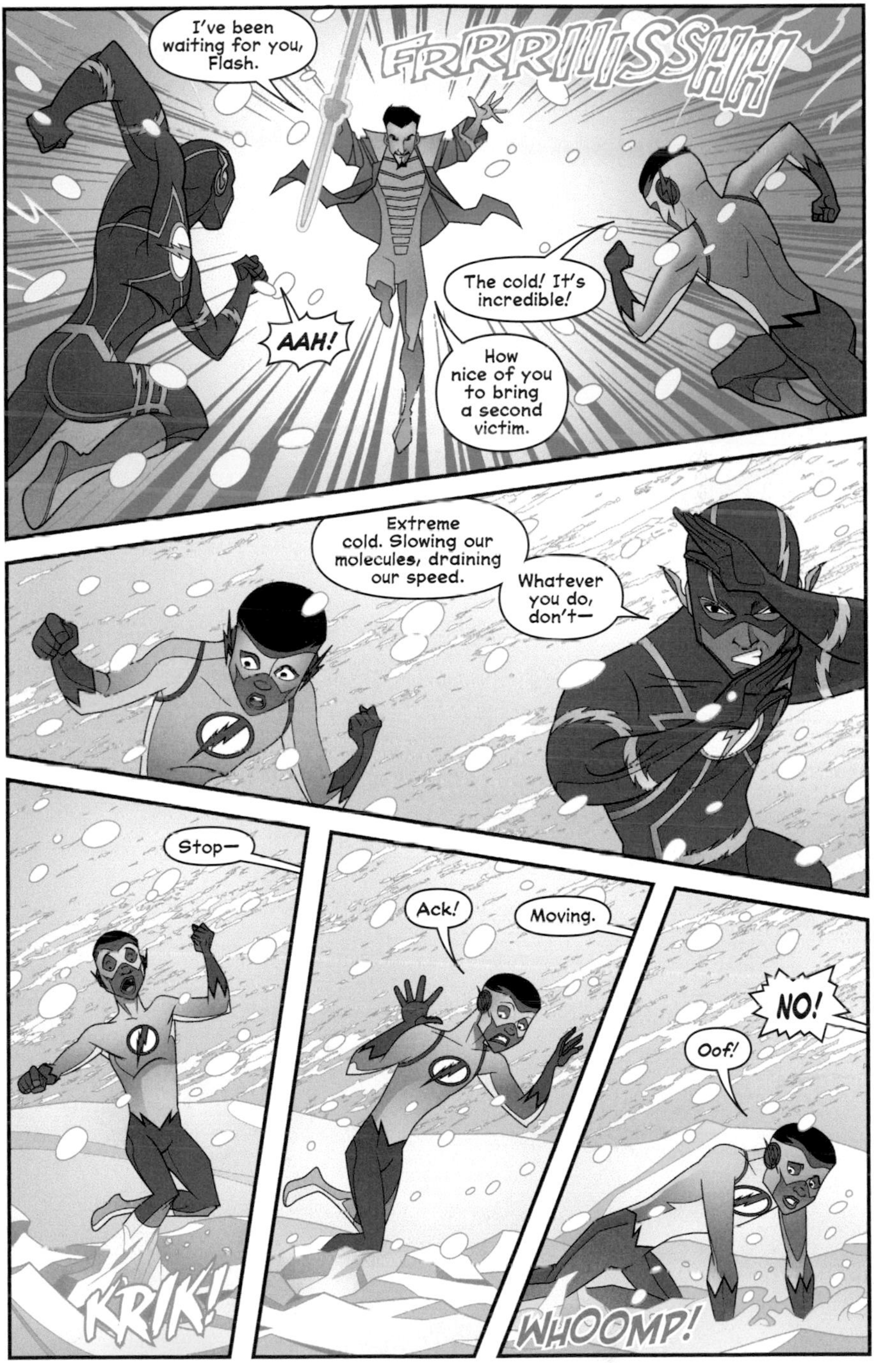
I've been waiting for you, Flash.
FRRRIIISSHH
AAH!
The cold! It's incredible!
How nice of you to bring a second victim.
Extreme cold. Slowing our molecules, draining our speed.
Whatever you do, don't—
Stop—
KRIK!
Ack!
Moving.
NO!
Oof!
WHOOMP!

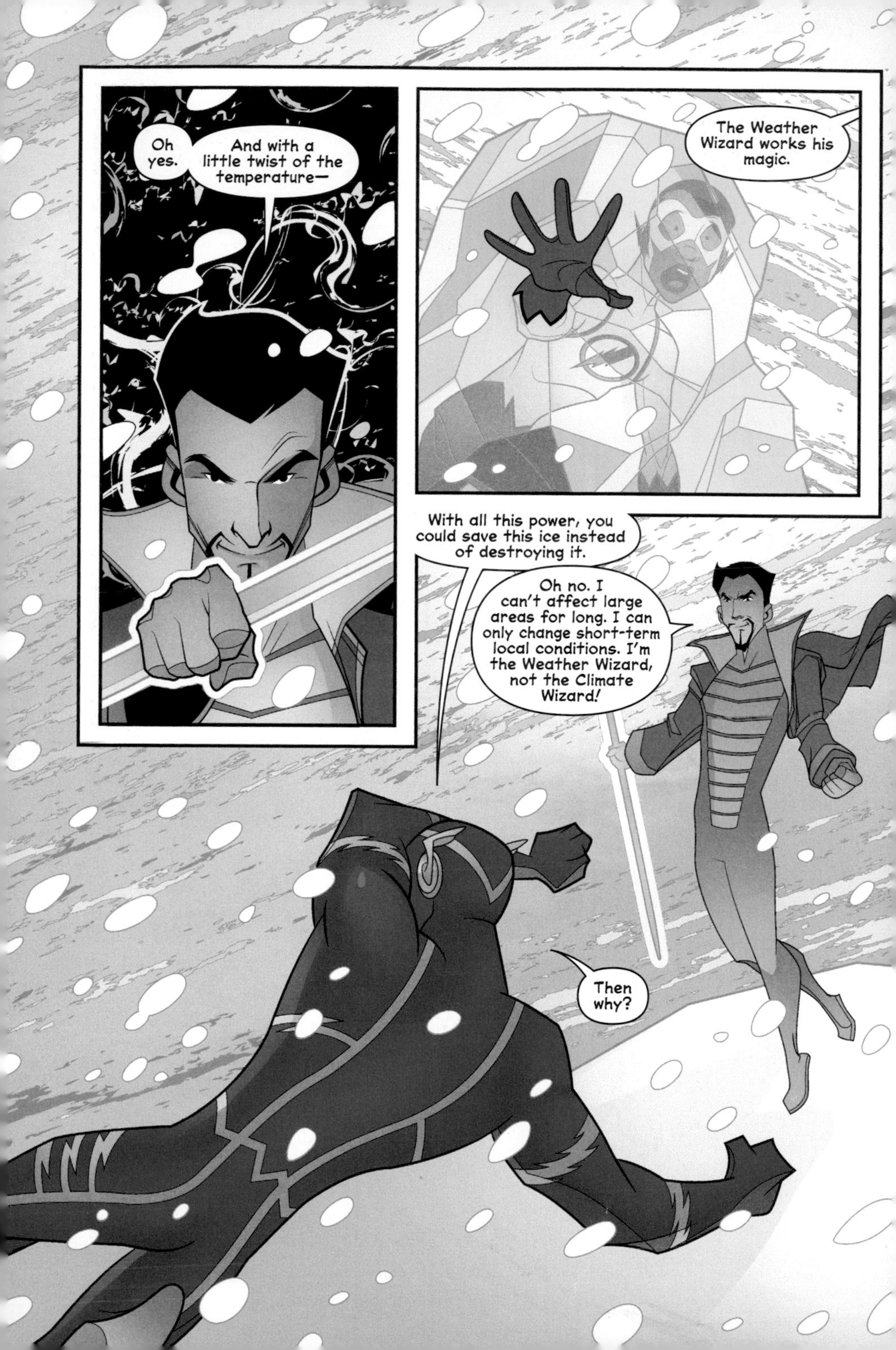
Oh yes.
And with a little twist of the temperature—
The Weather Wizard works his magic.
With all this power, you could save this ice instead of destroying it.
Oh no. I can't affect large areas for long. I can only change short-term local conditions. I'm the Weather Wizard, not the Climate Wizard!
Then why?

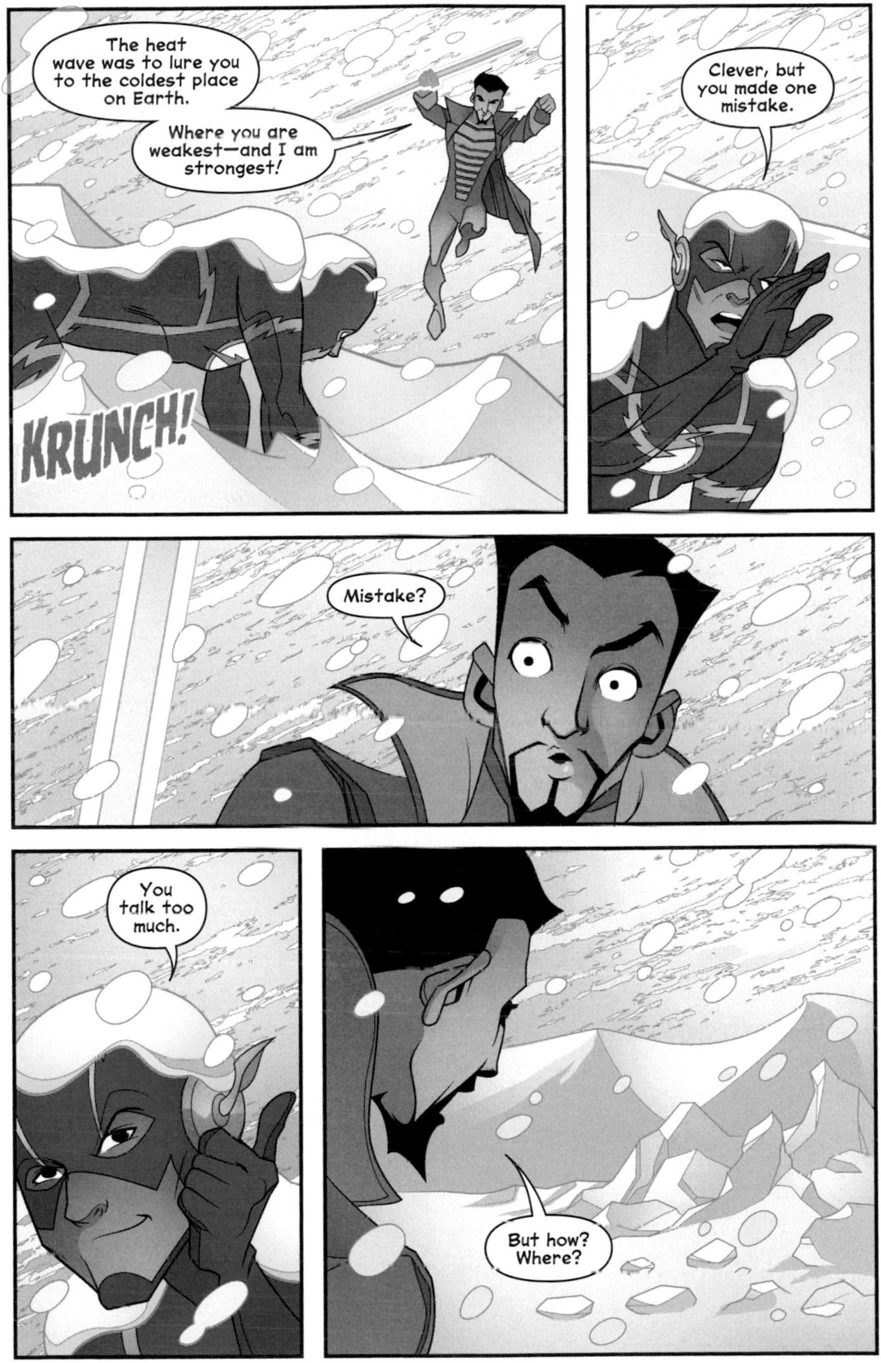

The heat wave was to lure you to the coldest place on Earth.
Where you are weakest—and I am strongest!
KRUNCH!
Clever, but you made one mistake.
Mistake?
You talk too much.
But how? Where?

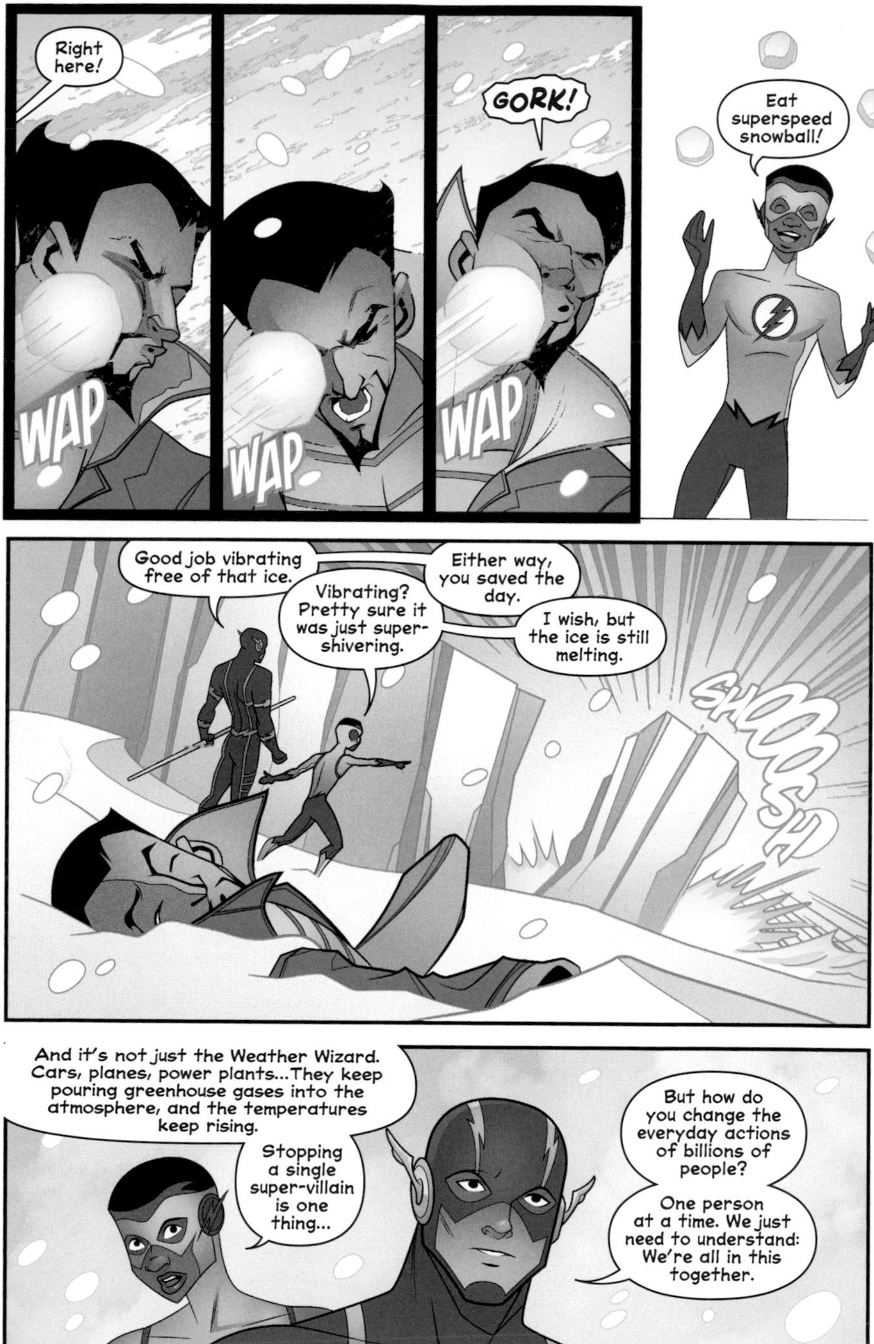
Right here!
WAP
WAP
GORK!
WAP
Eat superspeed snowball!
Good job vibrating free of that ice.
Vibrating? Pretty sure it was just super-shivering.
Either way, you saved the day.
I wish, but the ice is still melting.
SHOOOSH
And it's not just the Weather Wizard. Cars, planes, power plants...They keep pouring greenhouse gases into the atmosphere, and the temperatures keep rising.
Stopping a single super-villain is one thing...
But how do you change the everyday actions of billions of people?
One person at a time. We just need to understand: We're all in this together.

CHAPTER TEN

HUMAN
EXTREMES

WRITTEN AND ILLUSTRATED BY KIRK SCROGGS

LETTERED BY STEVE WANDS

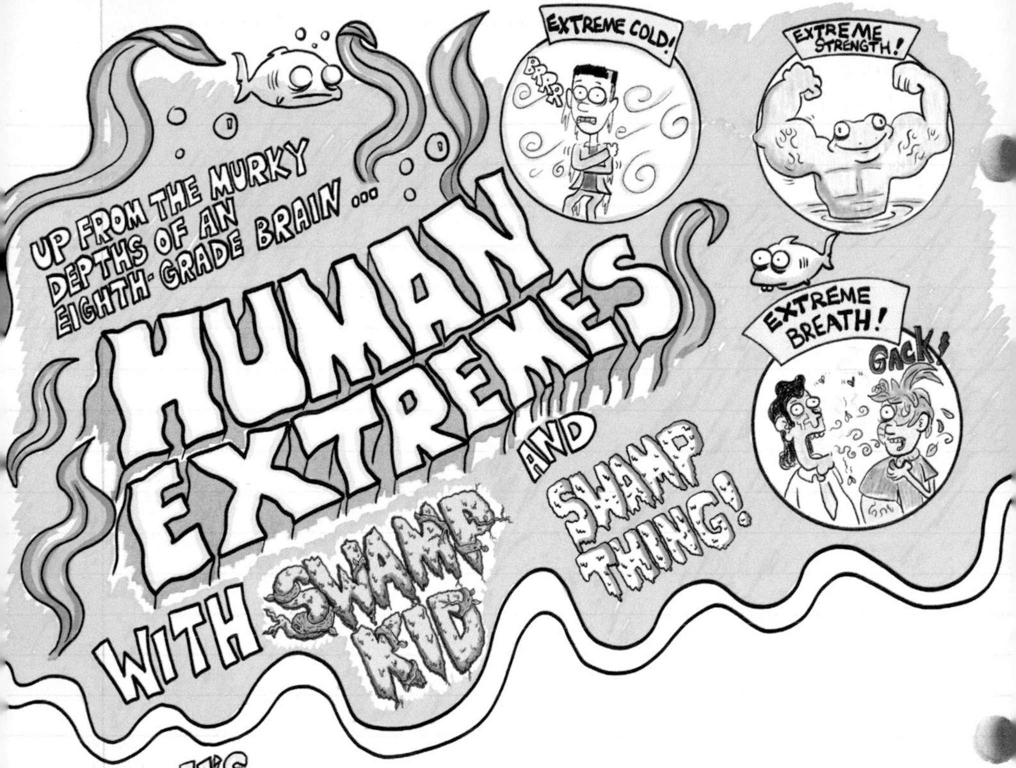
UP FROM THE MURKY DEPTHS OF AN EIGHTH-GRADE BRAIN...
HUMAN EXTREMES
WITH SWAMP KID
AND SWAMP THING!
EXTREME COLD!
BRRR
EXTREME STRENGTH!
EXTREME BREATH!
GACK!

RUSSELL'S SPIRAL

MONDAY 4:20 P.M.

Russell here. I'm so exhausted I can barely write. Today was my first practice for the cross-country track team! Why oh why did I let Charlotte talk me into it? I swore I'd never run again after my last track fiasco!

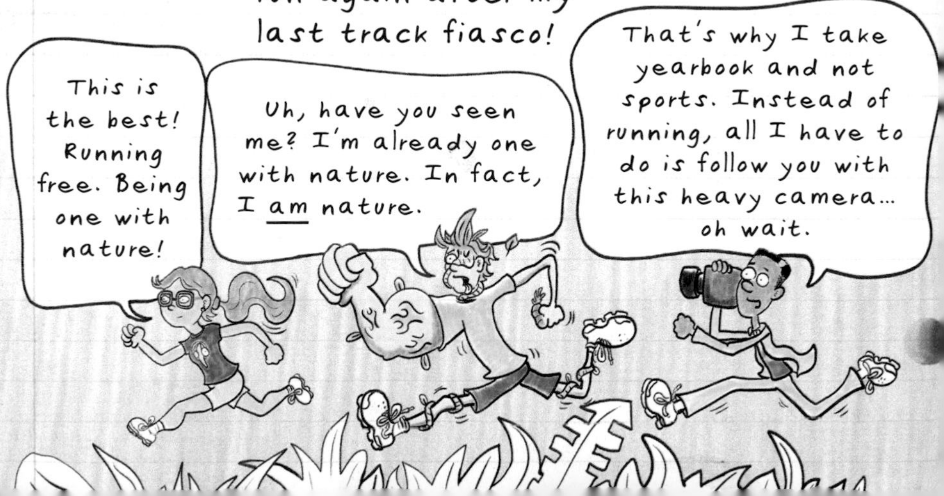
This is the best! Running free. Being one with nature!
Uh, have you seen me? I'm already one with nature. In fact, I am nature.
That's why I take yearbook and not sports. Instead of running, all I have to do is follow you with this heavy camera... oh wait.

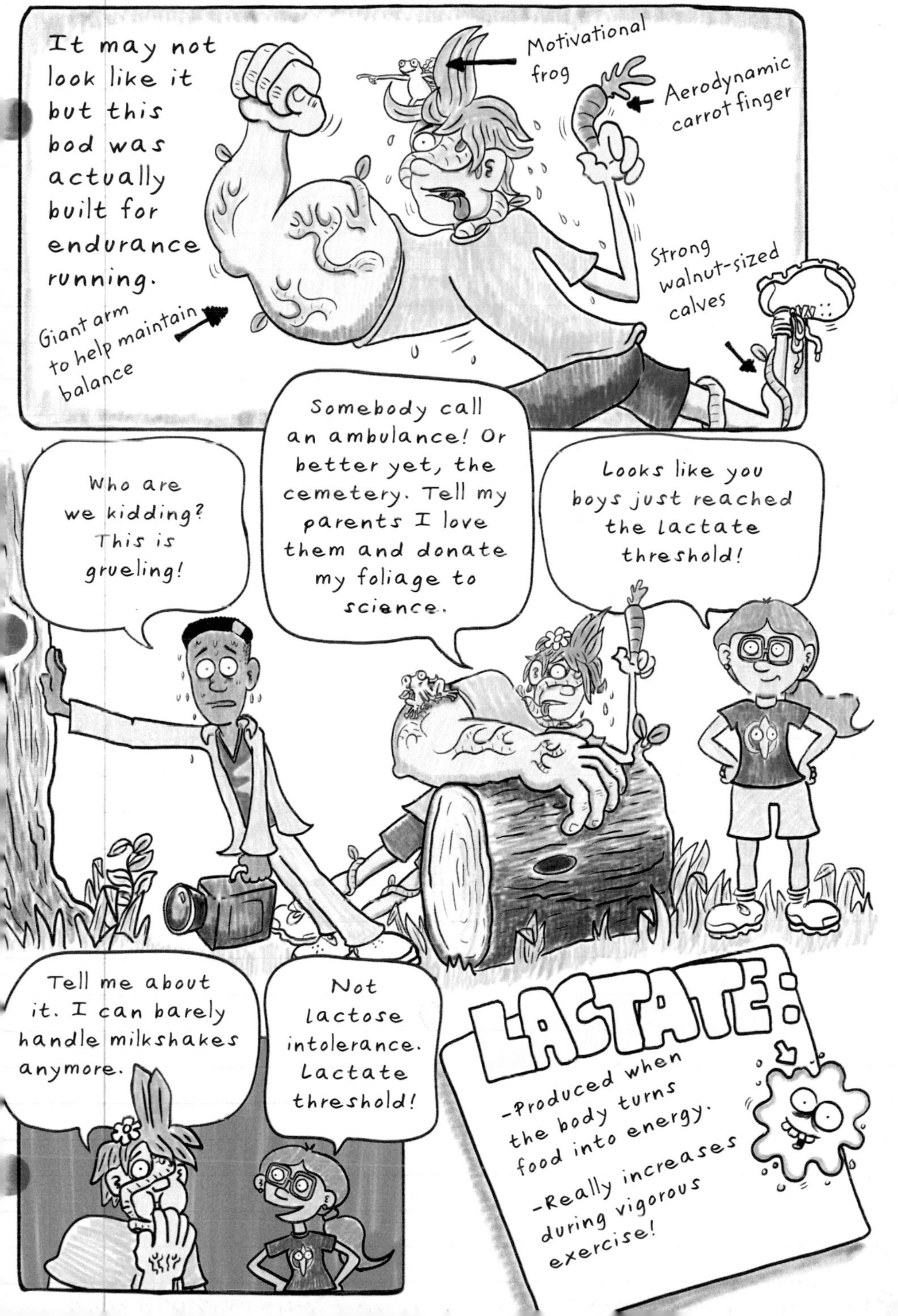

It may not look like it but this bod was actually built for endurance running.
Motivational frog
Aerodynamic carrot finger
Giant arm to help maintain balance
Strong walnut-sized calves
Who are we kidding? This is grueling!
Somebody call an ambulance! Or better yet, the cemetery. Tell my parents I love them and donate my foliage to science.
Looks like you boys just reached the lactate threshold!
Tell me about it. I can barely handle milkshakes anymore.
Not lactose intolerance. Lactate threshold!
LACTATE:
-Produced when the body turns food into energy.
-Really increases during vigorous exercise!

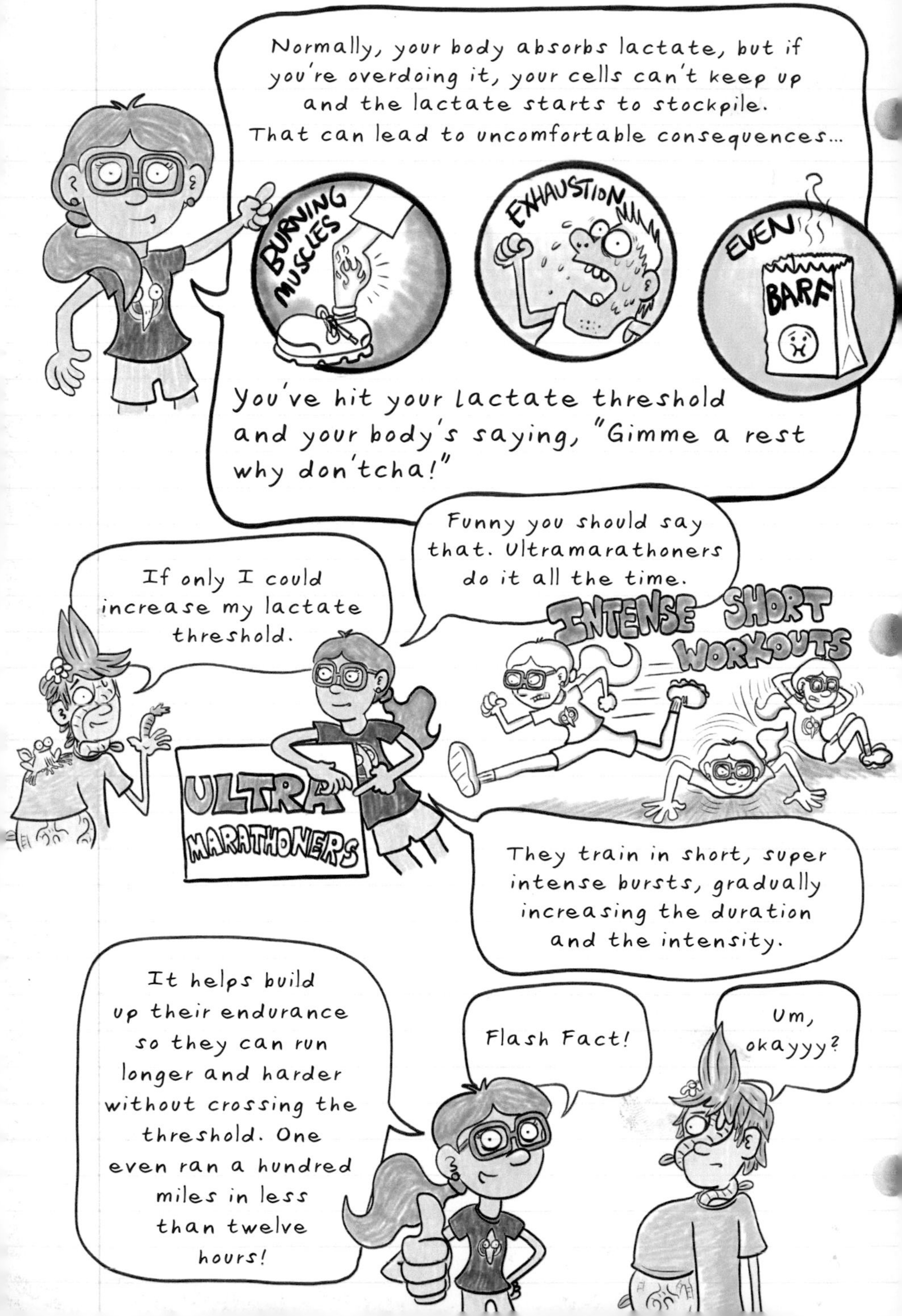
Normally, your body absorbs lactate, but if you're overdoing it, your cells can't keep up and the lactate starts to stockpile. That can lead to uncomfortable consequences...
BURNING MUSCLES
EXHAUSTION
EVEN
BARF
You've hit your lactate threshold and your body's saying, "Gimme a rest why don'tcha!"
If only I could increase my lactate threshold.
Funny you should say that. Ultramarathoners do it all the time.
ULTRA MARATHONERS
INTENSE SHORT WORKOUTS
They train in short, super intense bursts, gradually increasing the duration and the intensity.
It helps build up their endurance so they can run longer and harder without crossing the threshold. One even ran a hundred miles in less than twelve hours!
Flash Fact!
Um, okayyy?

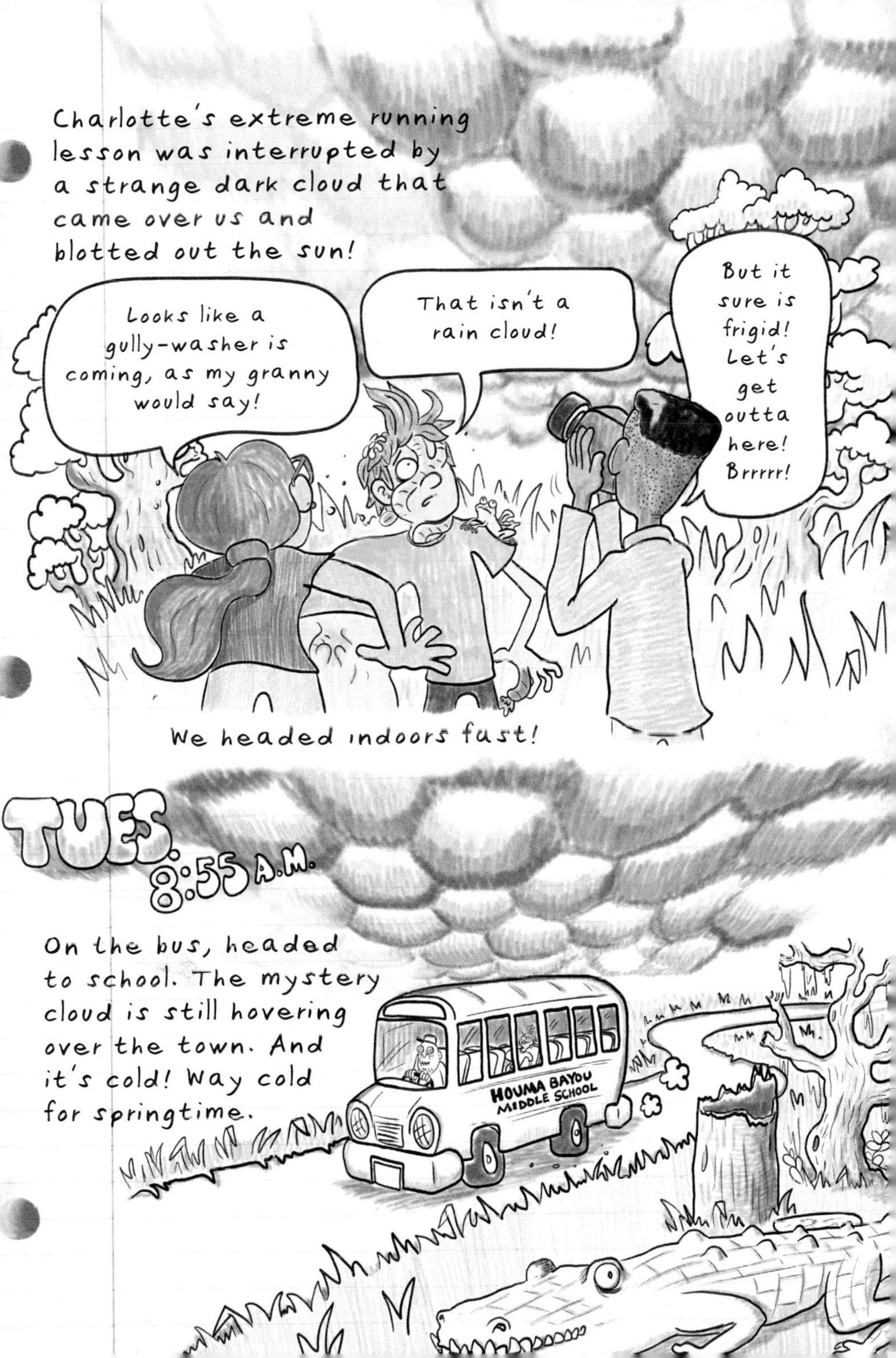
Charlotte's extreme running lesson was interrupted by a strange dark cloud that came over us and blotted out the sun!
Looks like a gully-washer is coming, as my granny would say!
That isn't a rain cloud!
But it sure is frigid! Let's get outta here! Brrrrr!
We headed indoors fast!
TUES. 8:55 A.M.
On the bus, headed to school. The mystery cloud is still hovering over the town. And it's cold! Way cold for springtime.
HOUMA BAYOU MIDDLE SCHOOL

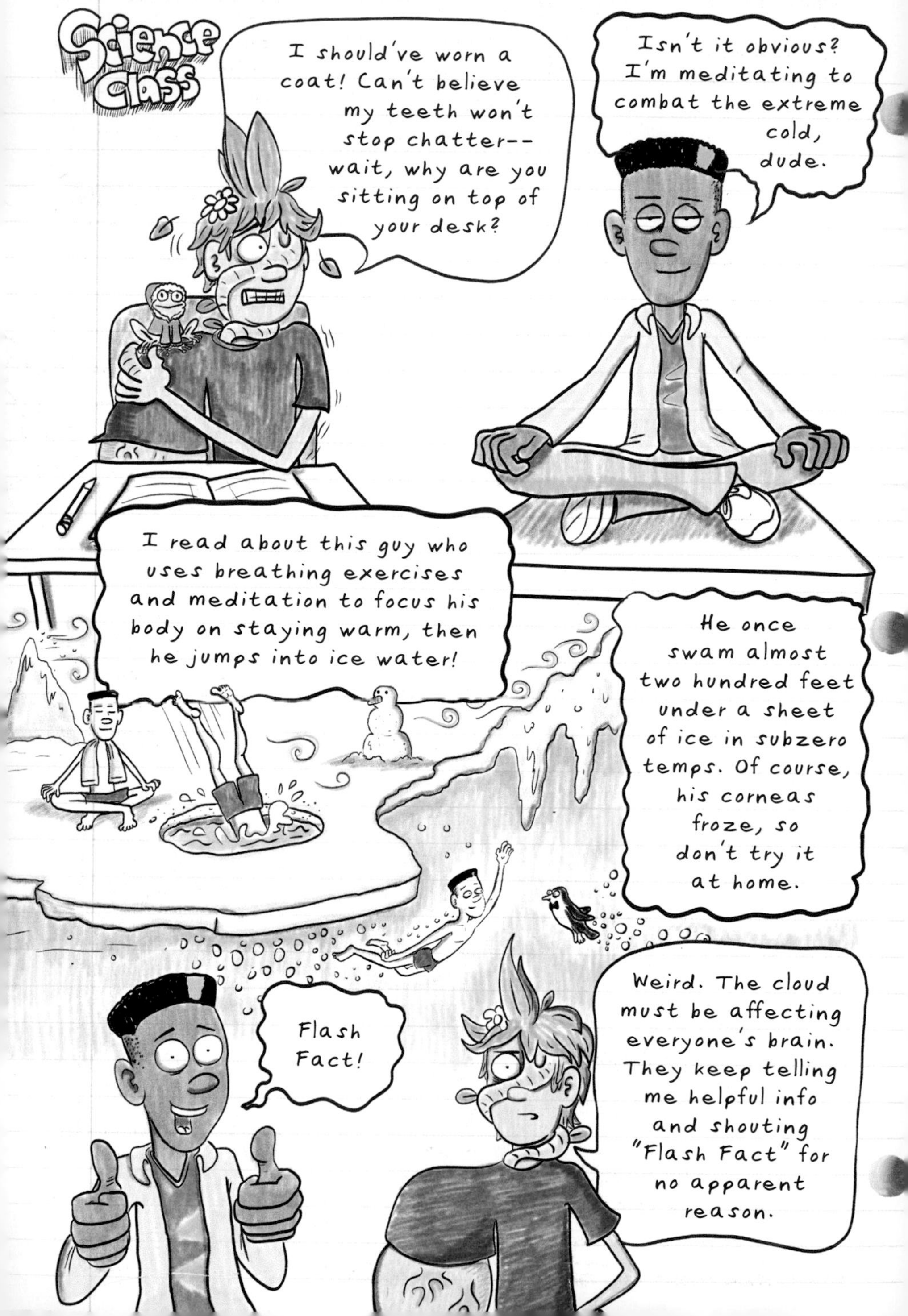
Science Class
I should've worn a coat! Can't believe my teeth won't stop chatter-- wait, why are you sitting on top of your desk?
Isn't it obvious? I'm meditating to combat the extreme cold, dude.
I read about this guy who uses breathing exercises and meditation to focus his body on staying warm, then he jumps into ice water!
He once swam almost two hundred feet under a sheet of ice in subzero temps. Of course, his corneas froze, so don't try it at home.
Flash Fact!
Weird. The cloud must be affecting everyone's brain. They keep telling me helpful info and shouting "Flash Fact" for no apparent reason.

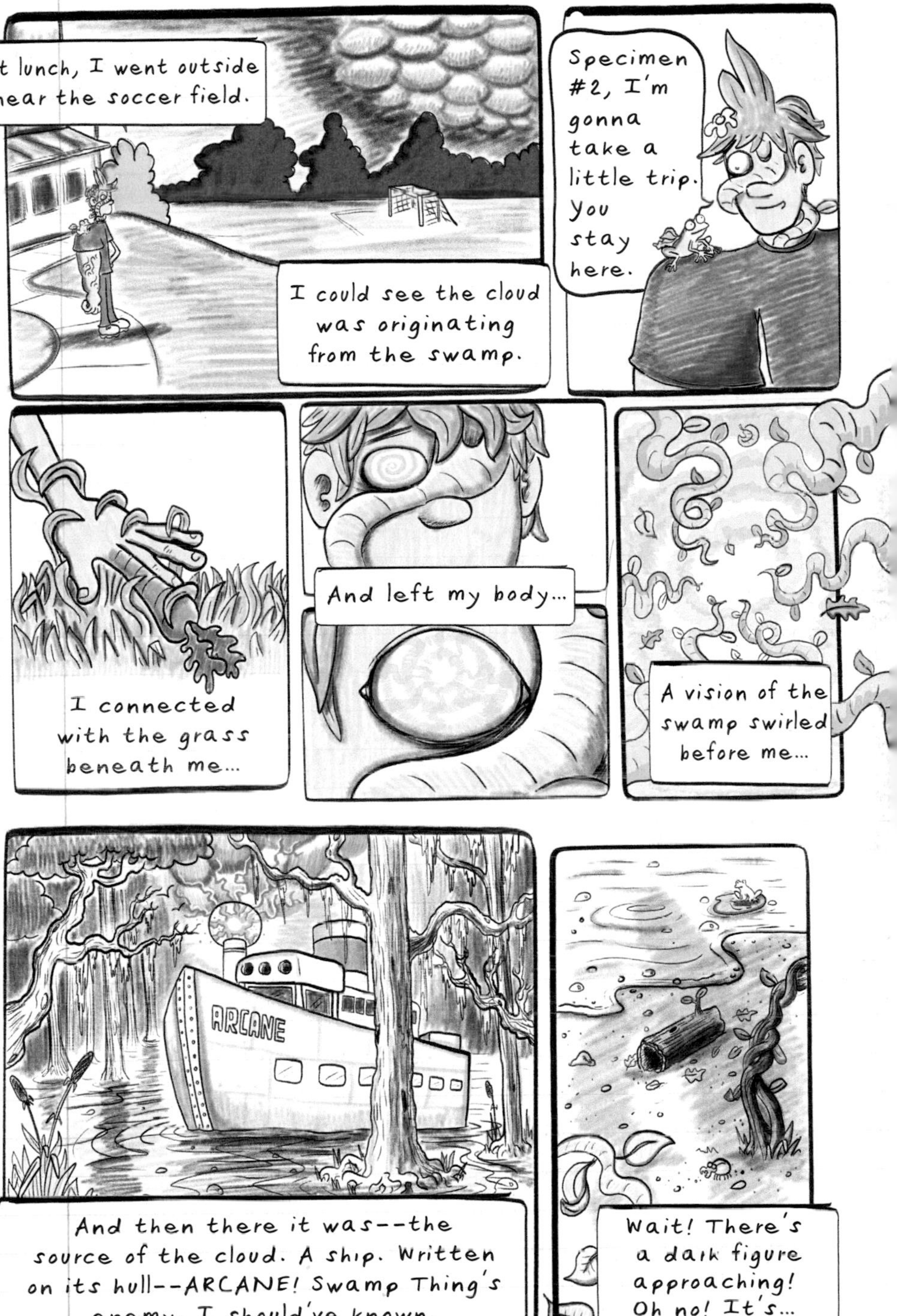
At lunch, I went outside near the soccer field.
I could see the cloud was originating from the swamp.
Specimen #2, I'm gonna take a little trip. You stay here.
I connected with the grass beneath me...
And left my body...
A vision of the swamp swirled before me...
ARCANE
And then there it was--the source of the cloud. A ship. Written on its hull--ARCANE! Swamp Thing's enemy. I should've known.
Wait! There's a dark figure approaching! Oh no! It's...

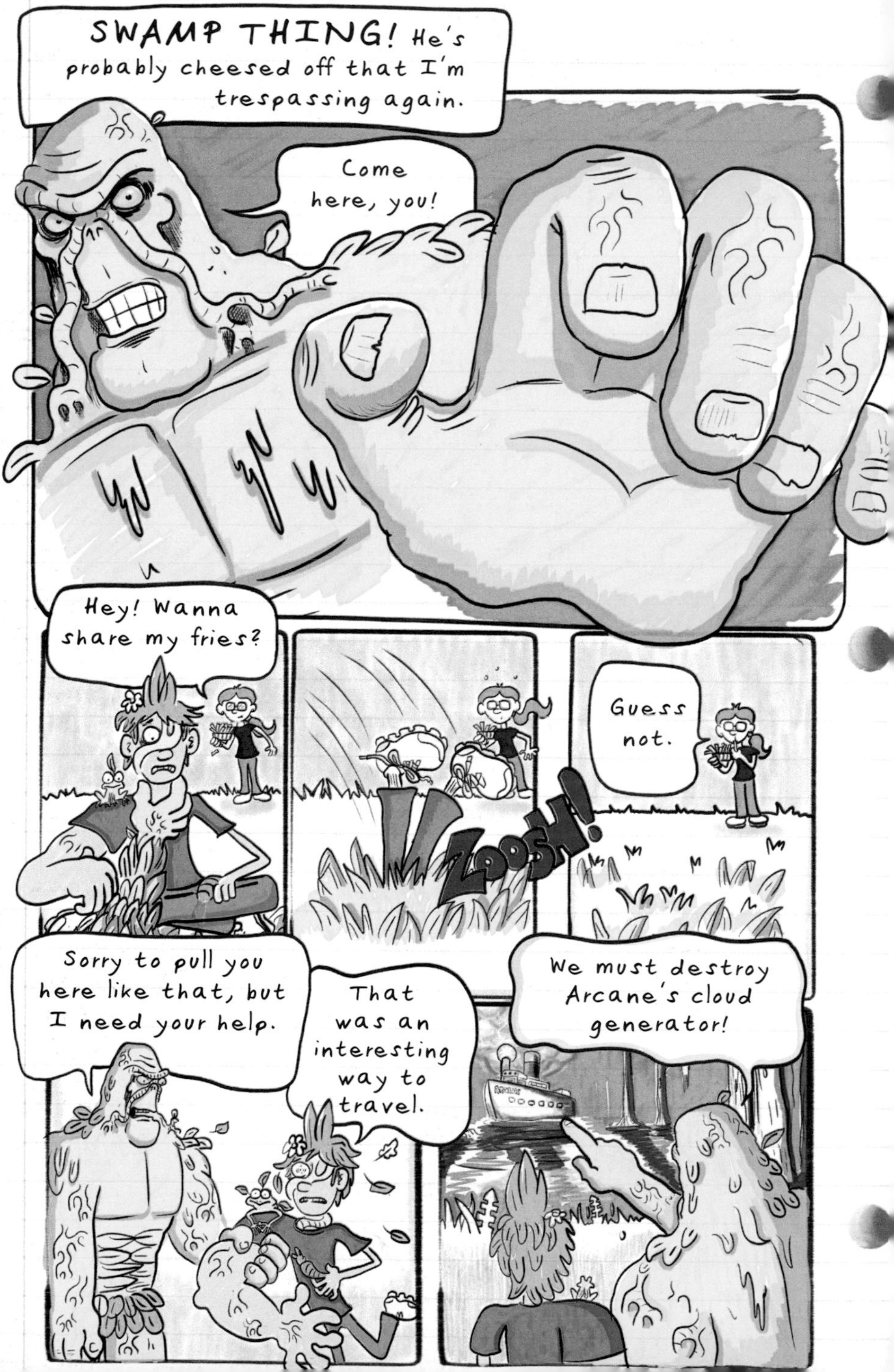
SWAMP THING! He's probably cheesed off that I'm trespassing again.
Come here, you!
Hey! Wanna share my fries?
ZOOSH!
Guess not.
Sorry to pull you here like that, but I need your help.
That was an interesting way to travel.
We must destroy Arcane's cloud generator!

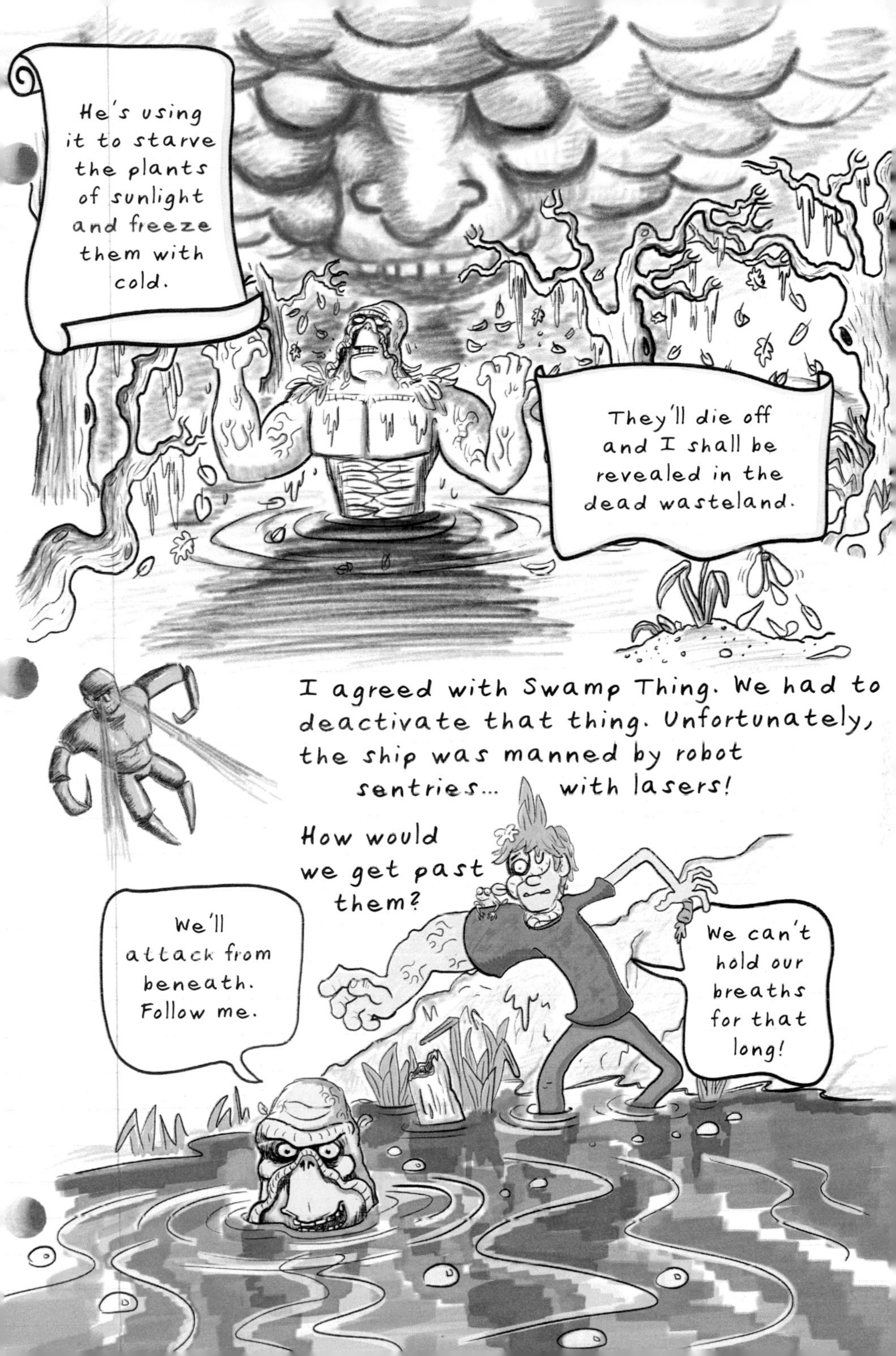
He's using it to starve the plants of sunlight and freeze them with cold.
They'll die off and I shall be revealed in the dead wasteland.
I agreed with Swamp Thing. We had to deactivate that thing. Unfortunately, the ship was manned by robot sentries... with lasers!
How would we get past them?
We'll attack from beneath. Follow me.
We can't hold our breaths for that long!

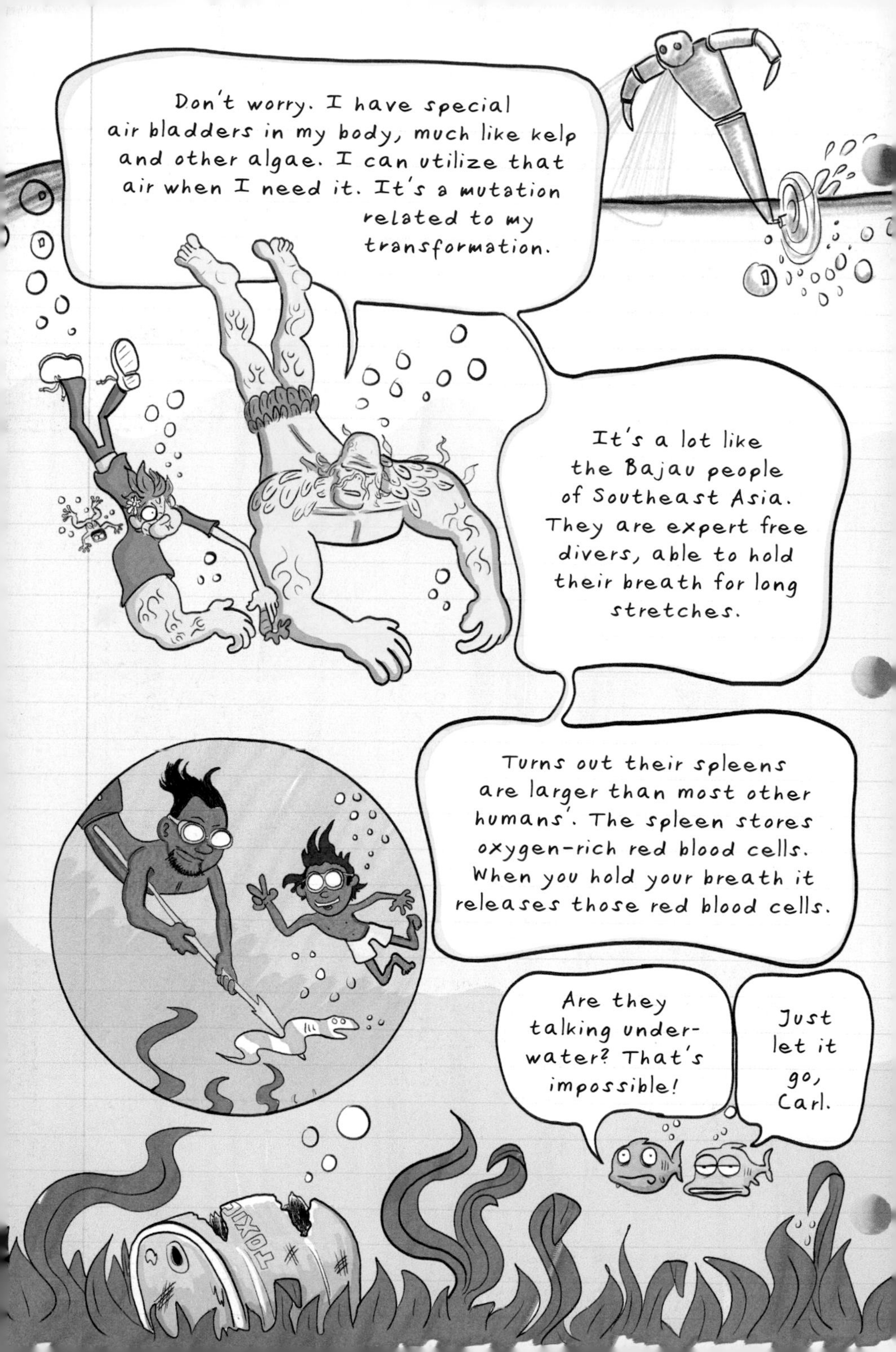
Don't worry. I have special air bladders in my body, much like kelp and other algae. I can utilize that air when I need it. It's a mutation related to my transformation.
It's a lot like the Bajau people of Southeast Asia. They are expert free divers, able to hold their breath for long stretches.
Turns out their spleens are larger than most other humans'. The spleen stores oxygen-rich red blood cells. When you hold your breath it releases those red blood cells.
Are they talking under-water? That's impossible!
Just let it go, Carl.

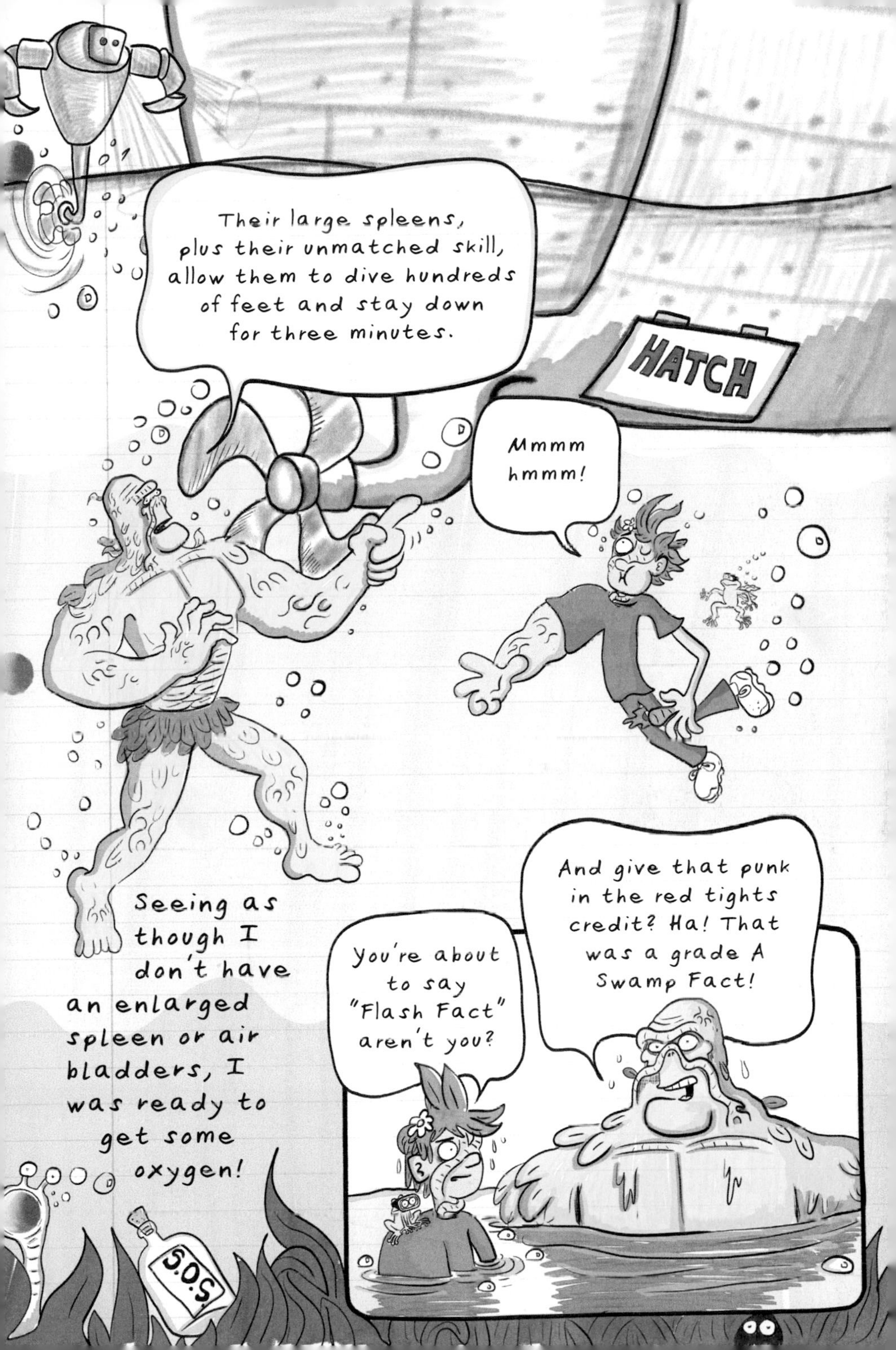
Their large spleens, plus their unmatched skill, allow them to dive hundreds of feet and stay down for three minutes.
HATCH
Mmmm hmmm!
Seeing as though I don't have an enlarged spleen or air bladders, I was ready to get some oxygen!
And give that punk in the red tights credit? Ha! That was a grade A Swamp Fact!
You're about to say "Flash Fact" aren't you?
S.O.S.

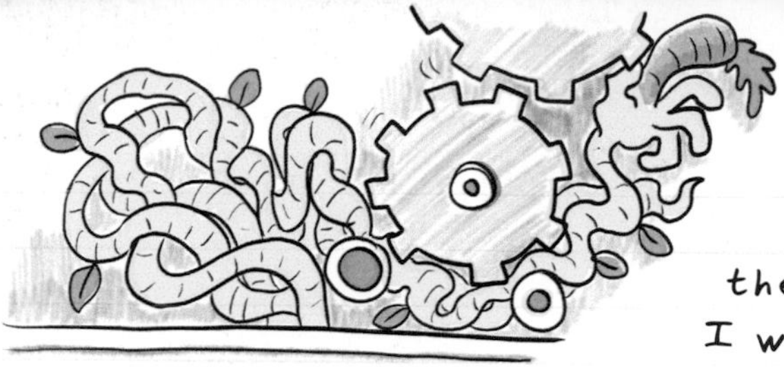

Through a small opening in the hull of the ship I was able to send some of my super stretchy vines in.

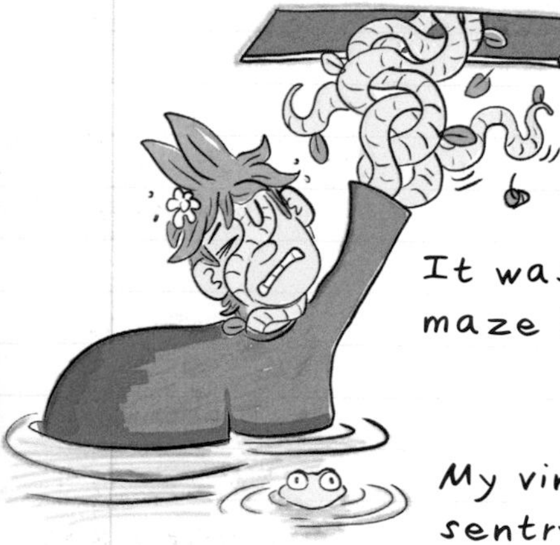

It was like a maze in there.

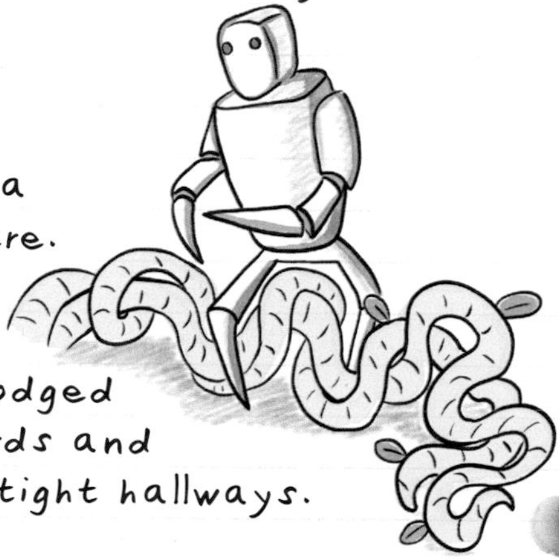

My vines dodged sentry guards and navigated tight hallways.

Then I found it! A lever thingy. And pulling lever thingies in movies always seems to cause trouble, so why not try it in real life?

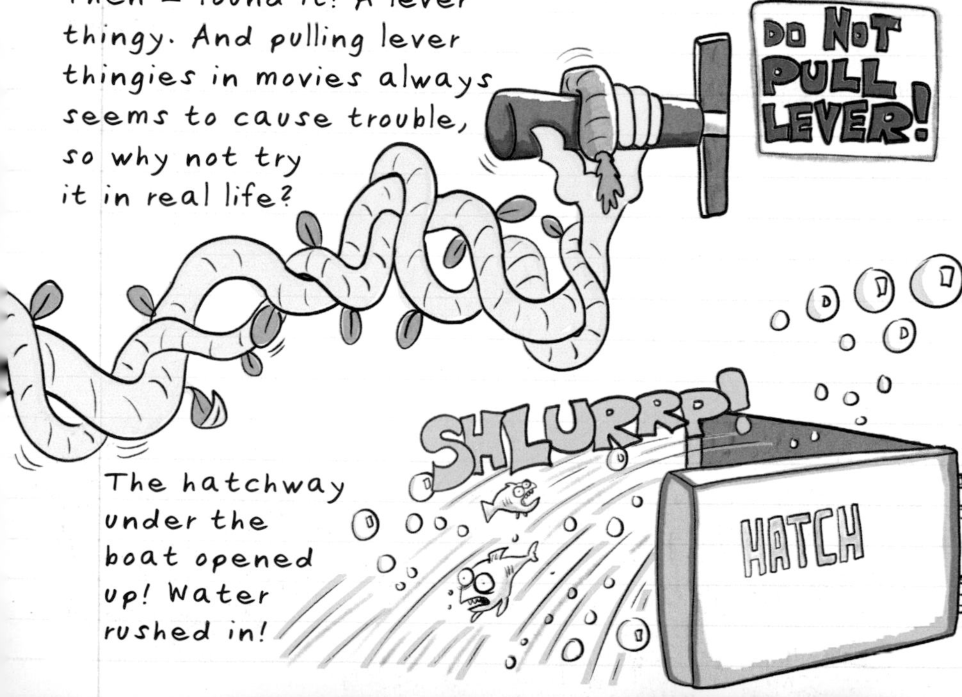
DO NOT PULL LEVER!
SHLURRP!
HATCH

The hatchway under the boat opened up! Water rushed in!

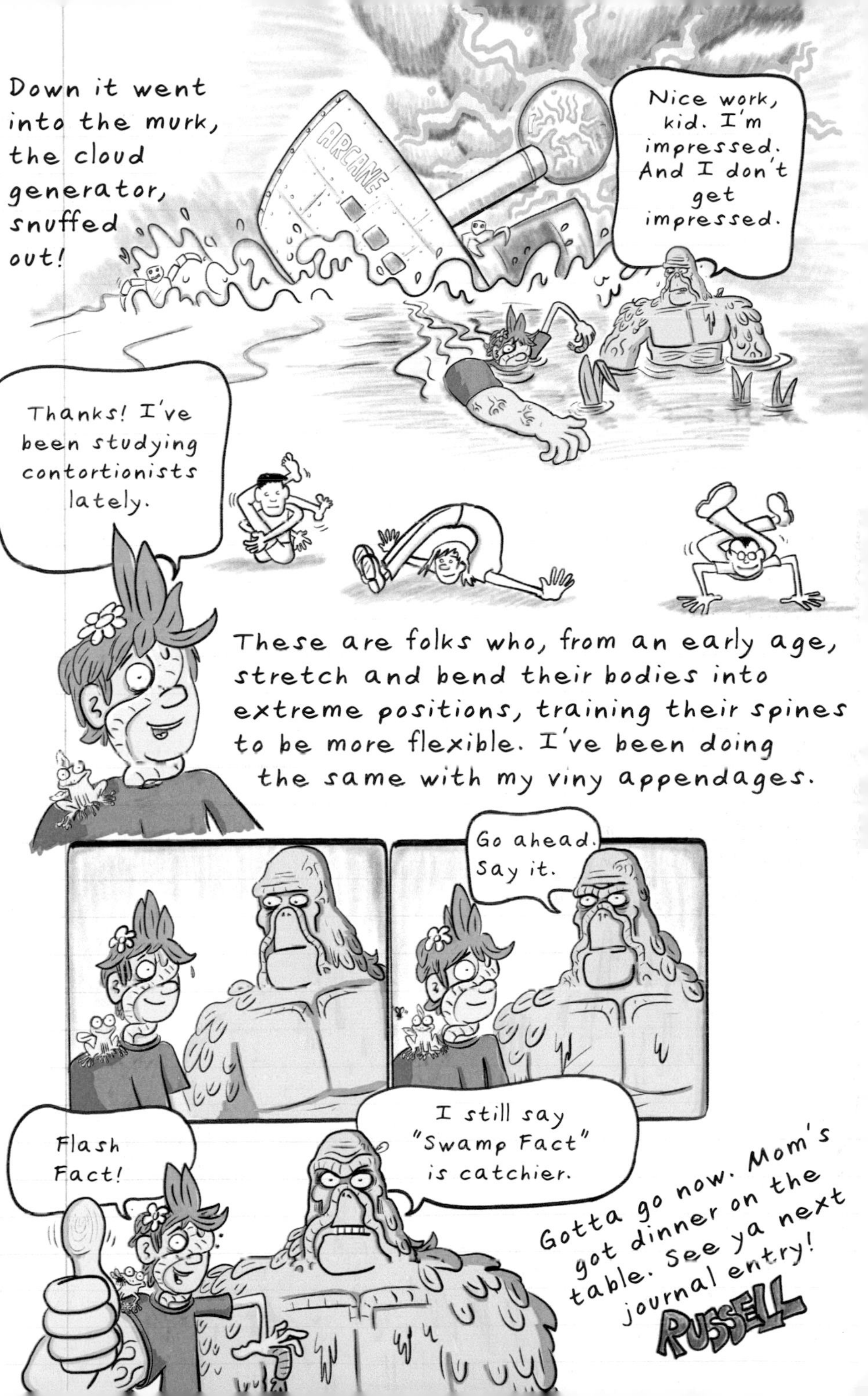
Down it went into the murk, the cloud generator, snuffed out!
ARCANE
Nice work, kid. I'm impressed. And I don't get impressed.
Thanks! I've been studying contortionists lately.
These are folks who, from an early age, stretch and bend their bodies into extreme positions, training their spines to be more flexible. I've been doing the same with my viny appendages.
Go ahead. Say it.
Flash Fact!
I still say "Swamp Fact" is catchier.
Gotta go now. Mom's got dinner on the table. See ya next journal entry!
RUSSELL

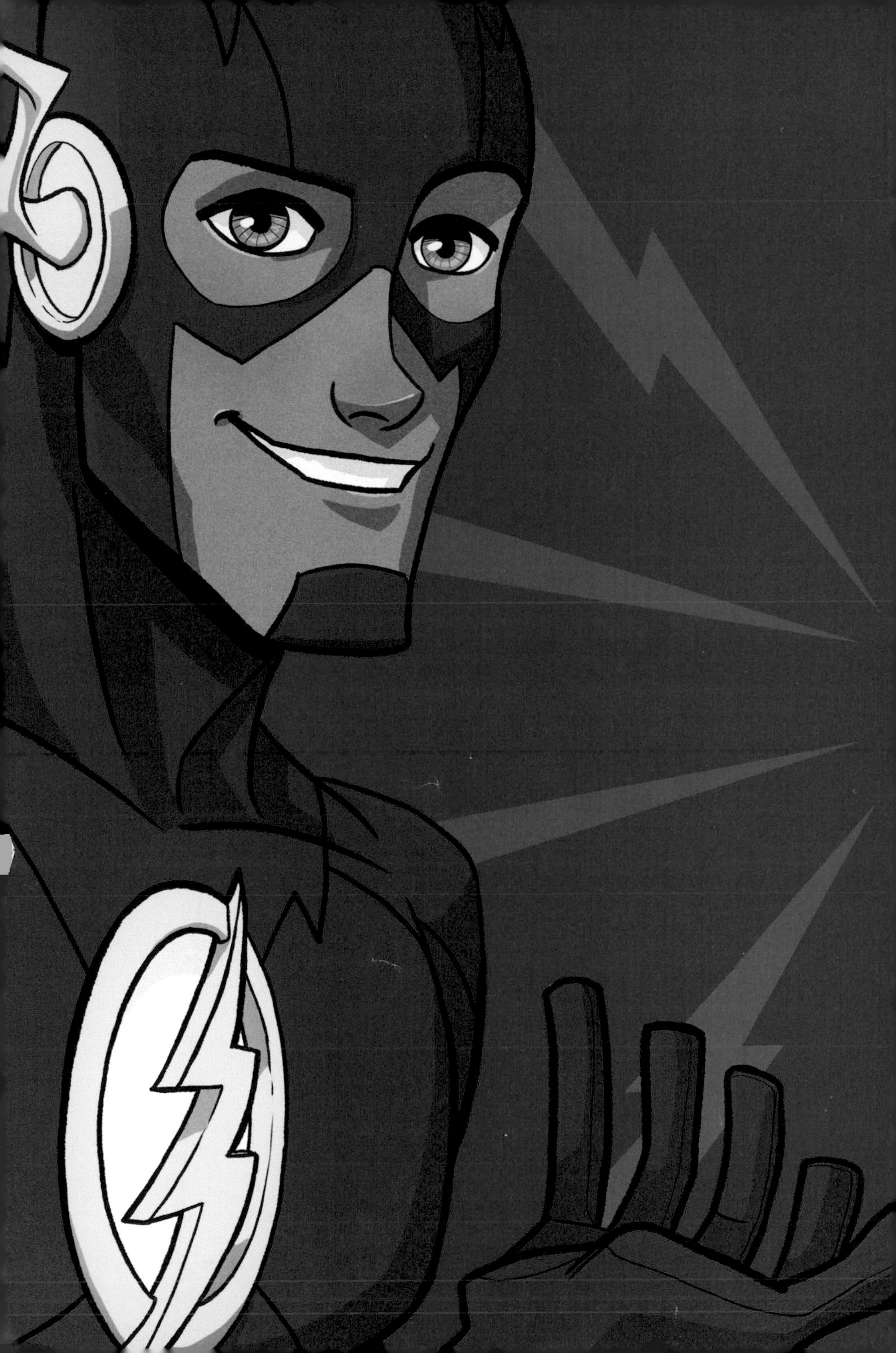

AFTERWORD

Boom! That was quite a ride, am I right?!

We've been through a lot together with *Flash Facts*. From understanding the effects of changes in weather to contemplating DNA as evidence to incorporating ourselves into unreality that is virtually real, what you have just encountered is the intersection of science and comics in a way you've probably never encountered them before.

The fields of science, technology, engineering, and math are changing the world we live in, and we are a part of that every single day. The world is full of wonder, mystery, and infinite possibility, and all of it is within our reach. But trust me: it is no small feat to understand the biggest concepts around— such as the universe!—as well as the tiniest things we can fathom, like atoms and molecules.

I feel confident that everything my friends at DC know about science, from the HUGE to the teeny tiny, is now in your brain—and we think it will stay in there for a long time! One of the most amazing things about being a young thinker now is that the possibilities really are endless in a way they never have been before. We live at a time when our technology and our understanding of the tech world allow us to dream really big. And we can have experiences that we previously could only dream about. I mean, we can think about living on other planets. We can see cars that drive themselves being tested. It's an incredible world!

Maybe you are interested in one day solving crimes like a detective of the future. Maybe you want to make the air we breathe safer for everyone. Maybe your skill set is more along the lines of charting the unknown for future exploration or designing new technology that helps us better understand our world. Whatever effect you have on the world, we hope this book has offered you a fresh look at all of the incredible ways we are touched by the powers of the universe. Let's see what you do with your powers—and make sure to take your parents and friends along with you. You're now empowered with *Flash Facts* knowledge—and we couldn't be happier to be along on this journey with you.

Mayim

REFERENCES

WANT TO DIVE DEEPER INTO THESE TOPICS?

HERE ARE A FEW RESOURCES TO HELP YOU GET STARTED!

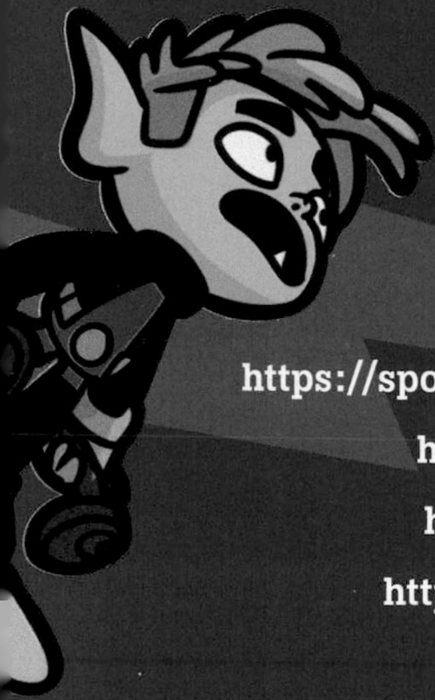

LINKS

https://spaceplace.nasa.gov/

https://spotthestation.nasa.gov/sightings/index.cfm

https://online.kidsdiscover.com/

https://learn.genetics.utah.edu/

https://oceanservice.noaa.gov/kids/

https://kidshealth.org/

YOUTUBE CHANNELS

Teacher's Pet

Crash Course Kids

Amoeba Sisters

Sci Show Kids

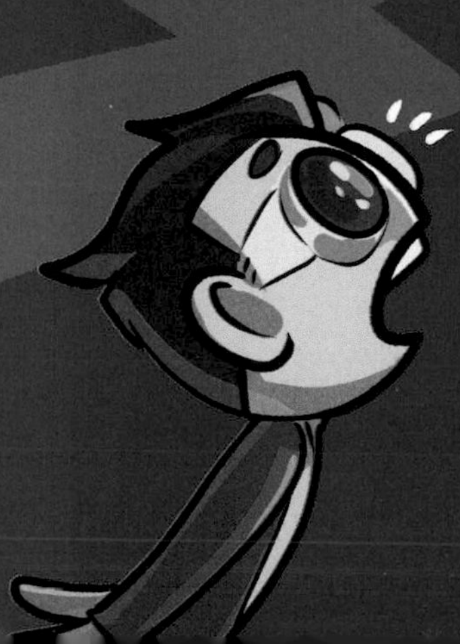

EXPERIMENTS & ACTIVITIES

CHECKING OUT LOCAL SPACE

BACKGROUND:

Finding objects in space is really fun and easy to do. Every object in space, whether it's a satellite that sends a GPS signal to a phone, the International Space Station (ISS), the moon, Mars, or even Jupiter and planets farther away, follows rules when it moves. Thanks to these rules, finding things in the night sky is just a matter of knowing where to look...and maybe having an idea of what to look for.

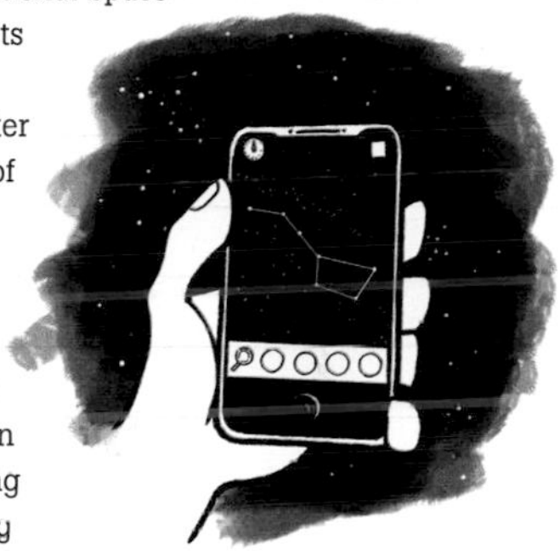

WHAT YOU NEED:

A stargazing app for your mobile device, or a stargazing website for your computer. Usually, the apps for a mobile device show the stars in a map that you can hold up against the sky to spot the objects you're looking for. There are many available—just search for "stargazing apps" to get started.

WHAT TO DO:

On a night with no clouds (or maybe just a couple), go outside with an adult and friends—it's always fun to point out something new to people—figure out which direction is north, and start looking to the skies! Our solar system neighbor, Venus, is very easy to spot—it's really bright! Mars is pretty easy to find as well, and it looks reddish, due to the rusty red dirt that covers it. Jupiter and Saturn are often easily spotted, at the right times of the year for your location, as well. Once you've found our neighbors, you can start spotting the stars and the constellations, which are patterns that we've put stars into over the years.

WHAT'S GOING ON?

Looking out into space is lots of fun and can be really exciting! The planets and stars are visible at certain times on certain nights during certain seasons because while the Earth is moving around the sun, the other planets are moving too. We see different sets of stars at different times during the year because we move in relation to them. They're so far away from us that it's difficult for us to see their motion.

TAKING IT FURTHER:

You can use most apps to look for and spot satellites high overhead as well! Satellites are devices that we've put into space that orbit the earth, so they're much, much closer to us than planets or stars are. One satellite that is really fun to spot is the International Space Station (ISS), where astronauts from all around the world live and work. Due to its orbit, it's not always visible, so you'll want to check out "Spot the Station" at nasa.gov to see when it's over your neighborhood. It's bright and moving very fast, so it will come up on one side of the sky and quickly travel across to the other. Wave to the astronauts as they cross the night sky!

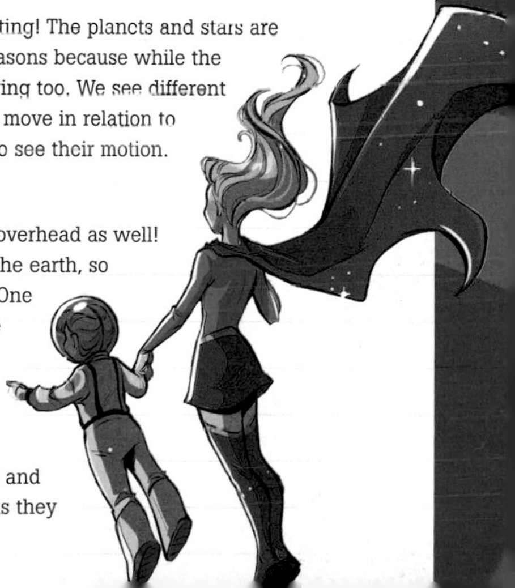

SEA ICE

BACKGROUND:

Oceanography is the science that studies the oceans—everything in them and how they work. Some oceanographers study icebergs—the huge chunks of ice that float near the North and South Poles.

Along with icebergs, there's a lot of other ice in the oceans near the poles. Vast shelves of ice spread and grow from Antarctica, while the North Pole is covered over in ice (although the amount of ice is shrinking due to climate change) in the Northern Hemisphere's winter months.

But all of that ice that you've seen? Even though the oceans are salt water, all the ice floating in it is fresh water. Icebergs come from glaciers, which are huge masses of ice on land that flow into the ocean, but what about that ice that forms on the ocean? How can that be fresh water? That's what you're going to find out!

WHAT YOU NEED:

1. A piece of black (or very dark) paper or cloth that lies flat
2. Table salt
3. Bottled water (distilled is best—some tap water has lots of dissolved solids in it, so you want water that's just...water)
4. A small plastic cup

salt water
ice
salt water after ice

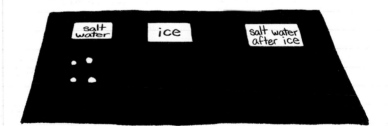

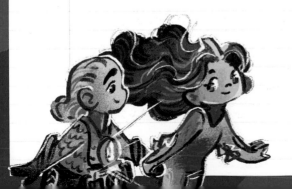

WHAT TO DO:

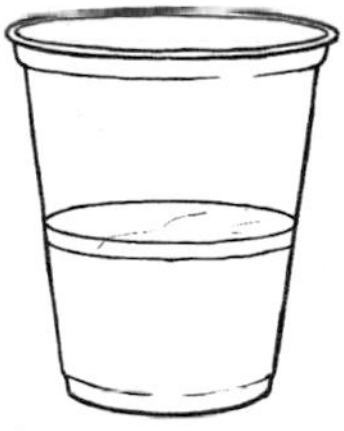

1. Put about a quarter of a cup of water in the plastic cup and then add a spoonful of salt. Stir until all the salt has dissolved and the solution is clear.
2. Label an area of the dark paper as "salt water" and place a couple of very small drops on the paper. You're going to let these drops evaporate and leave their salt behind.
3. Place that salt water cup in the freezer and check on it every 10–15 minutes to see if ice has formed on the surface.
4. When the layer of ice is about a quarter of an inch thick, take the cup out of the freezer and pull the ice out of the cup.
5. Give the ice a very quick rinse in cold water to remove any salt that might be holding on, and place a couple of small bits of ice on the dark paper in a spot labeled "ice." Let these drips evaporate and see if anything was left behind.
6. Label another spot on the dark paper "salt water after ice" and put another couple of very small drops of water from the cup on the paper.
7. Once all the water has evaporated, compare the amount of salt left behind from each source. You may need a magnifying glass or to use your phone's camera to zoom in.

WHAT'S GOING ON?

When salt mixes with water, the salt water that results has a lower freezing point than the water alone did. In other words, salty ocean water doesn't freeze at 32°F (0°C), but around 28°F (-2°C). When it does get that cold, the water part of seawater freezes, leaving almost all the salt behind. The result is freshwater ice, and a saltier area of water near the ice.

TAKING IT FURTHER:

Try this experiment again and see if you can get another layer of ice to form on your remaining salt water. Label the paper and keep track of the samples you're evaporating. Does the remaining water get saltier and saltier? Does it take the ice longer to form? Seawater is about 3.5 percent salt by weight, so if you want to simulate the saltiness of ocean water, try your experiment with about 1½ tablespoons of salt in 16 ounces of water to see how much ice you can form and how salty your water will get!

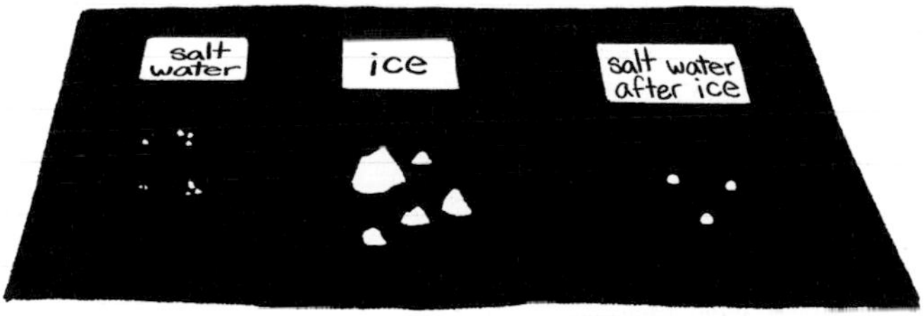
salt water
ice
salt water after ice

ENERGY

BACKGROUND:

For electricity to do useful things, it has to move. That means there has to be a pathway both to and from the device that uses it, as well as a source of electricity for something to work. And along with that, the pathway has to allow the electricity to travel easily—or in other words, the pathway has to conduct electricity. Then these three things together—a source of electricity, a pathway, and a device to use the electricity—are called a circuit.

Making circuits is easy when you have the right pieces!

Be careful! With this activity, you are going to be using electricity from batteries—have an adult help you, and never, ever play with electricity from outlets or anything larger than small batteries.

WHAT YOU NEED:

1. Two short wires with the metal ends exposed from the rubber insulation coating (called "stripped" ends)
2. A small light bulb from a flashlight
3. At least one battery (a D cell works fine, as does a nine-volt)
4. Tape—either cellophane or masking tape

WHAT TO DO:

Look at the battery—one terminal (or end) will have a (+) sign by it while the other will have a (-) sign. This means the positive (+) and negative (-) terminals of the battery. Tape one end of one of your wires to that end/terminal, and then tape one end of your other wire to the other terminal. Touch both of the opposite ends of the wires to the light bulb. You may need to adjust how the wires touch the light bulb a little to get it to light. It's okay, you can touch the bare wires— the amount of electricity is so small you won't even feel it.

You made a circuit!

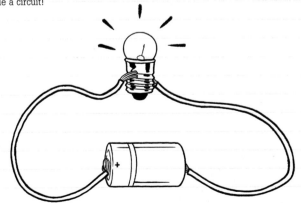

WHAT'S GOING ON?

What you've made is a series circuit. In series circuits, electricity flows in one direction "out" from the positive terminal of the battery, through the wire and the device, and back into the battery at the negative terminal. When you're talking about something being powered by batteries, they're almost always powering a series circuit.

And remember, to keep the light bulb lit you need to have all three parts of the circuit touching each other. If they're not touching, there's no way for the electricity to flow through the circuit.

TAKING IT FURTHER:

How bright was your light bulb with one battery? What do you think would happen with two D-cell batteries? Try it out! What about those wires? Do you think you could find other things that would allow the electricity to flow through them? What about a paper clip? A dollar bill? An eraser? A plastic spoon? A metal spoon? Things that allow electricity to pass through them are called conductors, and they're everywhere! After a few tests, you should be able to figure out what types of materials make good conductors, and which ones don't conduct electricity at all!

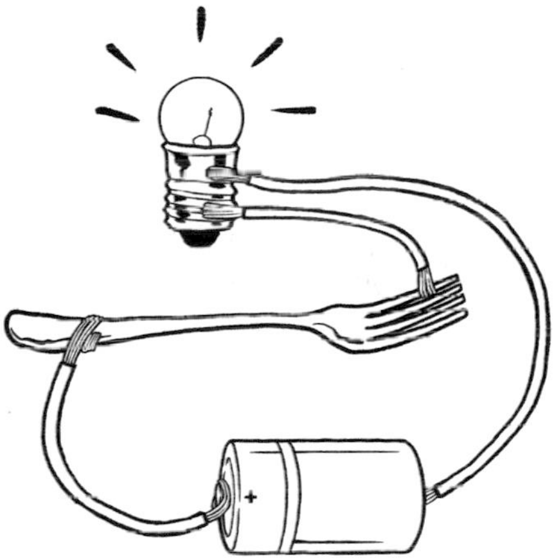

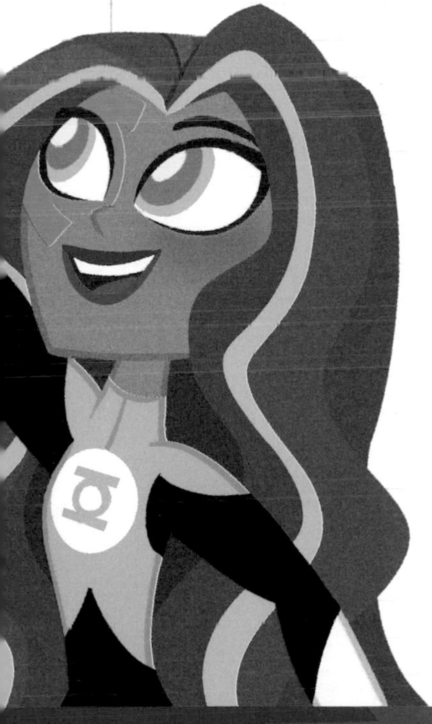

SUBATOMIC— ATOMS IN ACTION!

BACKGROUND:

One of the ways chemists and physicists understand matter is called the kinetic molecular theory. One of its main ideas is that everything—all matter—is made of small particles (either atoms or molecules) that are always moving. And when you heat up the particles, they move faster.

This constant motion explains why solids, liquids, and gases act the way they do. The particles in solids are barely moving, those in liquids are moving more than those in solids, and the particles in a gas, like air, are constantly zooming around, bouncing into one another and the walls of whatever container they're in.

While atoms and molecules are far too small to see with our eyes, we can see their actions— and we're going to use some food coloring and water to do it!

WHAT YOU NEED:

1. A clear glass or plastic cup
2. Food coloring—a dark color works the best

WHAT TO DO:

1. Fill the glass about three-quarters of the way full with warm tap water.
2. Set the glass on a flat surface and let the water settle so its surface is flat.
3. Carefully drip three drops of food coloring into the water.
4. Observe what happens to the food coloring.

WHAT'S GOING ON?

The food coloring spreads out throughout the water, almost like it's alive—but there's nothing alive here. Think small! The molecules of the water are warm, so they're moving around very quickly in the glass, sliding past and sometimes bumping into one another. When you added the food coloring, you put something new into the water for the molecules to hit. While you're seeing the food coloring spreading out, what's really going on is billions and billions of crashes between the water molecules and the food coloring particles. Put all those crashes together, and it looks like the coloring is gently spreading through the water. You're seeing the effect of moving molecules!

TAKING IT FURTHER:

What do you think would happen if the water in the glass were hotter? What if it were colder? Ask an adult to help you, and repeat the steps above, but this time, use very hot water and very cold water (let the glass sit in the freezer for a few minutes). When everything's ready, line your three glasses up—hot, warm, and cold—and drip food coloring in. Did it match what you thought would happen? What's going on with the molecules of water at the different temperatures?

HUMAN EXTREMES

BACKGROUND:

Have you ever wished that you were faster than a speeding bullet? Or could leap tall buildings in a single bound? Well, you may be more super than you think. Reflexes are what allow us to make split-second decisions even before we are consciously aware of doing it, and it's this ability that can save lives or at least stop you from getting burned when you accidentally touch the hot stove while making your ramen.

How fast are we really? And is there a difference between age groups and genders? Does it matter if you're team Xbox or PlayStation? We could list questions all day long (that's what makes science interesting), but how do we go about answering these questions? You've come to the right place. Find a friend and let's get to sciencing!

WHAT YOU NEED:

1. A ruler at least 12 inches long (30 cm)
2. Pen and paper
3. Friends (or enemies)

WHAT TO DO:

1. Hold the ruler between your thumb and forefinger with your arm straight out. You should be holding the ruler at the end with the largest measurement.
2. Ask your friend to put their thumb and forefinger slightly open at the base of the ruler but not touching it.
3. Randomly drop the ruler and record the measurement where your friend catches it. It's important not to let them know when you are going to drop the ruler.
4. Repeat three times and average your data. (Add up your measurements and divide by three.)
5. Winner gets bragging rights.

WHAT'S GOING ON?

Reflexes refer to the time it takes for your eyes to see that the ruler is falling and send a signal to the brain, which then tells the muscles to move the fingers. It all happens very fast. The smaller the number, the faster your eyes, brain, and fingers were able to communicate.

There are many types of reflexes, but protective reflexes are very important. Aside from being able to move our hands away from something hot, we sneeze or cough when something foreign enters our respiratory tract and we blink and produce tears when something gets into our eyes.

TAKING IT FURTHER:

Try comparing reflexes of different groups of people and see if there are patterns to how fast someone reacts. Can you think of other ways to test reflexes?

WEATHER & CLIMATE

BACKGROUND:
Living on the surface of the Earth, we've got anywhere from 10 to 15 miles of air above us. All that air is matter and has mass—in other words, it has weight and it pushes on everything on the surface, from all directions. We don't feel it or even notice it because we have always lived with it pushing on us. This push from the air is called air pressure. If you climb a mountain or go up in an airplane, there's less air above you, so there's less of a push, and your ears pop.

How air pressure works on everything around us is easy to show with some water and a plastic bottle!

WHAT YOU NEED:
1. A plastic bottle—this can be a two-liter bottle or any size smaller, like a water bottle. One important thing—it has to have a screw-on cap.
2. Something to poke a small hole in the bottle.

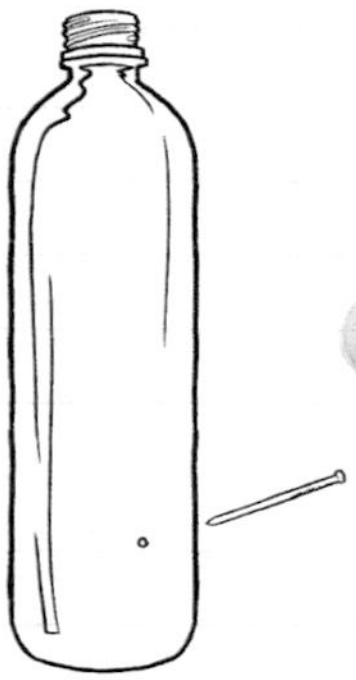

WHAT TO DO:
1. With a grown-up's help, poke a small hole ($3/8$ of an inch is perfect) about one-quarter of the way up from the bottom of the bottle. Hey, adults—if you're using a small nail, heating it up really hot and then poking it through the bottle works just great! Be careful with your smaller helpers, though…

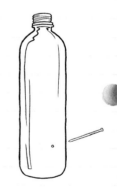

2. Put your finger over the hole, and then fill the bottle with water all the way up to the top. Place the cap on the bottle and screw it down tight. It's okay if you lose a little bit of water.
3. Gently set the bottle down on a level surface that you won't mind getting wet—beside the sink is great. Remove your finger from the hole. What's happening?
4. Now, this is a little tricky, and done best with a helper. Put your finger over the hole again and ask a helper to gently unscrew the cap just a little—but leave it on the bottle. Remove your finger from the hole. What's happening?
5. Take the cap all the way off the bottle. What's happening?

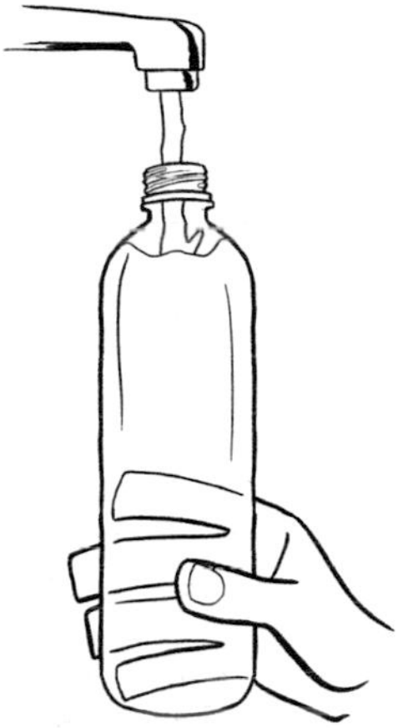

WHAT'S GOING ON?

When the cap is tightly screwed down on the bottle, there's no way for the air pressure to get into the bottle, so there's nothing pushing down on the water to force it out of the hole. The pressure in the bottle is lower than the pressure outside the bottle. When the cap is unscrewed, even just a little, the pressure from the air can go up and under the cap to press down on the water, which means the pressure inside the bottle is equal to the pressure outside, so the water flows out the hole. Air pressure is awesome!

TAKING IT FURTHER:

With the cap on the bottle and water inside, all it takes is a slight increase in pressure to make the water come out of the hole. Anything from a gentle tap to a squeeze on the bottle will increase the pressure inside the bottle and push the water through the hole. This is a time where science looks like magic if you don't know what's going on!

Can you think of some other times and places where you interact with air pressure?

Here are two to start your list: the weather and a straw.

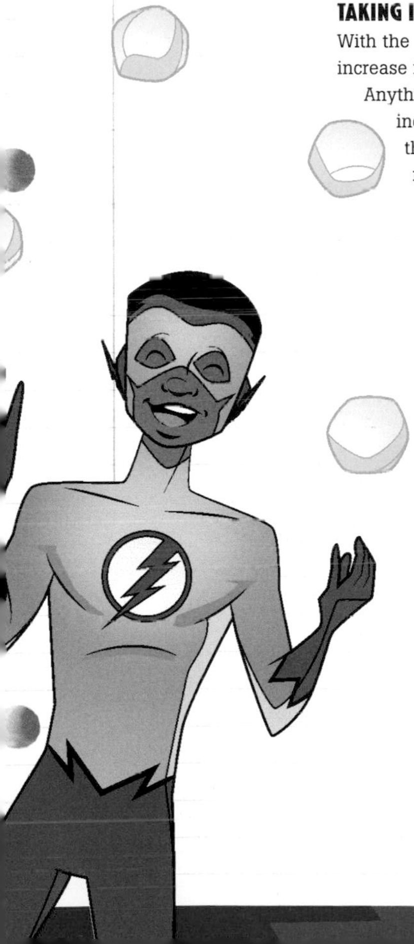

FORENSICS

BACKGROUND:

Forensics is the science used to help solve crimes. It includes biology, chemistry, physics, and good old-fashioned sleuthing. Even with all of the fancy tech we have currently, nothing is as simple and as powerful as fingerprint data. A fingerprint is generally always left behind on the surface of an object when touched with a bare hand due to the natural oils in our skin. It's pretty simple to lift this print and compare it to another one as a means of identifying the person who left it behind.

Fingerprints are unique to each individual and are a great tool for identification. But what about identical twins? Great question, but even twins have different sets of fingerprints because the patterns are set while still in the womb, and while genetics plays a role, the position of the fetus during this time plays a large part in determining the specific pattern of loops, whorls, and arches that make up the final fingerprint.

WHAT YOU NEED:

1. A smooth, flat object such as a microscope slide, small mirror, or even a plastic report cover taped down on a table
2. Fingerprint powder—this can be cornstarch or cocoa powder
3. Fingerprint brush—any small paintbrush with very soft bristles
4. Clear adhesive tape

WHAT TO DO:

1. Touch the flat surface with your finger a few times to leave prints. You can rub a soft pencil lead over your finger or touch the side of your nose for more obvious prints.
2. Gently shake a very small amount of the powder evenly over the prints. A kitchen strainer could help get this evenly spread. Gently brush away the excess or blow it away if it won't be too messy. This may take some practice. It should leave the fingerprint intact.
3. Stick a piece of tape firmly over the print and then lift it up. The print should stick to the tape. Stick the tape to a piece of contrasting paper to preserve it.

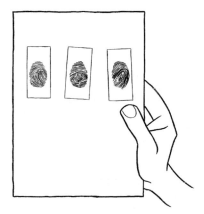

WHAT'S GOING ON?

The patterns are formed by ridges in the bottom layer of your skin called the dermis. Oils from your fingers left an impression of your prints on the flat surface. The powder stuck to these oils, and the pattern was transferred to the tape. This is why using the graphite from the pencil or adding extra oils to your fingers can lead to better prints.

TAKING IT FURTHER:

After you become an expert at doing this, try lifting prints from other surfaces around the house such as a doorknob, faucet handle, or cell phone (be careful with the powder if using a cell phone, and make sure to lift the prints from a screen protector rather than the surface of the phone). You can also lift prints directly from your fingers if using the graphite. Simply color on a piece of paper with a pencil and rub your finger over the graphite left behind. Place the tape directly onto your finger and then onto a piece of white paper. Collect family members' prints and see if you can determine any similarities or maybe solve a mystery in your own home.

BIOTECH

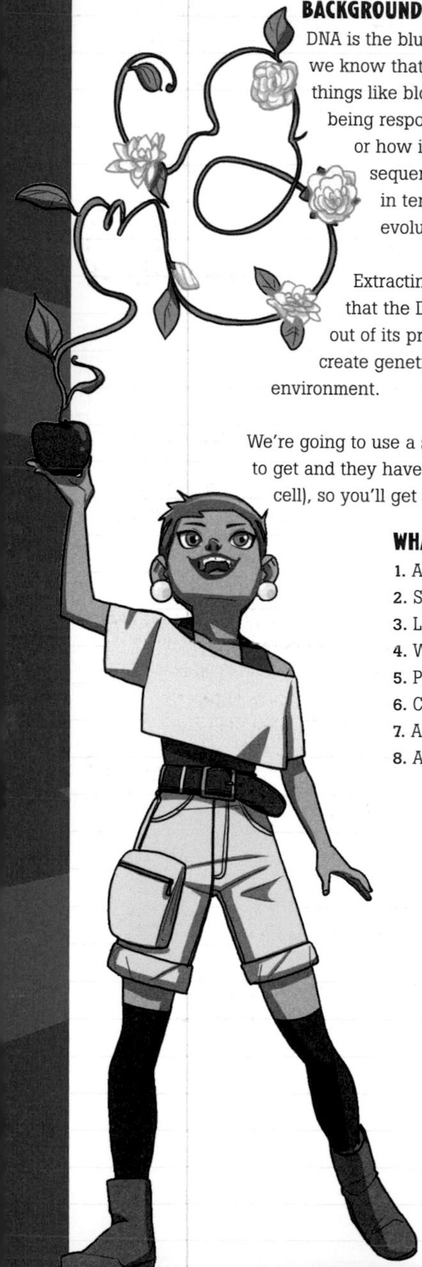

BACKGROUND:

DNA is the blueprint for all living things on the planet, past and present. Yeah, we know that the information contained in the DNA molecule is responsible for things like blood type and hair/eye color, but we never think of it in terms of being responsible for things like how we create energy from the food we eat or how it tells a plant to make glucose out of sunlight. It's these conserved sequences that not only allow us to use this molecule to drive the future in terms of bioengineering but also give us a window into our past evolutionary history.

Extracting DNA from living organisms is relatively simple, but keep in mind that the DNA you extract here will degrade pretty quickly once it's pulled out of its protective nucleus. Molecular biologists who bioengineer DNA to create genetically modified organisms do so in a very sterile, highly controlled environment.

We're going to use a strawberry for our experiment today for two reasons: they're easy to get and they have eight copies of their entire genome (total DNA sequence in the cell), so you'll get a lot of DNA out of one strawberry.

WHAT YOU NEED:

1. A resealable plastic bag
2. Strawberries (fresh or frozen)
3. Liquid dish detergent
4. Water
5. Plastic cups
6. Cold rubbing alcohol (place the bottle in the freezer for a few hours)
7. A coffee stirrer or toothpick
8. A paper coffee filter

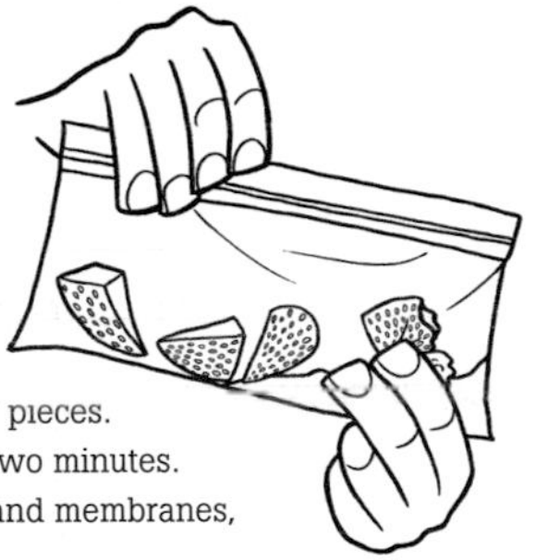

WHAT TO DO:

1. Pull off any green leaves that may still be on the strawberry and cut the remaining fruit into three or four pieces.

2. Place into the plastic bag and *gently* crush for about two minutes. This starts the process by breaking open the cell walls and membranes, releasing the cellular contents.

3. In a plastic cup make the DNA extraction liquid by mixing together two teaspoons of liquid dish detergent, one teaspoon of salt, and ½ cup of water.

4. Add two teaspoons of this liquid into the bag with the strawberries. Reseal and *gently* smash for another minute. Try to be gentle and avoid making too many bubbles.

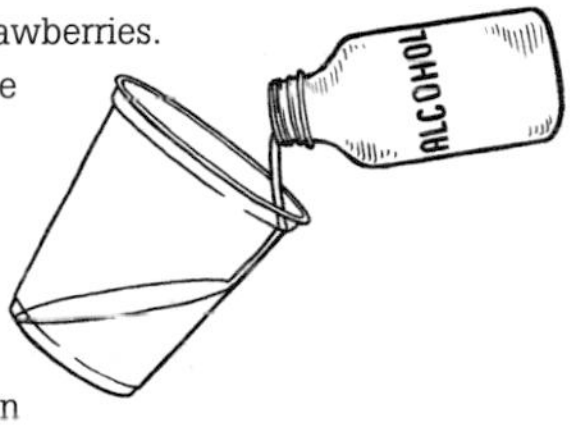
ALCOHOL

5. Place the coffee filter inside a clean plastic cup and pour the strawberry liquid into the filter. You can twist the filter closed and gently squeeze the remaining liquid into the cup. Be careful not to break the filter. Throw away the filter.

6. Take the alcohol out of the freezer and gently pour it down the side of the cup at an angle. Do not mix or stir at this point. You are beginning to isolate the DNA from the rest of the cellular material.

7. Within a few seconds you should see a cloudy white substance form in the alcohol layer. Take your coffee stirrer or toothpick and gently swirl it around—your DNA will stick to the end of the toothpick!

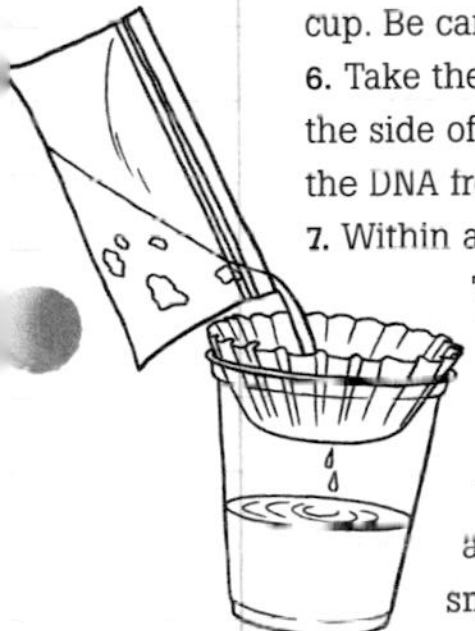

WHAT'S GOING ON?

The DNA is found inside the cell in a smaller compartment called a nucleus. These are all surrounded by cell membranes that are made of lipids. When you initially smash the strawberry you start to break apart the hard outer cell wall (only found in plants, by the way). The addition of the soap helps to break apart the lipids in the membrane, much like how soap will wash away grease and oil from your dirty dishes. The DNA will not dissolve in alcohol, so when you pour the alcohol over the top of the strawberry liquid, the DNA present will precipitate (fall out of solution) and form a white substance you can see with your eyes.

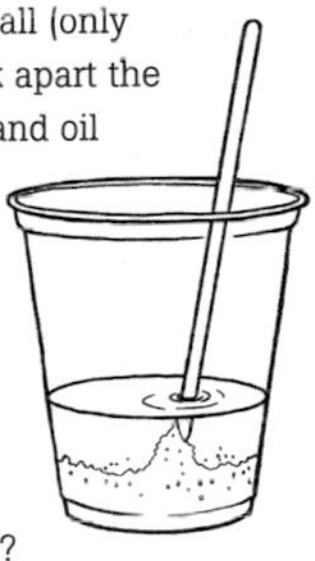

TAKING IT FURTHER:

So pretty cool, huh? You have a lot of extraction buffer left over, and it will keep in the fridge for a few days, so why not try other fruits and vegetables? Compare the amount of DNA in a strawberry to a banana or an apple. What about you? Using a similar technique, this is possible. You won't get nearly as much DNA as from the strawberry, but it is certainly possible. Do some research and write your own procedure to extract your own DNA!

BIOS

MAYIM HOYA BIALIK

is best known for portraying Bette Midler's character as a child in *Beaches* as well as for her subsequent lead role as Blossom Russo in the early-1990s NBC television sitcom *Blossom*. Bialik most recently appeared regularly on the #1 comedy in America, CBS's *The Big Bang Theory*, playing neurobiologist Amy Farrah Fowler, a role for which she has been a four-time Emmy nominee and two-time Critics' Choice Award winner. She will star in an upcoming multicamera sitcom, *Call Me Kat,* airing on Fox in fall 2020.

Bialik earned a BS in neuroscience and Hebrew and Jewish studies from UCLA in 2000, and a PhD in neuroscience, also from UCLA, in 2007. Her book about attachment parenting, *Beyond the Sling*, was published in March 2012 (Simon and Schuster). Her vegan cookbook, *Mayim's Vegan Table*, was published by Da Capo Press in the spring of 2014. Bialik also has two *New York Times* bestsellers with *Girling Up: How to Be Strong, Smart and Spectacular* (Philomel Books, 2017) and *Boying Up: How to Be Brave, Bold and Brilliant* (Philomel Books 2018).

COVER

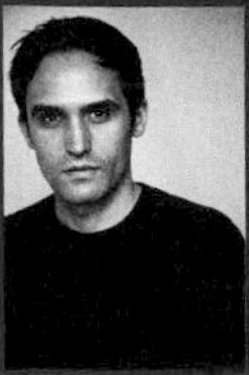

DEREK CHARM is an Eisner Award–winning comics artist and illustrator living in New York. He was the artist on *Jughead, The Unbeatable Squirrel Girl, Star Wars Adventures*, and the upcoming graphic novel *The Mystery of the Meanest Teacher*. His favorite feature of our solar system is the Oort cloud.

photo credit: Rémi Lamandé

FAST TRACKS

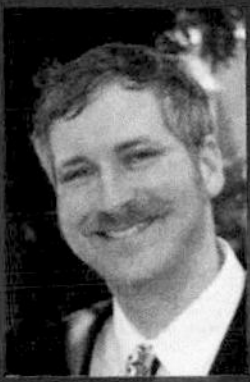

Bitten by a radioactive typewriter, **SHOLLY FISCH** prowls the night writing comics like *Scooby-Doo Team-Up, Teen Titans Go!*, and *The All-New Batman: The Brave and the Bold*. His comics for kids have won a *Comics Buyer's Guide* Fan Award, and have been nominated for an Eisner Award and four Diamond Gem Awards. Several of his Superman stories for older readers appeared in two #1 *New York Times* bestselling graphic novels. By day, Sholly is a mild-mannered developmental psychologist who has helped produce educational TV shows and games, including *Sesame Street, Cyberchase, The Magic School Bus Rides Again*, and lots of things you've probably never heard of.

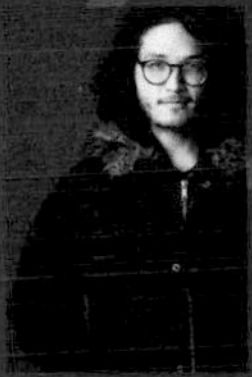

ISAAC GOODHART got his start in comics in 2014 as one of the winners of the Top Cow Talent Hunt. After drawing *Artifacts* #38, he moved on to illustrating Matt Hawkins's *Postal* for 26 consecutive issues. He recently illustrated *Under the Moon: A Catwoman Tale* and *Victor and Nora: A Gotham Love Story*, both written by Lauren Myracle and published by DC Comics.

photo credit: Cecile Vaccaro

IF YOU CAN'T TAKE THE HEAT

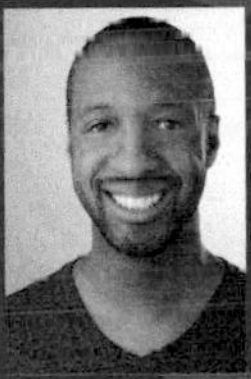

VARIAN JOHNSON is the author of numerous novels for young readers, including *The Parker Inheritance*, which was named a Coretta Scott King Honor Book, and the graphic novel *Twins*. Prior to becoming a full-time author, Varian worked as a structural engineer, designing bridges all across Texas. He currently lives outside of Austin, Texas, with his family, and can be found online at varianjohnson.com.

photo credit: Kenneth Gall

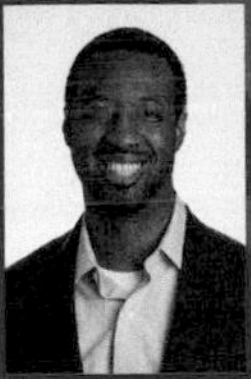

DARIAN JOHNSON works for a large technology company where he leads major cloud computing initiatives. Darian is also a hobbyist maker of electronic and 3D printed projects. His projects have been granted patents, have won multiple awards, and have been featured in numerous publications. Darian and his family reside in Dallas, Texas. He can be found online at darianbjohnson.com.

photo credit: Alex Claney Photography

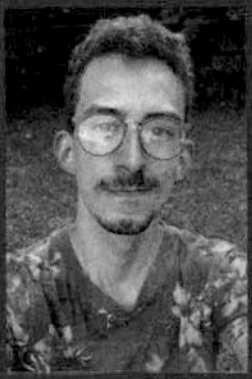

VIC REGIS is a freelance illustrator and comics artist hailing from Brazil. He is best known for his colorful pieces and his webcomic *Hexile*—under the alias TheDamnThinGuy—which was of one of Tapas's and Webtoon's staff picks in 2016 and 2019, respectively. He is passionate about roller coasters, video games, and fictional characters that could bench-press him.

photo credit: Vic Regis

THE FACTS OF LIFE

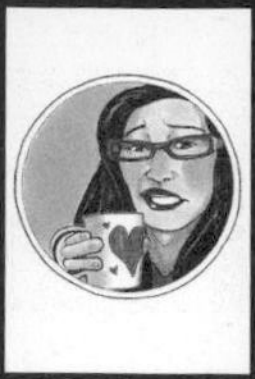

AMY CHU is a writer for comics, graphic novels, and TV. She has written popular characters such as Wonder Woman, Deadpool, Ant-Man, and Iron Man. She wrote Poison Ivy's first solo miniseries, and is the first woman to write the *Green Hornet* and *KISS* comics series. She is also the author of children's graphic novels including *Sea Sirens* and the sequel, *Sky Island*, published by Penguin Random House. She holds degrees from Wellesley College, M.I.T., and Harvard University and enjoys coffee, Lego, and donuts.

image credit: Janet K. Lee

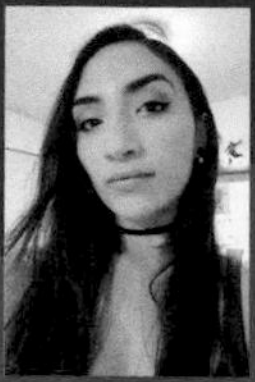

ILE GONZALEZ illustrated her first comic strip while in kindergarten and she grew up to study fashion design in college. Deciding graphic storytelling was her first true love, she refocused her creative efforts and landed her first paid work at the digital storytelling company Madefire, working exclusively for them and co-creating their popular middle grade series *The Heroes Club*. Ile most recently illustrated the Super Sons trilogy for the DC Graphic Novels for Kids imprint.

photo credit: Ile Gonzalez

MORE THAN MEETS THE EYE

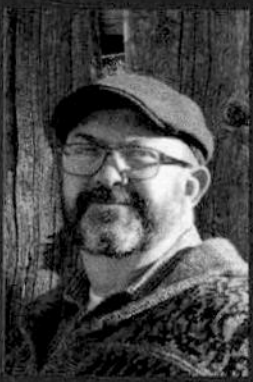

DUSTIN HANSEN has been making video games, drawing comics, and writing stories for nearly 30 years. His latest graphic novel is *My Video Game Ate My Homework*, which is an actual excuse he may or may not have used in the past. He lives in Utah on his little farm with his fine family of fellow artists.

photo credit: Jodi Hansen

LIGHTS-OUT

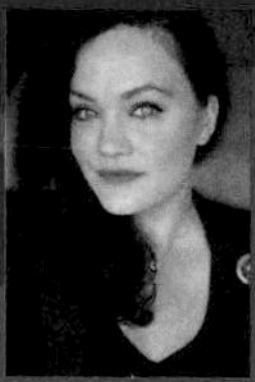

AMANDA DEIBERT is an award-winning television and comic book writer. Her work includes *DC Super Hero Girls*, *Teen Titans Go!*, *Wonder Woman '77*, *Sensation Comics Featuring Wonder Woman*, and a story in *Love Is Love* (a *New York Times* #1 bestseller) along with comics for IDW, Dark Horse, Bedside Press, and Storm King. She's written TV shows for CBS, Syfy, OWN, Hulu, and Quibi, and for former vice president Al Gore's international climate broadcast, *24 Hours of Reality*. She lives in Los Angeles with her wife, Cat Staggs, adorable daughter, Vivienne, and kitty, Raven.

photo credit: Cat Staggs

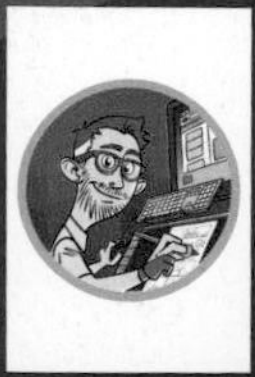

ERICH OWEN is the co-creator and illustrator of the graphic novel series *Mail Order Ninja*, which was published from 2005 to 2006 by Tokyopop. Since then, he has illustrated fun projects for companies like Viper Comics, IDW, Andrews McMeel, CBS, and DC Comics. Currently, he's creating *DC Super Hero Girls* and *Teen Titans Go!* stories for DC Comics from his home in San Diego, where he lives with his wife, two teen daughters, and five cats. Oh, and one time he ate lunch with Captain Kirk himself, William Shatner, to discuss a comics project; he was great!

image credit: Erich Owen

EDUCATIONAL EXPERTS

MATT BRADY teaches high school physics and chemistry and uses a lot—a lot—of pop culture as examples to engage and excite his students. Along with his wife, Shari, he co-founded thescienceof.org where he writes about the intersection of pop culture and science and, with Shari, preaches the gospel of pop culture and STEM at science education conferences, comic cons, and more. He is also the author of *The Science of Rick and Morty.* He and Shari live in Winston-Salem, North Carolina, and have one son who thinks his parents are nerds, but who loves and respects them just the same.

photo credit: Shari Brady

SHARI BRADY is a high school biology teacher by day and adjunct professor of education by night. Teaching from both sides of the mirror gives her a unique perspective on what makes good science teaching. She has a strong science background with a master's degree in marine biology and a PhD in K-12 science education. In addition to teaching, she runs thescienceof.org—a non-profit with a mission to make science accessible and engaging for everyone—with her husband, Matt Brady. She lives in Winston-Salem, North Carolina, with Matt. Together they have one son away at college and a dog, Jack, that is happy to replace him.

photo credit: Shari Brady

EDUCATIONAL REVIEWER

TRACY EDMUNDS, MA Ed, is an educator and author specializing in both hands-on STEM learning and the use of comics in K-12 education. She currently works with DC Comics, Andrews McMeel, Teacher Created Resources, and the nonprofit Reading with Pictures, and was the chair of the children's jury for the 2020 Excellence in Graphic Literature Awards. Tracy, her husband, two daughters, and two Labrador retrievers live in Southern California where they enjoy spending time at local dog parks and Disneyland. Tracy loves volunteering at a local wildlife zoo where she works with rescued animals including bears, beavers, porcupines, and turkey vultures.

SEA FOR YOURSELF

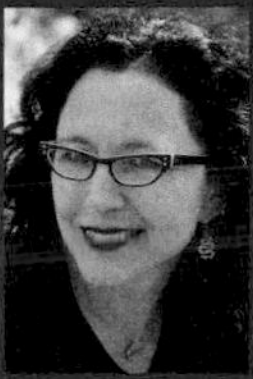

CORINNA BECHKO is a Hugo- and Eisner-nominated *New York Times* bestselling author who has worked for numerous publishers including DC, Marvel, Dark Horse, Boom!, and Sideshow on titles such as *Star Wars: Legacy*, *Savage Hulk*, *Angel*, *Once Upon a Time*, *Court of the Dead*, and *Green Lantern: Earth One*. She co-writes *Invisible Republic* with Gabriel Hardman. Her book for young readers, *Smithsonian Dig It: Dinosaurs and Other Prehistoric Creatures*, co-written with Brenda Scott Royce, appeared last year, at last allowing her day job as a fossil preparator to meld with her writing endeavors. There are more endangered parrots living wild in Los Angeles than there are in many of their native ranges, a fact Corinna knows well because she's a transport volunteer with a naturalized parrot rescue in San Diego, helping to get injured birds to their specialized facility from all over LA County.

photo credit: Gabriel Hardman

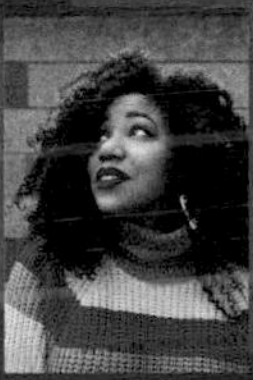

YESENIA MOISES is an Afro-Latina illustrator and designer with a specialty in toy design. Her work proudly portrays people of diverse backgrounds in fantasy worlds where they lead adventures that are brimming with color. Yesenia is the illustrator of *Honeysmoke: A Story of Finding Your Color* and *Stella's Stellar Hair*, her first picture book as both author and illustrator. She aspires to be able to take great photos, like her wildly photogenic dog Divom, someday.

photo credit: Christina Mallas

WEATHER OR NOT...

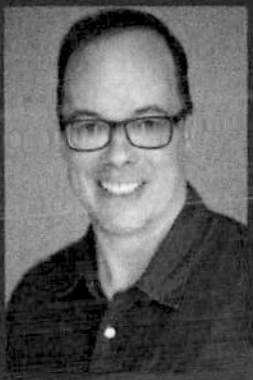

MICHAEL NORTHROP is the *New York Times* bestselling author of 13 books for kids and teens, including the hit graphic novel *Dear Justice League*. A former senior editor at *Sports Illustrated Kids*, he now writes full-time from his home in New York City. Visit him online at www.michaelnorthrop.net. Fun fact: Michael once stepped on a yellow jacket nest and was stung more than 75 times. (It wasn't fun at the time.)

photo credit: Francine Daveta

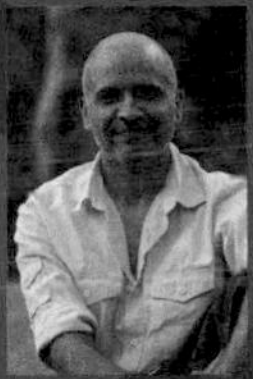

YANCEY LABAT is an illustrator of the DC Super Hero Girls original graphic novels and three-time recipient of Diamond Comic Distributors Gem Awards for Best All-Ages Original/Reprint Graphic Novels. He is also a winner of the 2018 Ringo Award for Best Kids Comic or Graphic Novel. He has two superhero girls of his own and lives in San Carlos, California.

HUMAN EXTREMES

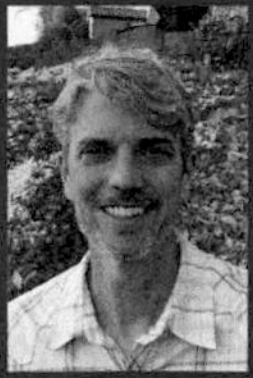

Ever since he started writing and illustrating for DC Comics, **KIRK SCROGGS** has been running around in full body armor, shouting stuff like "Shazam!" and "In brightest day, in darkest night!" and generally driving everyone crazy. He is the author and illustrator of *The Secret Spiral of Swamp Kid* and *We Found a Monster* and is currently saving Los Angeles from almost-certain destruction.

photo credit: Stephen Deline

(SUB)ATOMIC

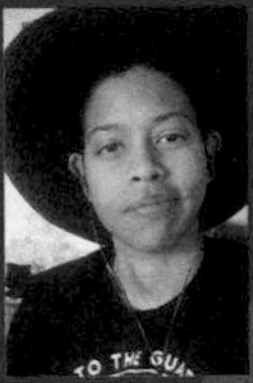

VITA AYALA is a queer Afro-Latinx writer born and bred in New York City, where they grew up dreaming dreams of dancing on faraway worlds, fighting monsters on the block, and racing the fish along the bottom of the ocean. Their work includes *The Wilds* (Black Mask Studios), *Submerged* (Vault), *Quarter Killer* (Comixology), *Supergirl* (DC), *Xena: Warrior Princess* (Dynamite), *Magic: The Gathering: Chandra* (IDW), *Morbius, the Living Vampire* (Marvel), and *Livewire* (Valiant), among others.

photo credit: Vita Ayala

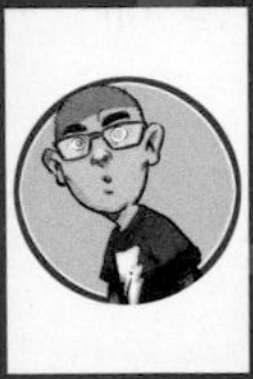

ANDIE TONG's past comic book and illustration experience includes titles such as *Green Lantern: Legacy, The Batman Strikes!, Spectacular Spider-Man* (UK), *Tron: Betrayal, Plants vs. Zombies, Star Wars, Tekken, The Wheel of Time,* and Stan Lee's *The Zodiac Legacy.* Andie has also illustrated children's books for HarperCollins for more then ten years and has had the opportunity to work on multiple books with the late Stan Lee. Malaysian born, Andie migrated to Australia at a young age, and then moved to London in 2005. In 2012, he journeyed back to Asia and currently resides in Singapore with his wife and two children.

image credit: Andie Tong

HOME SWEET SPACE

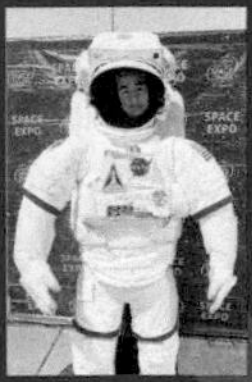

CECIL CASTELLUCCI is the award-winning and *New York Times* bestselling author of novels and comics for young adults including *Batgirl*; *Shade, The Changing Girl*; *The Female Furies*; *Soupy Leaves Home*; and *The Plain Janes.* She is the daughter of two scientists and is a huge space enthusiast. She follows all things astronaut and space related and always has her eyes and heart pointed toward the stars. Her favorite moon is Enceladus and she loves comets. She lives on the planet Earth in the city of Los Angeles.

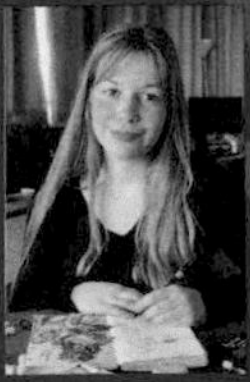

GRETEL LUSKY is an illustrator and character designer who worked for several years in animation before moving to the comic book industry. She recently illustrated *Primer* for the DC Graphic Novels for Kids imprint, and has also worked on projects for other clients including IDW Publishing, Simon and Schuster, and Netflix, among others. She's one-third mermaid and two-thirds chihuahua enthusiast.

photo credit: Nahuel Ruiz